Jodi Taylor is the internationally bestselling author of the Chronicles of St Mary's series, the story of a bunch of disaster-prone individuals who investigate major historical events in contemporary time. Do NOT call it time travel! She is also the author of the Time Police series – a St Mary's spinoff and gateway into the world of an all-powerful, international organisation who are NOTHING like St Mary's. Except, when they are.

Alongside these, Jodi is known for her gripping supernatural thrillers featuring Elizabeth Cage together with the enchanting Frogmorton Farm series – a fairy story for adults.

Born in Bristol and now living in Gloucester (facts both cities vigorously deny), she spent many years with her head somewhere else, much to the dismay of family, teachers and employers, before finally deciding to put all that daydreaming to good use and write a novel. Over twenty books later, she still has no idea what she wants to do when she grows up.

JODI TAYLOR

ABOUT TIME

HEADLINE

First published in Great Britain in 2022 by
HEADLINE PUBLISHING GROUP

First published in Great Britain in paperback in 2023 by
HEADLINE PUBLISHING GROUP

1

Cataloguing in Publication Data is available from the British Library

ISBN 978 1 4722 8694 9

Typeset in Times New Roman by CC Book Production

Printed and bound in Great Britain by Clays Ltd, Elcograf S.p.A.

Headline's policy is to use papers that are natural, renewable and recyclable
products and made from wood grown in well-managed forests and other
controlled sources. The logging and manufacturing processes are expected
to conform to the environmental regulations of the country of origin.

HEADLINE PUBLISHING GROUP
An Hachette UK Company
Carmelite House
50 Victoria Embankment
London EC4Y 0DZ

www.headline.co.uk
www.hachette.co.uk

PROTECTING THE PAST

TP

TO ENSURE YOUR FUTURE

Roll Call

TIME POLICE PERSONNEL

Commander Hay	Commander of the Time Police. About to endure the longest day ever.
Captain Farenden	Her adjutant. Looking on the bright side has never been more difficult.
Amelia Meiklejohn	One half of the perfidious Meiklejohn siblings. About to embark on a new career with the Time Police. What could possibly go wrong?
Major Ellis	New head of BeeBOC (Big Business and Organised Crime, for the uninitiated).
Lt North	New head of Records/Historical Briefing. And heading up the first team to boldly go where no man has gone before.

TEAM 235

Lt Grint	Team leader. Still stumbling down the rocky road of romance.
Officer Kohl (Socko)	
Officer Hansen	
Officer Rossi	

vii

TEAM 236 – TEAM WEIRD

Luke Parrish	Self-appointed team leader – but not for much longer.
Jane Lockland	Actually – she isn't.
Matthew Farrell	Right in the middle and not happy.

SECURITY TEAM

Lt Filbert	Head of security.
Officer Varma	Persistent. Always gets there in the end.
Officer Wu	
Officer Harvey	
Officer Jessup	
Officer Miller	

MEDCEN

The doctor	Possibly even more depressed than ever.
Kelly	Medical orderly.

POD BAY & LOGISTICS

Senior Mech	Unhappy about the number of women in his life. The *unnecessary* number of women in his life.
Oti	From Logistics. Crate provider.

OTHER OFFICERS

Major Callen	Using his initiative.
Lt Dal	
Lt Chigozie	All of these are relatively normal officers.
Lt Fanboten	

Officer Curtis   Just don't mention sentient poo.

Officer Rockmeyer   Unwillingly hosting Officer Curtis's naked buttocks. Don't ask.

ST MARY'S PERSONNEL

Dr Maxwell   Supposedly in charge of evacuating St Mary's but easily distracted.

Leon   Heroically fire-fighting while his pod takes a bit of a bashing. Again.

Dr Peterson   Both disappointed at not being involved

Mr Markham   but still happy to shove their oar in.

Mr Dieter   Very nearly squashed.

Adrian Meiklejohn   The other half.

CIVILIANS

Mrs Lockland   Jane's grandmother.

Mrs Farnborough   The Home Counties' Valkyrie. In all sorts of trouble.

John Costello   It's his pod, so it's not really stealing, is it?

Nikola Tesla   Yes, him.

Henry Plimpton   Still rocking the benevolent grandfather look but he'll shoot you dead if you cross him. Sometimes, even if you don't.

His men   Assorted minions, including: Blue Coat/ Broom, Jim, Tucker, Clore, Trip, Fisher, Otto and Andy.

Raymond Parrish   On really top form and rather enjoying himself.

Lucinda Steel	His PA. Sadly unable to bring the world to its knees this time round, but there's always hope for the future.
Ernesto Portman	
Anthony Portman	Portmans, so no one likes them.
Bradley Portman	
Portman Security	Not having a good day.
Lola	Cat-loving call girl.
Lift attendant	Now knows not to mix his lights with his darks.
Waitress	Provider of very welcome coffee.

SUNNYSIDE NURSING HOME

Dr Anne Summers
Nurse Suti
Their patient

MISCELLANEOUS

Mellor	Time Police helicopter pilot.
Miles	Civilian pilot.
A small box of emergency tissues	Doesn't get out much. The Time Police do not have a procedure for sobbing.

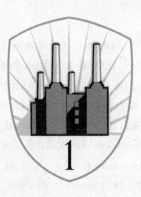

1

Commander Hay settled herself comfortably at her desk and picked up her mug of coffee.

'Right then, Charlie. Hit me with today's calamities.'

The usual procedure, established during their long working relationship, was for Captain Farenden to ease his commanding officer gently into a list of yesterday's disasters, following through with today's pending catastrophes, and then, depending on how things had gone so far, offer a teasing glimpse of tomorrow's possible misfortunes. As adjutant to Commander Hay, it was his job to expect the unexpected. The bizarre. The sudden. The inexplicable. And the downright stupid. *Especially* the downright stupid.

This last week, however, he had been spending his working days dealing with the Time Police's latest ... 'recruit' was the wrong word. 'Acquisition' was perhaps more appropriate. Amelia Meiklejohn – one half of the perfidious Meiklejohn siblings and former illegal – was now, unbelievably, a member of the Time Police.

A much-decorated and resourceful officer, Captain Farenden was struggling daily with all the feelings of exasperation and frustration traditionally experienced by anyone in a supervisory category coming into contact with either or both of the Meiklejohn siblings. However, he was an officer in the Time Police and challenges existed to be risen to. The alternative – and rapidly becoming his preferred option – was to shoot her dead, drop the body in the Thames and disclaim all knowledge of anything. This was a tactic that had always worked well for the Time Police in the past and he saw no reason why it should let him down now.

Captain Farenden was roused from these happy thoughts by his commanding officer enquiring whether he had gone to sleep.

He gritted his teeth. 'No, ma'am. I was merely arranging my thoughts in order to present today's agenda in a timely and efficient manner.'

'Good God, Charlie – you are in a bad mood.'

'Not at all, ma'am. Merely . . .' He paused.

'Merely . . . ?'

'Nothing, ma'am.'

Commander Hay, having herself endured several frustrating interviews with Miss Meiklejohn over the last couple of weeks, had gone on to dump the whole business of their new recruit in her adjutant's lap, citing her need to concentrate on securing additional funding from a reluctant government. Having, therefore, a very good idea of the cause of his tensely uttered 'Merely . . .', she simply grinned and waited.

Captain Farenden pulled himself together. 'Well, ma'am. The situation at the moment is as follows: everyone involved in the Paris Time-Stop and Acropolis incidents has completely recovered. Lt Grint is to be formally discharged later today, although he's been up and about for some time now. Ten days' light duties and if nothing drops off then it's a full return to work for him, as well.'

'That's good news. He's rather unique and I was worried we'd lost him in Paris.'

'Indeed, ma'am. And before you ask, there's no news of Henry Plimpton anywhere. If he has any sense, he'll go to ground for a good while. He must know we'll put the word out that he's a person of considerable interest with whom we would like more than a quick word after his recent attempt to stop Time. I've circulated rumours of a substantial reward.'

'Have we discussed this worrying tendency of yours to spend money the Time Police does not possess?'

'We have, ma'am. On several occasions.'

'And did we come to any conclusions?'

'I believe you expressed the appropriate sentiments, ma'am.'

'I'm certain I did and yet . . .'

'Would you like me to continue, ma'am?'

'Spending money we don't have, or today's sitrep?'

Recognising provocation when he heard it, Captain Farenden continued.

'Second stage reorganisation, ma'am. I've pulled together your thoughts on the latest changes to staff structure and this is how things look now.'

He activated a data stack. 'As you directed, Major Ellis is now the new head of BeeBOC with Lt Grint as his number two. And Officer North is promoted to lieutenant.'

'Well deserved. She kept her head at the Acropolis.'

'Indeed, ma'am, and she's now heading up the new Records/ Historical Briefing section.'

Hay nodded. 'I'll see her after this meeting.'

'Yes, ma'am.' He made a note. 'And in today's good news – unbelievably, Team Two-Three-Six have finally made up their minds which department to grace with their presence. Form D12s have been completed and submitted and it would appear they have come to rest in BeeBOC, thus remaining the responsibility of Major Ellis. Much to the joy of everyone not Major Ellis.'

'Are we aware of Major Ellis's thoughts on this matter?'

'We are not, ma'am, but I suspect they may easily be guessed. Everything else stays the same. And Major Callen remains in charge of the Hunter Division.'

Captain Farenden paused invitingly but there was no visible reaction from his commanding officer. To be fair, there rarely was. Commander Hay had been injured in an accident during the Time Wars. The door had blown off her pod. She had been the only survivor. Half of her face was now considerably older than the other half. People found the effect disconcerting. Commander Hay found it useful.

'Actually,' she said. 'Just while we're on the subject of Major Callen, please can you instruct all personnel to cease referring to him as the Vomit Magnet. Within my hearing, at least.'

Casually, she reached over to blank her screen saver.

'Of course, ma'am.' Discreetly, Captain Farenden turned his scratchpad face down. An unfortunate incident involving Dr Maxwell from St Mary's, their own Major Callen, and a record-holding amount of vomit had led to the acquisition of a substantial number of unofficial but amusing screen savers.

'And while we're discussing our last assignment, Charlie . . .'

'Yes, ma'am?'

'Your work minimising our part in the Paris Time-Stop and the Tunguska event was exemplary. I intend to promote you to major. I should actually have done it a couple of years ago but quite often a commander is only as good as her adjutant. I've been selfish, but I can't hold you back any longer – it's not fair to you. What do you say?'

Captain Farenden slowly shut down the data stack and closed his file. 'Well, first thoughts, ma'am – thank you very much.'

She nodded. 'And your second thoughts?'

'With grateful thanks, may I decline?'

'You may, of course, but why?'

'Several reasons, ma'am. I'm not A1 fit. I'm only A2.' He laid a hand on his bad leg.

She shrugged. 'I'm not A1, either – doesn't stop me.'

'True, ma'am, but there's no getting around the fact that my days of leaping in and out of pods are over and done. But mostly, ma'am, I like this job, I'm at the centre of things. I'm able to use my initiative.'

'Such as spending the entire annual budget covering up our actions in Paris and Siberia.'

He looked at her reproachfully. 'You omitted the word "successfully" from that sentence, ma'am.'

'I also omitted the word "expensively", Charlie. Be grateful.'

'Yes, ma'am.'

Hay swivelled her chair to look out of the window. 'My sight is not improving. I may not be able to command the Time Police for much longer. My successor would certainly promote their own people. Refuse a promotion now and it might never be offered again.'

'I'll happily take that risk, ma'am.'

'I can promote you and still keep you on as adjutant.'

'It would be unusual to have such a high-ranking officer in the post.'

5

She sighed. 'Do you want some time to consider this?'

'No, I don't think so, ma'am, thank you. I'm not likely to change my mind – but my grateful thanks for your consideration.'

'Very well. Moving on.'

He took a deep breath. 'Well, ma'am. Last item but one – our latest acquisition.'

'The one lurking in our deepest darkest dungeon.'

'Her *workroom*, ma'am. If you remember, you decided workroom was a much nicer word than dungeon.'

'It is the deepest darkest one we've got, though?'

'And correspondingly remote, ma'am. Accessed through the Pod Bay, past Logistics, past Storerooms 1 and 2 and right at the very end of a very long corridor. Behind the newly installed blast doors. I thought I could sell the location to Miss Meiklejohn on the grounds of health and safety.'

'And did she buy it?'

'She seemed completely unaware of the concept, ma'am. I gave up in the end. It was sapping my will to live. I'm not sure if you're aware of this, but she can be a . . . provocative . . . conversationalist.'

'Well, never mind – I'm sure you're giving it your best shot, Charlie.' She paused. 'Obviously, I'd attend to all this myself if only I wasn't so taken up with our funding issues. Alas . . .'

'Indeed, ma'am. Your regret shines through your every word. Fortunately, I find myself in a position to alleviate this disappointment.'

'Oh?'

He picked up his scratchpad again and flicked. 'I have good news.'

'Great Scott – we have good news? Actual good news?'

'We have very good news. I'm certain you will receive confirmation from the Right Honourable Mrs Farnborough very shortly, but my own sources tell me it looks as though the bill approving a substantial budget increase for the Time Police will soon be before the House and is certain to go through. Well done, ma'am. A complete turnaround from a few months ago when they were threatening us with cutbacks.'

'Well, I think our success in saving the Acropolis went a long way towards that.'

'Yes, we were lucky there. Failure could have meant the end of us. The Time Police went from zero to hero, ma'am.'

'In a single bound, no less. Arising from that, Charlie, please tell me Dr Maxwell has been returned to St Mary's.'

'Two days ago, ma'am.'

'I honestly thought her legendary luck had run out this time. Any lingering effects from her . . . experience?'

'She's St Mary's, ma'am, so it was hard to tell, but the doctor says probably not and it's not our problem anyway. I believe she passed the time in MedCen by assisting Meiklejohn with her investigation into the effects of using portable Time-travel devices.'

'And their conclusion?'

'Don't.'

'Fair enough, I suppose, given what happened to them both. They were lucky. They might not survive next time.'

'With luck, there won't be a next time, will there, ma'am? Amelia Meiklejohn is now a member of the Time Police and safely ensconced within our walls. Not sure how safe that will be for us, though,' he added reflectively. 'Still, I expect we'll soon find out.'

'I think you should look on the bright side, Charlie. There is an outside chance that both we and Meiklejohn will not only survive her time here but actually benefit from it.'

'Speaking of benefits, ma'am, and the final item today – I've rejigged the standard employment contract to reflect her . . . unique status.' He opened another file.

'And how have we defined the undefinable Miss Meiklejohn?'

'Consultant, ma'am.'

'Interesting.'

'The document clarifies her position and, I think, lessens the possibility of any future misunderstandings over what does and does not constitute reasonable behaviour.'

'You're imposing guidelines upon Miss Meiklejohn?'

'Rules, ma'am.' He sighed. 'I don't feel this is an area where ambiguity would be our friend.'

Commander Hay, who knew her adjutant very well, hid a smile and settled back. 'Let's hear these rules, then.'

Captain Farenden cleared his throat. 'Well, ma'am, in no particular order: no experimenting on anything alive. Or dead, for that matter.'

'Sensible,' commented Commander Hay.

'Everything remains the property of the Time Police. Except for any blame, liability or expense, which will automatically revert back to the blamee – i.e. Meiklejohn.'

She nodded. 'Yes, good.'

'Any and all fines are to be met by the employee.'

'Good.'

'All gaol time to be served by the employee herself.'

'Well, I'm not doing it.'

'Exactly, ma'am. The Time Police reserve the right to repudiate the employee and all her works at any time.'

'Good thought, Charlie. That could come in very useful.'

'The employee is to report to you every Friday afternoon with a detailed account of her week's activities together with her proposed schedule for the upcoming week.'

'Thus buggering my peaceful Friday-afternoon run-up to the weekend. Thank you, Captain.'

'My pleasure, ma'am. At the discretion of the commander of the Time Police, the employee may be terminated at any moment. And her employment, too.'

'Can I shoot her myself?'

'I don't see why not, ma'am, although I only put that one in as a joke. To lighten the mood, so to speak.'

'No, I like that one best. Make that Rule One.'

'Yes, ma'am.'

'How is the Senior Mech coping with this addition to his empire?'

'Meiklejohn has a sign up which reads, "This way to the Batcave", so he's deeply unhappy, ma'am.'

'And how is she dealing with that?'

'Waves merrily every time she sees him.'

'I meant her office accommodation. Is she finding it adequate?'

'It has four walls and a workbench, ma'am, and she's from St Mary's, which means she's accustomed to primitive. She's probably grateful she has a roof over her head.' He paused. 'For the time being, at least.'

'You're quite enjoying this, aren't you?'

'Actually, ma'am, I am. I have all the entertainment of

watching the cat among the pigeons without being the one responsible for actually putting the cat among the pigeons.'

Hay sighed. 'Have I done the right thing, Charlie? Bringing her here?'

'Oh, I think so. There's no doubt she could be useful to us. She's brimming with ideas. And as Dr Maxwell said, we don't want those ideas falling into someone else's hands. Now those ideas can benefit the Time Police.'

'Unless she manages to blow us all up first.'

'I was very carefully not going to mention that.'

'Your restraint is greatly appreciated, Charlie. What else does the contract say?'

'Not a lot more. Just the standard terms and conditions. She'll start on the same rate of pay as a Junior Mech but I've built in performance increments. Nothing extravagant, but I don't think this is an occasion on which to be stingy. Not that she seems to care much for money.'

'No, you've done the right thing there.' She paused. 'One thing that does cause me concern, Charlie – Meiklejohn is on the radar now and I can't help feeling Henry Plimpton won't give her up so easily. Especially after their showdown in Paris. And given the brutality with which he eliminated the residents of Beaver Avenue, we all know he doesn't like loose ends. At some point, he will come after her.'

'Yes, ma'am, in fact . . .'

'Yes?'

'Have you considered assigning her additional security? She's safe enough here at TPHQ, but it would be easy for him to snatch her off the street.'

'I take your point, Charlie, but I can hardly confine her to

TPHQ for the rest of her life.' She appeared to consider this option again and then shook her head regretfully. 'No – sorry. Besides, it's Meiklejohn. She and her idiot brother evaded us for years. I can't help feeling anyone attempting to force either of them to do anything against their will would very soon regret it.'

'Including us, ma'am?'

'That is a possibility, I suppose.'

'Well, if I could just draw your attention to Clause 10 open bracket iii close bracket letter c, her contract does give us the right to shoot her if she doesn't do exactly as she's told.'

'Have the whole thing typed up and laminated with something heatproof and bombproof, and nail it to her office wall. Actually, put a copy on every wall in her workroom. We don't want her claiming ignorance of the rules, do we?'

Captain Farenden passed the document across the desk. 'I'll just leave this with you then, ma'am.'

She took it very reluctantly. 'Why?'

'For your meeting this afternoon.' He noticed her blank look. 'It's Friday, ma'am.'

Commander Hay regarded him coldly.

At 1500 hours promptly, the Time Police's latest recruit presented herself in Captain Farenden's office, clutching several
files and festooned with data cubes.

'I'm here,' she announced, presumably in case he hadn't
noticed.

In modern holos, scientists are always depicted wearing
white coats. Mad scientists clutch a phial of bubbling green
stuff – while wearing white coats. Scientists up to no good
carry briefcases, thus reminding the viewer that they are
smuggling sensitive material out of their top-secret labs –
but still wear white coats while doing so. Even truly evil
scientists – the cackling kind who habitually gather in
hollowed-out volcanoes – wear white coats. No one knows
why they all do this. Presumably there's a scientists' code
somewhere.

All attempts to persuade Amelia Meiklejohn to wear the
standard Time Police uniform had failed. Ditto with the white
coat.

Time Police officers – who tend to like things cut and dried –
were somewhat confused by her attire, which consisted of a
brand-new leather flying jacket – the old one had met a terrible

end in Paris, 1902 – and goggles. But at least she didn't cackle. Yet.

Captain Farenden frowned at her. 'Your meeting with Commander Hay was scheduled for 1400 hours. You're late.'

'Am I? Oh. Sorry. Forgot the time. I can go away again if you like.'

She made gestures indicative of going away again.

Aware that boundaries were being tested, Captain Farenden paused to give her time to contemplate her sins. Sadly, very little contemplation occurred.

'Stay put. I'll tell the commander you're here. She may still be able to fit you in.'

'OK.'

He limped into Commander Hay's office. 'Miss Meiklejohn is here, ma'am.'

Hay's reply drifted back through the open door. 'So soon? I hope she hasn't cut short anything important. Ask her to wait two minutes, please.'

Captain Farenden nodded and returned to his office.

Mikey, who knew very well why she'd been told to wait, merely grinned at him and asked what was wrong with his leg.

'Helicopter crash,' he said, briefly.

'Did your leg cause the crash or was it damaged in it?'

'Most people are polite enough not to mention it.'

She beamed. 'Are they?'

Captain Farenden had no sisters but recognised deliberate provocation when he saw it.

Fortunately – or deliberately – or both – Commander Hay appeared at her door. 'Would you come in, please, Miss Meiklejohn? Yes, you too, Captain. I think we'll need minuting.'

13

She grinned at him as he entered because even a commander is occasionally at the mercy of her adjutant and revenge is sweet.

Amelia Meiklejohn had been gracing the Time Police with her presence for a fortnight now, but this was her first official visit to Commander Hay's office. That she was impressed was apparent.

'Cool.' She rushed to the window to stare out at the view.

The London skyline rose before her – all geometric shapes and flashing glass. The Gherkin, the Startled Hamster, the Shard, the Box of Tissues and the Sea Slug dominated the skyline, along with half a dozen giant mooring towers for docking airships. Just a little way downriver, the Wibbly-Wobbly Bridge continued to provide a challenge to pedestrians and a delight to small children.

Overhead, a number of smaller airships ground to a halt and trod water – figuratively speaking – as Concorde took off from Heathrow's Runway Seven, clawing her way into the heavens before sticking out her nose and heading to Bahrain at Mach 2.5.

'Wow,' said Mikey, temporarily awed.

The Thames meandered past, glittering silver on this sunny afternoon. Public clippers queued at their moorings to discharge their passengers. Boy racers and the river police battled for supremacy in the fast lane and water taxis zipped in and out of the traffic, cutting up slower-moving vehicles without a second thought.

Commander Hay cleared her throat and gestured for everyone to seat themselves at the long briefing table.

'Well, Miss Meiklejohn, have you familiarised yourself with your operating instructions?'

'Not really. I thought it would be easier and quicker just to make a start on things and see what happens.'

'Have you had time to read your copy of . . . ?'

She shrugged. 'I sort of skimmed the first few lines but you seem to have an awful lot of rules and I'm not really very good at remembering that sort of thing, so I think the best thing for everyone is that I just keep going until someone tells me to stop.'

'I think you'll find things here are very different from St Mary's. The Time Police will expect you to take just a little more responsibility for your own actions.'

Mikey cocked her head to one side. 'No – I don't think that argument would work in a court of law. According to the rules – your rules – you own me and you own my work. It follows, therefore, that you own the consequences of that work, good or bad. I'm pretty certain that should I come up with something ground-breaking you're not going to sit back and say, "Well done, Amelia. What a clever girl. Do enjoy spending all the money this will make you." We both know that everything I create – and sadly for you, that includes the stuff that goes horribly wrong – will automatically become the property and responsibility of the Time Police and not me. I think a good defence lawyer would pounce with delight on that particular contractual inconsistency, don't you? Just prior to having me acquitted from whatever you've accused me of.' Mikey gestured at her files and cubes. 'Shall I begin? So you can tell me to stop?'

Both Commander Hay and Captain Farenden sat in cold silence which their newest recruit, busy arranging her files and cubes, completely failed to notice.

'Firstly,' she said, 'you have a problem with your portable power source.'

Hay frowned. 'What portable power source?'

'Exactly. I mean, yes, you have solar panels on the pods and whatnot, but they're not a lot of use in Scandinavia in the middle of winter, are they? And the panels become less and less effective as a mission drags on, so in the end, before power drops to critical levels, the pod is forced to return to base for a proper recharge. I don't know how long-term some of your assignments are, but I bet it's a bit of a bugger if, after months of careful surveillance, you're all prepared to pounce but you can't because you're getting low on power. And, of course, using the camo thingy really eats into your power levels.'

Commander Hay opened her mouth but there was no chance.

'So, I've had some thoughts and I think I could convert a pod into an actual power source.'

'But what about . . .'

'I'd strip out all the innards – everything not essential would go – then I'd pack it full of cells, batteries, power packs – the lot. I'd leave just enough room for a mech to pilot and do the hooking up. It needn't be a big pod, either. In fact, it shouldn't be because it's going to have to be able to access everywhere. And, if I can rig a couple more Parissa fittings – without damaging the shell, of course – then possibly it could recharge more than one pod at a time. And that could double – possibly triple – the length of time your pods can spend on site. And then the power pod returns to base, either swaps out its cells – you'd need a constant supply – or recharges itself again and then nips off to service someone else. I think that could be quite useful, don't you, but I'll stop if you want?' She looked up. 'Yes? No? OK – we'll call that a yes, then. If you can persuade Old Porky to give me a pod to tinker with, then I should be able to have something to show you in about a month.'

'Old . . . Porky?'

'Yes, you know. Fat bloke. Never smiles. Bald spot. Old. Shouts a lot.'

'I suspect you are referring to our Senior Mechanic.'

'Yes, him. Doesn't like women.' Mikey grinned. 'And he especially doesn't like me.'

'I suspect that has very little to do with your gender and more to do with your attitude.'

Mikey gave this serious consideration. 'Could be. Could be. Anyway, yes or no on getting me a pod?'

Commander Hay nodded at Captain Farenden who said, 'The matter will be addressed. Is there anything else?'

'Oh God, yes. Loads. I was talking to someone. Can't remember his name. Big bloke. Looks like a puzzled mammoth.' She paused, but neither Commander Hay nor Captain Farenden were going to admit they'd recognised Lt Grint from that unflattering description. 'He was telling me about a time when an illegal pod got away from him because he couldn't get the EMP going quickly enough. Actually, as he progressed with the story, I rather think it might have been me and Adrian he'd been pursuing at the time. We used to get away from you quite a lot, didn't we? Remember that time in Pisa? Love the way you denied all responsibility for the Leaning Tower. And the eleventh stone at Stonehenge? That definitely wasn't our fault. Anyway, I'm thinking some kind of mesh. Or net, possibly. Light and flexible. You chuck it over the pod, switch it

17

on and it neutralises the field in much the same way as an EMP but ten times quicker, and targeted as well. It would prevent the illegal pod from jumping away before you can get to it. You can't always spare the time it takes to set up an electromagnetic pulse and you always have to be careful not to disable your own pods, so I should imagine you'd find something like that quite useful.'

'I rather suspect,' said Captain Farenden, 'that an illegal pod would be able to jump long before a couple of officers were able to creep up behind it and somehow manage to throw a net over it, don't you? It's not like catching chickens.'

'Drone deployed,' said Mikey, already moving on to her next project. 'The net would be packed underneath. At a given signal, it would be released. I'll weight it so it falls properly and as long as your people can get it lined up correctly, it should work well. What do you say? Yes? No?'

'Yes,' said Commander Hay. 'Well, thank you, Miss Mei—'

'And then there's the invisibility field.'

'What invisibility field?'

'Exactly.' Mikey waited. No one spoke.

'Oh, you want me to continue. OK. Using bracelets to generate an invisibility field . . . well – a bit of background first.'

'I don't think . . .' began Captain Farenden.

'No, it's OK – I'll keep it simple.'

'That wasn't what I meant.'

He was wasting his time.

'There have been various approaches over the years: meta-materials, negative index of refraction – which has proved impossible, by the way. Tons of time and money have been wasted on that. And yes, the Time Police have done things with cameras and sophisticated computer equipment, but it's not perfect. Everything depends on the background and the point of view of the observer. Sometimes it's still possible to make out an image. Especially if you know it's there.'

She leaned forwards in her enthusiasm. 'And then – along comes Henry Plimpton and his Time-travel bracelets and he inadvertently showed me a new approach. His bracelet wasn't calibrated properly. The field-to-power ratio was all wrong. Not entirely his fault – the concept itself was faulty. But I was wearing the bracelet and when he activated his pod, I was close enough for the pod's field to do something to the bracelet's field and I vanished. I honestly thought I'd be invisible forever until Max appeared with *her* bracelet and her field knocked mine back off and suddenly you could see me again. I wasn't actually invisible. You couldn't hear me and I couldn't really touch anything, so it wasn't true invisibility, but close enough. I could knock up something that could do the same – but under our control. It might mean people have to travel in pairs, though . . . You'd need the two fields to interact . . . unless, of course . . .'

Unconsciously twiddling her pen, Mikey lost herself in thought for a while before remembering her audience, who were regarding her with varying expressions of concern, dismay, alarm and trepidation.

Mistaking the cause of these kaleidoscopic reactions, she smiled in what she imagined was a reassuring manner. 'Oh, don't worry – I'll sort it all out.'

Captain Farenden surprised both Mikey and his commanding officer. 'Would this be anything to do with invisibility via the fourth dimension?'

19

She regarded him with approval. 'At the moment I don't think so, but that would be an interesting approach, wouldn't it? Another thing I've been thinking about . . .'

Commander Hay intervened. 'I think, for the time being, three projects are enough to be going on with. Our budget is somewhat constrained at the moment . . .' Captain Farenden looked carefully at the carpet, 'and our resources are limited. You can keep me updated on your progress through our weekly meetings. Successful completion of one project will open up opportunities for the next.'

Mikey, possibly familiar with this approach from her days at St Mary's, nodded. 'Fine. I'll be off, then. See you next Friday. Same Bat time? Same Bat channel?'

Commander Hay regarded her blankly. 'I beg your pardon?'

Mikey sighed. 'Never mind.'

The door closed behind her.

'Dear God,' said Commander Hay, faintly. 'What have I done?'

3

A new day was dawning for Team 236, two of whom were downstairs in their office and benefitting from a new and definitely illegal piece of equipment.

'It's a coffee machine,' announced Luke. 'They can't possibly expect us to keep drinking that stuff from the vending machines. I'm no expert but I'm pretty sure coffee shouldn't be grey. Anyway, I dipped into the bank account I'm not supposed to have and treated us to this.'

He gestured to the magnificent chrome edifice glittering illegally on top of their illegal bookcase. It is possible that Jane might have drawn breath to utter a comment of some kind but, as was frequently the case with her team leader, she wasn't given the chance.

'It's brilliant, isn't it? We're breaking all the rules. And we can have delicious coffee whenever we want. And it's pissing off everyone else along this corridor with the aroma of said delicious coffee. There is no downside, is there?'

As it turned out, he was wrong. The downside turned up in the form of Team 235 – Officers Rossi, Hansen and Kohl (known for reasons never disclosed as Socko), who crowded into the tiny office. 'What's that smell?'

Luke frowned. 'Well, that's not very polite. I'm certain Jane showered this morning.'

Rossi waved this aside. 'What is that smell?'

Luke indicated the newly installed illegal machine snorting illegal steam and foam in the corner. Like a chrome dragon.

Team 235 regarded it in wonder and envy. 'Where's the water coming from?'

Luke gestured vaguely. 'Pipe behind the wall. Mikey did something and hey presto – water.'

Hansen gaped. 'What? You've tapped into . . .? You can't do that.'

'We didn't. Mikey did.'

'But . . .'

'Apparently it's called research. Was there a water source and if so, could she connect to it? Research is like family values – you can get away with murder if you do it right.'

'What if someone finds out?'

'Like I say – research. And how would they ever know?'

'They will if we tell them.'

Luke sighed. 'Well, in that case we'll have to kill you now. Don't just sit there, Jane.'

'Kill them yourself,' said Jane, not moving. 'I'm enjoying my coffee.'

'That's the spirit, sweetie,' said Bolshy Jane, approvingly. 'He'll have you darning his socks next if you're not careful.'

Jane concentrated on her coffee. Should she mention these voices in her head at her next medical? Probably not.

The door opened but only a little way because it was a very small office and now there were five of them in it.

'What's going on in there?' said a voice. 'Open this door.'

They all shuffled around until the door could open properly.

Major Ellis, their former team leader and now their head of department, stood on the threshold. 'What's that smell?'

'We've been through all this,' said Luke wearily. 'It's all good.'

Ellis was staring across the room. 'What the hell is that and why is it making that noise?'

'Well, that's rather rude,' said Luke. 'We all know Jane is never at her best in the early morning but that's rather dehumanising, don't you think? Pay no attention, Jane. We who know and love you are . . .'

'Shut up, Parrish,' said Ellis. 'I know an illegal coffee machine when I see one.'

'Are you certain? Jane has many skills, you know, camouflage being not the least of them, and . . .'

'Shut up, Parrish, or I'll put you on a charge.'

'For what?'

'I shall seek suggestions from your colleagues. Who will, I am certain, be delighted to assist me in my search for something that will mean your certain incarceration for a considerable period of time.'

'Oh, please,' said Rossi, putting up his hand. 'Could you start with me, sir?'

'Shut up, Rossi. Parrish, get rid of that thing.'

'Can't. It's attached to the wall.'

'Why?'

'Health and safety.'

'You are a Time Police officer, Parrish. You should be unfamiliar with either concept.' Ellis eyed Jane, quietly sipping the best cup of coffee she'd ever had in her life. 'I'm surprised at you, Lockland.'

Jane nodded. She was quite surprised at herself, too.

North appeared at the door. 'What's that smell?'

'Oh God,' said Luke, wearily.

'Only I thought I smelled coffee.'

'No, you didn't.'

'Is that an illegal coffee machine?'

'No, it isn't,' said Luke.

'Yes, it is,' said Jane, Socko, Hansen and Rossi.

North frowned. 'I should report this.'

Luke stood in front of the illegal subject of their conversation. 'No, you shouldn't.'

Ellis frowned. 'That's "No, you shouldn't, *ma'am*".'

North's eyes narrowed. 'As a responsible officer in the Time Police, it is my duty to report this.'

'Why?' demanded Luke. 'It's not doing anyone any harm.'

'It's doing me harm.'

Luke spread his arms in bewilderment. 'How?'

'Because I haven't been offered any.'

'But . . .' said Luke.

'Continued use of this illegal machine – even continued *possession* of this illegal machine – will not come cheap.'

'What?' said Luke, indignantly.

'Allow me to simplify things, Officer Parrish. It's going to cost you.'

'What?'

North sighed. 'That illegal coffee machine. It's going to cost you.'

'Hold on a minute,' protested Luke.

'Are you arguing with me, Parrish?'

'No. Well, only a little bit.'

She stared at him.

Luke sighed. 'Exactly how much is providing a much-needed resource for my team – and out of my own pocket, too – going to cost me?'

'One mug at the beginning of every shift. Just to ease me into the day. And one at the end of the shift. Just to ease me back out again.'

Luke sighed. 'You can't do this.'

'That's "You can't do this, *ma'am*",' said Ellis, keeping a straight face with difficulty.

'And the same terms for your respected head of department. Officers' privilege,' said North.

Luke appealed to Ellis. 'Can she do that?'

'I'm sorry,' said Ellis pleasantly. 'I don't always hear very well first thing in the morning. Not until I've had my first cup of coffee anyway.'

'But . . .'

North folded her arms. 'Take it or leave it, Parrish.'

Luke sighed and turned to his head of department. 'Are you here for a reason, Major? Other than to render the junior members of your department's day even more traumatic than usual.'

'Ah, thank you for reminding me.'

'I've heard that lack of decent coffee can affect your memory, sir,' said Rossi brightly and was ordered from the room with the rest of his team.

Ellis shut the door behind them. 'Team Two-Three-Six, I have pleasure in announcing your first BeeBOC assignment. Something gentle after your Paris experience. We've had a tip-off. The usual thing. Someone somewhere's doing something naughty. Interrupt Officer Farrell's love affair with the

Time Map and assemble in Briefing Room 3 in ten minutes. Black – no sugar.'

The finding of a clean mug and making coffee for Major Ellis took Luke more than a few minutes. Consequently, when he stepped out into the corridor, it was empty. Until the sudden appearance of Lt Grint, newly released from MedCen.

Protocol decreed that Luke should step aside for the more senior officer. Especially one the size of Lt Grint. Sadly, Luke Parrish had never really got the hang of protocol.

He planted himself squarely in the middle of the corridor and waited.

Grint ground to a halt. Rather in the manner of India seeking to avoid a collision with the Isle of Wight. Both parties took a step backwards and blinked.

'Get out of the way,' said Grint, proud possessor of slightly fewer social skills than your average spleen.

'Or what?' said Luke, proud possessor of slightly fewer appeasement skills than your average Mongol horde.

'What do you want, Parrish?'

'Jane.'

'What about Jane?'

'Mess her about,' said Luke affably, 'and we both know what I'm talking about – and I will come after you.'

Grint stared down at him. Not a muscle moved. 'Get out of my way or I'll crush you like the useless piece of crap you are but Jane hasn't realised yet.'

Luke's eyes blazed. The moment went on and on and then he stepped to one side. Grint curled his lip and continued on his way.

'You're late, Parrish,' said Ellis as Luke entered Briefing Room 3.

Luke placed the coffee on Ellis's desk and glanced at the clock. 'Yes, I am. I intend to blame Lt Grint who detained me in the corridor.'

'Let's get started.' Ellis activated the screen, bringing up an image of a scruffy individual with a great deal of facial hair. The picture was somewhat blurred so it seemed safe to assume the subject had been travelling at speed. 'Pay attention, people.' Jane and Matthew sat up straighter. Luke lounged. Ellis pointed. 'This is John Costello. Alias James Costello. Sometimes alias Jack Costello.'

'Not very imaginative,' said Luke.

'Our Mr Costello sells rare historical artefacts.'

Matthew looked up. 'You mean like the flying auctions people?'

'I do not. Mr Costello operates much further down the social and commercial scale, offering his customers such rare pieces as the eye that Harold lost at Hastings, the shroud cloth of Genghis Khan – complete with the manufacturer's washing instructions recommending a thirty-degree wash and short spin – a horseshoe from the apparently sixteen-legged Black Bess and so forth. All of it completely unverifiable, which is not surprising because all of it is extremely fake. He's been known to us for some time but we haven't bothered because he's never been that important. He usually hovers around the big boys, picking up unwanted scraps.'

'Like a remora,' suggested Luke.

'Exactly. Although that might be slightly overstating his status. Anyway, we now have the time, the resources and the info to deal with Mr Costello, who recently came to the attention of another team. Sadly, they were unable to engage with him at the time since they were busy chasing down a group of inebriated students who had mistakenly thought 1746 would be a good place to celebrate their graduation.'

Jane put up her hand, feeling the usual blush sweep across her face.

'Sweetie, have you thought of seeking medical assistance for that?' enquired Bolshy Jane.

Jane ignored her. 'Do we know what Costello was doing there? In 1746?'

'From what the team could see as they raced past, Mr Costello was attempting to sell the head of Charles I.'

'The severed head?' said Jane, faintly.

'The skull,' said Ellis. 'Not the actual . . .' He made head gestures. 'Anyway, the students enthusiastically resisted arrest, matters became even more lively than Team One-Three-Eight had anticipated, and they didn't have time to stop and add Costello to their collection. But they have generously passed on the info and Team Two-Three-Six are today's lucky winners.'

'Oh great,' said Luke. 'Right in the middle of the Jacobite rebellion. What an idiot.'

'The rebellion has petered out,' said North.

'Yes, but no one in 1746 knows that, do they?' said Luke. 'For all they know, the Scots are poised to do it all again. A Stuart skull – is the bloke insane? Is the recent rebellion, Culloden and "Butcher" Cumberland not enough to worry about without adding Catholic relics to the mix?'

Ellis blinked. 'Gratifying to see the cash splashed on your education wasn't entirely wasted, Parrish.' He addressed Team

236 in general. 'Obviously, given your track record, I hesitate to say, "This should be a piece of cake," but I doubt even you will be able to screw this one up. Mr Costello has no record of violence, although he is reported to possess a serious turn of speed in a crisis so put your running shoes on. We want him, his pod and his merchandise. We'd also like details of his contacts – buyers, sellers, fences and so forth – so bring him back intact. You'll find him in London 1746 and Lt North will provide brief details of what you can expect to find there.'

North stood up.

'London – the whole country – is in a state of high tension after the recent Jacobite rebellion. The attempt to replace Hanoverian George I with the exiled Stuart line has failed. The Stuart Prince – Bonnie Prince Charlie, as he's popularly known – has been defeated at Culloden – incidentally the last battle fought on British soil. Until the Civil Uprisings, of course. The government forces were led by the Duke of Cumberland – "Butcher" Cumberland as Officer Parrish so vividly describes him.

'As it so often is, the aftermath was brutal and bloody. Attempts to integrate the Scots were neither sympathetic nor successful. Oaths of allegiance were required. Wearing the kilt was banned. The clans were disbanded. Yes, government reprisals were harsh, but please remember the rebels penetrated as far south as Derby. The French were poised to attack the south coast. The situation was critical and the government came down hard. Bonnie Prince Charlie escaped with the aid of Flora MacDonald and was never really a threat again. By the time you will arrive, Francis Towneley, together with fellow members of the Jacobite Manchester Regiment, has been hanged, drawn and quartered at Kennington Common. Their heads were the last to be displayed on Temple Bar. The Earl of Kilmarnock and Lord Balmerino have been beheaded in the Tower. Lord Lovat is awaiting execution. Treason is still in the air. People are jumpy. There will be soldiers everywhere. Caution and discretion are strongly advised.'

Jane was scribbling frantically. Alone among the Time Police, she still preferred her trusty notebook to a scratchpad. Luke folded his arms and looked bored.

Ellis looked around. 'Any questions, anyone?'

There were none.

'Then why are you still here? Collect your gear and be on your way.'

'No helmets,' said Luke as Team 236 entered their pod. 'Londoners will still be jumpy after '45 and we don't want to draw attention to ourselves with outlandish headgear.'

That Team Weird had never been able to avoid drawing attention to themselves – outlandish headgear or not – was not mentioned.

'Yes, because everyone wore sinister black clothing in those days,' said Matthew, looking down at his uniform. 'I really think it's time we reconsidered our public image.'

'Oh, I don't know,' said Luke. 'I quite like the whole shock-and-awe thing we have going for us. After all, we want people to wet themselves when they see us coming. For me, that's the best part of the job. Jane, what the hell is that? Have you taken to wearing your knickers on your head for some reason?'

'It's a mobcap, actually,' said Jane, busy laying in the coordinates. 'There are now so many women in the Time Police that . . .'

'Twelve,' said Luke. 'There are twelve women in the Time Police. Thirteen if you count the Map Master and don't accept the popular view she's not from this planet. I don't call that "many".'

'And you're going out with four of them,' said Matthew.

Jane persevered, '. . . that someone . . . high up . . . and not being a member of the gender who would have to wear it . . . decided there should be some sort of camouflage for us. Hence the all-purpose mobcap.'

Luke sneered. 'Are you wearing a pinny under your cloak as well?'

'No, I'm wearing a small but perfectly formed blaster, a fully charged sonic, my trusty baton and two lots of liquid string, because now that you're our team leader, I expect to have to use all of it before we eventually manage to overcome John Costello, dismantle his operation, impound his pod and illegal hoard and barely escape with our lives.'

There was a pause. 'That was very hurtful,' said Luke. He turned to Matthew. 'Matthew . . .'

Matthew grinned at him. 'What she said.'

Luke sighed impatiently. 'Are we done yet?'

'Um . . .'

'Just finish the coordinates and let's go.'

Silence fell. 'Coordinates laid in,' said Jane. 'Go on, team leader. Engage the AI.'

Luke threw himself into a seat and waved a vague hand. 'I'll leave all that to you.'

'But you're the team leader,' said Jane, carefully not catching Matthew's eye. 'You should be the one who . . .'

'That's just tradition,' said Luke. 'I don't think we . . .'

'No, it's not. The rules specifically state that it's the team leader's responsibility to initiate . . .'

'All right. Jeez, give it a rest, will you.' He drew breath. 'Pod – commence jump procedures.'

The AI responded in its pleasantly female voice. 'Unable to comply.'

'Here we go,' muttered Matthew, making himself comfortable.

'What? Why not?' demanded Luke.

'Protocol failure. You have failed to identify yourself.'

Luke looked at Jane. 'Don't you usually do that?'

'Usually, yes.'

'Well, why haven't you . . . ?'

'You only told me to finish the coordinates.'

'Jane, I expect this sort of behaviour from our wildly misnamed artificial intelligence but not from you. Could you enter the team ID and let's get on before the Senior Mech starts banging on the door to ask if we've forgotten how to jump?'

'Won't that make Jane the team leader, though?' murmured Matthew provocatively.

'For God's sake, can we just go?'

Jane swivelled her chair back to the console and entered the team ID. 'Pod, commence jump procedures, please.'

Luke sighed in exasperation. 'I keep telling you – it's a machine. You don't have to say please.'

'Jump procedures commenced.'

Jane smiled. 'Thank you.'

'You're welcome.'

Luke sat up in a hurry. '*What* did you say?'

'Which of us are you talking to?' enquired Jane.

32

Luke gestured. 'It said, "You're welcome."'

'No, it didn't,' said Jane, not looking at Matthew.

'You said, "Thank you," which you don't need to say, Jane, I keep telling you, and it said, "You're welcome."'

'No, it didn't.'

'Can we go?' said Matthew. 'Before the Senior Mech starts banging on the door to find out if we've forgotten how to jump.'

'But it shouldn't . . .'

The world flickered.

4

'We're exactly where and when we should be,' reported Jane. 'Southwark, 15th December 1746.'

'Let's have a look, then,' said Luke.

They all peered at the screen.

'Trees?' said Luke. 'I can see trees. Why can I see trees? For God's sake, Jane, have you put us down in the Forest of Dean?'

'We're in a churchyard,' said Jane, calmly. 'It has trees.'

'Are you sure?'

'If you take a moment to recover your composure,' said Matthew, 'you'll be able to make out the headstones. Oh, look – is that a patch of disturbed earth? Do you think something's clawed itself free of its grave and is waiting to rip out our throats?'

Luke stared at Matthew. 'Only if I'm very lucky.'

'Not a nice day out there,' said Jane, consulting her instruments. 'Cold and damp.'

'And foggy?'

'No, I think that's old-fashioned smog. From all the fires. Caused by wet wood and cheap coal, I expect.'

'Oh God. So we can add respiratory diseases to everything else we're going to pick up here.'

'It's a time of massive social unrest,' said Matthew comfortingly. 'You're much more likely to end your days with your head on a spike on London Bridge than live long enough to cough black sputum all over the pod.'

Luke glared at him. 'I still don't know why we bring you.'

'I'm the morale officer.'

'Well, stay at home and cheer us all up.'

'Or *you* could stay at home and cheer *us* up.'

Jane, who had occupied her time by being a proper officer and donned her cloak all ready to go, stood at the door and cleared her throat. 'In your own time, gentlemen.'

They opened the door and stepped out.

'Bloody hell, it's a bit nippy,' said Luke, pulling his cloak around him.

'Yes, it's winter,' said Jane. 'As in the date. Fifteenth of December.'

Luke stamped his foot on the hard ground. They were indeed standing in a dank and gloomy churchyard. The dark bulk of St Saviour's loomed behind them. The ground was rutted and frozen. Tufts of dead, brown grass, ancient wooden crosses and toppled tombstones provided additional trip hazards. The sun hadn't been strong enough to melt the larger icy puddles. In fact, the weak sunshine struggling through the smog only emphasised the bitter cold. They could see their own breath.

That they were in a heavily populated area was evident. There were smoking chimneys everywhere. The smoke would climb a little way and then stream sideways to hang over the houses in a dirty, yellow-brown cloud.

Luke coughed extravagantly. His team ignored him.

Jane sniffed delicately. Smoke wasn't the only smell on

the block. The river, sewage, cut wood, earth and cooking – although what was being cooked was debatable – all with top notes of stale urine.

Surrounding the churchyard was a waist-high stone wall over which they could see a wider street off to their left, lined each side with haphazardly built stone and timber buildings. There was a bizarre mixture of good and bad. One or two houses were stone-built and of good quality with tiled roofs. These stood alongside fragile-looking wooden structures – some only part-roofed and a few with no roofs at all. From where Team 236 were standing, it was impossible to see whether the street was paved or not but, going on past experience of London streets, even if it was, the stones would long since have disappeared under regular floods of mud, rubbish, sewage, rotting vegetables and animal shit.

The street was not particularly crowded. Possibly everyone who could was staying indoors. And not just because of the weather. The country was suffering the aftermath of a major coup. A failed major coup. No one would be on the streets who didn't have to be. And no women at all that Jane could see. Not even the ladies of briefly purchased affection. Jane reflected briefly on the folly of lifting your skirts in this weather and then wished she hadn't.

Those who were out and about wore layers of coats, cloaks, shawls, blankets, even tattered rags. Every piece of clothing they owned, probably. The good news was that Team 236 would be able to get around more quickly in the empty streets. The bad was that they'd be more noticeable.

Staring around him, Luke groaned.

'Makes the 20th century look good, doesn't it?' said Matthew cheerfully.

36

'For God's sake, watch where you put your feet,' said Luke, looking down at the frozen mud. 'We don't want any broken ankles.'

'Pod, send a street map of 1746 Southwark to our scratchpads, please,' said Jane. 'Overlay with pod signatures.'

'Dear God,' said Luke, staring at Matthew's scratchpad. 'How many Cock Alleys does one city actually need?'

'That one leads to Naked Boy Yard,' said Matthew, pointing.

'I am not going down there and neither are you. Jane, I think *you* should wait in the pod.'

'I keep telling you,' said Bolshy Jane in exasperation. 'Kill him now. Why won't you listen to me?'

'Actually,' said Wimpy Jane timidly, 'I think he might be joking.'

'I wouldn't bank on it,' said Actual Jane, darkly. 'But whether he is or not, I'm still not waiting in the pod.'

'That way leads to Dead Man's Place,' said Matthew, now pointing in another direction. 'I don't think we want to go there either, do we?'

'Lord, no,' said Luke. 'Although I wouldn't mind a peek at Whore's Nest. Just think how fascinating it would be to study, close up, the nesting habits of the . . .'

'How do we get to Costello's pod?' enquired Jane, before Luke's plans for the team's social education could derail the entire mission.

Matthew frowned at his scratchpad. 'Um . . . the direct route would be through the gate over there, into Church Alley, turn right into Green Dragon Court and then left into Frying Pan Alley.'

He paused invitingly for the inevitable comment but Jane

was frowning at her notes and apparently Luke was too cold and grumpy to make the effort.

'Or, if you want a less direct route, we could go via Stoney Street, down Dirty Lane, turn right into Foul Lane, left into Green Dragon Court and turn right into Frying Pan Alley. Whichever we choose, Costello's pod is about halfway down. Quite a good pitch because there's what passes for a main road at the end which leads directly to London Bridge, so he's probably after any passing trade cutting through to Stoney Street.'

'Can we just get on?' said Jane, plaintively.

'What's the rush?'

Jane blushed. 'Some of us forgot to go before we came out.'

'Well, nip behind that headstone over there.'

Jane contemplated that headstone over there. Wild horses could not induce her to relieve herself in a churchyard – what sort of person weed on the dead? – and she didn't even want to contemplate the muddy, shit-ridden area on the other side of the churchyard wall.

'I can wait.'

'Sure?' said Luke. 'We can stand guard if you're that worried.'

'Quite sure,' said Jane, quite sure she couldn't, but she'd cross that bridge when she came to it.

Rumour had it that St Mary's pods had toilets. Of course, rumour also had it that St Mary's were a bunch of reckless, irresponsible half-wits with the life expectancy of a mayfly chatting to a trout at teatime, which was probably true, but that still made them reckless, irresponsible half-wits, etc. *with a toilet*.

She sighed. Would it kill the Time Police to build a small toilet into each of their pods? It wasn't as if they didn't have the technology. Actually, that was a point. Not only did they have the technology, now they had a Mikey. Hmm . . . In the meantime, she tried to think of deserts, scorched earth and arid plains.

Luke pulled his cloak around him again. 'Let's get moving before we freeze into the mud. I'll take the lead, with Jane in the middle. Matthew, you bring up the rear.'

'Roger that,' said Matthew.

'Very good,' said Luke. 'Just like a real Time Police officer.'

'Yes,' said Jane. 'Just think how good we could be if we had a real team leader.'

That time was closer than they thought.

In single file they made their way through the deserted churchyard. Naked trees stood silently, their thin, black branches clutching at the heavens. An appeal on behalf of the inhabitants, perhaps. The heavy wooden gate creaked as they let themselves out into Church Alley. The only sound was their breathing and the occasional drip of moisture from the bare branches to the hard ground beneath.

Tomorrow's icy puddles, thought Jane.

Compared to their last visit to London – nearly a hundred years before this – the streets and alleyways were almost completely deserted. Back in 1663, the popular Charles II had just ascended the throne, the long years of Puritanism were ending and Londoners were packing the streets, eager to make up for lost time. Then, the streets had been filled with the noise of the crowds, clattering hooves, wheels rumbling across the cobbles and the many and varied cries of street vendors. Now there was just a sullen, cowed silence.

Such people as were about moved quickly, hugging the sides

of the narrow streets, their eyes on the ground. Partly to watch where they were putting their feet, Jane guessed, and partly to avoid drawing any sort of attention to themselves. These were uncertain times. No one wanted their final address to be London Bridge, third spike from the left. Many shops and houses had their doors and lower windows boarded up. Were people still afraid of the rebels? Soldiers? Rioters? Even of each other?

They moved quickly but not too quickly. As Luke had said, no one wanted to turn an ankle on the frozen ruts. Jane watched her breath cloud the air in front of her and wondered why the place stank even in winter. What must it be like in the summertime?

At the head of Frying Pan Alley, Luke brought them to a halt and they crowded around Matthew's scratchpad.

'There,' said Jane. 'The signal's quite strong. Set back a little. Behind the fourth – no, fifth – building on the left.'

'OK, people,' said Luke. 'Eyes peeled. Stay behind me. Matthew . . .'

'Yeah, I know,' said Matthew. 'Watch our backs.'

They set off. Frying Pan Alley was not wide – certainly not wide enough to catch the last rays of the setting sun. The words 'dark' and 'dank' were almost too complimentary. The tiny houses on either side were unlit. Those that had shutters had closed them early. If, indeed, they ever opened them at all in these uncertain times. No lights showed. The smoke-smelling mist eddied around them.

They inched their way cautiously towards a tiny gap between what looked like a very informally built pigpen and someone's possible kitchen. The two structures were remarkably similar and there was no sound from either.

Jane felt Matthew close up behind her. She increased her pace to stand directly behind Luke and placed her hand on his shoulder to let him know she was there.

Luke halted, whispering, 'Over there. That must be the pod. And look – there's our boy.'

'Boy?' said Jane, looking at the figure holding something aloft as he harangued the small and incredibly uninterested crowd.

The narrow gap widened into a small area of lumpy waste ground large enough to accommodate their target – the entrepreneur known as John Costello – together with his pod and a rough wooden table covered with a grubby purple cloth. This was strewn with interesting-looking objects. Interesting to the Time Police, that is. No one else was showing a great deal of enthusiasm.

Mr Costello, muffled in a long, heavy coat that could have come from any century, had managed to attract a crowd of about eight or nine men – all of them nearly as down at heel as he was himself – and none of them showing even the slightest spark of interest in the marvels laid out for their approval. In fact, they bore all the marks of people pausing only very briefly on their way home. Or on their way to the pub, for which they would certainly be saving their money.

For all his sales talk, Mr Costello was clearly not winning them over.

'The headcloth of sainted Queen Jane Seymour, gentlemen. Bequeathed to an ancestor of mine who served that gracious lady and passed down through the family to me. Guaranteed – *guaranteed*, gentlemen – to cure dropsy, sweating sickness, the pox, whatever ails you. Look at the workmanship, gentlemen, fashioned by the hand of the queen herself . . .'

There was a lot more along those lines. From what Jane could see, as Team 236 drew back into the rapidly deepening shadows, John Costello was around forty years old. An ageing hippy, she thought, with his long hair turning grey and his skimpy, already grey beard. He was tall and lanky and sagged in the middle – almost as if he lacked the strength to hold himself up and his massive coat had to do it for him.

'Is anyone else looking for Scooby Doo?' murmured Luke.

Lacking any kind of sound system, John Costello was reduced to shouting at the small, indifferent crowd. His thin, reedy voice cracked occasionally. Jane wondered how long he'd been at this. No one could fault his enthusiasm, however. Standing in front of his table of marvels, he selected another item. The failing light made it impossible to see what it was from this distance, but he'd obviously given up on the head-cloth of Queen Jane.

They'd been lucky, reflected Jane. The day was drawing to a close and Costello was winding down. Ten minutes later and they might have missed him altogether.

'I can't see what he's offering,' she whispered.

'And I can't hear what he's saying,' said Luke as another couple of punters drifted away. Those left showed no signs of snapping up the remaining bargains. Another one disappeared into the shadows.

'Hold on,' said Matthew, fumbling at his belt for binoculars because none of them were wearing helmets or visors. He focused. 'Yep – definitely at least one skull on the table. Don't know if it's King Charles's . . .'

'It can't be,' said Jane swiftly, tilting her trusty notebook to catch the last of the light. 'Charles I is buried in St George's Chapel, Windsor Castle. With his head.'

'It could be anyone's skull,' said Matthew.

'Yes, because they're so easy to come by, aren't they?' said Luke sarcastically. 'You go online and order a charming young lady, milk, newspapers, cheese, a couple of bottles of wine and – oh, two skulls, please. Just to see me over the weekend.'

Matthew and Jane ignored him. Not for the first time.

'They might not even be real skulls,' said Matthew, still squinting. 'No one here would recognise something plastic-based.'

'Plastic's illegal,' said Jane, sharply.

Luke turned. 'Seriously? We have an illegal and his pod selling dubious artefacts that he acquired God knows how and you're banging on about unlawful plastic?'

Jane reflected briefly on the ease with which she continued to ignore her team leader.

'What's the plan?' enquired Matthew. 'There aren't many people left and he's going to know who we are as soon as we step out of this doorway.'

'I'll go around behind him,' said Jane.

'Stay between him and his pod,' warned Luke.

'I will.' She disappeared back past the pigpen to work her way behind Mr Costello.

'Com check,' said Luke as she rounded the corner.

'Loud and clear.'

'Right, team, stay on your toes. Remember the embarrassing saga of our first meeting with Henry Plimpton and everything that led to. So no sob stories. No second chances. No pity. In – grab the bastard – string him and straight back to the pod.

Sonic him if he looks at you wrong. Let's make sure we get this one right.'

They waited, the seconds ticking by.

'I'm in position,' reported Jane. 'If you approach now, then I can nip in behind him while he's wondering who the two clowns in black cloaks are.'

'OK, everyone,' said Luke. 'Sonics and string only to begin with. We don't want to start another riot. It's becoming our signature move. Let's go.'

They went.

Sadly, so did their target.

He didn't appear to have clocked their appearance at all so Jane could only assume he had some kind of sixth sense concerning the Time Police. Given his lifestyle, that seemed extremely likely.

In one movement, he tipped over the rickety table on which he had been displaying his wares. A deliberate act, Jane assumed, since the very small pile of grubby coins tinkling to the ground were pounced on by the few people remaining to watch his sales pitch. Word travels fast when there's loose change flying about and, within seconds, the size of the crowd had doubled as more people darted out of the shadows and joined the scrum.

Not that this drastic action did Mr Costello much good. Whirling around, he found himself almost face to face with Jane, who had taken very good care to situate herself between pod and pod owner.

'John Costello . . .'

He whirled around again. Luke and Matthew were being hampered by the people scrabbling around in the mud. Jane was on her own. Without a second thought, she aimed and stringed. Long and hard. Thick yellow tendrils wrapped themselves around Mr Costello's lower legs. In theory, he should have crashed to the ground, surrendered immediately, and allowed himself to be taken back to TPHQ, where he would enthusiastically tell them everything they wanted to know.

Sadly, this was real life and that sort of thing rarely happened to the Time Police. And to Team Weird not at all.

The fire-trucking stuff doesn't harden quickly enough, thought Jane, not for the first time.

This was a perennial complaint from hard-working Time Police officers, forced to watch their target disappear over the horizon trailing useless tendrils of still-soft yellow string. She yanked out her sonic to give Costello a quick burst and someone chasing a tiny coin knocked into her. She fell painfully into the frozen mud, skinning both her hands as she tried to save herself.

Grabbing sonic and string, she pushed herself to her knees just in time to see a tendril-festooned Costello vanish into the dark. The next second, Luke and Matthew had arrived.

'Hurt?' said Luke.

'Only my pride.'

The crowd, having grabbed all the money it could find, had disappeared, leaving Team Weird alone with an upturned table and a considerable amount of worthless tat. Queen Jane's headcloth, on closer inspection, turned out to be an old pillowslip purloined, at some stage, from the Station Hotel in Gloucester, shortly after it was built in 1880 and apparently not washed since.

'We're in the wrong job, aren't we?' sighed Matthew. 'Even our first brush with Henry Plimpton went better than this. Do you think this is some kind of record?'

'*Nil desperandum*, team,' said Luke. 'We've got this.' He slapped the side of Costello's pod. 'He has to come back. We'll simply wait and get him as soon as he reappears.'

His team regarded him dubiously.

'You know,' said Jane, brushing off her knees, 'when they wanted to put me to work in Records and send Matthew to the Time Map, they might have had a point.'

'What about me?' demanded Luke, indignantly.

'I think the smart money was on a dishonourable discharge by close of play on your first day.'

Luke stared around. The sun had gone. Dark shadows stretched towards them. The day seemed suddenly much colder.

Righting the table, they picked up and examined the remainder of Mr Costello's dubious wares.

There were a number of cheap-looking lockets containing various locks of hair. Unlabelled, so presumably the astute businessman could sum up the punter standing before him and then offer the appropriate curl of probable cat hair.

'From Queen Catherine herself, sir, a lovely lady.'

Or, 'From Our Lady of Walsingham – given to my father with her dying breath.' Which would work very well provided the customer couldn't do maths.

Or, 'A lock of hair from the sainted Thomas Becket – a cure for whatever ails you.'

Or, 'From the Old Queen herself – guaranteed long life and luck.'

Jane rather thought that not only had Queen Elizabeth I been as bald as a coot at the end of her long reign, but even when she had possessed a full head of hair, anyone attempting to take a lock therefrom would speedily find himself in the Tower and bereft of nadgers.

A much-dented goblet stood at the back. From the table of the Merry Monarch himself, no doubt.

Luke peered at – but was careful not to touch – a small pot of ointment, purpose unknown but probably guaranteed to make your nadgers drop off altogether should you be unwise enough to apply it to such a sensitive area.

There were goodluck charms a plenty, including an astonishing number of not very lucky for their original owners rabbits' feet. Jane was pretty sure several of them were anatomically impossible for a rabbit. A duck, perhaps.

There were also several phials of a suspiciously bright red fluid – no doubt the blood of the Blessed Saint Insert Name of Choice.

And finally, a couple of skulls, none of which, Jane was confident, belonged to His Majesty Charles I.

'Should we gather up his merchandise?' she enquired.

'No,' said Luke. 'I'm pretty sure he'll come back for it. It's his livelihood. He's probably watching us at this very moment.'

'Actually,' said Matthew, thoughtfully. 'I've had a Brilliant Idea.'

Luke groaned. 'Oh God, no.'

'Which is?' enquired Jane, dubious but loyal.

'One of us jumps back to HQ.'

He was regarded in silence. Eventually, Luke said, 'Why?'

'Because,' said Matthew, triumphantly, 'this is an excellent opportunity to test out Mikey's net.'

He was regarded in more silence. Luke frowned. 'Is "Mikey's net" perhaps a euphemism for . . . something else?'

Matthew turned an interesting shade of crimson. Jane was surprised to see this sort of thing could happen to other people as well and it wasn't just her.

'No,' he said, crossly. 'She's come up with something to prevent illegal pods escaping those who haven't had the fore-thought to bring an EMP with them.'

There was more silence, during which he stared at his team-mates. Who stared back again.

'Sorry,' said Luke, finally. 'I think we're going to need more.'

Matthew sighed. 'You chuck the net over the pod and it neutralises it. The pod. It's not going anywhere. If we loudly declare that Costello's been too clever for us – which is true – and that we're returning to base for a search party, then I can nip to TPHQ and bring back the net, which we then chuck over the pod. From that moment on, his pod's not going anywhere. We hide, collect John Costello as he's unsuccessfully trying to jump away, and then triumphantly return with him, his pod and his merchandise. Team Two-Three-Six and Mikey collect some well-deserved brownie points. As our revered team leader would be the first to say – no downside.'

His colleagues considered this for a moment.

'Yeah, OK,' said Luke.

Jane, however, had doubts. Possibly due to her twanging bladder. 'He'll never fall for that,' she said.

Luke shook his head. 'He can't afford not to. We've got his livelihood and his only means of getting out of here. He has to come back to get his pod or risk spending the rest of his life in 1746.'

'And you think this will work? Suppose the net fails?'

'Then we're no worse off, are we?'

'Why is Matthew going?'

Matthew opened his mouth but Luke got there first. 'Matthew's the best person to persuade Mikey. And I have to stay because I'm team leader and important.'

Jane swivelled to stare at him. 'Meaning I'm *unimportant*?'

'You know what to do,' murmured Bolshy Jane. 'A single thrust to the jugular. Quick step back to avoid the spurting blood. Job done and go.'

Matthew frowned. 'The only downside is that you two will be here without pod or back-up.'

'I'm sure even we can manage for thirty minutes or so.' Luke gestured around at the empty streets and silent houses.

'And if Costello turns up in the meantime?'

'If we can't take down an old man like Costello, then we don't deserve to be in the Time Police.'

'Will Mikey be allowed to give you the net?' asked Jane.

'She's a consultant. And we're consulting. We can call it a field trial.'

'Hay won't be happy,' she said. 'No one will be happy.'

'That clinches it for me,' said Luke. 'We'll do it. Good plan, Matthew. We'll ostentatiously depart, saying things like, "Well, he was just too clever for us", and "We'll have to give up now and return to base for reinforcements". Jane and I will huddle together under a tree or in an icy doorway and grab him as soon as he comes out of hiding. Or await your return to save the day. Whichever comes first.'

'OK,' said Matthew, on whom sarcasm rarely worked. He set off back towards their pod.

'Oh,' said Luke, loudly. 'We have failed in our mission and must return to our pod to seek further instructions.'

Jane nudged him. 'Shut up.'

'But . . .'

'Just shut up, Luke.'

Luke sighed. 'This is classic Team Weird behaviour, isn't it? Staring failure in the face and bickering about it is what we do.'

'Now you're getting it.'

5

Jane and Luke watched Matthew disappear into the cold and the dark. A few minutes later his pod signature faded from their screens.

'I hate it when that happens,' said Jane. 'Suppose we're stuck here forever.'

'Yes,' said Luke. 'Because Matthew's bound to get lost on his way back to TPHQ. And no one knows where or when we are. And Ellis and North, to say nothing of Grint, certainly wouldn't move heaven and earth to get to you. I suspect I'm a bit of an optional extra, but I can handle that. Let's go and find somewhere warmer to huddle.'

'Here,' said Jane, slipping into a deeply recessed doorway and leaning against the stone wall. The step was thick with sodden leaves, making the stones slippery and treacherous underfoot.

'This doorway's warm, is it?'

'Well, actually I chose it because it has a good view of Frying Pan Alley, but yes, it's very warm.'

Luke squeezed up beside her.

'You sure?'

'Oh yes,' said Jane with confidence. 'This doorway is much warmer than all the other doorways.'

'Well, no, actually my main concern is that this is the first doorway you meet if you're coming out of the pub down there and therefore the most likely to be urinated in, if you see what I mean.'

With some alacrity, Jane ceased to lean against the wall but it was probably too late now. She wished Luke hadn't mentioned urination. She also wondered what were the chances of Luke waiting in silence.

'Absolutely none, I should think,' said Bolshy Jane. 'Stab him now. There's a churchyard over there, for heaven's sake. There's bound to be a fresh grave somewhere. Just scrape off the topsoil and roll him in. You'll never have a better opportunity.'

'I have to ask,' said Luke, mercifully interrupting this train of thought, 'because every other officer is dying to know – how're things with you and Grint?'

This was actually the question on everyone's lips. There had been a great deal of unit-wide speculation over which of them – Jane or Grint – was the odder of this very odd couple.

Forty-eight per cent said it was Jane. Thirty-four per cent said it was Grint.

Of the remaining . . . um . . . eighteen per cent, four per cent reckoned they were both odd and the relationship should be encouraged, as it prevented them spoiling two other couples.

Three per cent objected to the relationship altogether on the grounds that it was unnatural, but since that particular three per cent all belonged to the Religious Nutters section, no one was inclined to take them too seriously. Especially since the RN's definition of unnatural was very, very different from everyone else's.

Religious Nutters wasn't the section's official name,

obviously, but no one could remember the official designation – or cared – so Religious Nutters it was. Their purpose was to prevent any and all Time Crimes committed by those who thought producing incontrovertible proof that their god actually existed would be a good thing for the world in general. Luke Parrish generally referred to these as those for whom the pendulum of religion had swung too far. Members of the RN section – possibly in sheer self-defence – tended not to believe in anything at all. Gods, Tuesdays, personal hygiene, social interaction, women, gravity, ankles – all this and more were lies put about by weak and foolish misguided wretches who had no idea the world around them was a hollow sham behind which Dark Forces waited to consume the unwary – i.e. anyone who wasn't them. Sadly, society has always been burdened with those unable to deal with the knowledge that not everyone says, does and believes as they do. A few join the Time Police. Those rejected – even by the Time Police – as being too far gone to mix with people on a daily level usually went on to become internet trolls. Or politicians.

Anyway, for those still following the plot, of the remaining eleven per cent, ten couldn't give a rat's arse about either Jane or Grint, and the remaining one per cent wished them well.

'Everything's fine,' said Jane. 'How're things with your blonde? And your brunette? And everyone else you've acquired since we last did a headcount.'

Luke rubbed his nose. 'Well, we all know the path of true love never runs smooth.'

'Your love must be truer than most, then,' said Jane. 'Judging by all the yelling coming from your room the other night. What did you do this time?'

'It wasn't clear. There's so much that women object to that it would probably be easier and quicker to ask what was going right.'

'In your case, nothing, I should imagine. What did she throw?'

'My Two-Three-Six mug,' he said, gloomily. 'I was quite fond of that one.'

'Have you ever thought of restricting yourself to just one woman at a time?'

'No,' said Luke truthfully. 'Never. Anyway, less of me, fascinating though the subject is – what of you and Grint?'

Jane took a deep breath to speak, thought better of it and subsided.

'What?' said Luke. 'Spit it out, Jane.'

'He's back to work soon.'

'Yes . . .'

'But before that . . .'

'Yes . . .'

She craned her neck. 'Is Costello's pod still there? I can't see.'

Luke consulted his scratchpad. 'Yes. Don't change the subject. What's the problem with you and Grint?'

'There isn't one. Everything's fine. Except . . .' She broke off.

Luke reviewed the facts. 'OK – you've had three, no, four dates?'

She nodded.

'Everything going well?'

She nodded again, not meeting his eye. 'We usually go to that little restaurant just round the corner. You know – where we went to celebrate when we qualified. It's nice there. And the staff are great. And they know us. Only now . . . now . . .'

She stopped, certain that her glowing face would alert Costello to their presence.

Luke regarded her shrewdly. 'Ah – got it. He's moved on to the next stage – serious making out. It's *my room or yours?* time, is it? Always tricky, I must admit. There's no privacy at TPHQ and you certainly don't want something the size of Grint trying to creep down the corridor to your room at the dead of night and everyone knowing why.'

'Well, yes, that's part of it,' said Jane, feeling her face flame like a setting sun. 'There's always someone around and . . . and, as we know from you and the other night, the rooms aren't particularly soundproof . . . or even soundproof at all . . . but the thing is . . . he hasn't actually said anything . . . so perhaps he doesn't . . . want . . . I mean . . . but he's quite . . . shy sometimes and . . . I mean, he hasn't tried anything, so perhaps he . . . well, I'm not . . . pretty . . . so perhaps he doesn't . . . find me attractive . . . and doesn't know how to . . . well, dump me.'

She stopped, awaiting inevitable self-combustion.

Luke cleared his throat. 'Much though it goes against the grain to say anything even remotely pleasant about him, I don't think Grint's that sort of bloke. You're right. He's just awkward. And so are you. Look, why don't you pick a moment – when the two of you are alone and well away from anything inflammable – and just talk to him about it?'

Jane was horrified. 'I couldn't do that. What would he think?'

'The chances are that he will be as relieved as you to have it all out in the open. The two of you can have a nice chat. And you never know, one thing might lead to another and the pair of you will drift through a romantic evening to the sound of birdsong and flowers . . .'

'What sort of sound do flowers make?'

'Don't interrupt me.'

Jane shuffled her feet, privately of the opinion this was a recipe for disaster and not only would her relationship with Grint crash to the ground, but the pair of them would spend the rest of their lives cringing with near terminal embarrassment every time they caught sight of each other.

'No, that's um . . . the thing is, Luke . . . that's not quite the . . . um . . . the whole problem.'

'Well, what then . . . ?' Luke paused and reviewed his audience and her life experience. 'Oh.'

It was far too dark to see her feet but Jane stared at them anyway.

'All right,' said Luke. 'Fact-finding time. Has he even kissed you yet?'

'Yes,' said Jane, doing her best to assume the expression of one who was kissed all the time and was actually slightly bored by the whole kissing thing. 'Obviously.'

'Anything else?' enquired Luke. 'Hands?'

'Um . . .'

'Has he tried it on?' demanded Luke. 'Do I need to go and sort him out?'

'No. No. No. No,' cried Jane, trying to shout in a whisper and very nearly luminescent with embarrassment. Far from trying anything on, Lt Grint had been a model of restraint. Jane, initially concerned that too much might happen too quickly, was now beginning to wonder why things that, according to all the romances she'd read, *should* be happening – weren't. There had

56

been the very lightest of touches – enough to make her gasp – and whether this had been misinterpreted by the other half of the relationship . . . she had no idea. Lt Grint hadn't been the only one groping in the dark. 'For God's sake, no. It was just a little bit of . . . you know . . .'

Fortunately, Luke was more than well acquainted with a spot of . . . *you know*. 'Are you saying that now he wants a bit more than just . . . you know . . .'

Jane swallowed. 'That's just it. I don't know. I don't know anything. And . . . I'm not sure he does either.'

Slightly taken aback, Luke considered this. It seemed unlikely, given his age, experience and occupation, that Lt Grint was completely unaware of the world and how it worked, but Luke was willing to bet Jane was his first proper girlfriend – that he hadn't had to pay for, anyway – and certainly his first serious relationship. It was very likely he was as much at sea as she was. Given the lack of privacy at TPHQ, and with so much mutual ignorance sloshing around between the pair of them, the possibilities for disaster were enormous, and while he could take or leave Lt Grint, Jane was his friend. And after she'd kept him alive in the snow at Site X, he owed her.

Jane was struggling on. 'The thing is, Luke, I think we've reached the . . . the point where . . . and . . .' Oh God, when did the night become so hot? 'I know the . . . the technicalities – obviously – we did it at school – but I don't know . . . some things . . . and I don't have anyone . . . to . . . ask and . . .' She tailed away again.

'Ah, gotcha,' said Luke, pulling himself together. 'And you've sought out the master. Wise move, Padawan. What do you want to know?'

'There's someone out there,' whispered Jane, thankfully.

Luke didn't move. 'Where?'

'Behind you.'

'Not Matthew?'

'No.'

'Within sonicking range?'

'No. Difficult to tell without visors, but I don't think so. Wait.'

On the other side of the street, a shadow moved and then settled again.

'He's taking his time,' whispered Jane.

'I suspect he's done this before.'

Jane drew back behind Luke and pulled out her proximity alert, shielding the glow with her hand. 'Only one signature. Not moving.'

'He's waiting,' breathed Luke. 'He suspects we're here somewhere. He'll be working out whether he can make a break for his pod before we get him.'

'I'm getting another pod signature,' whispered Jane, suddenly. 'Matthew's back.'

'This should be interesting. Ready?'

Jane nodded. 'Whenever you are.'

'We are not finished with our conversation, Jane.'

'Oh, um . . .'

Luke tilted his head, listening. 'Matthew's reporting in. Doing the biz with the net, I assume.'

Jane nodded. Good move. Disable the getaway vehicle before moving in.

There was a very faint sound above her. She wouldn't have

58

heard it if she hadn't been listening. A shadow ghosted through the night sky.

'Costello's about twenty yards from the pod,' whispered Jane, staring at her proximity meter. 'Still not moving.'

They waited in what was now solid darkness. Jane tossed back her cloak, pulled out her sonic and checked her string was accessible. Any minute now.

'Net deployed and working,' said Matthew in her ear. 'I'm behind Costello. He hasn't seen me. Wait – he's making a dash for it. Towards his pod.'

'Close in,' whispered Luke.

He ghosted out of the doorway, Jane right behind him. Leaving the shelter of the doorway, they crept towards the pod. The night was bitterly cold. And utterly silent. Jane followed Luke, placing her feet with care. She didn't want to trip.

Ahead of her and a little to her right, she heard Matthew shout, 'Time Police. On the ground. Now.' Followed by the sounds of a struggle.

Jane and Luke abandoned caution. Jane had her torch ready. Shouting, 'Time Police officers,' they picked up the pace, arriving at what seemed to be a scrum of panting, cursing, heaving limbs.

Even as they arrived, Costello tore himself free. Jane heard Matthew shout, 'Light,' and flicked on her torch. The brilliant white light lit up the scene. Costello scrabbled at the door of his pod. Matthew lunged for him at the same time as Luke. They bounced off each other and Costello disappeared inside.

'Fire truck,' shouted Matthew in frustration. 'I had him, you tosser. Why did you get in my way?'

'What do you mean?' shouted Luke. 'I had him in my

59

sights but couldn't use my sonic because you had hold of him. Idiot.'

They glared at each other.

Jane ignored them both, shining her torch over the scene.

'Hey,' said Mikey, strolling from behind the pod.

'What . . . ?' said Luke, abandoning a complicated sentence concerning Matthew's parentage and abilities. 'What are you doing here?'

'Field trial,' said Mikey. 'Checking out performance under mission conditions.'

Luke looked at Matthew. 'Are you mad? Two women in one pod – asking for trouble.'

'Three,' said Officer Varma, strolling from behind the other side of the pod. 'You made a complete dog's breakfast of that one, didn't you? Presumably security will have to save the day. Again.'

Luke raised his arms in exasperation. 'What the hell are *you* doing here?'

'Lt Filbert said Two-Three-Six was in desperate need of both muscle *and* brains. So here I am.'

'Were those his actual words?'

'No, actually it was more like – "I don't know what those morons in Two-Three-Six are up to – nor do I want to know – but it seems they've screwed up again. You'd better go along too, Varma. Any of them give you any trouble, then shoot the lot of them and make sure you're back in time for your training session this evening."'

'So thoughtful,' murmured Luke.

'Additionally, the Time Police felt it necessary to safeguard their new investment.' Varma regarded Mikey closely. 'There were concerns over said investment possibly seeking to escape the hospitality of the Time Police.'

'Nah,' said Mikey dismissively. 'If I wanted to go, I'd be gone by now.'

Varma narrowed her eyes. 'I wouldn't be too sure.'

That Mikey was unimpressed by this threat was apparent.

Varma continued, 'I wasn't doing anything important and I don't get out as often as I would like, so here I am. On the other hand, the last time I went out with you three, you nearly killed me.'

'Don't take it personally,' said Luke. 'We nearly killed everyone.'

'Should we move back a little?' said Jane, who had been nervously watching the pod. 'Just in case he does jump away?'

Mikey shook her head confidently. 'This pod's not going anywhere. Trust me.'

'In that case,' said Varma, 'and since it's not getting any warmer, perhaps we should persuade the occupants to surrender themselves into our tender care.'

'There's only one,' said Luke.

Varma sighed in an unnecessarily exaggerated manner. 'So – five of us and one of him.' She shook her head. 'Your move, Officer Parrish.'

Luke thumped on the door. 'This is the Time Police. Your pod has been disabled. Come out with your hands up. Don't make me send for a clean-up crew.'

There was a long pause, during which John Costello was presumably still running through the various procedures for initiating a jump – none of which would be successful.

Luke, Matthew and Mikey stood by the door. Varma stood

well back – because this was Team Weird, after all. Jane moved off a little to scan their surroundings for any unwanted attention. There was none. The aftermath of a failed rebellion was not the time to investigate unexplained shouting in the dark. She was confident they wouldn't be disturbed.

Luke banged on the door again. 'Come out, Mr Costello.'

'Costello?' said Mikey, startled.

Luke looked at her. 'Yeah. You know him?'

She turned to Matthew. 'You didn't say.'

'I didn't know you knew him.'

'If it's who I think it is, then I do. Slightly.'

'We'll talk about this later,' said Luke. 'Can you persuade him to open the door? Jane has a full bladder.'

Mikey shifted her feet. 'So you can arrest him?'

'Well, yes. We're the Time Police. It's what we do.'

'He's harmless.'

'He's selling the head of Charles I.'

'Well, if people are stupid enough . . .'

'He has an illegal pod.'

'If you arrest everyone who has one of those . . .'

'We'd be doing our job,' finished Luke. 'You are aware of who you work for, aren't you?'

'I thought you'd be arresting real criminals. Like Henry Plimpton. Not persecuting harmless . . .'

'Con men,' finished Luke. 'He's selling fake heads.'

'There's no crime in that. Religions everywhere deal in so-called religious artefacts. There are enough pieces of the one true cross out there to replant the rainforests.'

'You do realise it was your net that prevented his getaway, don't you? It's your fault he's not a free man any longer.'

Mikey glared at him and sighed. She tapped on the door. 'Hey, Jake. It's me, Mikey. Remember me? Your pod's disabled and you can't get away. Yes, they're the Time Police, but this bunch are more likely to fall over their own feet than do you any harm.'

'Hurtful,' said Luke.

'But true,' murmured Bolshy Jane.

'You can come out. They won't hurt you; I promise.'

There was a very long pause. And then, slowly, the door swung open.

6

Jane thought afterwards it was like something from a classic horror film. The door creaking open to reveal the sinister and possibly monster-filled darkness within. Of course – the pod had no power and the emergency lighting had obviously failed. Mr Costello hadn't kept his batteries charged.

'Jakey,' said Mikey brightly. 'It's me. How you doing?'

'Mikey? It *is* you.'

'Course it is. Who else?'

'*You're* in the Time Police?'

'*With*, my friend, not *in*. I'm a consultant. Are you going to come out?'

Slowly, in the best *Hammer House of Horror* tradition, a figure emerged through the swirling fog. Jane struggled not to laugh.

Team 236 crowded around.

'OK,' said Mikey, obviously regarding herself as the doyenne of their little social event. 'Introductions, I think. This is Mr Costello.' She paused as if to add some kind of job description and wisely decided against it. 'And these are Officers Varma, Parrish, Farrell and . . .'

'Never mind that. What do you want? I wasn't doing any harm.'

Luke intervened. 'You're selling fake artefacts and . . .'

'I'm selling mementos of past events. No one claims they're genuine. No one even cares.'

'You are the owner of an illegal pod.'

'No, I'm not.'

Luke gestured at the dark pod. 'Excuse me . . .'

'It's not mine,' said Costello, swiftly.

'Really? Whose is it, then?'

He closed his mouth. 'No comment.'

Luke sighed.

Jane was shining her torch around the pod interior searching for something – anything – that might be a door to a small toilet. She wasn't even that bothered about the state of it – which wouldn't be wonderful if the rest of the pod was anything to go by, but she was past the point of being fussy.

Like owner – like pod. Mr Costello was unkempt and dishevelled and so was his pod. The air was stale – she suspected the air con had long since packed up. The torchlight picked out scuffed patches on the walls and floor and dubious stains everywhere. Boxes of probable junk were stacked around the walls, leaving just enough room for one person to access the primitive console. The screen wasn't working – nothing would work while Mikey's net was still in place, and even when it was removed, the pod would have to be rebooted – but Jane wouldn't mind betting the screen had more dead pixels than living. The console was littered with plates of half-eaten food that had congealed in self-defence. Stained mugs contained fluid. What sort of fluid was impossible to say without chemical analysis. A bucket stood in one corner. Its purpose could easily be guessed at. Her thoughts returned to the Atacama Desert.

With Jane dwelling on desiccation and drought, Luke was drilling down to the point of today's mission. 'What's in the boxes, Costello?'

John Costello remained silent.

Matthew stepped inside, took out his knife and made a neat slit across the top of one of the boxes. Reaching inside, he pulled out a cheap plastic skull. Reaching inside again, he pulled out another one. Both were labelled.

Jane obligingly shone her torch. Matthew read the first label. 'Head of the martyred Charles I.'

He read the second label. 'Head of the traitor, Charles I.'

'Pandering to every market,' said Luke admiringly. 'I like it.'

Matthew frowned at the skulls. 'Why is this one so much smaller than that one?'

Mr Costello never missed a beat. 'That's Charles I as a child.'

'Oh, mate,' said Luke, more in sorrow than in anger. 'You are so nicked.'

'Can you all excuse me for one moment,' said Jane. Never mind the entrail-strewn surroundings – privacy was suddenly her overriding priority.

She had only just stepped out through the door when she was knocked to the ground for the second time that night, as Mr Costello, showing an astonishing turn of speed, made his getaway. Also for the second time that night.

The only one to move was Officer Varma, who shoved Luke and Matthew out of her way and disappeared after him.

Jane heaved herself to her feet and also disappeared into the night, but for entirely different reasons.

The remaining two-thirds of Team Weird, together with their consultant, stared out into the pitch darkness.

'And he's gone again,' said Matthew.

'Well, fire truck me,' said Luke. 'This was supposed to be an easy assignment. Now what?'

'We wait,' said Matthew.

'What for?'

'I'm sure Officer Varma has everything well in hand, so let's see what happens next.'

They waited. But not for long.

There was a female scream in the dark. Closely followed by a male shout of surprise. Followed by another female scream in the dark. Followed by a male cry of alarm. Followed by the sounds of someone on the receiving end of a really good seeing-to.

'Sounds like Varma got her man,' said Luke, cheerfully. 'I hear she's clear favourite for the inter-departmental Punch Your Opponent's Lights Out Competition next week.'

'Actually, I think he might have fallen over Jane,' said Matthew as the sounds died away. 'Should we go and save him, do you think?'

'Oh, I don't think so,' said Luke. 'Jane's not going to be in the best mood and Varma's still out there somewhere, as well. We'll guard the pod, shall we? By which I mean, let's stay here out of harm's way until everyone sorts themselves out.'

Matthew pulled out his torch and switched it on. A sharp white beam cut through the darkness.

'Hoi,' shouted Jane from not that far away and foreshadowing the Blitz by some one hundred and ninety-five years. 'Put that light out.'

'Sorry,' shouted Matthew. He put that light out.

There was a short pause.

'OK, you can put it back on again now.'

'Follow me, team,' cried Luke, striding dramatically into the dark.

Mikey and Matthew exchanged glances but followed in his footsteps anyway.

'Are you decent, Jane?' called Luke.

'Yes, of course I am,' said Jane, crossly. 'I didn't actually have time to get going before this idiot fell over me.'

'So you *still* haven't . . . ?'

'Can we talk about something else, please.'

'Like how you took down John Costello all by yourself,' said Matthew, admiringly staring at the groaning figure in the frozen mud. 'You don't really need us, do you?'

'I bring you two along to make me look good,' said Jane.

Varma arrived out of the darkness. 'Did you get him?'

'I did. If you care to assist Mr Costello to our pod, we can be getting home. To some proper facilities.' Jane turned to Mikey. 'Never mind nets, power sources, invisibility bracelets and all the other stuff – could you build in a toilet?'

''Spect so,' said Mikey, suddenly thoughtful.

'Speaking of which, we need to get your net back and secure the illegal pod,' said Matthew.

'And organise a clean-up crew,' said Luke.

'And I can't wait that long,' said Jane, disappearing into the dark again.

While Matthew and Mikey shot off to retrieve their equipment, Varma and Luke escorted the considerably shaken John Costello back to their pod. Jane had been seriously displeased at being interrupted at a critical moment and had reacted accordingly.

He made no resistance as they pushed him into a seat and used the restraints. Wrists *and* ankles because Costello had form. As Luke said, 'To lose your prisoner once is a misfortune. To lose him twice is a monumental cock-up. To lose him three times is to have to live in Ulan Bator for the rest of your life because no one in the Time Police would ever let you forget it.'

Varma seemed amused. 'Your team really does have its own style, doesn't it?'

'A style soon to be emulated by every other officer in the Time Police,' said Luke, with dignity. 'How long before we can get back to TPHQ?'

Varma shrugged. 'Depends. Got a date, have you?'

'Of course,' said Luke, as in *doesn't everyone?*

'Well, we can perhaps make a start while waiting for your colleagues to materialise.' She stood before John Costello. 'You said the pod was not yours. To whom does it belong?'

'Not saying.'

'All right. Who do you work for?'

'Myself.'

'Not for the owner of the pod?'

He shook his head vigorously.

She regarded him for a moment. 'Did you steal it?'

Costello paused just that moment too long. 'No.'

'So you stole it. From whom?'

'No one.'

'So if we were to disable your pod, tie you to the seat, leave you and it here, and broadcast your whereabouts to everyone we knew – no one would come looking for you?'

'No,' he said, but his voice lacked conviction.

'We could do that quite easily,' said Luke. 'Chuck him out

into the night, engage our camo device and wait to see who turns up.'

'And see what they do to Mr Costello here. Good scheme, Officer Parrish.'

'Thank you. And we could while away the time by laying bets on *who* turns up for our friend here.'

'And whether our prisoner survives the experience.'

'Oh, I think it's a given he won't,' said Luke. 'I think we should get as much out of him as we can now since he's unlikely to last the night.'

'Another good scheme, Parrish.'

'Yes,' said Luke. 'I really think I'm getting the hang of this Time Police business. Give it a couple of weeks and I'll be as big a bastard as the rest of you.'

'You wish. For instance, five minutes into our interrogation and I can't help noticing the prisoner is disappointingly undamaged.'

'Well, give me a chance. Why don't you take a quick stroll for ten minutes or so? You know. So I can work up a real man's sweat.'

'I'm not saying anything,' declared John Costello. Very unconvincingly.

'Hush, John,' said Varma. 'The grown-ups are talking.'

'It's Mister Costello.'

'Actually, it's *Prisoner* Costello.'

Prisoner Costello made no response.

The door opened to admit Mikey and Matthew.

'Bad news,' announced Mikey, cheerfully. 'The net melted. It's made a dreadful mess.' She turned to Prisoner Costello.

'Not sure how much damage has been done to your pod. Fingers crossed, eh?'

'Should it do that?' enquired Luke. 'Overheat and melt, I mean.'

'Not really, but it doesn't matter – the result is the same. That pod's going nowhere.'

'Leave it,' said Varma. 'I'll send a clean-up crew to sort things out.'

'Yes,' said Mikey. 'It's too hot to handle at the moment, but could they make sure they bring back as much of the net as they can, please? I really need to take a look at it. Although I think I know what went wrong.'

'That's very comforting to the rest of us,' said Varma. 'Any sign of Lockland yet?'

John Costello looked up. 'Who?'

'Officer Lockland,' said Luke. 'You trod on her while she was attempting to avail herself of the local facilities.'

Varma frowned at their prisoner. 'Is there some significance to Officer Lockland?'

He shrugged but wouldn't meet her eyes.

'I asked you a question, Costello. What about Officer Lockland?'

'What about Officer Lockland?' said Jane, coming through the door and closing it behind her. 'It's freezing out there.'

She busied herself stowing her cloak away in a locker and then became aware of the silence around her. 'What? Has something happened?'

Varma ignored her. 'Do you know this officer?'

Costello cast Jane a fleeting glance and then looked away again. 'No.'

71

He was obviously lying.

'Lockland, do you know this man?'

'No,' said Jane, puzzled. 'I've never seen or heard of him before. In fact . . .'

'Sweetie,' said Bolshy Jane very quietly. 'Something's going on here. Don't say another word until you know what it is.'

Jane shut up.

Not that anyone noticed. Mr Costello was gabbling like a maniac who couldn't get the words out fast enough. 'Did you do this on purpose? Why else would you send her?'

White-faced and trembling, he faced Jane. 'I never told anyone. I swear I never told anyone.'

Jane had never had this effect on anyone before. Not even when acting the part of badass Time Police officer.

'I don't understand,' she began.

'Hush,' said Bolshy Jane. 'I've got a very bad feeling about this.'

'But . . .' Which was as far as she got, because at that moment, John Costello rolled up his eyes and collapsed back in his chair.

'Oh my God,' said Jane, stepping back. 'Have we killed him? What did we do?'

Everyone looked accusingly at Varma, who held up her hands. 'Hey – it wasn't me. I'm all the way over here. Is he still breathing?'

Matthew felt for a pulse. 'I think so. Should I get him some water?'

'He's unconscious. Are you going to bathe him?'

Matthew brought water anyway.

Mikey moved back against the wall, out of the way. 'I have

72

got to get me a job as a field officer. I had no idea your missions were so exciting.'

'He's coming round,' said Matthew. 'What do we do?'

'Put his head between his knees.' Luke paused. 'To be perfectly clear: Costello's head between Costello's knees. No part of Matthew's anatomy is involved.'

'Yes,' said Varma.

'No,' said Matthew. 'I mean yes. No, I mean no.'

'I am definitely going out with this team again,' said Mikey. 'This is the funniest thing I've seen since Adrian set fire to Dieter's boots. And he was in them at the time.' She considered this sentence. 'Dieter, I mean.'

John Costello's eyes fluttered open. He hauled himself upright, leaned back, closed his eyes again and took a deep breath. Then another.

'Steady on,' said Varma. 'Don't start hyperventilating. Just take things slowly. We won't jump until you're ready.'

Costello nodded and sipped the water Matthew held to his lips. Slowly his colour came back. He drew a couple of deep breaths and looked at Jane.

'Your name is Lockland?'

'Yes.'

He looked at the rest of them. 'Who are you?'

'Time Police, mate,' said Luke. 'Like I said. You really need to cut back on the wacky baccy.'

Costello looked up at Jane. 'I don't understand. Why are you here?'

'All right – enough,' said Luke in exasperation. 'Tell us what this is about, for God's sake.'

'It's about her.'

'Lockland?'

Costello shook his head. 'Her mother.'

'My mother?' said Jane in astonishment. 'Helen Lockland? What about her?'

Costello closed his eyes and, as much as he could with such restricted movement, began to rock backwards and forwards.

Varma looked from Costello to Jane and back again. 'Be quiet, Lockland.'

'But . . .'

'That's an order.'

Jane subsided.

Varma turned to Costello. 'You're talking about Helen Lockland?'

He shook his head. 'No.'

'Helen Lockland was my mother,' said Jane, disobeying a direct order and not for the first time.

He shook his head. 'That wasn't her real name.'

Jane felt the ground shift under her feet. Finding her voice, she whispered, 'What was her real name?'

John Costello closed his eyes as if he thought it might help.

'Your mother was Helen Portman.'

7

Historians are always banging on about pivotal moments – whether you want them to or not, actually. Moments when, without warning, events pivot and everything is different. Not what you thought. Same events – different point of view. Different interpretations.

Not immediately, of course. Often there are long, blank moments of incomprehension as everyone struggles to catch up and reorient themselves in a suddenly strange, new world.

This was the moment when, as so many had predicted it would one day, Team Weird fell apart. Shattered into a million fragments.

The silence in the pod was so complete that Jane could clearly hear the faint hum from the console. She stared at John Costello, his words running through her mind on some kind of loop as she grappled with their meaning. Her mother was Helen Portman.

Luke stood like a pillar, staring at Jane as if he could hardly believe his eyes. Or his ears. Or the words that had just been uttered.

Matthew looked from one to the other and then instinctively took a protective step towards Jane.

Luke found his voice first. 'You're a *Portman*?'

'So are you,' said Matthew, swiftly.

'Your mother was a Portman?'

'So is yours,' said Matthew. 'It's no big deal.'

'No big deal?' shouted Luke. *'No big deal?'* He rounded on Jane. 'You . . .'

Varma moved swiftly. 'Sit down, Parrish.'

It is possible Luke never heard her. His entire attention was focused on Jane, who still stood, stunned.

Varma was in his face. Full on. *'I said, "Sit down, Officer Parrish."'*

Still not taking his eyes off Jane, Luke backed into a seat.

'And you, Lockland.'

Matthew nudged Jane into another seat. One, not coincidentally, as far away from Luke as was possible in such a small space. A small space so thick with bewilderment, disbelief and shock that Matthew could have reached out and touched it.

It was generally reckoned afterwards that had Officer Varma not been present, then the situation could have turned very ugly indeed. Standing in front of Costello, she said quietly, 'John Costello, you are under arrest for crimes yet to be determined. You will accompany me back to TPHQ to answer all questions put to you. Sit down, Miss Meiklejohn. Officer Farrell, if you could take us home, please.'

Matthew nodded dumbly and seated himself at the console. He ran his eyes over the various read-outs, using the time to pull himself together.

'Greens across the board.'

'Whenever you're ready, Officer Farrell.'

76

'Commencing jump procedures.'

The world flickered.

Their landing was gentle. Under normal circumstances Matthew would have demanded congratulations. As it was, the thought never entered his mind. He busied himself shutting things down. The silence in the pod was thick and heavy and dangerous.

'Fall in, everyone,' said Varma, releasing the prisoner from his restraints. 'Follow me to security.'

'Actually . . .' said Luke, between clenched teeth.

'That's an order, Parrish.'

They fell in as instructed. Mikey exchanged worried glances with Matthew and then, unsure whether she was included or not, trailed along some yards behind.

Varma marched them all out of the Pod Bay, past the astonished mechs and straight into security.

Lt Filbert looked up at their entrance, shock written all across his face. 'What on earth . . . ?'

'One prisoner to book in,' said Varma. 'John Costello.'

A long-standing and experienced officer, Lt Filbert was generally reckoned to be a bit of a bastard and with even less of a sense of humour than your average member of the Time Police, but he had recovered himself and was grinning now. 'Only one prisoner, Varma? There's so many of you, I thought you were bringing in an entire army.'

'The mission suffered some unexpected developments, sir,' said Varma, stiffly. 'I'm about to take statements from everyone.'

Filbert paused and looked at the group more closely. Luke, still rigid with rage. Jane still stunned. Matthew still concerned.

Mikey last in through the door and still slightly bewildered. John Costello still Prisoner Costello.

Filbert turned to Varma. 'Look, if you want to get this done more quickly then I'll process the civilian. Shouldn't take me too long.'

'No, it's OK, thank you, sir,' said Varma, typing the details into the duty report. 'I think initially I'll interview them as a group.'

The lieutenant hesitated. 'Are you sure, Varma? I didn't want to say anything, but some of you look – and smell – as if you've been rolling around in a manure heap.'

'Very perceptive of you, sir. That's exactly what some of us have been doing.'

'Not to hurt your feelings, Varma, but you and your prisoner are stinking out my lovely facility.'

She sighed. 'Point taken, sir.' She looked at Team Weird. 'Get yourselves cleaned up, then report back here.'

Filbert frowned and took her aside for a moment. 'What's the problem here?'

Varma glanced over her shoulder at the disappearing Team Weird and lowered her voice. 'Not sure, sir. An issue within the team.'

'I'm assuming something more serious than their usual malfunctioning team dynamics.'

'I think so, sir. There could be repercussions. Certainly something we should keep in-house until we find out exactly what's going on.'

Filbert grunted and ran his eyes over the prisoner. 'This Jake Costello. What exactly has he done?'

'Possession of a pod which may or may not be his. Illegal sale of fake historical artefacts. Breathing . . .'

'Is he injured?'

'Possibly, sir, he fell over Officer Lockland in the dark. And then I think he fainted.'

Filbert frowned. 'We'd better get him checked out first, then. I don't want him slipping through our fingers by claiming Time Police brutality. Or that he banged his head and didn't know what he was saying.'

'Yes, sir.'

He headed towards the door. 'Interrogation Room 1 is free – put him in there. I'll call for the doctor.'

'Thank you, sir.'

'And then take yourself off for a shower, as well. You're still stinking out my lovely facility.'

Fifteen minutes later, a freshly showered Matthew went to meet Mikey in her workroom/dungeon. As has already been mentioned, this wasn't the easiest place to access, although notices saying *This Way to the Bat Cave* posted at regular intervals were certainly an aid to navigation. As was the handwritten poster on the door.

> This is no longer an accident-free workplace.
> It has been 0 days since the last incident.
> Has anyone seen the Senior Mech today?
> Anyone?

He grinned and pushed his way inside.

Mikey's domain was quite large. A big room about thirty feet square. There were no windows, of course, but that left more room for the floor-to-ceiling racks of shelving along the walls.

Despite her short tenure, these were already stuffed full of bits of tech – purpose unknown and unguessable – together with books; a shoe – not one of hers; a plate with something once edible welded to it; a couple of torches; a handless clock – for some reason; a first-aid kit still in its wrapping; a length of rubber hosing; half a dozen mugs in different stages of cleanliness; a box of data stacks; a cluster of lightsticks; more books; various notebooks – some unused, some not, and one which looked to have been immersed in something unpleasant; two tins of biscuits; a caddy of what looked very much like tea but couldn't possibly be because that would be illegal, wouldn't it?; half a dozen tins of beer lightly disguised as toilet rolls; half a dozen actual toilet rolls; a banjo; what looked like a mechanical octopus; half a dozen canisters of string; a whole North Sea fishing fleet of nets in various sizes and mesh; a box of face masks; two Bunsen burners; two staplers; a struggling air freshener; and a six-inch-square sound system that could probably produce enough decibels to cause birds to drop from the sky.

A long wooden table was pushed against another wall with what looked like two of Henry Plimpton's bracelets, each enclosed in its own Faraday cage. An enormous dust hood hung from the ceiling. A poster of the periodic elements had been duct-taped to one wall, alongside a kitten peering from a wellington boot, alongside a poster promoting an infamous Swedish death-metal band. Copies of Captain Farenden's carefully compiled *Time Police House Rules* lay unregarded on the floor. Seven variously coloured fire extinguishers had been placed at strategic intervals around the workroom – one for every conceivable type of fire and a couple more for new types Mikey hadn't come up with yet – together with three buckets of sand should the extinguishers prove ineffective. Two blasters were propped up in a corner, almost certainly fully charged. And a dartboard had been fixed to the back of the door at exactly the right height to take someone's eye out should they open the door at the wrong moment.

A smaller table in the corner supported a kettle, some very iffy-looking milk – Matthew's mother would almost certainly take this opportunity to inform everyone that all milk is iffy – and a catering-sized pack of sugar.

Mikey beamed at his entrance. 'Hello.'

He smiled back. 'Ready?'

'Yes.' They stepped out into the corridor together. 'What's this all about, Matthew? Both Luke and Jane looked as if they'd seen a ghost.'

Matthew sighed. 'The Portmans and the Parrishes are long-standing business rivals. There was some sort of arranged marriage between Luke's father and Alessa Portman. Possibly it wasn't so much a marriage as a merger. You know – big family dynastic stuff. So Luke's mother is a Portman. Which came as a bit of a shock to him. Then this bloke called Eric Portman was mixed up in that Site X business and supposedly topped himself to avoid discovery. The jury's still out on whether it was suicide or not, and if not, then who did it.'

'I still don't see . . .'

'Eric Portman was the person who involved Imogen Farnborough in illegal Time travel. And some other things, too. For which she was executed. By us.'

'Even so . . .'

'She was Luke's girlfriend. Or had been at one time. He was still quite fond of her.'

81

'Oh. And now we discover that Jane . . .'

'Is a Portman. Half a Portman anyway.'

'But, surely, so is Luke.'

'Yes,' said Matthew.

'This is . . .' She stopped, thinking through the implications.

'This is going to be nasty,' said Matthew. 'Luke has . . . not yet learned not to make mistakes in his life.'

'Nice way of putting it,' said Mikey, pushing through the door. 'What's going to happen now? And how is all this connected to Jakey?'

'Don't know yet. It's the first I've heard of any of this. And Jane looked utterly gobsmacked, didn't she?'

'She did, yes.'

Turning a corner, they found Jane in the corridor just ahead of them. Luke was already waiting for them outside Interrogation Room 1. Varma arrived at the same time as Mikey and Matthew.

'Right,' Varma said, addressing them all. 'Rules. With which you will comply. Initially, I will interview you all as a group. Anyone misbehaving will be evicted on the toe of my boot and a complaint lodged with Major Ellis. Anyone anticipating problems with complete obedience to my every word – speak now.'

There was silence.

'Right, then. In you go.'

Luke hit the control and the door hissed open.

To reveal John Costello lying on the floor in a pool of dark, shiny blood.

'Shit,' said Varma, pushing her way to the front. 'Everyone stay well back. Parrish, get a medic up here fast.'

'No need,' said the doctor, appearing with Lt Filbert. 'What's happened here?'

'Unknown,' said Varma, stiffly. 'The situation is just as you see it. No one's touched anything.'

Filbert took in the situation at a glance. 'All of you – hand over your weapons. Lay them on the table there. Yes, you too, Parrish. Varma – clear the area. Move everyone into Room 2. Keep them there. No one leaves. Including you.'

He followed the doctor into the room and closed the door in their faces.

'You heard the lieutenant,' said Varma. 'Interrogation Room 2. Now.' She opened her com. 'Major Ellis? Sir, we have a situation in security involving members of Team Two-Three-Six. Your urgent attention is required.'

They filed into the second interrogation room.

'Sit,' said Varma. 'No one speaks. No one moves. We wait.'

The wait seemed endless.

Someone brought coffee. Jane buried her nose in her mug. Luke looked everywhere except at Jane. Matthew stared at the table. Mikey stared at the wall. Varma watched them all.

After what seemed like hours, Filbert strode through the door.

'Right,' he said. 'As you will be aware, the prisoner Costello has been attacked and sustained a severe head trauma. He's been removed to MedCen where he will remain under armed guard. He is expected to recover, although when, and how completely, is not yet known.'

'Does this mean you think it was one of us?' demanded Luke.

'All the evidence certainly points in that direction.'

Filbert gestured to the guard who had followed him in. 'I'll interview you all one at a time. You're all under observation,' he glanced up at the camera, 'and Miller here will remain to discourage any inadvertent wandering.' He paused, meaningfully. 'Or colluding.'

'You mean we're actually suspects?' demanded Luke, outraged.

'I do indeed, Officer Parrish. Please feel free to register your displeasure with Officer Miller, who will be delighted to ignore your every word. Varma – you're up first.'

Their actions, as described to Lt Filbert, were all similar. Varma hadn't left security, showering and changing in the female locker room. No witnesses.

On leaving security, Luke had showered and enjoyed an illegal drink in his room. No witnesses.

Jane had showered and tried to think about the implications of what Costello had said. No witnesses.

Matthew had showered and then gone to collect Mikey. Who had not showered – because, as she pointed out, she hadn't been rolling around in the mud because that wasn't what she was paid to do.

When asked, sarcastically, what she *was* paid to do, she replied, 'To discover how my net managed to melt all over Jake Costello's pod,' before going on to enquire whether this was going to take much longer because she had work to get on with.

Establishing all of this took some considerable time.

As their department head, Major Ellis was invited, as a courtesy, to sit in on every interview, which he did, making no comments of any kind. At the end of Lt Filbert's interrogation, Ellis instructed Team 236 and Miss Meiklejohn to wait for him in his office. Such was his tone of voice that even Luke forbore to argue.

Major Ellis watched them trail out through the door and then turned to Filbert. 'Do we yet know how this happened? What do the cameras show?'

'Nothing, sir. The cameras in Room 1 were disabled from the control room. Which,' he set his teeth, 'was temporarily unmanned. Jessop discovered a minor electrical fault and went for a new handset. He was gone less than two minutes. In his absence the cameras were switched off. He was about to raise the alarm when Varma did it for him. And before you ask – he's been bollocked rigid but has an alibi for the period in question. Oti from Logistics was with him the whole time.' He sighed. 'No one saw a thing. Including me. I was in my office summoning the doctor. But that only took a minute.'

Ellis said nothing. Mutterings that Filbert was getting too old for the job had been doing the rounds for over a year now. He suspected that Filbert, having spent all his working life in the Time Police, had nowhere else to go and had, possibly in an attempt to put it off for as long as possible, made very little provision for retirement. It happened all too often. He suspected the same thing would happen to Grint. And Fanboten, perhaps. And Dal. Not Varma. Definitely not North. And until an hour ago, he'd have said not Team 236 because none of them were likely to live that long. There was now every possibility Team 236 wouldn't exist for long enough to bear out his theory.

He was on the point of leaving when the news came through that the prisoner was awake. He pulled himself to his feet. 'With your permission, Lieutenant, I'd like to hear what he has to say.'

'Of course, sir.'

MedCen wasn't far away. Through several sets of double doors and they were there. The prisoner, Costello J, was enjoying his own private cubicle in the ward set aside for senior officers. Two armed guards sat outside.

'Two?' said Ellis.

Filbert stopped, turned away and muttered, 'One to watch the other.'

'You're taking no chances.'

'Not until we know what we're dealing with here, sir. After you.'

Other than his pallor, John Costello looked remarkably chipper for someone who, so far, was having a very bad day. The only other sign of his injury was a large wound dressing taped to a shaved patch in his scraggy grey hair.

'Sorry about the smell,' said the doctor. 'We've cleaned him up a little but it's definitely him – not us.'

'Is he making sense?' said Filbert. 'Can we rely on anything he says?'

'He's not too bad,' said the doctor. 'He knows who he is and can speak coherently. Which is actually more than can be said of most officers.' He consulted his scratchpad. 'Fifteen minutes. No longer. If your questioning doesn't kill him then you can come back this evening for another go.'

He disappeared, leaving them alone with the patient, who grinned amiably at them. Something that convinced both officers that Costello was slightly more out of things than the doctor had led them to believe. Very few people grinned amiably at the Time Police.

In an unfamiliar attempt to look less threatening, they both sat down.

Filbert opened the batting. 'Do you know who I am?'

Costello squinted at him for a long time, struggling to focus, and then shook his head. And winced.

'Do you remember me from before your injury?'

Costello regarded him warily. 'Should I?'

'No. Do you know where you are?'

'Not really.'

'You're at TPHQ. You've been arrested on comparatively minor charges. It's very possible those charges might disappear completely if you cooperate. Do you understand what I'm saying to you?'

'Yes, I think so.'

'All right. Do you remember being arrested?'

'Yes. I think so.' He squinted. 'But not by you.'

'No, neither of us were your arresting officers. We're here about your injury. Do you remember what happened?'

Costello frowned. 'I was sitting at the table. Someone said coffee . . . I think. I was thirsty.'

'Did you hear the door open?'

'Think so.'

'Who came in?'

He shook his head again. And winced again.

'Did you hear anything? Any particular sound?'

'No.'

Ellis had a thought. 'Did you *smell* anything?'

Costello frowned. 'No.'

'Any clues at all as to who attacked you?'

'None.' He looked at Filbert. 'Is that what happened?'

'It would seem so,' said Ellis. 'Unless you threw yourself backwards off your chair, of course.'

87

Costello's forehead creased. 'No, don't think so.'

'Chair was upright when we found him,' muttered Filbert. He turned to Costello. 'Can you give us anything – anything at all – that might help us identify your attacker?'

'No. Sorry. It's a complete blank.'

Filbert sighed and went to stand up.

'I have a few more questions,' said Ellis.

'Sorry, sir.' Filbert sat back down again.

'Helen Lockland.'

Costello's eyelids flickered.

'Or should I say Helen Portman? Please think very carefully before telling us you don't know who she is.'

'Did know her. She's dead now.'

'Do you know what happened to her?'

'Well, yeah. You bastards killed her, didn't you?'

8

Commander Hay was not in the best mood.

'Where the hell did all this blow up from, Charlie? We despatch Two-Three-Six to pick up some minor illegal, and two hours later it's World War Four out there. Any news on who attacked John Costello?'

'No, ma'am. None.'

'One of us, obviously.'

'Major Ellis and Lt Filbert are conducting a thorough investigation.'

'And getting nowhere.'

'I'm afraid so. Officers Lockland, Parrish and Farrell have all been instructed to remain in their quarters. Just keeping them out of the way until the situation is clearer. Varma is back on duty but is being monitored.'

'Meiklejohn?'

'Given the remote location of her workroom, ma'am, and that St Mary's advised us to keep her occupied at all times, I've allowed her to return to work.'

Hay nodded. 'Wise. And Costello himself has no idea who attacked him?'

'None, ma'am. He thinks he remembers hearing the door open behind him but nothing more.'

She sighed.

'I have Lt Filbert's official report on Costello's interrogation, ma'am.'

'Give me the gist.'

'Well, in order of revelations, ma'am, I'll begin with Lockland's parents – Aaron and Helen Lockland. Or Helen Portman, as she apparently was.'

Hay settled back. 'Go on.'

'It's not good, ma'am. It's especially not good for us.'

'No. Not one of our finest moments, I believe.'

'Our understanding is that, acting on information laid by old Mrs Lockland, her son and his wife were the subject of a Time Police action.' He sighed. 'Which, as we already knew, they did not survive.'

'Do we have any details as to what happened? Reports filed at the time and so forth?'

'It all took place some fifteen or more years ago, ma'am. Preliminary searches haven't turned up anything, so I've set Lt North on it. She'll find something, I'm certain.'

'We know that Lockland's parents were illegals, resisted arrest and we shot them. Unfortunate, but . . .'

'According to the prisoner, Costello, Lockland's parents weren't involved in illegal Time travel at all, ma'am.'

Hay suddenly sat forwards. 'What?'

'Well, they were, but not in the way we thought. They were running a safe house.'

Hay frowned. 'What sort of a safe house? Safe from whom?

Us? Lockland's hag of a grandmother claimed they were illegals. Were they illegals hiding other illegals?'

Farenden sighed. 'It would appear not, ma'am. Whether old Mrs Lockland was aware of the true facts – which I doubt – Lockland's parents were part of an underground group that resettled those suffering domestic abuse.'

Hay groaned.

'They had access to a pod owned by the prisoner Costello. They would borrow Mr Costello and his pod – for a price – and use it to transport the victims to a safe location. Apparently, it's the initial escape that's key. Getting those in need away from a dangerous environment as quickly and quietly and untraceably as possible. Which is what the Locklands did. They would then pass them on to someone else and so on. There was a network that stretched all across the country.'

'Still illegal Time travel, Charlie, no matter what the reason. Like robbing a bank and giving all the money to charity.'

Captain Farenden looked up. 'Has anyone ever done that?'

'Not to my knowledge. Just as a matter of interest, how many people did they manage to rescue?'

'That Costello knows about? A couple of men. About eleven women. Four or five children.'

Hay sighed again. 'And then we killed them. The Locklands, I mean.'

'Well, ma'am . . .'

'What?'

'It's worse than that. Our actions panicked the other members of the network and the whole thing was shut down more or less overnight. If you really want to beat yourself up, we might, indirectly, have been responsible for many more deaths and injuries.'

'How did this scheme actually work? Do we know?'

'Oh yes, ma'am. Mr Costello was quite forthcoming. Until he fell asleep, of course, but I think we have the gist of it. For amateurs, they didn't do a bad job. Obviously, the biggest problem for them was accidentally finding themselves in the same time twice, which they solved by setting the coordinates for one or two days hence and at the other end of the country. They would then drop off their passengers . . .'

'And return to their own time?'

'No, ma'am. They knew better than that. They would return to their own location but in the new time. Hence: if I rescued you from Manchester on, say, Wednesday 10th, I would then jump you to Truro on Thursday 11th, pass you on and then return to my original location but on Friday 12th. Mr Costello made it clear that all teams – including the Locklands – were always very careful. They only ever jumped forwards. They had scrutineers, rotas, data stacks – the lot. All to ensure there were no unfortunate accidents.'

'And all this was going on right under the noses of the Time Police?'

'It was, ma'am. But to be fair, there was a lot more important stuff going on at the time and all this was very low-key.'

'What went wrong? For the Locklands, I mean?'

'Old Mrs Lockland obviously tumbled to it somehow. She must have. Sensing the opportunity to rid herself of a hated daughter-in-law and make a little money at the same time, she dobbed them up to us. A team was despatched and, as we know, Lockland's parents did not survive the arrest.'

Hay thought for a moment. 'Precisely how long ago did this happen?'

'I don't have exact dates, ma'am – we'll have to consult the records. But as I said earlier, at least fifteen or sixteen years, I think. I understand that after all the dust over the deaths had settled, there was a considerable struggle to persuade Mrs Lockland to shoulder her familial duties, and Jane Lockland was in the care of local authorities for some time. I believe there were several court appearances before, eventually, Mrs Lockland was "persuaded" to undertake the care of her granddaughter.'

He sighed. 'I suspect Lockland received only the very minimum education mandated by law and as soon as she was old enough – while she was still at school, in fact – she was designated as her grandmother's carer. For which she received the usual allowance – most of which she paid to Mrs Lockland for board and lodging. That was the state of play until Lockland joined us, knowing almost nothing of her past.'

Hay got up to stare out of the window again.

Farenden paused. 'Except . . .'

Hay turned around. 'Yes? Except . . . ?'

'I find it suspicious there's no record of the incident. Anywhere. According to us, the arrest and shooting never happened.'

Hay sat back down. 'Presumably all this occurred during Colonel Albay's regime?'

'Towards the very end, ma'am, yes.'

'Well, there you are. Lots went on then that we don't want people knowing about.'

'But this was such a minor incident in the grand scheme of things, ma'am. What would be the point of covering it up? And the very fact there's no record is suspicious in itself, don't you think?'

She sighed. 'I do, yes.' She played with her paper knife. Always a disquieting sign. 'And the next one?'

'I beg your pardon, ma'am.'

'You said "revelations" plural. What's the next one?'

'Lt Filbert attempted to address the other issue, ma'am – namely the ownership of the pod Costello denied was his.'

'I gather he – Filbert – was unsuccessful.'

'Yes, by then the prisoner was beginning to exhibit signs of drowsiness and disorientation. However, just as Major Ellis and Lt Filbert were getting up to go, he said . . .' he flicked through his scratchpad, 'quite chattily . . . "He's mad, you know. And if he gets them, we'll all be in trouble. You should do something."

'Then it says that Major Ellis sat back down again and said, "But we will. We're already on it. You were giving me all the details."

'To which the prisoner replied, "Was I? Yes, I was, wasn't I. He's given up on the man. It's the papers he's after."

'To which Major Ellis replied, "Yes. The papers are key. Where are they?"

'To which the prisoner replied, "Very tired. Safe."

'To which Lt Filbert said, "Yes, you're safe now."

'To which the prisoner seemed to look around and then said, "Hotel."

'To which Lt Filbert said, "No, not a hotel. Hospital."'

Commander Hay sat very still. Her adjutant would not be mentioning this seemingly unimportant dialogue without a reason.

'To which the prisoner, now falling asleep, responded, "No. Safe. Hotel." He then displayed signs of considerable agitation, grasping the major's arm and saying, "Dangerous." Apparently fighting to stay awake, he muttered again, "Death." Followed by, "Raisable. To do. If he . . . Forbidden," and then fell soundly asleep. We can only hope Costello's as helpful when he next opens his eyes but the doctor says that will be unlikely. His chattiness is probably the result of his injury and the drugs he's been given. We won't know until he wakes up again.' He looked expectantly at Commander Hay. 'Well, ma'am. How would you like us to proceed?'

Hay pushed back her chair and began to pace. 'There are a number of issues here, aren't there?'

Farenden nodded.

'Who's "he"? And what's forbidden? And what is he raising? I swear, Charlie, if someone's raising the devil, then just let them get on with it. It could be a merciful release for all of us.'

'So noted, ma'am.'

She sighed. 'First things first. As soon as we've finished this meeting, get Lockland up here. This is going to get out no matter how careful we are. It's even possible, given her acquaintanceship with the prisoner, that Meiklejohn knows something about it. I want Lockland to hear it from me. Properly. Not a bit of corridor gossip.'

'Yes, ma'am.'

'Widen your search for anything relating to the deaths of her parents. Do you have any contacts in the civilian police?'

'Several, ma'am.'

'Good God, Charlie. Is there anyone you don't know?'

'No,' he said, simply.

'See if they can help at all. Discreetly.'

'Yes, ma'am.'

'Inform Lt Filbert he is to persevere with Costello. I want

to know everything he knows. Especially the owner of his pod. Is that the mysterious "he" Costello was talking about? What's dangerous and what is he raising? Depending on what the doctor says, we may have to hold off on any truth drugs. Or the cuff. Let's see what a little kindness can do. Tell him to use his own judgement, but Filbert can offer Costello amnesty if he thinks that will work.'

'Yes, ma'am.'

'Anything else?'

Captain Farenden looked up from his scratchpad. 'It would appear, ma'am, that as the result of these revelations, Team Two-Three-Six has suffered a ... fracture. I suspect Officer Parrish will be applying for a transfer. Or even submitting an application to leave us altogether.'

'Major Ellis can handle that. Better than me, probably.'

'Yes, ma'am.'

'Shit, Charlie – how could one minor mission blow up like this?'

'I don't know, ma'am. It's Team Weird. This sort of thing seems to happen to them all the time. We despatched them on a routine mission to monitor Henry Plimpton and the next moment we were up to our necks in Site X and the Paris Time-Stop.'

'Well, let's hope their fracture is only temporary. In the meantime, Charlie, we should get cracking.'

He stood up. 'Yes, ma'am.'

He was on his way out when she called him back. 'Just a thought. Give that last bit – the bit about the papers – to Meiklejohn. She's a puzzle-solver. Let's see if she can make anything of it.'

He sighed. 'Are you sure, ma'am?'

'Yes, I think so. You can talk to her while I see Lockland.'

He sighed again. 'Yes, ma'am.'

Jane had assumed the purpose of the meeting was to talk about her connection to the Portmans. She was wrong. As Hay's opening words demonstrated.

'How aware are you, Lockland, of the circumstances leading up to your parents' deaths?'

'Um, well. Not a lot. They were killed in an accident when I was very young. My grandmother was always very reluctant to talk about it. I hardly remember them at all.'

'Where did you all live?'

'In my grandmother's house.'

'Do you have *any* memories of them?'

Jane frowned. 'I honestly don't remember a time before my grandmother, ma'am. Not clearly. I have a few pictures in my head, but that's it. If there ever were any images of them, I think she threw them away. And all their belongings as well.'

Hay had thought long and hard about how much or how little to tell Lockland and had come to the conclusion that her purpose was best served by complete frankness. Lockland had been fed enough lies.

'Sit down, Lockland.'

She waited while Jane perched nervously on the edge of her chair.

'Stay calm, sweetie,' advised Bolshy Jane. 'Just listen and don't panic.'

'You will remember, a little while ago, I despatched an

officer to investigate your grandmother's claim that her ill health necessitated your leaving the Time Police to nurse her.'

Jane nodded dumbly. She certainly did remember that. She also remembered her overwhelming relief at hearing the claim had been denied. Had the matter been reopened? Had her grandmother refused to accept Hay's ruling and reapplied? And now this Portman business. Would Hay be glad of the opportunity to rid herself of someone who might turn out to be an embarrassing problem?

'Arising from that, I requested a more thorough investigation of the circumstances of your parents' deaths. It would appear your grandmother's version is not quite correct. At this point I have to ask you – do you wish to hear more?'

'Yes, yes, I think so.'

'You are certain?'

Jane wasn't certain at all but what sort of person would she be if she said no?

'Yes,' she said, as firmly as she could. 'I am.'

'Very well. Your parents were engaged in illegal Time travel.'

'Were they?' said Jane, genuinely astonished. 'Are you sure?' And then blushed with embarrassment at the implication that Hay might not be sure of her facts. Worse – might even be lying.

'I meant . . .'

'No, that's quite all right, Lockland. I think a certain amount of disbelief is understandable, but the initial information came from your grandmother herself and since it shows her in a less than creditable light, I think we can assume the facts are more or less correct.'

'Sorry,' muttered Jane.

'I ask only that you hear me out to the end before passing any comment.'

Jane braced herself. 'All right, ma'am.'

Hay's voice was quiet and level. 'Your parents were engaged in illegal Time travel but for a supposedly noble purpose. As far as we can ascertain – and the matter is still under investigation – they used a pod to transport sufferers of domestic abuse to a safe time and place.'

'Oh,' said Jane. And then as the implications dawned on her . . . 'Oh.'

'Precisely. Somehow your grandmother got wind of this, and in an unlikely effort to do her public duty, she informed on them to the Time Police.'

Jane's mouth fell open.

'A squad was sent to arrest them – we don't yet have details. Apparently, shots were fired. Your father died at the scene. Your mother died a little later. I will give you a minute.'

She touched her intercom. 'If you please, Captain . . .'

Captain Farenden entered, bearing a glass of water which he set gently in front of Jane. Jane, who had always rather liked Captain Farenden, was dismayed at the grimness of his expression. She had, however, been asked not to comment until the end and so she wouldn't. She sipped her water and tried to get her thoughts in order.

The Time Police had killed her parents. Who were illegals. But in a good way. If that was possible. But the Time Police had killed her parents. She couldn't get past that. The Time Police had killed her parents. Very, very carefully – because at that exact moment she couldn't rely on her hands to do as she wanted – she placed the glass of water on Hay's desk.

She waited while Jane perched nervously on the edge of her chair and then seated herself. 'I want to assure you, Lockland – this was before my time as commander. To give you some context, the worst of the Time Wars was over. We were beginning to prevail, but a lot of things still weren't . . . as they are now. If it helps at all, almost everyone serving at that time isn't in service any longer.'

Jane nodded, still unsure what to say. Still unsure she *could* say anything.

'However, there are one or two things that don't quite add up and so I am conducting a thorough investigation as we speak. I hope to be able to tell you more very soon. Do you wish to be kept informed?'

Jane nodded. 'Yes, please, ma'am.' She paused and then lifted her chin. 'I have to tell you, ma'am – illegals or not – I'm quite proud of them and what they tried to do.'

'That is understandable. Even I applaud their actions. It's only their getaway vehicle with which I have an issue. Did your grandmother ever speak of this to you?'

'Never.'

'I should warn you we will probably need to interview her. Here – at TPHQ.'

Jane nodded miserably. Her grandmother tainted everything she touched. Even Jane's new life here in the Time Police was to be irrevocably tarnished by her old life.

'I'm sorry, Lockland. This must be an enormous shock for you. I'm assuming if you'd known of this, you might not have joined us.'

Jane stared blankly. 'I don't know, ma'am.'

'No, of course you don't. I can imagine your thoughts are all over the place at the moment. On top of everything, I understand there is an issue within your team?'

Jane nodded.

'Might I suggest you return to your room and consider today's events in peace and quiet? And should you find yourself in any difficulties, I recommend you speak to Lt North. You probably won't get any sympathy, but you will get understanding and good advice.'

'Yes, ma'am. Thank you, ma'am.'

Her face burning, Jane escaped.

Captain Farenden's interview didn't go nearly so well.

'What ho,' said Mikey, breezing through the door. Since her return from 1746, she had found time to divest herself of her jacket and goggles and, at this precise moment, looked comparatively conventional.

Captain Farenden nodded and continued writing. 'I shan't keep you a moment.'

'No problemo,' she said cheerily, crossing to a notice board and beginning to read the notices posted there.

He looked up and frowned. 'Those are confidential.'

'Not a good idea to pin them up where everyone can see them, then, is it?'

'Most people aren't so nosey.'

'Didn't we establish I'm not most people? Anyway, what do you want?'

He glanced towards the closed door to Hay's office. 'Commander Hay has just spoken to Officer Lockland.'

Mikey nodded. 'Yeah. Bummer.'

'You know what's going on, presumably?'

'I don't know anything specific. No one does. Doesn't stop tongues wagging, of course.'

'I can imagine.'

'Yes. For instance, did you know Lockland is Callen's love child?'

If Captain Farenden had been on his feet, he would have staggered. 'What?'

'And he's eliminating witnesses.'

'To what?'

'His torrid affair.'

'With whom?'

'Opinion is divided on whether that would be her mother, her grandmother or a completely unknown third party.'

'What?'

'And Costello knows everything.'

'No, he . . .'

'Varma was despatched to despatch him. You know – actually despatch. Before he could talk.'

'Could we just return to reality for one—?'

'OK. How about – Lockland's a double agent planted by the Portmans?'

'Oh God . . .'

'She's a sleeper and . . .'

'No. Enough. Shut up.'

'Well, you asked what I knew.'

'And I now know never to do that again. Sit down, stay quiet and listen to this.'

He played the end of the recording. John Costello's sleepy voice filled the room.

Mikey looked at him angrily. 'What did you do to him?'

'*I* didn't do anything. So far, he has received first-class medical treatment and, if he cooperates, an offer of amnesty may be made to him, together with the opportunity to start a new life elsewhere, so go and be judgemental over someone who cares.'

Mikey subsided. 'OK. Let's hear it again.'

She listened, staring into the middle distance and absently twiddling an elastic band she had found on his desk.

Captain Farenden, who had discovered this did not mean inattention, imbecility or even bad manners, waited silently.

Abruptly, she stood up, reached over his desk and grabbed a marker. Many officers were still old-fashioned enough to use whiteboards and Captain Farenden was one of them. His was covered in scribbled reminders and spider charts. Mikey swept all this away with her sleeve and – without so much as a by your leave – drew an X. From this she extended a line. From there, everything descended into pointless doodling. Arrows, boxes, unreadable squiggles and dotted lines were scribbled in an apparently random and haphazard manner all across the board, and when that was full, she moved on to the wall itself. Stepping back, she muttered to herself for a while and then turned to Captain Farenden, saying in surprise, 'You're still here?'

'That would be because this is my office. And you've just destroyed my notes for next week's senior officers' meeting. And written across my walls – for a reason which escapes me since my office is generally reckoned to be ground zero for paper.'

He indicated the shelves lining his office walls, all neatly stacked with identical binders labelled *Wages – Junior Ranks* (a woefully thin file); *Wages – Senior Ranks* (only marginally

103

thicker); *Senior Officers' Meetings*; *Budget Reports*; *Probationary Reports A–L*, *Probationary Reports M–W*, *Probationary Reports X, Y & Z* (which frequently led the uninitiated to wonder what on earth X, Y & Z could possibly have been up to that necessitated their own personal binder); and *Complaints* (four thick volumes and counting). The point being that Captain Farenden's office was either a model of neatness and organised thinking or the sign of a diseased mind, depending on whether you were Luke Parrish or not.

She ignored all this. 'The "forbidden" bit is quite interesting, don't you think? Can I use your scratchpad? I forgot mine.'

'No.'

He might as well have spared his breath.

She tapped and flicked at the screen. Then tapped some more. Then flicked some more. Then some more again.

The window in Captain Farenden's office was nowhere near as large as Commander Hay's but a stray sunbeam found its way through somehow. Captain Farenden watched it light up her hair like a golden halo.

She muttered to herself for a while and then said abruptly, 'When was jumping to America illegal?'

'Do you mean when was the legislation passed or during what years is jumping to America forbidden?'

'Interesting. You just used the word *forbidden*.'

'I just . . .'

He'd lost her. Head down, she was flicking through his scratchpad again. 'I've had a thought. It incorporates all the known facts but, of course, we might not know all the facts. In fact – see what I did there – we certainly don't know all the facts, but from what we do know . . . yes, my thought would fit. But others might have other thoughts which would also fit. We need more information.'

'And with luck we will have it when Mr Costello wakes again.' She looked at him. 'Do you want me to talk to him?'

Captain Farenden was silent.

'Yes, I know what you're thinking. *Bit of a double-edged weapon.* Closely followed by the always popular *just a little chit of a thing. What could she possibly know?* Followed by *known troublemaker.* Closely followed by *wish she'd get out of my office.* OK – your wish is my command. I'm off.'

Mikey headed for the door.

'Stop. Come back.'

Mikey did neither. 'Why?'

'Because I wasn't thinking any of that. I was actually thinking *look at the mess she's made of my whiteboard.* Followed by *she's written on the bloody walls.* Followed by *she's walking off with my scratchpad.* Followed by *bloody hell, she's irritating, why has no one ever boxed her ears before now?* Followed by *I wonder if she's cracked it.* Followed by *does she want some coffee?*'

'A definite yes to the last one and a possible yes to the one before that. Try it and see what happens to the one before that. And hang on to that whiteboard – it will be worth a lot when I'm dead. White. Strong. Two sugars.'

'I'll swap you a coffee for my scratchpad back.'

She smiled and handed it back, sipping her coffee as he flicked through what she'd been looking at.

'Bloody hell. Could this be . . . ?'

Mikey nodded. 'Yeah. I might be completely wrong, of course, but I definitely think I need to talk to Mr Costello.'

9

The Time Police are famous for not letting the grass grow under their feet but events moved swiftly, even for them.

A quick catch-up for those whose attention has been wandering.

Jane had returned to her room and was quietly reading. Well, staring at a book anyway. Until someone knocked at her door.

Matthew had been in his room but was now knocking on Jane's door.

Luke was in his room alternately drinking and seething.

And Mikey had taken herself down to MedCen to talk to John Costello.

She smiled sunnily at the two guards, who showed no signs whatsoever of smiling sunnily back again.

'Let me go in. I want to talk to him.'

Neither guard moved or spoke but it was clearly understood that there was no chance.

Mikey had always been a big fan of persistence. And chocolate, of course. And alcohol. And unlimited Time travel for talented siblings but, mostly, at this precise moment – persistence. Because persistence overcomes resistance. Everyone knows that.

'Please let me talk to him.'

'No visitors. For his own safety.'

She beamed at a guard. 'Doesn't apply to me – we're old friends.'

The guard scowled. 'All the more reason.'

'Captain Farenden sent me.'

Which was nearly true. That had certainly been her impression, anyway.

Sadly, it wasn't that of the two man-mountains – menmountains? – standing in front of her.

She raised her voice. 'Hey, Jakey – are you awake? Can you hear me?'

'For God's sake,' said the first guard, 'stop shouting. They can probably hear you all over the building.'

'Just give her a bit of a slap,' said the second guard. 'That'll shut her up,' and suddenly found himself face to face with Mikey – which, given that her head was barely level with his breastbone, was no small feat.

'I have no huge objection to being shot,' she said quietly, 'but slap me and I'll . . .'

The guard scoffed. 'You'll do what?'

'Nothing – not right now – but one night, when you least expect it, I will come for you.'

'And kill me in my sleep, I suppose?'

'Oh no,' said Mikey, very softly. 'You won't die. Not for a very, very long time. I'll make absolutely certain of that.'

They stared at each other for a long moment and then Costello shouted, 'Mikey? You still there?'

She raised her voice. 'I am indeed. I've come to yell at you about a number of private and confidential matters. Can you hear me or should I shout even louder?'

'Where are you?'

'Just on the other side of the partition.'

'Why are you shouting?'

'So they'll let me in. Tell me whose pod you stole.'

The doctor turned up. 'What the hell is all this noise?'

Mikey smiled so hard her cheekbones ached. 'Captain Farenden sent me.' Which, as she kept telling herself, was very nearly true.

'I've had no instructions to let her in,' said the first guard.

'And heaven forbid you should use your initiative,' said Mikey, brightly.

The guard scowled. He hadn't joined the Time Police to use his initiative.

'If you like,' said Mikey, pressing home her advantage, 'the prisoner and I can continue to yell at each other, thus giving loads of people an opportunity to hear our confidential conversation. In fact, let's open all the doors so they can hear us in security. And Logistics. And the Pod Bay. And . . .'

'Shut up,' said the doctor. He turned to the guard. 'Get Captain Farenden down here.'

'Tried that,' said the second guard. 'He's with Commander Hay.'

'Then get security. Or Lt North. Anyone. Just stop everyone yelling at each other in my MedCen.'

North arrived at the same time as Lt Filbert. Both summed up the situation with one glance. Filbert grinned and said to North, 'Your call.'

'Coward.'

'Too right.'

North sighed. 'It's probably quicker and easier to let her in.'

Filbert shook his head. 'No – it's probably quicker and easier to shoot her.'

Both guards brightened visibly.

'That can be our second option,' said North, smoothly. 'To be enjoyed – I mean employed – when all else fails.'

Filbert nodded at the guards. Who nodded at Mikey.

'Alone,' said Mikey.

'Not a chance,' said Filbert.

'There's only a partition,' said North. 'We can hear every word they say.'

Filbert glared at Mikey. 'You'd better not mess us about on this.'

Mikey shook her head.

Filbert sighed. 'Against my better judgement – OK.'

Mikey slipped into the cubicle and smiled at Mr Costello. 'Hey there, how are you feeling?'

'All right, actually. Not sure what they've given me but it's really good stuff.' He lowered his voice. 'Could you get me some more?'

'I don't know. Tell me who you're working for and I'll see what I can do.'

His eyes shifted sideways. 'No one. I'm not working for anyone.'

'Oh, come on. We all know it's not your pod. I'm guessing you stole it and someone somewhere is quite cross with you.'

Costello lowered his voice, suddenly nervous. 'Mikey – drop it. Tell them . . .' he gestured to TPHQ in general, 'to drop it as well. He's not a good man. If he finds me . . .' He stopped and pulled up his covers, quite plainly terrified despite all the happy drugs waltzing around his system. 'He's not quite normal. He . . .' He stopped.

Mikey waited hopefully but it seemed no more was forthcoming so she changed tack. 'And you were daft enough to steal a pod from someone like that?'

He tried to sit up straighter. 'Yes. But no, actually.'

'OK,' said Mikey, carefully. 'Too many happy drugs, perhaps?'

'No – I mean – yes, I did steal it, but it was mine originally so it's not. Stealing, I mean. I simply reclaimed my own property.'

'And he's been chasing you ever since?'

'Off and on.'

'How long has this been going on?'

He shrugged. 'Dunno. A long time. But it was *my* pod.'

'I'm sure it was. He took it from you and you stole it back again. Very understandable. I'd have done the same thing myself. The thing is, you're safe here. There's nowhere safer. So you tell us everything you know about this bloke – the one who's after you – we take him down and you'll be safe forever.'

'With my pod?'

Mikey hardened her voice. 'Your pod's finished. And so will you be if you don't talk.'

'But it's . . .'

She leaned forwards, whispering, 'This can go one of two ways, Jakey. Either you die, horribly murdered by the pod's previous owner – who stole it from you,' she added hastily as he opened his mouth to protest. 'Or, you survive all this, your problems melt away – a bit like my net, now I come to think of it – and you live happily ever after. Your choice.'

His mouth set in a stubborn line. 'You can't make me talk.'

'I can't, but they can.' She gestured to the two guards standing

110

at the entrance to the cubicle and watching their every move. 'Fail to cooperate and they'll simply escort you to the front door, publicly thank you for all the very helpful information you provided, drop a small sum into your bank account, wait to see who murders you, and arrest *him*. None of which will help you because you'll be very painfully and very messily dead, won't you?'

Costello licked his lips, staring at the officers outside his cubicle. At some point, Varma had turned up and was standing alongside North. Lowering her voice, she said, 'Hay wants you when you've finished here. Something about Lockland's parents.'

North nodded, never taking her eyes from John Costello. Who was shaking his head, saying, 'I don't know what to do.'

'Hang on,' said Filbert, stepping into the cubicle. 'Let me see if I can help. Shift out of the way, Meiklejohn.'

Mikey scowled but moved out of the chair.

Filbert took her place, making his voice gentle. 'I've been authorised to offer you amnesty, Mr Costello. Help us with our enquiries and you'll be protected for as long as necessary. When it's all over, you'll be given a new identity and enough money to start another life wherever you want. As long as you don't do anything stupid . . .' he glared at the cowering Costello, 'you need never see *me* . . .' he gestured around, 'or any of this lot ever again. Free and clear, Mr Costello. My word on it.'

Costello stared at him, indecision written all over his face. 'I . . . I don't know . . .'

Filbert leaned forwards. 'Mr Costello – you're quite safe. If you cooperate. What do you say?'

Costello licked his lips. 'You mean it? A genuine offer?'

'I do. A genuine offer. A genuine reward. A genuine new life. If you do the *sensible* thing.'

John Costello looked from Filbert to Mikey and back again. 'I . . .' He floundered in a daze of indecision and happy drugs.

'Jake,' said Mikey, who had her own agenda. 'I think I can guess a lot of this. You don't have to tell me anything – I'll tell *you*. All you have to do is say yes or no. Cooperate – and as the nice officer says, all your problems will disappear. OK?'

'OK,' said Costello, reluctantly. They both looked at Filbert.

'Just me,' said Mikey.

'No chance,' said Filbert.

'Actually,' said North, 'if it gets us what we want to know . . .' She looked at Filbert and raised an eyebrow.

'All right,' he said, grudgingly. 'Don't make me regret this, Costello. Anyone here will tell you not to cross me. Understand?'

Costello nodded.

Filbert edged past Mikey and headed for the exit. 'Everyone else out as well. Yes, you too, please, doctor.'

Within a minute the cubicle was clear. The two guards remained on the other side of the partition, just out of earshot. Mikey could see their shadowy outlines.

'OK,' she said. Leaning forwards, she began to whisper. When she'd finished, she sat back. 'Am I right?'

Still not saying a word, Costello nodded. Just once.

'Yes,' breathed Mikey, punching the air. 'Thanks, Jakey. Get some sleep if you can,' and she left the cubicle at a trot. She needed to get hold of Hay. And quickly. This was no time to mess about with daft Time Police protocol and rank and formal procedures.

'Whoa,' said a guard, moving to block her exit. 'Where do you think you're going?'

'Need to see Hay,' said Mikey, trying to peer around Mount Time Police Officer.

'No, you don't,' he said. 'You tell us, we report to Filbert and he decides whether to pass on the information to the commander.'

'Oh,' said Mikey, meekly. 'Yes. Of course. How silly of me.' She peered up through her eyelashes in a manner that would have had Captain Farenden moving to DEFCON 1 without bothering to pass Go or even collect his two hundred pounds.

'Silly of you, but not of me,' said the guard, unmoved. He opened his com.'Captain Farenden? Meiklejohn has information . . . Yes . . . Yes, sir.' He closed his com and nodded at his mate. 'You're to go with her.'

Mikey looked him up and down. 'Will you be able to keep up?'

'Only if I want to.'

'Then come on,' said Mikey impatiently, already heading for the door. Where she paused to look back, suddenly doubtful.

'I'm watching him,' said the first guard, cradling his weapon and moving to stand at the foot of Costello's bed.

'Yes, but who's watching you?'

'Yeah,' said the guard, heavy on the sarcasm. 'I'm in sole charge of the prisoner and something happens to him. No one's ever going to suspect me, are they?'

The second guard pushed her out of the door. 'Get a move on.'

Meanwhile, back to the almost forgotten quick catch-up . . .

113

The wrong time to be caught sneaking out of anyone's room is usually in the small hours of the morning when all sorts of interesting – and usually perfectly correct – conclusions can be drawn. On this occasion, however, the wrong time for Matthew to be caught sneaking out of Jane's room was the exact moment Luke Parrish snuck out of his own room in search of more vodka.

They stared at each other for a moment. Matthew instinctively took refuge in silence. Luke leaped effortlessly to the wrong conclusion. 'What the hell were you doing in there?'

'Talking to Jane. She's just learned her parents were killed by her employers. And that they weren't who she thought they were. Her parents, I mean. And that one of the people she's come to rely on to have her back – doesn't. In fact, that one person is being such a tosspot he doesn't even want to have anything to do with her. Which, incidentally, is fine by her.'

Typically, Luke ignored all of this. 'She can't stay on the team.'

'I don't see why not.'

'She's been lying to us. All this time. Why didn't she tell us she was a Portman?'

'She didn't know.'

'So she says.'

'Luke, what is wrong with you?'

'Think about it, Matthew – it all makes sense now. The Portmans pay Hay to take Jane Portman into the Time Police . . .'

'What?'

'. . . where she can report back anything that threatens their empire. She gets herself involved with the Site X undercover operation . . .'

114

'How?'

'. . . after Nuñez and Klein were murdered and . . .'

'Are you saying Jane killed . . . ?'

'Of course not. The Portmans have people to do that for them . . .'

'This is ridiculous. You're being ridiculous.'

'She gets herself to Site X . . .'

'Luke, you have to stop this. She – you both – nearly died at Site X.'

'She finds the snowsuits that keep us alive. The ones put there for her to find. No wonder she was so calm. She knew she'd be rescued.'

'The Time Police rescued you. Are you even listening to yourself?'

'For God's sake, Matthew, how can you be so thick? Haven't you grasped it yet? Jane Lockland is not who she appears to be. Just like everyone else in this world.'

Matthew struggled not to lose his temper. 'Only a few weeks ago you were convinced your own father was behind Site X. Luke, for God's sake, stop. Just stop. Let's get a drink and talk about this calmly and you'll soon see . . .'

'Didn't we recently discuss a possible traitor at TPHQ? During the Paris Time-Stop? Someone who knows what the Time Police are doing even before we do? Well, look no further.'

'Don't be so fire-trucking stupid. Of course it's not Jane. How could it be?'

'I'm telling you – it all adds up and you're just too dense to see it. Or too naïve.' Luke narrowed his eyes. 'Or you don't want to see it.'

Matthew stared at him. 'There is something seriously wrong with you.'

'I tell you, she's a traitor. Let her try to prove otherwise.'

Matthew's eyes blazed a fierce gold. With sudden violence, he pushed Luke back against his own door. 'Jane doesn't have anything to prove. She saved you at Site X – although God knows why – and she held her own against that arse-wipe Sawney. She stood her ground in Tutankhamun's tomb. She laid you out in the corridor to unit-wide approbation. If you're expecting people to take your side against her, then you'll be disappointed. She's the same Jane today as she was yesterday and last week. The only difference to the status quo is you. Because you're a spoiled, entitled, self-obsessed dick-head completely incapable of seeing the world in any other terms than yourself. So *you* fire truck off out of it, Parrish. We don't need you and we don't want you. The one leaving the team is you.'

He gave Luke one final push and then strode off down the corridor, his head and his heart thumping with rage.

Luke stood still, shocked to his core. Matthew never lost his temper. He was well known for steering clear of arguments, disputes, quarrels, any sort of situation where voices could be raised. He disliked violence. He didn't avoid it and you could always rely on him in a fight, but unlike many officers, he never looked for it. That he would even raise his voice . . . and to a teammate . . .

Luke adjusted his clothing and set off to see Major Ellis. He knocked, entered and scowled at North, who was also present.

'I'll come back,' said North, standing up.

'There's no need, Lieutenant,' said Ellis.

116

'No, sir, I think this is BeeBOC business. Besides, Hay has asked me to do some research for her.'

She closed the door. Ellis and Luke regarded each other.

'Why have you left your quarters?'

As usual, Luke ignored anything not concerned with his own agenda. 'I'm requesting a transfer to another team.'

Ellis frowned at him. 'You think there's a team out there who will take you?'

'If Two-Three-Five won't, then I'll buy myself out. And don't bother sending Hay along to do her usual "Don't make any hasty decisions" speech. I won't work with Jane Portman.'

Ellis controlled himself with an effort. 'Parrish, I'm urging you to reconsider. Look at the progress you've made over the last year. Being a member of the Time Police has given you a sense of responsibility. A purpose. You're a team leader . . .'

'Fine. You've denied my request. You'll have my application to buy myself out within the hour.'

A sudden jag of temper ran through Ellis. He thumped the desk. '*Enough*. I've done patient. I've done understanding. I've even, God help me, had a go at caring, but enough is enough. You don't take that tone with me or anyone else in this building. I will speak to Lt Grint concerning your request to join his team and you will await his decision, although I suspect we both know what it will be. You can't just flounce in and out of teams as the fancy takes you. And if he does say yes, then you'll need to find someone from that team willing to exchange into Two-Three-Six. If no one will, then your transfer won't happen.'

'Hay moves people around all the time.'

'No, she doesn't, and when she does, it's for operational reasons. Not because someone's having a hissy fit.'

117

'Lockland's a Portman.'

'She's always been a Portman. You weren't bothered this time last week.'

'I didn't know this time last week.'

'Enough, Parrish. I'm not entering into a dialogue over this. Go for a long run. Then schedule yourself some time in the gym. I tell you now, if you don't calm down and view this matter more rationally, then you'll be on no one's team.'

'Not a problem for me.'

'Jesus, Parrish, you're hard work.'

They glared at each other for a while. Eventually, Ellis drew breath and struggled for a more patient tone. 'I've given you good advice, Luke. You've made a place for yourself here. Don't throw it all away in a tantrum.'

Luke's face was stony. 'Anything else, Major?'

Ellis sighed. 'No. Dismissed.'

Leaving Ellis's office, Luke rounded a corner and walked straight into a wall. At least, that's what it felt like. His face exploded with pain. Strange. Even stranger was when the wall bent down, picked him up, set him gently on his feet and then knocked him down again.

Again, Luke crashed to the floor. The wall heaved him to his feet and threw him hard against a door. His face took most of the impact. He both heard and felt his nose crunch. He hung for a moment and then his legs gave way and he slithered down the door to land in a sprawling heap. With a faint and far-off voice in his head shouting that it really wasn't a good idea to be lying helplessly on the floor, he struggled to get his limbs moving again.

The wall seized him by the scruff of his neck, shook him as a terrier shakes a rat and then hurled – there was no other word for it – hurled him violently down the length of the corridor.

Luke actually felt himself fly through the air and just had time to realise that the landing was really, really going to hurt, when it did. It hurt like buggery.

This time his inner voice advised him to stay put and he was happy to obey. In fact, he was still staying put in a heap some minutes later when Matthew, on his way down to the Pod Bay, nearly fell over him and was genuinely horrified.

'Jesus, Luke, what happened? No, don't try to move. I'll get a medic up here.'

Luke's lips weren't working properly. 'No.'

'Luke, I don't think you realise . . .'

'No. Help . . . me . . . up.'

Not without some difficulty, Matthew heaved him to his feet. Luke's face was a mess. Blood streamed from his nose and a cut across one cheekbone. His eyes were swollen shut.

'Can't . . . see . . .'

'I'm not surprised.'

Luke groped helplessly. 'Where's . . . my room?'

'Sorry, mate. It's MedCen for you. Can you walk?'

'Course.'

They set off very, very slowly. Luke's head was spinning. The journey to MedCen was a long and painful one.

The medtec took one look and rang for the doctor.

Who stared in silence and then said, 'Cubicle 1.'

'No,' said Luke. ''M fine.'

'That's an order. Kelly, get the portable X-ray up here. You can go, Farrell.'

119

'Will he . . .? I mean, will he be OK?'

The doctor ignored his question with one of his own. 'How did this happen?'

'I don't know,' said Matthew, happy to be telling the truth. 'I found him on the floor. I think . . . I think he might have fallen down some stairs.'

'You might want to rethink that story, lad, but not here. Off you go now.' He turned to Luke. 'OK, I'm asking and you're going to tell me. Don't bother me with *falling downstairs* bullshit. What happened?'

'Genuinely . . . don't know,' said Luke. 'Didn't see it . . . coming. Or hear . . . either.'

'Can you see anything?'

'No,' said Luke, panic bubbling to the surface despite his best efforts. 'Nothing. Nothing at all.'

'All right, lad. No cause for alarm. Let's take a look, shall we?'

10

Matthew was reluctant to leave Luke, but with his leave application approved, the faint glimmerings of an idea were ... glimmering.

He was deposited at the St Mary's Institute for Historical Research by the usual grumpy mech who took one look at the ominous pall of smoke issuing from several of the upstairs windows, made a curt *you're on your own, mate* gesture and made haste to return to a safer world.

Matthew trudged across the grass towards Hawking Hangar where he was met by a harassed Mr Dieter.

'Your dad's busy fighting the fire and your mum's supervising the evacuation.'

'OK,' said Matthew amiably. 'Anything I can do here?'

'Only wait. The blast doors are down so you can't get into the main building at the moment.'

'What happened?'

'Guess.'

'Not Greek fire again? Has the professor still not got the recipe right?'

'Slightly more complicated than that. It struck him that it would be much quicker and easier to acquire an *actual* sample of *actual* Greek fire, rather than mess about with various combinations of chemicals. So off they went . . .'

'Off who went?'

'Professor Rapson, Dr Dowson, Lingoss, Bashford, Roberts, Sykes . . .'

'All the usual suspects . . .'

'Indeed.'

'Not Mum?'

'Well, your mum doesn't really do this sort of thing any more, does she? Not since . . .'

'No. So what happened? Everything obviously went horribly wrong.'

'No – everything went fine. They got their sample, carried out an on-site analysis, argued a little bit, jumped back, argued a little bit more, mixed up some stuff . . .'

'Yes . . . and . . . ?'

'And were successful.'

'Wow – they finally managed to produce Greek fire? The real thing?'

Greek fire was first used by the Greeks to besiege Constantinople. The recipe has, probably fortunately, been lost to the modern world, which hadn't stopped St Mary's experimenting at regular intervals. Unsuccessfully to date, which was just as well because the problem with Greek fire is that it's very difficult to put out. Water just makes it burn more fiercely. Actually, nearly everything makes it burn more fiercely, as St Mary's had discovered to their cost in the past. Today, however, it would appear they had finally achieved success. That is, the St Mary's definition of success, which tends to be different from that of the real world.

Dieter nodded. 'They did and it is.'

'Interesting,' said Matthew.

Dieter rolled his eyes. '*Interesting* is not the word currently being bandied about. Apparently, the stuff ignited – as it should – and there were typical History Department cries of "ooh" and "aah", followed by typical History Department screams of panic and alarm when they discovered they couldn't put it out. The Security Section is up there now, grappling with a hazard that will, no doubt, kill us all. I suspect there's a very good reason the secret of Greek fire was lost, and now St Mary's has unleashed it upon the world again.'

'Yay, St Mary's,' said Matthew vaguely. 'I wondered why there was no Security presence when I landed. How long, do you think, before . . .'

'Before it engulfs St Mary's and then the entire world?' said Dieter, calmly. 'Who knows? Are you in a rush? Fancy a nice cup of tea?'

'Oh yes,' said Matthew, the events of the day suddenly catching up with him. 'So much.'

Half an hour later and Matthew was sitting with his mother under a tree watching the hoses being coiled, equipment being stored away and the smoke disperse.

'That went quite well, I thought,' said Max, sipping her tea.

'Well, you all lived to tell the tale,' said Matthew.

Once, he would have said, '*We* all lived to tell the tale.' Max smiled sadly and then straightened her shoulders. 'What can I do for you?'

'I've come to see how you're doing. You know – after the Acropolis business.'

123

'I'm fine, thank you. Your father now only mentions it three or four times a day, so he's over it, too. Again, what do you want?'

'Nothing. Well, just to see how you are. And perhaps to ask your advice about something.'

'I'm fine. What's the problem?'

'It's a biggie.'

She leaned back against the tree trunk. 'Everyone's safely evacuated and nothing's happening here until Security declare the building fit for human habitation again, so hit me.'

Matthew spoke solidly for ten or so minutes. Possibly a personal best.

Max frowned. 'Have you ever met this grandmother?'

He shook his head. 'Although from the little Jane has said about her, she's not a nice person.'

'Why do you want to investigate this? Why can't Hay send someone back to find out what happened?'

'She can't. None of them can jump to that date.'

'Why ever not?'

Matthew frowned. 'It wasn't long enough ago.'

This incomprehensible sentence made complete sense to Max. 'Oh. Right. Gotcha.'

'No one can go and investigate because they were all alive at the time. They'd have to track down a couple of officers who were in another time during the attack and that won't be easy,' finished Matthew. 'The only person who can check it out *now* is me.' He looked at his mother. 'Can you steal me a pod?'

'Of course. But only if I go too. Thief's privilege.'

'Mum . . .'

'Hush, dear, Mummy's plotting. Do we know when and where the attack takes place?'

'Jane gave me the date. And supposedly it happened outside her house in Lacey Gardens. So, we have when and where.'

'Let's stop and think for a minute,' said Max. 'Let's assume Jane was quite young and her parents were reasonably conscientious.'

Matthew nodded.

'They'd be gone for several days so they'd have had to leave her with a babysitter.'

'I've been thinking about that,' said Matthew. 'What they were doing was quite dangerous. They'd have to cope with the possibility of interference from people's abusive partners and the subsequent risk of violence to themselves. To say nothing of the Time Police discovering what they were up to. They wouldn't want strangers anywhere near them.'

'But they were gone for at least three days, Matthew. No matter how old Jane was at the time, they wouldn't have left her alone. They had to leave her with someone.'

'Someone they thought wouldn't grass them up,' said Matthew, thoughtfully.

'Well, they got that wrong, didn't they?'

'But they didn't know that. Jane's grandmother must have seemed the best choice at the time. Keeping it in the family, so to speak.'

'Do you honestly think they'd have left her with old Mrs Lockland?' said Max, doubtfully.

Matthew nodded firmly. 'I do. Not only because they lived with her, but if there were any other family relatives around, then Jane's granny would have made very sure orphan Jane was foisted on to them and not her.'

Max nodded. 'Good point.' She grinned. 'Wouldn't you have liked to see her face when she realised she'd shot herself in the foot? That she was the one stuck with a young child? I bet she loved that. If it wasn't for the way she treated Jane, I would say it served her right.'

'Do you think they told her – Jane's grandmother – what they were doing?'

Max sipped her tea again. 'Doesn't seem likely. Why would they?'

'That's what I thought. So – we have to ask ourselves – how did Mrs Lockland find out about their activities?'

Max blinked. 'That's another very good point, Matthew.'

Matthew nodded. 'The intel she passed on to the Time Police must have been good enough and specific enough for them – us – to take it seriously, since we despatched at least one team to bring them in.'

Max sighed. 'And they took no prisoners. Literally.'

'Again – how could Mrs Lockland have known? Did she just guess what they were doing during their absences?'

'She could have, I suppose, but how? How could she have acquired enough knowledge to convince the Time Police? Someone *must* have told her.'

Matthew frowned. 'But who? And why? Why didn't they just go directly to the Time Police and collect the reward for themselves? It doesn't make sense.'

Max was thinking. 'What happened to the pod?'

'What?'

'What happened to their pod? Afterwards. Presumably the

Time Police impounded it. Or destroyed it. Or whatever it is you do with other people's pods.'

'Depends. Sometimes a clean-up crew wipes it from the face of the earth; other times we download everything we can and then strip them down. Anything useful is kept. Everything else is destroyed.'

'So, either way, there wouldn't be anything left?'

'Not after all this time.'

They looked at each other in silence.

'We're going to have to check it out, aren't we?'

'Mum . . .'

'It's not going to be easy. I'm still in a tiny teaspoonful of trouble with your father.'

'What happened at the Acropolis wasn't your fault.'

'Exactly what I told him. Several times. I went to TPHQ in all good faith – not that you have a lot of choice when the Time Police start banging on the door. I thought it was just a quick historical briefing on the History of the Acropolis. I had no idea I was actually going to end up there.'

'You volunteered, Mum. Actually, you absolutely insisted on going.'

'Did I?' said his mother, vaguely. 'I remember so little about the events of that night. Shock, you know.'

Matthew grinned. 'Was he cross? Dad, I mean.'

'He was very, very cross. I had to mention the Cretaceous, Constantinople, Nile crocodiles, France, and all the other times I've had to save *him*. Sometimes I think he shouldn't be allowed out on his own.'

'I thought you weren't supposed to be doing this sort of thing these days. You know, after . . .'

'And I'm not,' said his mother indignantly.

'Mum, you were in Rome when Julius Caesar was assassinated.'

'Yes, but . . .'

'You led the team to the King's Arsenal. Where you took over the building, tied up and interrogated the staff. It was practically an act of war.'

'Nonsense. That was . . .'

'You muscled your way into the Acropolis thing, and given half a chance, you'd have been at the Paris Time-Stop as well.'

'I know, but . . .'

'Honestly, Mum.'

'You sound just like your father.'

'I don't know whose father you expect me to sound like.'

'It's the Time Police, isn't it? They've done this to you. I warned you.'

'Mum . . .'

'I said. Didn't I say?'

'Mum . . .'

'I still wonder if we shouldn't send you to one of those organisations and get you de-culted.'

'The Time Police are not a cult.'

Mother and son regarded each other with mutual exasperation.

'We're doing it, then,' said Matthew.

'Well, obviously,' said Max. 'Isn't that why you're here?'

Mother and son grinned at each other.

11

At her request, Captain Farenden was updating Commander Hay concerning the recent attack on Luke Parrish.

'I gather we have blood up the walls again, Charlie. Literally, in this case.'

'Yes, ma'am. Someone has finally given Luke Parrish the seeing-to that half the building thinks he richly deserves. I can instruct Lt Filbert to investigate the matter, but he has more than enough on at the moment, and since we all know who is responsible anyway . . .' He tailed away.

'How is Parrish?'

'Broken nose. The two most magnificent black eyes in history. Sprained wrist. Extensive bruising to his chest and ribs.'

'Nasty,' commented Hay.

'There is some support for Lockland, ma'am, and the general feeling is that Parrish not only got what he deserved but that it was long overdue.'

'Well, in a way, that solves our problem of what to do with him at the moment.'

'Indeed, ma'am. He's going to be off sick for a while.'

'How much fuss is he making?'

'He's being strangely silent, ma'am.'

'That's concerning.'

'Yes, ma'am. This was more serious than the usual scuffle in the corridor. If he wants to make a formal complaint then he might have a case.'

'Hm. Suggest to Lt Grint that he might benefit from a few days' holiday. Somewhere out of the building.'

'Yes, ma'am. On a related note, Officer Farrell requested and was granted leave of absence.'

Hay stared out of the window. 'That's . . . interesting.'

'It's another one of them out of the way, ma'am.'

'Yes . . . although . . . given Officer Farrell's propensity to return to St Mary's . . . I wonder . . .'

'Ma'am?'

'Oh, nothing. If only we could find something to keep Meiklejohn occupied in Outer Mongolia . . .'

'She's been visiting John Costello, ma'am.'

Hay sat up straight. 'What? For God's sake, tell me she was supervised.'

'Lt North, ma'am. I've received a message that Costello cooperated fully and that Meiklejohn is on her way up here now.'

'Well, given their previous relationship, I suppose she might have got something from him, although I suspect he's still too afraid to . . .'

The outer door to Captain Farenden's office burst open. Something fell to the floor.

'That will be her now,' said the captain wearily, getting to his feet. 'No one else enters a room quite like that.'

Commander Hay rubbed her eyes and groped for her spectacles. 'This has been a long day, Charlie.'

She didn't know the half of it.

Captain Farenden moved towards the door. 'I'd better . . .'

He was too slow. The door to Commander Hay's office burst open and a dishevelled Mikey, face alight with excitement, tumbled into the room.

'I was right. I thought I was. I usually am. I know what he was on about. I know who he was working for. Until he stole his pod back, anyway. And you definitely have a problem.'

'Given the way today is going, I would have been greatly surprised if we didn't,' said Hay drily. 'Which particular catastrophe is about to engulf us all now?'

Mikey was pacing furiously, adrenalin spiking in the excitement of her discovery.

'I know who Costello was working for. He told me. Well, he didn't, but he didn't say it wasn't.'

'Sit down, please, Miss Meik—'

'And I know what he was after. Will be after. He said it wrong. Not surprising considering all the drugs he'd been given. And taken over the years. But he said it wrong. And we heard it wrong.'

'Said what?' said Captain Farenden. 'Heard what? Why is it so difficult for you to report in a calm and coherent manner?'

'Because calm and coherent doesn't work for me. You listened to him – calmly and coherently – I didn't. But I heard what everyone else missed.'

'And what exactly was it that you heard but everyone else missed?'

She opened her scratchpad. 'It's all about spacing and emphasis. You heard . . . blah blah blah . . .' Her fingers danced. 'Here we are. This is what you heard.'

She began to read. '*Dangerous.* Then *Death.* Then *Raisable.* Then *To do. If he . . . Forbidden.*'

She stopped.

Commander Hay blinked. 'And?'

'Listen.' She repeated herself.

'Again,' said Hay. 'And?'

Mikey sighed in frustration. '*This* is what *I* heard: *Dangerous Death Rays. Able to do if he . . .* and so on. Then he went on about *forbidden* and that was the final clue. But I think we should be able to get there first.' She ground to a halt. 'If you're not too particular about whose rules you follow.'

'Could you please . . .'

'Although you are the Time Police, of course. Shoot first then go home for tea. I'd need to modify a pod. Overcome the safety protocols. And if anyone ever finds out, there will be hell on, but that's your problem, not mine. No proof, of course, before you ask – just Costello's unspoken nod – because he didn't want to speak – confirming my inspired conjecture – at which I'm rather good.'

'Miss . . .'

'And it would certainly solve a long-standing mystery. People have speculated for—'

Hay sighed and pinched the bridge of her nose. 'Captain Farenden, if you would be so good, please.'

He nodded, placed himself in her path and drew a deep breath.

'Stand. Still.'

Mikey blinked and ground to a halt.

'And shut up.'

A somewhat tense silence fell.

Mikey stared up at him. A stricken dandelion flower trampled by brutal boots on the cruel path of life. 'Why are you shouting at me?'

'Is there any other way to attract your attention?'

'I was making my report. You know, the way the Time Police like and . . .'

'You were not reporting. You were pacing the commander's office spouting some sort of stream of consciousness babble and thoroughly irritating the hard-working Time Police officer who has to spend his days dealing with you. It may interest you to know, Miss Meiklejohn, that these days the greater part of my time is taken up with you, your demands, your work, the results of your work, your behaviour and your attitude. I used to have an office where people knocked politely before barging in. Where people didn't write on the walls. Where people didn't start their end of a conversation halfway down the corridor and then burst in demanding to know what I'm going to do about something I don't have a clue about. In short, Miss Meiklejohn, you are irritating, provoking, bloody hard work and I'm becoming increasingly convinced you're not worth the effort.'

If possible, the silence became even more tense.

Commander Hay reached stealthily for her paper knife and prudently removed it from Captain Farenden's reach.

Mikey sat down with a bump, her eyes huge and stricken. Two large tears ran down her cheeks. Her bottom lip quivered.

Commander Hay became busy with an important file. Statistics of some kind. Captain Farenden was on his own.

Two more tears followed the first.

'Um,' he said.

Obviously lacking any kind of nose-wiping equipment, Mikey dragged her sleeve across her nose.

'Oh, for heaven's sake,' said an exasperated Captain Farenden.

Without looking up, Commander Hay opened her bottom drawer and took out her box of emergency tissues. It didn't see a lot of use. Sobbing was not a Time Police–approved activity. The box sat on Commander Hay's desk, blinking in the unexpected sunshine and, rather like its owner, waiting with interest to see what would happen next.

'Here.' Captain Farenden thrust the box at Mikey.

She took one and held it to her face, apparently too overcome to speak. The dreadful silence went on and on. Captain Farenden, who had never – to his knowledge, anyway – actually made anyone cry before, was unsure how to respond.

He was rescued by his commanding officer who said drily, 'Stop milking it, Miss Meiklejohn.'

'Oh. Right. Yes.'

Mikey sat up. Not a trace of a tear anywhere. She handed him back the tissue and twinkled at him. 'Thank you so much.'

Commander Hay closed the file and spoke. 'Miss Meiklejohn, this behaviour might have been tolerated at St Mary's – although I very much doubt you ever tried this nonsense on Dr Bairstow – but it will not be tolerated here. I gather you have important information to impart. Please, in future, take a moment to pause – on the other side of the door, preferably – to arrange your thoughts and then, having done that, present your information in a calm and coherent manner. You are an intelligent and talented young woman and it would be a shame if your contribution to the Time Police is, in future, either ignored or disparaged simply because, through your own irresponsible behaviour, you lack credibility and are regarded as a clown.'

There was even more silence.

Mikey stared at her feet. Eventually, she said, 'Sorry.'

'Don't apologise to me.'

She looked at Captain Farenden. 'Sorry.'

He smiled. 'Apology happily accepted, Miss Meiklejohn.'

She nodded.

'Now then,' said Commander Hay, returning the box of tissues, saddened but grateful for any small break in its monotonous existence, whence it came. 'I believe you have some information for me.'

Mikey nodded.

'Then please may we hear it? Charlie, can you stay for this, please. Go ahead, Miss Meiklejohn.'

'Mikey,' said Mikey, suddenly.

'I beg your pardon?'

'It's Mikey. I'm sorry, but this *Miss Meiklejohn* business brings out the worst in me. I'm Mikey.'

Hay nodded. 'Very well. First things first – has John Costello revealed for whom he is working?'

'Yes. Although he keeps telling me he's working for himself – and that might be true now, but it hasn't always been the case. Yes, he stole the pod, but he's justifying that on the grounds it was stolen from him and he simply reclaimed his own property.'

'And the name of this person?'

Mikey sighed. 'I suspect you already know.'

'Well, I have made a guess. It's Henry Plimpton, isn't it?'

Mikey nodded.

'And Costello's not prepared to divulge any details about him at all?'

Mikey shook her head. 'No, but he was prepared to talk about the other matter. The one he mentioned to Ellis and Filbert.'

'Major Ellis and Lt Filbert,' reminded Captain Farenden, gently.

'Yes – them.'

'And what did he have to say?' enquired Commander Hay.

Mikey drew herself up and prepared for her big moment. 'I was right. I thought I was. I usually am, you know. It's Tesla.'

Hay blinked. 'The old-style car or the man?'

'The man. Nikola Tesla. Inventor of lots of amazing things.'

'Including a Death Ray, it would seem?'

'Yes. There was a lot of interest at the time but no one ever found his papers. Well, they did. Some of them. But no Death Ray details. And, people argued, if he had actually invented one, then he wouldn't have died poor, bankrupt and alone. Which he did.'

'In America,' said Hay, beginning to see where this was going. '*Forbidden*. Of course.'

'I bet there's a lot goes on there you don't know about,' said Mikey.

'They signed the treaty, along with everyone else,' said Hay, neutrally. 'We have no reason to believe they aren't abiding by it.'

'If I could just point out,' said Captain Farenden, 'with the greatest of respect, of course, that if we pursue this matter – this Death Ray thing – then we could be the ones responsible for breaking the treaty.'

Commander Hay sat back in her chair. 'Continue, please.'

Mikey leaned forwards in excitement. 'Tesla's papers disappeared after his death. Not all of them, but the ones that were discovered were quite insignificant. Tesla always said he had something important stashed in his safe, the promise of which he was using against payment of his hotel bills, but when they opened the safe after his death, there was nothing in there. Well, there was, but not what they expected to find, and now I'm wondering if that's because someone else got there first.'

Captain Farenden had been flicking through his scratchpad. 'A brilliant man.'

'Yes,' said Mikey, her enthusiasm rising again. 'Tesla coils, remote control, neon lights, alternating current, robotics, lasers, wireless transmission and . . .'

She paused for the big finish. 'And this supposed Death Ray. Which got everyone very excited at the time. Suppose . . .'

The room fell silent.

'Yes,' said Commander Hay, staring thoughtfully out of her window. 'Just suppose . . .'

Captain Farenden frowned. 'And John Costello told you all this?'

'Well, actually, I told him but he didn't contradict me. And before you congratulate me on my perspicacity . . .' She paused for a moment but the silence was discouraging so she sighed and continued. 'I think it was the combination of a friendly face, head wound and a cocktail of drugs that did the trick.'

'Do you believe him?'

'Yes, I think so.'

'Why? How do you know all this wasn't just the result of a cocktail of drugs, his head wound and . . . ?'

137

'A friendly face,' said Mikey, helpfully. 'Because he was thinking clearly enough to stipulate that if we can successfully recover Tesla's papers, he wants a reward. A sizeable reward.'

'Not too injured to negotiate,' said Farenden. 'Good to know.'

Hay nodded. 'Well, thank you . . . Mikey. Can you put all this in a written report for me?'

Mikey produced a data cube. 'You should find everything I've got so far on this.'

There was a lengthy and surprised silence and then Hay said, 'Thank you. Excellent work.'

'You're welcome,' said Mikey, and left. Surprisingly quietly for her.

Captain Farenden followed her out into his office, closing Hay's door behind him. 'Are you all right?'

'Always,' said Mikey, keeping her face turned away.

'How's Adrian these days?'

'Fine.'

'Still at St Mary's?'

'Yes.'

'She meant it, you know. That was good work.'

Still not looking at him, Mikey nodded.

'Where are you off to now?'

She shrugged. 'Back to the Batcave. Sorry – my workroom.'

Farenden smiled. 'You're not going to blow us all up, are you?'

She turned back angrily. 'Is that what you think?'

'No. It was just a bad joke on my part.' He paused and then said, 'We started on the wrong foot, didn't we?'

She shrugged. 'The Time Police spent years trying to catch me and Adrian and we all know what would have happened

138

if you had. Yes, I'm here with Matthew – which is good – but I've got you – all of you – trying to control me, my work, every aspect of my life. I know why I'm here. You don't want me, but you don't want anyone else to have me. People like Henry Plimpton. Yes, I have a roof over my head and a place to work, but we both know I'm not free. I'm not my own person any longer.'

She dragged her still-sticky sleeve across her nose again.

'Hey.' He pushed forwards a chair and pulled out another one for himself. His desk was no longer between them. 'Almost everything you said is true. But you're a known illegal, Mikey. There's a price to pay and this is it. You're not in gaol. Neither is Adrian. And what we do here is important. You can make a contribution. You'll have to work for acceptance and respect, but so does everyone else.'

She looked out of the window for a moment and then nodded.

'And it's for your protection as well. You don't want to end up with Henry Plimpton again. Or someone even worse. Imagine big business going around snatching up talented people like you. Imagine being one of many, shackled to a workbench, no freedom of movement or thought. That could still happen, Mikey. Modern slavery takes many forms and Henry Plimpton isn't the only unpleasant person out there.'

She nodded again. 'But you still control my work.'

'I think, if you don't blow us all up over the next couple of months, Commander Hay will relinquish some control. You can't blame her for being a little wary. We all still remember the teapot.'

'It was destroyed in the Thera eruption.'

'A noble end.'

'Yes, I suppose it was.'

'So back to the Batcave for six more exciting inventions before lunch?'

She looked at him. 'You should come down sometime. I'll give you a guided tour.'

'Thank you. I'd like that.'

She stood up. 'You're welcome.'

'And brilliant work on Tesla.'

She disappeared out of the door and the sun went in.

Next to see Commander Hay was Lt North. With disquieting news.

'Ma'am, as you instructed, I've searched our records for reports on the Lockland shooting. I've had an entire team on it. We have nothing.'

Hay was startled. 'Nothing at all?'

'Nothing at all. Past or present. Nothing on the Locklands or Helen Portman. There's no record of old Mrs Lockland laying any information or the subsequent operation to take them down. No details of the people involved, the pods used . . . absolutely nothing. I even went through the pod schedules for the time and every single one was accounted for elsewhere.'

She waited. Hay sat back. 'You said nothing on the Locklands. Does that include our Lockland?'

'No, ma'am. The records of Officer Lockland, Jane Christine, are all just as they should be.'

'Then how is this possible? Is the problem with us? Do we have a hole?'

A hole was a professional term denoting a place where information once was and now, for some reason, wasn't.

North shook her head. 'No – no hole. That's the really worrying part. It isn't that the info has been deleted, ma'am. Nothing has been removed or tampered with. The info was never there in the first place.'

'Have you cross-referred to Portman?'

'Yes, ma'am. All we have is the recent entry on Eric Portman and his involvement with Imogen Farnborough and Site X.'

Hay said thoughtfully, 'Well, this is interesting, isn't it? Mrs Lockland must have assumed her son and daughter-in-law were involved in the Time Wars – which were, at that time, in the closing stages – and she laid information against them. It turns out – according to Mr Costello – that Lockland's parents were actually helping those suffering domestic abuse to escape, so nothing to do with the Time Wars. Did we ignore her information because of that?'

'Unlikely, ma'am,' said North. 'It's the Time travel that was illegal, not the reason for it. And if anything, we would have been even more stringent in those days than we are now.'

'Yes,' said Hay, thoughtfully. 'Thank you, Lieutenant. Keep digging, please.'

North nodded and left the room.

Hay pressed her intercom. 'Charlie – can you come in.'

He found her staring out of the window. Without turning, she said, 'It would be a huge coup for us if we could acquire Tesla's papers.'

'What would we do with them?'

'Destroy them, of course.'

He stepped back. 'Ma'am?'

'We're not historians, Captain. Our job is to safeguard the Timeline and keep the peace. The last thing I want is to see

141

the details of Tesla's dubious inventions out there in the *Big Boys' Book of Death Rays*. No – we destroy everything we find, and if we can manage to take down an important illegal in the process, then I would be a very happy Time Police officer. Well, certainly a less depressed Time Police officer than I am at the moment.' She thought for a minute. 'I think, given Team Two-Three-Six's involvement in all this, I'll hand this one over to Ellis and BeeBOC.'

'With respect, ma'am – surely this is one for Hunter Division.'

'I think not, Captain. Not at this exact moment. The recent attack on TPHQ ... the business with Henry Plimpton ... missing information ... everything points to someone here at HQ who . . .' She paused.

'Whose first loyalty is not necessarily to this organisation?'

'Indeed. I think, from this moment on, you and I should be a little more careful with our information and with whom we share it.'

'Ma'am?'

'Compartmentalising everything gives us more control. And will enable us to narrow down the field of suspects.'

'Which at the moment is just about everyone.'

'Well, I'm pretty sure it's not me. And I'm almost certain it's not you, Charlie.'

'That's a relief, ma'am. Innocence is much more difficult to prove than guilt.'

'Could you get me Major Ellis, please?'

Ellis was there in minutes.

Hay looked up with a smile. 'Good day, Major Ellis. Thank you for coming.'

'My pleasure, ma'am.'

The smile disappeared. 'Pleasantries over with, Major, allow me to hand you a poisoned chalice.'

'Oh?' He raised an eyebrow.

'I am considering breaking the treaty as it relates to America.'

Ellis was startled. 'Ma'am?'

'Captain, could you update Major Ellis, please.'

Captain Farenden outlined the state of play in a few brief sentences. At the end of which there was a long pause.

Hay clasped her hands. 'As you can see, the situation is fluid in the extreme and I feel would best be addressed by your department. And please feel free to utilise the skills of Miss Meiklejohn, who has had some useful thoughts. Captain Farenden will flash full details to your scratchpad.'

Major Ellis fixed Captain Farenden with a look. 'Thank you, Captain.'

Captain Farenden grinned. 'My pleasure, Major. Miss Meiklejohn has been working the problem and her interview with Costello has confirmed her first thoughts.'

Major Ellis blinked. 'That was fast, but given her prior acquaintance with the prisoner, how much weight should we place on her findings?'

'That was my thought,' said Commander Hay, 'but she does appear to have had some useful insights – many of which are written on the walls of Captain Farenden's office should you care to inspect her workings on your way out.'

Major Ellis, who knew just how much Captain Farenden prided himself on his immaculate office, very carefully kept his voice neutral. 'Oh?'

Captain Farenden appeared to brace himself. 'I found her

promise to return with more information extremely disquieting, ma'am.'

'Never mind, Captain. Your sacrifice is greatly appreciated. What of Parrish, Major? How is he?'

'About to be discharged from MedCen. In a completely unrelated matter, I intend to suggest to Lt Grint that he might like to take a few days to finish his convalescence elsewhere.'

'Already in hand, major. Charlie will furnish him with whatever he needs – travel warrants and so forth ... Most immediately, I think we might all benefit from a quick chat with Mrs Lockland.'

'Agreed, ma'am. It will be interesting to see what she has to say for herself. And I must admit to some curiosity about her. Lt Grint's report was far from flattering. Given the current problems in security, I'll send one of my own teams to bring her in.'

'Thank you, Major.'

'Thank you, ma'am.'

12

Back at St Mary's, the fire was not so much raging as just muttering crossly to itself. The worst was obviously over with. In between shouting wholly disregarded helpful advice to those still clearing up, Matthew and his mother were busy making plans.

'We'll borrow your father's pod.'

'Won't he mind?'

'Yes, probably.'

'Would it help if I left a note saying everything was my fault?'

'That's very sweet, Matthew, but he'll have no difficulty laying the blame at the right door. I'll leave him a message telling him where and when we've gone. Just in case.'

'Mum, I don't want to get you into trouble.'

'Oh, I wouldn't worry about that. I usually manage to do that all by myself.'

'But . . .'

'We'll say it was to help Jane. He likes Jane.'

'Suppose one of us gets hurt.'

'How? We're only going to witness an event. Not even a major historical event in contemporary time – only a very minor one. We probably won't even have to leave the pod.'

'Two people will be killed.'

'Then we'll definitely stay in the pod.'

They turned their attention back to the formerly burning St Mary's. Soaked and scorched furniture and mattresses were being thrown from the upper windows. Some of them rekindled as soon as they made contact with fresh air. Warning shouts rang out.

'Your father's going to be ages yet,' said Max. 'We should go while we can.' She emptied her mug on to the grass and stood up. 'This way, I think. Avoiding the more exciting areas.'

They made their way around Hawking and in through the back door. From there they skirted the kitchens, then went down the Long Corridor and into the paint store.

'Dad might have changed the codes,' said Matthew as they slipped into the small pod no one was supposed to know anything about.

'He hasn't,' said Max with confidence.

He hadn't.

'Destination? Date?'

Matthew passed across a sheet of paper with the appropriate coordinates. Max sat down, fired up the console and set to work.

Matthew made himself comfortable and seized the opportunity to ponder recent events. Where would all this end? How would it end? Team 236 was finished. Luke, he knew, would request a transfer to another team. A complete waste of time – no team would take him. And if that happened, then Luke was finished in the Time Police.

Which would leave just the two of them. Traditional teams consist of four officers, so 236 was already pushing the boundaries with just three members and a junior officer for a team leader. A team of two was unworkable. He sighed. Jane could move into 235 – where she would be more than welcome – and he, Matthew, could revert to his original plan – to work on the Time Map. Which he wouldn't mind doing now that Mikey was around the place. They could work together. Yes, it would mean the end of 236, and he would always feel a pang of regret, but he could already hear the massive sighs of relief gusting through TPHQ.

Max had finished laying in the coordinates. 'Ready?'

'When you are.'

The world went white.

They arrived a few minutes after midnight. Max engaged the camo device, activated the screen and switched to night vision.

'We don't have a precise time for . . . the incident,' she said, 'so I've gone for just after midnight on the day in question. Which means we could find ourselves waiting here for hours and hours. Did you think to bring a book?'

'No,' said Matthew, stretching himself out on the floor. 'If you don't mind, I'll get my head down for a bit. Can you wake me in a couple of hours?'

Max nodded, folded her arms, settled back in her seat and looked around. For her, no book was needed. There were memories enough within this pod's four walls. She settled her chin on her chest, cast her mind back, and smiled to herself.

The sun came up with some reluctance. Slowly the details of their surroundings emerged from the early-morning mist.

For an allegedly poverty-stricken old lady barely able to muster the basics of life, Jane's grandmother lived in a surprisingly nice area. Tall, narrow, pleasantly shabby houses with wrought-iron balconies stood around the small public garden that gave the square its name. The trees were bare and the flower borders empty and prepared for spring planting, but the clumps of rhododendrons and laurels scattered around would provide them with plenty of leafy cover.

No one and nothing was moving at this time of morning. Lacey Gardens was a quiet, respectable, suburban area. Blinds or curtains were drawn at all the windows. A fat tabby cat jumped off a garden wall, trotted across the road and off into the shrubbery. All the front gardens were very neat. Polished door knockers would gleam in the sun – if the sun ever got going today. Everything was very peaceful. The residents must have thought nothing bad could ever happen here.

They got that wrong.

Time dragged on. The sun rose higher and the mist melted away. Still no early bird appeared through their front door, pulling on their coat, toast in one hand, briefcase in the other, and dashing off to work. Perhaps no one here did work. This looked to be an old person's neighbourhood. There were no toys in the gardens. No swings in the park.

Although Jane lived here, didn't she? Max focused on Jane's grandmother's house. The one next to a narrow alleyway. Nothing was stirring. Was a very young Jane in there somewhere? Fast asleep and dreaming of fairies and pink unicorns, with no idea that her world was about to fall apart? Matthew had said she had no memory of what had happened to her parents. She'd only ever had her grand-mother's version.

Matthew awoke to a mug of greatly appreciated tea. They

148

discussed going outside to make a quick recce of the area and decided against it.

'We have to be very careful,' said Max, who could record the number of times she'd uttered that sentiment on the fingers of one ear. 'We mustn't do anything that could somehow change the course of whatever happens here today. While you were sprawled on the floor snoring, I've set up the cameras. Two on Jane's house over there and one on the entrance to the square. I've left the others to be deployed as we need them. What time is it?'

'Six forty-five,' said Matthew, yawning. 'They'll all be getting up and setting off to work soon. Although I'm certain nothing will happen until nightfall. This is completely the wrong time of day for an ambush.'

'You'd think so, wouldn't you?' said Max, staring at the console. 'But check this out.'

Matthew leaned over her shoulder. 'Another pod signature? Where?'

Max toggled one of the cameras. 'There – that patch of shrubbery over there. By the gate. Can you see it?'

'Yes. I think I can see the corner of a pod.' He frowned. 'They haven't made much attempt at concealment, have they? A bit sloppy for the Time Police. This must surely be Jane's parents back from whatever it is they've been doing.'

Max was frowning. 'Could be, I suppose, but I'm not sure. For some reason it's just sitting there. Why would they do that? I think it might be the Time Police, after all. Let's keep watching.'

They watched and waited. Nothing happened.

Matthew was scowling at the screen. 'If that is the Time

149

Police, you'd think they'd be over here to check us out, wouldn't you?'

Max nodded. 'Is it possible they don't know we're here?'

'Unlikely. We've engaged the camo device but they would still be able to read our signature. They should have IDed us as soon as they landed and hit us with an EMP. They haven't, so my guess is – not Time Police.'

They waited some more. Nothing moved. No one left the other pod. The world waited.

'Something's wrong,' said Matthew, uneasily. 'They must know we're here. If they think we're Jane's parents, they should be banging on the door by now. If they know we're not Jane's parents, they should still be banging on the door by now. What's going on?'

'Perhaps they don't care who we are and they're getting ready to blast us out of existence. In which case, your dad's going to be really cross.'

'I think if they knew we were here then they would have done that by now,' said Matthew. 'Don't you?'

'I don't know. They're just sitting there. Why? Who are they? I'm beginning to have a really bad feeling about this.'

'Should we . . . I don't know . . . do something?'

'No,' said Max, gently. 'We shouldn't do anything at all. You know that.'

He sighed. 'Yes, I do. It's just coming up to seven. Keep your eyes peeled, Mum. I think Jane's parents will be along any minute now.'

'Funny time of day to make the return jump.'

'Actually, it's rather clever. Anyone emerging from the park in the small hours would always be suspicious, but at this time

150

of the day, people will assume they've simply been out for an early-morning walk.'

'True. But what makes you think Jane's parents will soon arrive?'

'From an operational point of view . . .' He gestured at the pod. 'This is tying up a whole team and a pod. They wouldn't spend all day on this. Jane's parents aren't important enough.'

Max shook her head. 'I don't think these people are Time Police either. I think they're someone else.'

Matthew stared at the screen. 'Well, that would explain a lot. Although who else they might be . . .'

'A third party?'

'We're the third party, Mum.'

'A fourth party, then?'

'An unknown element, certainly.'

'Hang on. Something's happening.'

The pod door had opened to reveal six men. All dressed in black. All armed. Splitting up, they deployed themselves around the square. One vaulted a low wall into someone's garden. Two concealed themselves behind the trees. One took himself off down the alleyway, presumably to cover the rear. The remainder disappeared into the bushes. Everyone knew exactly where to go. This had obviously been carefully planned. They were quick and quiet. Twenty seconds from start to finish and then, once again, the square was silent and still.

Matthew stood rigid, staring at the screen. 'They're not Time Police.'

Max turned to look at him. 'Are you certain? It's a while ago, remember. Different uniforms perhaps. Different tactics. Different style pods.'

151

He shook his head vigorously. 'No, that's not us. I mean – that's not a Time Police pod. Nor a Time Police team. What the hell's going on?'

They looked at each other. The moment was here. Any minute now, people were about to die.

'Matthew, are you all right with this?'

'I'm not thrilled but it has to be done.'

'OK, then.'

'Recorders on?'

'Yes. All of them.'

'OK. I don't think we'll have long to wait.'

Barely had he spoken when . . .

'There's another signature,' said Max, quickly. 'They're here.'

A small box had appeared some thirty feet away, partly obscured by a thick clump of laurel bushes. Now that Matthew knew what he was looking for, he could see a faint path trodden in the grass, leading in and out of the shrubbery. This was obviously their usual landing spot.

He shook his head. Careless. Very careless. Had they been doing this for so long that they were neglecting basic precautions?

Two figures emerged from the laurels. A man and a woman. The man was short and slim and had a beanie pulled down over his head. The woman led the way. She wore a tightly belted jacket with a sheepskin collar. Matthew felt his heart thump. She was older, obviously, but it might have been Jane herself emerging from the shrubbery. He felt his stomach slide sideways. This was going to be bad.

The foliage must have been damp. They were brushing drops

152

of water off their sleeves, not even looking around to see who was about. Definitely careless. Fatally careless. Matthew sighed. The next few moments would end their lives, change Jane's life forever, and her grandmother's, and by extension, his, Luke's, and everyone else with whom Jane would come into contact. As his mother was so fond of saying, 'Nothing happens in isolation. Every event is connected to every other event. Often, the connection isn't obvious, but it's always there.'

A third figure appeared. A little younger, shorter hair, more upright, less battered by life. Matthew stiffened. 'That's John Costello. That must be his pod. Are you sure you're getting all this, Mum?'

Max glanced at the console. 'Absolutely certain.'

The three figures conferred briefly. Arrangements for the next jump, perhaps. Costello nodded, made a farewell gesture and turned to go.

A man's voice shouted an order and six black figures leaped from their hiding places.

The squad may not have been Time Police but they were fast and professional nonetheless. Nor did they go in with all guns blazing in the manner so beloved of holo-makers everywhere. They didn't need to. Aaron and Helen Lockland surrendered immediately. Standing very still, they raised their hands and waited. Whether they thought they were being arrested by the civilian or Time Police wasn't clear. What was clear was that there was no thought of resistance on their part.

John Costello, however, had other ideas. Perhaps he thought that, as the owner of the pod, he'd be in the most trouble. Or perhaps he thought his pod was close enough for him to attempt an escape. Whichever it was, displaying the same speed which, one day, would so dismay Team 236, he turned and disappeared back into the bushes.

A single voice barked a command. Now they opened fire. Short, sharp bursts. Bullets ripped through the greenery. Leaves, twigs, whole bushes – all exploded in a hail of gunfire. The noise was loud in the early-morning stillness.

Aaron and Helen Lockland acted instinctively. The sensible thing would have been to throw themselves to the ground, cover their heads and pray nothing hit them. But that didn't happen.

Helen Lockland – closest to the shrubbery – turned to follow Jake. She must have had some thought of gaining the safety of the pod. She actually managed three paces before she was hit.

Aaron Lockland ran towards the armed men waving his arms and shouting, 'Stop. Stop. We surrender. Helen, stand still. Don't shoot. Don't shoot.'

A hail of gunfire ripped his chest apart. The force blew him backwards where he lay on his back, his red blood staining the bright green grass.

Helen Lockland had been hit in the back. The impact propelled her into the shrubbery where she lay for a moment, and then, unbelievably, painfully, inch by inch, tried to drag herself away.

John Costello reappeared briefly, seized her arm, and attempted to pull her further into the bushes. She was too heavy for him. Or he was too weak. He tugged but failed to move her and the next moment he was hit himself.

Matthew saw the impact spin him around, saw the bright red rose of blood high up on his shoulder, saw him pause for what could have been a fatal moment and then, clutching his shoulder, turn and stagger deeper into the shrubbery. Back towards his pod.

The clatter of gunfire died away.

Helen Lockland was still trying to crawl to safety.

'She's still alive,' said Max, in disbelief. Ignoring the fact that she couldn't possibly be heard, she shouted, 'Stay down. Don't get up. Lie still, for heaven's sake.'

Ignoring both civilians on the ground, the armed men plunged into the shrubbery. There was another brief burst of gunfire, presumably after the retreating Mr Costello, and then silence.

The whole thing had taken ten, perhaps twelve seconds.

Two men reappeared from the shrubbery. Ignoring Helen Lockland lying at his feet, one spoke into a hand-held com.

The next moment, the original pod door opened and a figure emerged.

'Shit,' shouted Matthew, stepping back in disbelief. Recollecting himself, he elbowed his mother away from the controls, seeking to enlarge and enhance the image. 'Shit. Fire-trucking fire truck. Bloody bollocking hell, Mum.'

'What?' said Max. 'Who's that? What's the matter?'

Matthew banged his fist on the console in frustration. 'That's the bloke who was responsible for the Paris Time-Stop.'

'But who is he? You know him?'

'Yes – and so do you, although you've never met. He also tried to blow up the Acropolis. That's Henry Plimpton. It wasn't the Time Police after all. Henry Plimpton killed Jane's parents.'

155

13

Jane was alone in her room. She had been there for quite some considerable time and was now stuck for something to do. She'd reorganised all her drawers. She'd sorted her underwear into colours. Which, since almost everything was white, had not taken very long. She'd tidied her shelves, rearranging her few books in order of enjoyment. Then by height. Then the more conventional alphabetically. She'd reordered her clothing. Which, since almost everything, including her uniforms, was black, had also not taken very long. Now, resources exhausted, she was simply staring out of the window and thinking.

She was a Portman. What did that actually mean?

Well, nothing, really. She felt no different today than she had yesterday. She knew nothing of the Portmans and cared even less. And presumably they felt the same about her. No one had ever knocked on her door with an offer of a better life, a better education, a job – anything. She could only assume that as small fry went, she was the very smallest. Which, she thought sadly, really was the story of her life.

She had just heaved yet another enormous sigh when someone tapped at the door. Automatically, she called, 'Come in,' and Lt Grint entered.

Jane blinked. 'Are you allowed in here?'

Grint shrugged.

'Only I think I'm not supposed to see . . . You're not supposed to . . . We shouldn't . . .'

Grint pulled open the door and bellowed out into the corridor, 'I'm in Lockland's room if anyone wants to come and tell me I shouldn't be here.'

They waited for the echoes to die away. Jane had her hand over her mouth, torn between alarm and amusement. Nothing happened. No sirens went off. No one was arrested for illegal entry into Jane's room.

'I'm beginning to like this bloke,' said Bolshy Jane with rare approval.

Grint closed the door. 'You were saying?'

Jane tried hard not to laugh. 'I think I was saying how nice it is to see you.'

'It's good to see you too, Jane. Um . . . I've brought you something.'

He tugged some books from his backpack. 'From the library. I . . . um . . . I hope you like them.'

He handed them to Jane. His knuckles were swollen and badly bruised. Matthew had mentioned that Luke had sustained an . . . impact . . . but had not gone into details and she hadn't asked.

She took the books. 'They're my favourites,' she said, not even looking at the titles. 'It's funny – I used to long for the peace and quiet in which to sit down and read all day.' She sighed. 'I think I should be more careful what I wish for. Thank you very much for these.'

Grint nodded, not looking at her. 'You're welcome.'

'It isn't just the books,' said Jane, awkwardly, 'it's knowing that someone out there hasn't forgotten me.'

'Farrell hasn't abandoned you, surely?'

'No, he brought me some chocolate and . . . and news . . . and we talked a little. Now he's gone on leave so I haven't seen anyone at all.' She smiled at him. 'It's good to know that someone out there still likes me.'

There was a deep and somehow meaningful silence.

Grint assumed the expression of one about to undergo a great ordeal. 'I like you.'

Jane blushed. 'I know.'

There was more silence.

Jane began to think something more might be required. Not looking at him, she said, 'I like you, too.'

Now the silence took on a different quality.

'I wondered,' said Grint, staring out of the window, 'I know we haven't talked about it . . . but perhaps . . . I've been given leave and I thought . . . if you want to, of course . . . I wondered . . . would you like to . . . we could go away . . . for a bit . . . a bit of a rest, I mean. Perhaps we could go down to the coast. Or stay in town and see the sights we're always too busy for. Um . . . what do you think?'

'I'd love to, but are you sure? With all this going on, I mean?'

'Of course I am. It was you I wasn't sure about. Whether you would want to. Go away, I mean.'

'Will they let me?'

Grint opened his mouth to say they'd probably be delighted to have her out of the building, but one of the less frequently accessed areas of his brain kicked in and suggested a better response.

'You haven't done anything wrong. You're not responsible for what that moron Parrish says and does. You're only in here to keep you out of his way. And now he's in MedCen anyway.'

'Is he?' said Jane, very carefully not looking at Grint's swollen hands.

'Mm,' said Grint, very carefully not looking at his swollen hands.

'Well,' said Jane, slowly morphing from scarlet to crimson and astonished at her own wanton behaviour, 'I have to say that getting away from here does sound . . . very nice.'

'Have a think about where we could go. Together. I did say together, didn't I?'

Jane touched his hand gently, wondering if her face could be seen from space. 'I think that would be the best part.'

'Me too,' said Grint. 'You being there, I mean. Not me. Although I would be there as well.'

The room felt suddenly much too hot.

'I must go,' he said.

'And I must stay,' said Jane, sadly.

'But not for long,' said Grint. He paused, looked uncertain for a moment and then, with the air of Hercules accomplishing an additional and unplanned Labour, kissed her cheek.

That Jane did not spontaneously combust was a small and unexplained miracle.

The door closed behind him.

'Aw . . .' said Bolshy Jane.

'Shut up,' said Actual Jane, picking up her new books.

14

Summoned to Major Ellis's office and instructed to bring in old Mrs Lockland for questioning, Team 235 exhibited signs of doubt. And some dismay.

'What?' said Ellis, who had to put up with this sort of thing from Team 236 and saw no reason why 235 should jump on the same bandwagon.

'Will Lt Grint be accompanying us, sir?'

'Just to pick up an old lady? Unlikely.'

'Only he's been there before and she knows him.'

'Lt Grint has requested forty-eight hours' leave.'

Team 235 regarded each other glumly.

'Problem, officers?'

'Well, she's an old lady, sir,' said Rossi. He appeared to be struck by inspiration. 'Perhaps we should take a female officer with us? You know, in case she . . .' He paused. Inspiration had disappeared even more quickly than it had arrived.

Ellis stared at him. 'In case she what?'

Rossi shrugged. 'I don't know. Don't old ladies have . . . needs?'

His two teammates stared at him.

'What sort of needs?' said Socko.

'Well, I don't know, do I? What does *your* granny need?'

'More shotgun cartridges usually,' said Socko. 'She shoots foxes.'

Now everyone stared at *him*.

'Why?' said Hansen, bewildered.

'Because shooting people is against the law.' He appeared to have second thoughts. 'Unless you're us, of course.'

Ellis stirred restlessly. 'If I might recall you all to the real world and your function within it . . .'

'Sorry, sir.'

'You may take either Lt North or Officer Varma if you feel you need protection. And if you can persuade them to abandon their normal duties for the purpose of holding your hands. Either is perfectly competent to deal with dangerous little old ladies even if you are not.'

'Yes, sir.'

'Dismissed.'

There was considerable corridor discussion over whether they'd be better off taking Lt North . . .

'Although *she'll* end up taking *us*. You know what she's like,' said Socko, checking over his shoulder to ensure Lt North hadn't suddenly materialised directly behind him.

. . . or whether they should invite Officer Varma.

Rossi shuffled his feet. 'Are we sure about that? She has full powers of arrest and won't hesitate to use them on us if things go wrong. And she's clear favourite in next week's annual inter-departmental boxing competition. Again.'

There was nodding. That was true.

'North it is, then,' said Hansen, to unanimous agreement, and they set off for Records.

* * *

161

The Time Police were the proud owners of two helicopters. Black helicopters, obviously. In these quieter days they were used mainly for transportation rather than gunships, although they both retained the facility to bristle with armaments and frequently did. They were nowhere near as big as the old Leviathans but considerably nippier. And more comfortable. Major Callen was known to make frequent use of them during his recruitment campaigns. Dramatic touch-downs on a spotlit helipad were one of his most effective recruitment tools.

Today, however, Delta Zero Two was scheduled to transport a potential prisoner to TPHQ. Together with a distinctly uneasy Team 235.

'All aboard,' said the pilot. 'Get a move on – the footie's on tonight. Battersea versus Fethiyespor. Second round of the qualifier.'

There followed an intense if pessimistic discussion as to Battersea's chances. In self-defence, North closed her eyes. And her ears.

A thirty-minute flight brought them to Jane's grandmother's house, outwardly unchanged since the recent Grint incursion.

The helicopter set down in the gardens – not too far from the spot where Jane's parents had landed all those years ago. The shrubbery had not survived the test of time but otherwise the gardens hadn't changed at all.

'I think,' said North, surveying the peaceful square and then the resources at her disposal, 'that I had better do the talking.'

Team 235 indicated this was an excellent idea. Rossi and Hansen disappeared around the back – not that anyone seriously expected old Mrs Lockland to climb out of a rear bedroom window, but, as Rossi said, they weren't Team Weird, well known for needing at least two or three attempts to bring in their prisoners, were they?

Socko and North marched to the front door and arranged their faces in pleasant, non-old-lady-alarming smiles. The door was opened by Mrs Lockland herself – obviously more mobile than Lt Grint had previously realised.

She took one look and tried to shut the door in their faces. Socko moved quickly, inserting an enormous boot. 'Mrs Lockland?'

'No,' she said, and tried to close the door again.

North moved in. 'Mrs Lockland, we are the Time Police. You are requested and required to return with us to TPHQ to assist us with our enquiries.'

Mrs Lockland cast a look around the square. Socko, somehow managing to watch their backs while still keeping the door open, was prepared to bet there were any number of inquisitive eyes behind all those lace curtains. He was also prepared to bet Mrs Lockland wasn't too popular with her neighbours at the best of times and wondered how much they were enjoying the scene.

'Well,' said the old lady, grimly. 'At least you didn't bring the monkey this time.'

Being involved at the Acropolis at the time, North had missed the sight of Lt Grint's broken and burned body being rushed to MedCen for emergency treatment. Now, contemplating the tiny but malevolent figure in front of her, she did not so much abandon sympathy and compassion as shove them into a lead box and drop them into the nearest river. 'Do you require assistance to access the helicopter?'

Mrs Lockland peered over North's shoulder at the presumably

hitherto unnoticed sinister black helicopter with its still-circling rotors, now occupying a large part of the communal garden, and changed her tactics, drooping pathetically.

'Where's my granddaughter? I need her to take care of me. I'm old and sick.'

North gave no signs of hearing a word of that. 'Do you require assistance to access the helicopter?'

Mrs Lockland abandoned drooping and pathetic as too difficult to sustain. 'I'm not going all the way to London. Wicked place. I'm too sick to travel. I should be in my bed. My granddaughter should be here. She's worthless but she's my blood and it's her responsibility to take care of me. Ran off, she did. Feckless little good-for-nothing. Just like her mother.'

Her eyes gleamed hatred. The passage of time had clearly not mellowed her in any way.

'Do you require assistance to access the helicopter?'

'I can't go anywhere. All my medication . . .'

'Can be provided by our MedCen. Do you require assistance to access the helicopter?'

Behind North, Socko raised his weapon. The whine of a charging blaster was very loud in this peaceful residential neighbourhood.

Furious and frustrated, Mrs Lockland fell back on an old favourite. 'I told you, I'm too sick to travel.'

North smiled pleasantly. Generations of peasant-oppressing ancestors lined up behind their favourite descendent. 'Not as sick as you will be if you *don't* travel. Do you require assistance to access the helicopter?'

'I'm not going anywhere.'

'Do you require assistance to access the helicopter?'

'I told you I . . .'

'Do you require assistance to access the helicopter?'

Rossi and Hansen appeared from the back of the house.

'Still here? What's the problem?' muttered Rossi.

'A bit of a Clash of the Titans,' whispered Socko. 'I'm staying well out of it. My money's on our girl, though.'

As if she had heard him – and it wouldn't surprise him if she had the hearing of a bat – Mrs Lockland glared at him. He smiled amiably.

There was a long silence. The world held its breath. Sonicking the old crow and forcibly dragging her to the helicopter was still everyone's favourite Plan A and possibly, on some level, Mrs Lockland was aware she had met her match. The Time Police rarely went away just because you wanted them to.

'If you please, Mrs Lockland.' North stepped aside and gestured towards the helicopter.

Even then there was a struggle. 'My house . . .'

'Will be perfectly safe. I shall notify the civilian police that you have been removed as a person of interest and they will automatically place a couple of officers on guard. At your front gate. Where everyone can see them. Do you have your keys? Do you require assistance to access . . . ?'

'No,' she snapped. 'For the love of God, stop saying that.'

Picking up her bag and keys from the hall table, she slammed the door behind her. Rossi and Hansen escorted her through the gate and across the road. North followed on behind, grinning to herself.

Mrs Lockland furiously resisted any attempt to help her even though it was very apparent she did, in fact, require assistance to access the helicopter.

Possibly impatient at all this fannying around and concerned he might be too late to witness Battersea's inevitable heavy defeat, the pilot performed the helicopter equivalent of revving the engine and in the end, Socko lifted Mrs Lockland off the ground and handed her up to Hansen, who strapped her into her seat.

About to climb in herself, North cast a glance around the square. Fascinated faces lined every window.

Mrs Lockland had also noticed. 'You've ruined my good name.'

'Oh, I wouldn't worry about that,' said North, cheerfully, closing the door and shutting out the noise of the engines. 'It's very unlikely you'll ever return to hear what they're saying about you. Whenever you're ready, Mellor.'

Mrs Lockland complained all the way back to TPHQ. They watched her bitter little mouth moving. Incessantly. She never stopped. But since they'd all had the forethought to put on their helmets and switch off the audible function, no one cared. Or even heard.

Mrs Lockland was deposited in Interrogation Room 1. Mr Costello's blood had been wiped away – although there had been considerable discussion on whether it should be allowed to remain as an effective interrogation technique – and Officer Varma was detailed to question her.

Ellis and North had both asked to observe the interview. For which they paid heavily. There were hours of whining, self-pity, bitter complaints about the cost of bringing up an ungrateful granddaughter, self-justification, condemnations of Jane, demands to be released, and general bitching about

166

everything under the sun for Mrs Lockland to work her way through first.

Varma summoned her professionally blank expression and persevered. 'Mrs Lockland, please can you tell me . . . ?'

'Where's my granddaughter? Why isn't she here?'

'What do you know about . . .?'

'Where's my medication? I'm sick and you're with-holding . . .'

'I've checked with MedCen and they advise you're not due anything until . . .'

'Where am I? What is this place?'

'Please can you tell me about your daughter-in-law's . . . ?'

'I'm sick. I can't answer all these questions. That thug who manhandled me into that helicopter has banged my hip. I'm in agony. Threw me in like a piece of rubbish.'

'Officer Kohl exercised the very greatest . . .'

'No, he didn't.'

'I've seen the visuals,' lied Varma. 'Yes, he did. Do you wish me to add falsifying an accusation against an officer to your charge sheet?'

Mrs Lockland stiffened. 'You've got nothing on me. What charge sheet?'

'Your charge sheet.' Varma stabbed at her scratchpad, bringing up next week's lunch menus. 'Consorting with ille-gals . . . sheltering said illegals . . . illegal Time travel . . .'

'I reported—' She broke off. 'I don't know anything about any of that.'

'Not according to my records. Look.'

Mrs Lockland shut her eyes. 'I'm not well enough to see properly. I want a doctor. A proper one – not one of your abortionists. I need treatment after what you people did to me. You can't withhold treatment. I know my rights.'

'Madam,' said Varma, pleasantly. 'In case you haven't already realised it – we are the Time Police. We answer to no one. We're utter bastards. You are currently being held by Time Police security officers who are regarded as utter bastards even by the Time Police themselves. And I am genuinely reckoned to be the utterest bastard of them all. Answer my questions.'

'My granddaughter . . .'

'Doesn't have the slightest idea you've been brought in for questioning.' Varma paused and then added softly, 'And never will.'

There was a pause as Mrs Lockland regrouped. 'I'm sick. I'm an old woman. I want to go home.'

And so on and so on and so on.

At one point, Lt Filbert entered the observation room bearing coffee, which Ellis and North both accepted with relief and gratitude.

North enquired whether one was for Varma.

Filbert shook his head. 'She's getting a nice rhythm going. She won't thank me for the interruption. Has the prisoner said anything useful yet?'

'Well, we know she's sick,' said Ellis.

'And she wants her granddaughter,' said North.

'And she banged our expensive helicopter with her hip,' said Ellis.

'And Lockland deserves a medal and some sort of official recognition for putting up with this woman for years,' said North.

'Otherwise, nothing.'

Filbert grinned. 'I'll spell anyone who wants a bog break.'

North shook her head. 'I'm OK at the moment.'

'And me,' said Ellis. 'But thanks for the coffee.'

'My pleasure,' said Filbert. He glared at Mrs Lockland through the screen – something of which she would be completely unaware – and pushed off.

Ellis and North sipped their coffee and resigned themselves to more tedium. Mrs Lockland wasn't saying anything worth listening to. Perhaps they should take her home and consider another approach. Ellis could see nothing of the rhythm to which Lt Filbert had referred and then, just when they were beginning to despair of ever learning anything at all from the prisoner, never mind anything useful, suddenly . . .

Varma had said nothing for some time, simply waiting for Mrs Lockland's monologue to run down. Which it must do sooner or later, surely. After several lifetimes, Mrs Lockland began to flag. The flow of words ran more slowly. Then finally stopped. She clasped her hands in her lap and stared defiantly at her interrogator.

Varma sat back and smiled. 'Mrs Lockland, you are an old lady and all this must have taken its toll on you. If you come with me, I'll take you to your cell. We can continue in an hour or so.'

'You're not dragging me off to your cells. I know what you do to people there.'

'Very true,' said Varma, brightly. 'Only this morning one of our prisoners was brutally assaulted. In this room. And in that very chair, too.'

She let that sink in.

'And in a further coincidence – really, you couldn't make it up, could you? – I believe you know him. What was his name now . . . ?' She paused, apparently racking her brains. 'Coe? Coster? No – Costello – that was it. John Costello. A very good friend of your son's, I believe.' She paused again. 'I wonder if he's still alive. Immaterial, really. As long as he confessed before he carked it. And I'm certain he would have. Confessed, I mean. We're really very good at what we do.'

Mrs Lockland said nothing, but her hands twisted.

Varma clasped her own hands on the table in front of her. 'And now, Mrs Lockland, you will stop wasting my time. What led you to believe your son and daughter-in-law were engaged in illegal Time activities?'

'Well, they were, weren't they?'

'They were indeed, Mrs Lockland, but how were you aware of that? Were you perhaps part of the same organisation?'

Mrs Lockland's head snapped up. 'Of course not. I reported that ungrateful, insolent little bitch to the authorities as soon as I was aware of what she was up to. And I never did get my reward. The officer said there would be a reward and a good one and I never got it. So where is it?'

'We'll come to that in a moment, Mrs Lockland. My priorities this afternoon are to determine your own involvement in this matter, how precisely you obtained your information and finally – should you still be capable of coherent speech – exactly what you did with this information.'

'I told you . . .'

'So – to summarise – your relatives were engaged in illegal activities while living under your roof. Activities you claim to know nothing about. And yet you laid information against them. So – if you weren't in it with them – how did you know?'

170

'I found out.'

'So you said, but how? I have to say, all the evidence leads me to believe you were equally involved.'

Mrs Lockland was silent, her jaws working. Eventually, and very reluctantly, she said, 'Someone told me what she was up to.'

Varma deliberately misunderstood. 'Your daughter-in-law told you?'

'Her? I wouldn't give her the time of day. Bad enough I had to have her in my house.'

'You didn't like her?'

'She was a trollop. Looked as if butter wouldn't melt in her mouth, but she had a real nasty tongue on her, she did.'

By which Varma understood that Helen Lockland had given the old besom as good as she got.

'I wouldn't have her in the same room as me. Or her brat, either. They knew to stay out of my way, they did.'

Varma reflected on Helen Lockland's lot. Sharing a house with this bitter old crone. Decried and disparaged at every moment. Physically keeping out of her sight. As if that was possible – the old bat would have been a lot more mobile in those days. Keeping her little girl quiet and as far away from her grandmother as possible. Perpetually afraid the slightest noise would unleash yet another torrent of complaint and abuse. Coping with the nightmare of a crying baby. Struggling to soothe a teething toddler. What must life have been like in that oh-so respectable house?

And what of Aaron Lockland? What had kept him living under the same roof as his mother? Money – or lack of it – probably. If ever a person showed every sign of maintaining a death grip on the purse strings, it was old Mrs Lockland.

Varma twitched her shoulders to rid herself of the thought. 'So, just to be absolutely clear, someone told you your daughter-in-law was up to something illegal.'

'Yes.'

'And what did Mrs Lockland say when you confronted her with these allegations?'

'Nothing. I mean, I didn't.'

'You made no attempt to verify the information you'd been given?'

'Why would I?'

'To ascertain the facts, of course.'

'It was true, wasn't it?'

'Yes, but how did you know that? Who told *you*?'

Mrs Lockland said nothing. This was plainly an area into which she did not wish to venture.

Varma changed tack. 'And your son? Was he involved in these illegal proceedings as well?'

'No, of course not. He was a good boy. He'd never have done it if she hadn't made him.'

'Done what?'

'Whatever it was she was doing.'

It was at this point that Varma reckoned she deserved some sort of award for not ridding the world of old Mrs Lockland on the spot and pushing off for an early tea.

Instead, she smiled and continued. No change to her voice. Not the slightest hint of frustration and impatience. Slow and inexorable. One who would never go away. 'Who was the person who told you what was happening?'

Mrs Lockland writhed in her chair. 'Someone who knew she was breaking the law. Which she was.'

Varma let the silence hang heavy for a minute or so, keeping her eyes fixed steadily on Jane's grandmother. As Ellis said afterwards, even he felt the urge to confess something, so heaven knew how the old lady was feeling.

'Mrs Lockland, let me be frank with you. And I advise you to listen because these are your last moments as a free woman. I can find no record anywhere of the information you say you laid. Extensive searches have failed to find any trace of you ever contacting the Time Police. Are you even able to furnish me with the name of the officer to whom you spoke?'

Mrs Lockland, shoulders hunched to her ears, shook her head. 'He never gave it.'

'I find that very hard to believe.'

Mrs Lockland said nothing.

'You see, Mrs Lockland, I am harbouring a strong suspicion that you yourself were part of this illegal activity. It seems obvious to me that when it was about to be discovered, you attempted to cover your tracks by inventing a mysterious informant about whom you can provide no details of any kind, together with a cock-and-bull story about laying information with the Time Police. About which you are also unable to supply any particulars. It is my duty, madam, to advise you that as an officer of the Time Police, I have the authority to regard you as an illegal and to prosecute you for your involvement in the crimes of your son and daughter-in-law – which, given the severity of the charge, will almost certainly carry a death sentence.'

Mrs Lockland turned white. 'You can't do that. I told you. I'm the one who tipped you off. Without me you'd never have caught them. You're just trying to wriggle your way out of paying me my reward.'

'There is no record of your tip-off. You will not name the officer with whom you spoke. You will not name your own supposed informant. Madam, I would be considered to be derelict in my duty if I did not immediately take you into custody.'

Mrs Lockland broke into hasty speech. Which as far as Varma was concerned was just as well since she had no evidence of any kind and, if Mrs Lockland had the sense to keep quiet, not much chance of getting any.

'You've got it wrong. All wrong. I *helped* you. I told you what they were up to.'

'And who told *you*?'

Silence. Varma contemplated the old lady in front of her. This made no sense. She'd threatened to charge Mrs Lockland with an offence usually punishable by death. By rights the old lady should be tumbling over herself to clear her name. To implicate someone else. Anyone else. And yet she wasn't. What – or who – could be more frightening to a little old lady than the thought of incarceration and possible execution?

'Mrs Lockland . . . you must see my position. How could you possibly know about any of this unless you yourself were involved?'

Still silence.

Varma stared, her eyes narrowed and her brain racing. 'How much did he pay you to lay the information on his behalf?'

Mrs Lockland said nothing.

'All right – how much did he pay you to stay silent about his identity?'

Mrs Lockland's eyes flickered.

Varma felt a tug of satisfaction. She was on the right track. The key was not Lockland's parents, or the pod, or Costello, or the rescue organisation to which they belonged. The key was the person who had used Mrs Lockland to lay the information. Knowing the identity of this person might help her discover why there were no records of the incident anywhere at TPHQ. Why all trace of the incident involving the Locklands had disappeared.

She slapped the table. 'Who, Mrs Lockland? Who was it? This is your last chance. Someone will be going down for this, and unless you can present me with a viable alternative, it will be *you* making the journey to Droitwich Execution Centre and never coming back.'

Noisily, Mrs Lockland began to cry. 'He said I wasn't to say.'

A chink. The prisoner was beginning to crumble. Normally, at this point, Varma would draw back a little, offer sympathy, refreshment, reassurance – whatever she thought would be most effective in securing the information she was after. Not this time, however. She contemplated the supposedly sobbing prisoner and found she had no pity. Time to push even harder.

'Very well. I am about to charge you formally. Please stand up and put your hands behind your back.'

'I can't. I'm just an old lady. A sick old lady.'

'Beatrice Elizabeth . . .'

'Stop. Stop.'

'Beatrice Elizabeth Lockland . . .'

Mrs Lockland began to cry in earnest now. Tears of self-pity ran down her face.

'He'll hurt me. He said he would if I ever told. You have to protect me.'

'Protect you from whom?'

'Him. He's a bad man. I knew it as soon as I saw him.'

175

'Who's a bad man? When did you see him? Tell me.'

Mrs Lockland was rocking herself backwards and forwards, her words lost in a torrent of sobbing.

'What?' said Varma. 'Take your hands away from your face. I can't hear what you are saying.'

'He came to my house.'

'Who came to your house?'

'He'll hurt me if I tell you.'

Varma slapped the table again. 'And I'll hurt you if you don't. *Give me his name.*'

Mrs Lockland lowered her hands. Her face was mottled purple and grey. Her eyes had lost their usual look of calculating malice, and now showed panic, fear, distress. Her thin frame shook with the effort. Varma drew back. Mrs Lockland was a boiler about to blow.

'Parrish,' she shrieked. 'All right? His name was Raymond Parrish.'

There was a long, long silence, during which no one moved.

Mrs Lockland sat hunched in her seat and stared at the table.

The words 'Raymond Parrish . . . Raymond Parrish' seemed to reverberate around the room.

On the other side of the wall in the observation room, Ellis and North stared at each other, the implications of Mrs Lockland's statement slowly dawning on them.

Varma sat back in her chair, thinking. Eventually, she opened her com. 'Lt Filbert, sir. I have a name.'

'On my way.'

Ellis and North were waiting in the corridor as Varma

emerged from Interrogation Room 1. Closing the door behind her, she rotated her neck and shoulders and stretched.

'Good work, Varma,' said Ellis. 'Very well done.'

'Who?' demanded Filbert, rounding the corner. 'What name?'

'Mrs Lockland's informant.'

'When you say informant . . . ? You mean . . . ?'

'The person who told her about Aaron and Helen Lockland – yes.'

'Who?'

'Raymond Parrish,' said Ellis. 'There's a turn-up for the books.'

Filbert's mouth dropped open. For a moment he seemed too astonished to speak. 'Is that what she . . . ? Luke Parrish's . . . ? You're kidding.'

Varma shook her head.

'We still need to find out which officer dealt with Mrs Lockland's tip-off,' said Ellis.

'Absolutely,' said Filbert. 'I think we should all take a moment to consider how best to proceed. Shall we reconvene in, say, ten minutes?'

'Agreed,' said Ellis.

Filbert nodded. 'You need a break, Varma. Get yourself a drink and then we'll both go back in. We'll tag each other. I'm sure Mrs Lockland will have a lot more to say.'

Varma hesitated.

'No, go on. I'll stay with her until you get back. Ten minutes.'

Varma opened her mouth but never had the chance to speak. A thousand alarms went off at once. Bells and sirens combined in an ear-splitting racket. Red lights flickered. The floor trembled beneath their feet as the blast doors thudded shut, signifying the building was under threat and had been locked down.

'That's the Pod Bay,' shouted Ellis over the racket. 'Unauthorised pod incursion. My God – is it possible—?'

He broke off, unwilling to put the thought into words. Was this actually an attempt to . . . what? Get to old Mrs Lockland? Or was it only a coincidence? What exactly was going on?

Filbert snapped into action. 'Varma – grab a team and get down there. Find out if that's connected to this and report back to me. I'll secure the prisoner.'

Varma leaned in close, shouting over the clamouring alarms. 'Sir, this could be some sort of diversion.'

Filbert pulled out his blaster. 'Good. I'm just in the mood. Go.'

Varma was going before he finished speaking, racing down the corridor with North on her heels.

Filbert turned to Ellis. 'We can pick this up as soon as we know what's going on here.'

Ellis glanced at the closed door behind Filbert, who growled, 'Don't worry, Major. Nothing will get past me.'

15

Back in Lacey Gardens, Max and Matthew were still glued to the pod screen, watching in disbelief as Henry Plimpton stood just outside his pod, surveying the carnage around him.

'Is that Henry Plimpton?' said Max. 'That's the bastard who tried to destroy the Acropolis?'

Matthew nodded.

'Are you sure? He looks like everyone's favourite uncle.'

'Oh, that's him,' said Matthew, grimly. 'You can always recognise him by the number of people lying dead on the ground at his feet. This is the bloke who blew up an entire street to protect his identity. Don't be fooled by the benevolent grandad look. We were – me and Luke and Jane, I mean – and a lot of innocent people paid the price.'

Max nodded, surveying the scene. Aaron Lockland lay dead on the ground.

Half in and half out of the shrubbery, the ignored Helen Lockland lay dying slowly.

'Bastard,' shouted Max. 'Two minutes to stop the bleeding and she might have survived.' She thumped the console. 'Bastard. Bastard.'

179

'Costello's pod has jumped,' reported Matthew, scanning the console. 'The signature's gone.'

'Was Costello in it? Do you think he managed to get away? Or did these bastards take it?'

Matthew shrugged. 'None of them have reappeared, so who knows.'

They watched Henry Plimpton say something into his com.

'It was the pod he wanted,' said Matthew, suddenly. 'Costello, the Locklands – none of them were his target. It was the pod all along.' He turned to Max. 'Perhaps that's how he operates – stealing pods and killing their owners. It's a lot easier to steal one than to build one.'

'There's a gun in the locker,' said Max. 'I've never been more tempted.'

Matthew nodded. Neither had he. He looked across to the house where young Jane lived. She didn't know it yet but her life had just changed forever. She had nothing but years of loneliness and soul-sapping toil ahead of her. If Luke had been here with him – had seen what he'd just seen – would his attitude to her being a Portman have changed? They'd never know.

Henry Plimpton stepped back into his pod.

'Last chance,' said Matthew, still thinking of the gun.

Max shook her head. 'No. It's already happened this way so it has to happen this way.'

The door closed and five seconds later his pod disappeared too.

Matthew had the door open in a flash. Seizing the first-aid kit, Max raced out behind him. It was obvious at a glance that nothing could be done for Jane's father. His chest simply wasn't there any longer.

Helen was still alive but barely.

Max knelt at her side, ripping open the kit. 'I don't think I can do anything.'

Matthew shook his head, whispering, 'It'll take a day or so but she will die of her wounds.'

Max looked around. People were coming out of their houses, running down the steps and across the road. Although not from Jane's house, where the windows were suspiciously blank and the door still firmly shut. Max stood up and waved her arms over her head to attract attention. 'Over here. Bring blankets if you can. Someone call an ambulance. Hurry.'

Matthew was kneeling at Helen's side, his head very close to hers.

Max looked around. 'Matthew – we have to go. The authorities will be here at any moment.'

He looked up. 'I thought . . . I just thought she might have some last words. About Jane. Or for Jane.'

Max gripped his shoulder. 'And if she has, will you tell her you were here? Tell her what you saw? And did nothing to prevent?'

He stood up angrily. 'Enough people have lied to Jane.'

'I know. It's your decision.'

He shook his head, suddenly looking very young. 'I don't know what to do, Mum.'

'Then do nothing until you do. Come on.'

There was no time to lose. They could both hear the sound of sirens in the far distance. A police helicopter clattered overhead.

A number of people were streaming through the gates into the garden. Residents and normal passers-by, he assumed. They did as people usually do – tried to help by milling around and staring helplessly. Max and Matthew drew back in case anyone had thoughts of taking photos of the bodies and selling them on. The last thing they needed was to make an inadvertent appearance in any news bulletins.

Matthew rubbed his face with his hands and then his hair. Which did his free-form hairstyle no good at all. 'What now?'

'The Time Police didn't kill Jane's parents.'

He shook his head. 'No.'

'They weren't involved at all.'

'No. Henry Plimpton killed Jane's parents.'

Max drew closer and whispered, 'But how did he know?'

Matthew whispered back. 'Mum – we think there's someone in the Time Police who's been selling secrets.'

Max stiffened. 'Well, that's not good. Are you absolutely certain?'

'Not absolutely, but if it wasn't the Time Police – if they're not here today – who did Mrs Lockland tell? Is she lying about informing the Time Police? Or did someone lie to her?'

'A very good question. *The* question, in fact. Here's another. Who knows you're here?'

'Well, specifically here and now – no one.'

'You're sure? Where do you normally spend your leave?'

'With you and Dad at . . . oh.'

'And who's possibly the only person in the entire Time Police who could, legitimately, be here, now, in this time?'

'Well, Mikey, perhaps – but mostly me. Shit, Mum.'

'Yes.'

'No, it's worse than that. I'm almost certain they'll bring her in for questioning. Mrs Lockland, I mean.'

'And if she's *not* lying about going to the Time Police,

there's a very good possibility she'll be able to identify the officer who originally interviewed her. Or at least name him. And who, if he's still there, will certainly take steps to ensure she won't be able to.'

'Mum, I have to get back and warn them not to bring her in.'

More and more people were appearing every moment, clutching blankets, bottles of water and pitifully tiny first-aid packs designed to treat minor domestic accidents, not violent trauma. They crowded around, shocked and disorganised and completely obliterating any traces of pods and people. Matthew silently wished the civilian police good luck with preserving this crime scene.

Before he could move, however, a voice was raised over the general clamour.

'It was the Time Police,' said a short man in a blue puffa coat, standing a little distance apart from the crowd. 'I saw them. The Time Police did this.'

'He's right,' said a woman who Matthew knew for a fact had only just left her house. 'It *was* the Time Police. I saw them, too.'

'And me,' said someone else.

The words Time Police ran through the crowd. People started to melt away. The Time Wars might be in their closing stages, but no one ever wanted to be involved with those bastards. Matthew nodded. Clever. The man in the blue coat had planted the seed, and by the time the civilian police got around to taking statements, the few people remaining would honestly swear they'd seen the Time Police gun down Aaron and Helen Lockland.

He and Max allowed themselves to be gently elbowed aside.

They stepped back, as if to allow others the room to work. Two more steps backwards took them clear of the scene. Another two steps took them to the edge of the shrubbery. There they paused, because the secret is not to run. Not to attract attention. And the helicopter was still overhead.

Matthew turned his back on what was happening behind him, masking Max at the same time. 'I think that man's a plant. If people think the Time Police did this, then the civilian police aren't going to make a fuss or ask awkward questions.'

'And I think we need to leave. Before we're swept up in all this. We mustn't do anything to alter . . .'

'I agree.' Matthew thought for a moment. 'That bloke. The one in the blue coat. What's he doing now?'

Max carefully peered around him. 'Walking around. Pointing. My guess is he's planting misinformation by telling everyone what he's just "seen", and everyone else is "remembering",' she hooked her fingers, 'that they saw exactly the same thing.'

'I think the Time Police need a word with him.'

'We could drag him into the pod and . . .'

Presumably having sufficiently contaminated people's memories, the man in the blue coat was slowly edging out of the gate.

The sirens drew closer. Only a few streets away now.

'I'm going to have a chat with him,' said Matthew. 'Mum – take the pod back to TPHQ. Download our recording and tell Hay what we've seen here. Standard instructions – don't get yourself shot. Don't argue with anyone. Try not to set fire to anything.'

'You sound just like your father.' Max hesitated a moment and then said, 'I'll come back for you.'

'Half an hour,' said Matthew. 'Be here. There'll be hell on if I don't get you back home by teatime.'

She patted his arm. 'Good luck.'

'And you.'

Max stepped back into the shrubbery and headed towards her pod. Matthew edged his way around the crowd and walked quietly out of the gate, his eyes fixed firmly on the man in the blue coat.

Blue Coat himself seemed equally anxious to avoid attention, slowly and casually crossing the road and taking the quickest route out of the square by turning down the alleyway next to Jane's house.

Matthew gave him a moment and then set off after him, matching his pace to his quarry's, holding his com to his ear and apparently engrossed in an important conversation.

At the end of the alleyway, he turned right. The man in the blue coat was about fifty yards ahead of him. There were other people on the street here, attracted by the sound of sirens, perhaps. The police helicopter still clattered overhead. Matthew was careful not to move too quickly.

Crossing the road, he found himself in a children's playground. Behind that, a small gate led to some allotments where, despite the still quite early hour, a few people were already about. His mother would have made some disparaging remarks concerning the unhealthy early-morning habits of people who actually grew and consumed green food. At the same time, she frequently offered useful advice on the wisdom of carrying something for the purposes of blending in. He looked around.

A small pile of pea-sticks, neatly tied up with string, leaned against a dilapidated shed – a real one. Definitely not from St Mary's. Matthew picked up the pea-sticks, mentally apologised to their owner and lifted them on to his shoulder. Thus heavily disguised, he continued picking his way around the various cultivated patches, eventually arriving at what appeared to be one of the communal compost heaps.

Blue Coat paused, as did Matthew, half turning away, his attention apparently all on inspecting his bundle of sticks. No one else was in sight. There would never be a better moment. Blue Coat was looking around. A man waiting for someone. Or some*thing*. Time to take a chance. What had he to lose?

'Morning,' he said cheerfully, drawing closer and still clutching his sticks. 'Got a message for you from Mr P.'

Blue Coat said nothing.

'Rendezvous has been changed. Other side of the kids' playground.' He gestured with his head. Blue Coat didn't move. 'So how did it go? Everything OK?'

Blue Coat stared suspiciously. Matthew sighed. This sort of thing always worked for his mother. Sadly, he himself didn't appear to have inherited that particular talent.

'Who're you?'

'Told you. Message from Mr P.'

The man peered at him. 'Nah, don't think so.'

Bollocks. Cursing his deficient genes, Matthew dropped his sticks and threw himself forwards. He had no sonic so this probably wasn't going to go well, but the important thing was just to hang on to Blue Coat until the cavalry turned up.

Matthew Farrell was not well built. His physique had frequently been compared – unfavourably – to that of a nine-year-old girl. By Luke Parrish, usually.

186

They rolled about on the ground. A couple of sharp punches to his ribs caused Matthew to wince but not relinquish his hold. He tried to wrap his arms and legs around his assailant. All he had to do was hold on until someone turned up. Those thirty minutes must be ticking away.

Wrenching an arm free, the man pulled out a gun.

Matthew immediately rolled away. 'You don't want to do that, mate. Time Police. Shoot me and they'll hunt you down. And when they find you . . .'

The man looked wildly around. No sign of the people he was presumably supposed to be meeting. No reinforcements. No one to tell him what to do next. No one to help him out. The gun wavered. Matthew could see his indecision. Would he shoot or run? Matthew didn't particularly want him to do either. Blue Coat throwing down his weapon and surrendering would be Matthew's first choice. He himself was still on the ground and not in any position to attack. Now was definitely the moment to look quiet and unthreatening. 'Just put down the gun, mate, and we'll talk about it.'

The man was bouncing on his feet, gun not quite pointed at Matthew, obviously unable to decide what to do for the best. Matthew could only hope that not shooting a Time Police officer was top of the list.

It was. With one last, desperate look around, Blue Coat aimed a vicious kick at Matthew's head from which he was easily able to roll away. By the time he sat up, the man was disappearing through a hole in the fence.

Ah well. You win some – you lose the rest.

He picked himself up, brushed off the worst of the mud, and leaned against the wooden slats confining this particularly malodorous compost heap, intending to get his breath back and have a bit of a think.

Alas – he wasn't granted the opportunity to do either. A pod materialised some twenty feet away. Not the Time Police. Nor Henry Plimpton's pod. And not his mother, either. Presumably, this was the person Blue Coat had been waiting for. He was unsure whether he'd been lucky or not. If they'd turned up thirty seconds earlier, they could have stepped out of the pod and shot him as he grappled with Blue Coat, but thirty seconds later and he'd have been safely on his way back to rendezvous with his mother. Uncertain what to do next, he stood still and waited.

The door opened. A complete stranger stood there. They looked at each other for a moment and then the man said, 'Well, don't just stand there. Get in.'

16

Max's pod landed neatly in the Pod Bay at TPHQ.

'Our second home,' she said, patting the console affectionately. 'Let's see if they manage to shoot me this time, shall we?'

The Time Police were providing enough drama to gladden any historian's heart. Flashing lights, ringing alarm bells, people running around and brandishing their weapons. Drawing on many past experiences, Max waited until they'd formed a nice semicircle around the pod and then slowly opened the door, being very careful to make her exit from the pod as undramatic as possible. Not being shot was her first priority. Without being asked, she crossed her ankles, lowered herself slowly to the floor and put her hands on her head. Such docility aroused the very greatest suspicion in the ungrateful Time Police.

She sat quietly until they had the sense to turn off the alarms and everyone could hear what was going on and then said, 'I have vital information for your security head. Or Major Ellis. Either. Or both.'

The Senior Mech, glowering at her over his enormous blaster, was inclined to be difficult. 'Identify yourself.'

'I threw up all over your atrium not so long ago.'

'I'm going to need more than that.'

'I could do it again if you like – you know – provide another sample for the purposes of comparison. Or you can get a security team here now. Or Major Ellis. Or even Lt Grint. Whoever you like, but can we get a move on, please – officer in need of assistance.'

Scowling over the unnecessary number of women currently in his life, the Senior Mech opened his com.

Before he could speak, however, a small team of security personnel headed by Officer Varma ran through the doors and took up their positions, guns raised. She blinked in surprise at Max sitting cross-legged on the floor. 'Oh, for heaven's sake, get up. You look ridiculous down there.'

Max sighed. 'Can't. One of the penalties of old age. Getting up is much more difficult than getting down.' She reached up a hand.

Surprised, Varma grasped it and hauled a supposedly elderly and infirm historian to her feet. She was even more surprised when Max failed to let go of her wrist, pulling her in close and whispering, 'We think you have a mole. At least one. If Jane's grandmother is here, you mustn't leave her alone. Not even for one moment. She's probably the only person who can identify him. Matthew is chasing down a lead at this very moment.'

Varma stared. 'Shit.' She stepped back, saying loudly, 'So you say you know the identity of an officer leaking information from TPHQ?'

Max blinked. 'What are you doing?'

'Saving Mrs Lockland's life.' Varma gestured around at the Senior Mech and his team, together with the few people from Logistics and Mikey, who had wandered in to see what all the noise was about. 'The more people who know this so-called mole's name, the better.'

190

Max leaned towards her, whispering, 'It would be if I knew it.'

'I thought you were from St Mary's. Improvise.'

Max stared for a moment and then raised her voice again. 'Yes, you have a mole at TPHQ and I know who it is.' She leaned forwards again, whispering, 'I might not have a bloody clue who it is, but I bet Mrs Lockland does.' She drew back again, saying loudly, 'And now, so do you.'

'Mrs Lockland is with Lt Filbert. Let's go and talk to her, shall we?'

Motioning to her team to follow, she and Max set off at a swift trot, out of the Pod Bay and back through the doors into security.

They were too late.

Two or three officers stood on guard outside the open door of Interrogation Room 1. They wheeled around as Varma approached, blasters raised. 'Halt.'

Varma swore softly and with great feeling. 'Don't shoot.' She shouldered her way through the guards.

Mrs Lockland lay back in her chair, her head resting impossibly over her shoulder, sightless eyes staring at the wall behind her. Her arms hung loosely at her sides.

Varma cursed again and stared around. 'Where the hell's Filbert?'

'MedCen. He's been injured. It's bad.'

'Is he dead?'

'Unknown.'

'Find out.'

Far from obeying her order, the guard drew back, gun raised, aiming mid-point between her eyes. 'You were the last person in there.'

Varma drew a deep breath. 'I was. She was alive when I left her, as Major Ellis can testify.'

'Ellis is reporting to Hay. He's not here.'

'He'll bear me out.' She narrowed her eyes. 'Where were you when it happened?'

Her question was unnecessary. More people were arriving by the second and already eyeing each other askance. The same question was on everyone's lips. 'Where were *you* when it happened?'

Max drew Varma back against the wall. 'What the hell . . . ?' she said, in a fierce undertone. 'How could this happen? This is *security*, for God's sake.'

Varma was very pale but had herself well in hand. 'Well . . . dealing with the practicalities – it wouldn't take any time at all. Her back is to the door. Enter – snap her frail neck – and straight back out again. I could do it in a second.'

'Did you?'

'No.'

'Don't you have cameras and things?'

'We do, but if it was me, I'd don a helmet, obscure my name badge, nip in and do the deed. The camera's in the ceiling so figures are foreshortened. Difficult to identify. Very risky, but not as risky as leaving her alive to tell everyone my name.'

'Remind me never to turn my back on you.'

'He's covering his tracks. Whoever he is.'

'And now we've told everyone that we know his identity. Do you think we'll be next? I swear, Varma, it's like one of those Agatha Christie stories. Do you think Hay will lock us down and we'll all be trapped inside with the killer?'

'Probably. Max, you stick with me. You don't leave my side for a second.'

Max stepped back. 'I don't think so.'

Varma's head snapped up. 'What?'

'Well, I know it wasn't me, but suppose it was you?'

'It wasn't. How could it have been?'

'For God's sake, Varma, people are dropping like flies in your so-called security department. You admitted you were one of the last people to see her alive. There's a very good chance it was you.'

'Or you,' said someone else.

Max wheeled on him. 'That's ridiculous. I've only just got here.'

'So you say.'

Officers were looking at her. Suspicion and hostility were in the air. Paranoia even. Max was suddenly aware she was surrounded by people who didn't like her very much and would probably welcome the opportunity to snap her own neck, no matter what secret knowledge she was supposed to possess. She edged backwards until her back was against the wall.

Varma opened her com. 'Commander Hay, please. No, Captain, her urgent attention is required.' There was a pause. 'Ma'am, I'm in security with Dr Maxwell ... yes, that Dr Maxwell. Could Major Ellis or Captain Farenden come down to collect us, please ... Because Mrs Lockland's been murdered under our very noses and I don't trust anyone any longer.'

Ten minutes later, Mrs Lockland's body had been discreetly removed to MedCen. On Commander Hay's instructions, Major Ellis had taken control of the security department and Max and Officer Varma were in Commander Hay's office.

Hay nodded at Max. 'You first.'

In a few brief sentences, Max described the events in Lacey Gardens and handed over the downloaded images. After she'd finished, the room was silent.

Hay turned to Varma. 'Now you, please, officer.'

Varma, standing rigidly to attention, gave her report. 'To summarise, ma'am – a prisoner has died in custody. Less than twelve hours after another was attacked. Also while in our custody. Furthermore, I was unable to discover the name of the officer who initially dealt with Mrs Lockland – if indeed that actually happened.'

Hay was silent for a long while. Finally, she said, 'Stand easy, Varma.'

Varma breathed out and relaxed a little.

Hay frowned. 'I think we can assume it did happen and that Mrs Lockland was silenced for that very reason.' She stared thoughtfully out of the window. 'Any news on Filbert?'

Captain Farenden replied. 'It's not good, ma'am. He was hit in the shoulder. Full blaster charge at very close range. He was almost certainly grappling with the attacker. Still unconscious and likely to remain so for some time.' He paused. 'If he lives – about which the doctor will not commit himself – he will never be the same again.'

Hay sighed. 'He was here when I joined up, you know. We were both present when the Alhambra went up. He was the last man into my pod. We only just got out in time. I handed him his long service and good-conduct medal five years ago. And his second citation for meritorious conduct last year.'

She stared at her desk.

'So was he face to face with the killer?' said Max.

Farenden nodded to her. 'He was almost certainly facing the person who shot him, yes.'

'Which wasn't Mrs Lockland, presumably?'

'No.'

'Filbert was armed?'

'All our officers are armed.'

Max frowned. 'Well. There's a policy you might want to revisit.'

Hay ignored this. 'Captain, do we know the whereabouts of Major Callen?'

'I believe Major Callen is in Delta Zero One and on his way back from Glasgow, ma'am.'

'Good. I want to see him on his return. Where is Officer Parrish?'

'At the time in question, he was still confined to MedCen. He was signed off sick and left the building about half an hour ago. The officers watching John Costello were able to confirm his alibi for the time in question, so he was allowed to leave.'

'How did the info about Raymond Parrish being the informant get out?'

Max blinked, but said nothing. It was Varma who answered. 'No idea at this moment, ma'am, but it did.'

'Who knew?'

'Me,' said Varma, unflinchingly. 'Lt Filbert. Major Ellis. Lt North. The officers in the monitoring room.'

'Who were?'

'Jessop and Wu. But other people would have been in and out all the time for one reason or another. It's security, ma'am, and they're security officers.'

'So,' said Max, thoughtfully. 'It could have been anyone from security.'

The words *and people gossip* hung in the air, unspoken.

Varma shook her head. 'That's where I would begin my enquiries, ma'am, but it could have been anyone on that floor. A mech, perhaps.'

'Or someone from Logistics.'

'Or MedCen. Or Meiklejohn. All within easy walking distance.'

'Or none of those.'

Hay shifted in her seat. 'The building is in temporary lockdown but . . .'

'But the offender could have left the building before the alarm was raised,' said Max, helpfully.

'That is possible, but a very short time elapsed between the murder being committed and the body discovered.'

'What do the cameras show?' enquired Hay.

Captain Farenden answered. 'Filbert entering and addressing Mrs Lockland. She has no time to reply. He whirls around, sees something that was carefully out of camera, and lunges out of shot. A few seconds later, a helmeted figure enters, snaps Mrs Lockland's neck and exits. Just four seconds from entrance to exit. We don't even know if it was male or female.'

'Corridor cameras?'

Farenden set his teeth. 'Motion activated, ma'am.'

'So?'

'Lt Filbert fell half in and half out of the door, ma'am. The door kept trying to close, encountered his body, retracted again, tried to close again, and on and on. Every camera, attracted by the motion, faithfully recorded that event. And that event only. And, of course, the alarms were sounding at the time.' He nodded at Max. 'Your arrival.'

'Are you saying my arrival provided the opportunity for this to happen?'

Hay nodded. 'Regrettably, yes.'

Max turned to Varma. 'The murder happened exactly as you said it did.'

Varma nodded. 'And a helmet was discovered kicked into a corner further down the corridor. To add insult to injury, it has been identified as Filbert's.'

'To implicate him?'

'Possibly. Or just a coincidence.'

Hay stirred. 'Anything on the weapon?'

'Left alongside him.'

'Whose is it?'

'Not one of ours, ma'am. And before you ask – unregistered.'

'And Filbert's own weapon?'

'Undischarged. He never got the chance to use it.'

'Any damage to his hands?'

'No, ma'am. He didn't even get a blow in.'

Hay swore long and bitterly. Three people regarded her with some sympathy.

'I want at least two guards on Filbert at all times. One from security and one from another section.'

Captain Farenden made a note.

Hay sighed. 'Moving on. You said Officer Parrish has left the building?'

'He has, ma'am. And given the speed and smoothness of the attack, I think we can assume it couldn't have been him.' Farenden paused. 'According to his leave sheet, he's gone to

197

visit his father. I think we can all guess what that will be about. Would you like me to have him recalled?'

'No, I don't think so.'

Captain Farenden was startled. 'Is that wise, ma'am? Given the possible implication of Raymond Parrish?'

'I've always said, Captain – *shake the tree and something useful always falls out*. However, flash a message to his com. Officer Parrish is to be back in two hours. No arguments. Tell him that if he gives any trouble, he'll end up in one of our cells. Where, given our current performance, he'll be lucky to last the night.'

'Yes, ma'am.'

'Turning to other matters – you and I can alibi each other, Charlie.'

'Indeed, ma'am, although I'd like to make it clear I never suspected you.'

Hay looked at Max. 'And you're out.'

'I am,' said Max, 'but I'm sure you'll soon come up with a reason for shooting me anyway.'

'Don't tempt me. It would be very convenient to be able to pin this on an outsider.'

Max beamed. 'Give it your best shot.'

'As I said, don't tempt me.' She paused and then, in a different voice, said, 'Max, I'm sending you back to St Mary's. Thank you for your assistance. And my thanks are genuine. Your discovery that Henry Plimpton was behind the murder of Lockland's parents has brought a whole new dimension to this affair. Yes, I know you would prefer to remain here and learn the outcome, but remember, you and Varma have publicly announced you know the identity of our mole. It makes sense to split you up. You'll be safer at St Mary's . . .' She paused, reviewing what she knew of St Mary's. 'Marginally safer. And yes, I will keep you informed of the outcome. Captain Farenden will escort you safely to the Pod Bay.'

'But—' said Max.

'Please, Max. Allow us to deal with our dirty linen in private.'

'I understand, but—'

'I'm sorry – I can't risk keeping you here. You must see that.'

'I mean – I need to go and collect Matthew.'

Commander Hay opened her mouth to say her own people were perfectly capable of handling that before she remembered why that wasn't possible and closed it again.

'You see,' said Max. 'You need me. Everyone in this organisation was alive at the time Jane's parents died. It's possible an older officer might have been on assignment some time else, but do you have time to trawl the records? And it's tying up another officer or even another team. I'll handle this for you.'

'Reluctantly,' said Hay, sighing, 'agreed.'

'I'll take a blaster though,' said Max, who had always had ambitions in this area. 'One of the really big ones.'

Hay looked at Farenden. 'One of the smaller ones, Charlie.'

'God, yes,' said Captain Farenden with feeling and departed with a grumbling historian.

St Mary's are always saying their pods will fit in anywhere, from Ancient Mesopotamia to a modern allotment. Max had already done Ancient Mesopotamia and now here she was in a modern allotment, surrounded by little plots of fruit and veg – mostly bare at the moment. Almost every one of them had its own shed, knocked together out of whatever could be scrounged or foraged, and all of them, it has to be said, looking considerably more respectable than the pod trying to emulate them.

Discretion had played a part in her choice of landing site. The police and media presence were rendering Lacey Gardens a bit of a no-go area, so she'd gone for the next street in the direction Matthew had disappeared.

On cautiously opening the door, she had discovered herself to be in a small children's playground – again deserted because of the superior entertainment elsewhere. Beyond the playground was a patch of municipal allotments. Neither playground nor allotments showed any sign of Matthew.

Frowning, she returned to the console.

A faint, a very faint, pod signature showed. About a hundred yards away at the far end of the allotments. As far as she could see, the whole area was still deserted. There would never be a better opportunity to check things out. She reset the camo device, picked up the – in her opinion – completely inadequate blaster, and let herself out of the pod to investigate.

If there had been a pod here, then she'd missed it. She stared around. Matthew should have returned by now – the thirty minutes had long since passed – but other than a discarded bundle of pea-sticks, there was nothing and no one. All the action was still in the next street. Here was just deserted silence. But there had been a pod here. Been and gone. As, apparently, had Matthew.

The day was crisp but the long-awaited sun had finally put in an appearance. And there was warmth near the compost heaps. Max took one final look around, found herself a quiet spot between a shed and its rain butt, squatted on an old stump – original purpose unknown but very handy for an informal squat – and prepared to wait.

Matthew didn't come.

Max sat quietly, blaster across her knees, waiting.

Matthew still didn't come.

After a while, it occurred to her that he might already be here, but injured or unable to make his presence known for some reason. That actually seemed very likely, so she got quietly to her feet again and set off around the allotments, this time looking for an injured or possibly unconscious Matthew.

Another thirty minutes later and she was back where she started. By now, Matthew was well overdue. All right – she had options. Return to TPHQ and seek assistance. But what assistance could they offer? She could return to St Mary's. But what could they do? Stand and wait with her? It wasn't as if both organisations didn't have enough on their hands. Rumour had it that Greek fire could only be extinguished by old urine so the mind boggled at what might be happening at St Mary's at this very moment.

Max was just resuming her log again when, staggeringly, and taking her completely by surprise, a pod materialised. And not just materialised – which implies concepts like *gently*. And *lightly*. And certainly *controlled*. This landing was none of those. This pod thudded into the soft soil, taking out someone's old raspberry canes and a gooseberry bush. Damaged or badly set safety protocols, possibly. Handled by amateurs, almost certainly. Whatever the reason, it wasn't more than about thirty feet away. Max crouched behind the rain butt and held her breath. Was this Matthew? It must be, surely.

It wasn't. The door was wrenched open but no Matthew

emerged. Instead, three men burst through the doorway, fighting each other to get out, panting, shouting, falling, scrabbling to get up, terrified. But of what? From what were they trying to escape? Max drew back.

As far as she could see, only one of them was armed and his weapon was nowhere near as big as hers. OK – one less thing to worry about. They were spinning around, trying to cover every angle at once. What were they looking for? Or were they trying to get their bearings? Didn't they know where they were? That seemed possible – these men were frightened out of their wits. Had they just grabbed the nearest pod and fled? Yes, that could make sense. Something had happened – they'd jumped into a pod – and if there had been no time to set different coordinates, then the chances were good this was probably the pod that had been here earlier. But these were grown men. Was something pursuing them? Was it in there with them? They certainly hadn't been able to get out of that pod fast enough. So fast they'd left the door open.

Whatever the reason, they obviously weren't thinking rationally. There would never be a better opportunity and Max was a great one for seizing opportunities. No time to think about who or why or what was happening. There were three of them, and any moment now they would disappear in three different directions and the opportunity would be lost forever.

She stepped out from behind the compost heap and raised her blaster.

'Halt. On the ground. Now.'

The buggers ran away. Whether as a deliberate strategy or whether in blind panic, they ran in three different directions and she couldn't get a clear shot off at any of them. Within seconds, every single one had disappeared behind sheds, bean poles smothered in dead foliage, or ancient fruit trees. Given the nearby police presence, Max thought it best not to draw attention to herself by firing wildly and uselessly. She wasn't a member of the Time Police, after all.

Sighing, she lowered the blaster. Well, that could have gone better, but all was not lost. There was the pod to check out. Very, very cautiously, she approached and peered through the open door.

Everything looked normal enough. Console, screen – currently blank – a couple of seats ... one was split with the stuffing coming out. Nothing was waiting in the corner, licking its chops ... She took one cautious step over the threshold. No, the pod was definitely empty.

Stepping back outside, she picked up the old stump – not without some difficulty – and wedged the door open. Because she'd once been kidnapped by a wayward pod and had no desire to repeat the experience.

This pod was well worn. There was a slight smell of bleach so it was clearly cleaned occasionally. There were scuffs and dents on the floor and walls but they looked more like wear and tear than neglect.

She crossed to the console and studied the controls. Simple and basic. Coordinates. Camera. Door control. Power levels showed low but not critical. No red lights showed anywhere. Nothing was about to blow. This pod still had a few more jumps in it, so what had caused such fear? There were no clues anywhere. The panic-stricken evacuation reminded her of the time during the Hatshepsut jump when a flock ... cluster ... clump ... swarm of bees had found their way into Number

Five via a door left open for some fresh air. There had been a more than rapid exit. Various people had been detailed to go in and get them out again and every single one of them had refused. Roberts and his team would be there still if the bees themselves hadn't decided there were more salubrious potential homes than this one and pushed off of their own accord. Today, however – no bees. Nor clues, either.

The easiest way to determine a pod's history is to check its coordinates. Starting with the most recent. Because something had terrified those three men beyond rational thought. Their only instinct had been to get away. As quickly as possible.

The console was scratched but grease- and fluff-free. Max seated herself gingerly and began to scroll through the coordinates. Nothing jumped out at her. Interestingly, this was apparently not the pod's first visit here. It had been here – call these coordinates A; then gone somewhere else – coordinates B; and then returned back here to coordinates A.

She frowned. Coordinates B were unfamiliar to her but it seemed logical to assume Matthew had encountered this pod at some point and, willingly or not, had jumped back there. And was probably still there. And was this pod connected with events in Lacey Gardens? It seemed likely.

It was tempting, but she couldn't do this alone. She kicked the log out of the way and exited the pod, making sure the door was firmly closed behind her. Sighing, she trudged back to her own pod.

Max's return to TPHQ followed the traditional routine. Alarms. Sirens. Flashing lights, etc., etc. Some things get old very quickly.

'Seriously,' she said, stepping carefully out of the door into the Pod Bay again. 'Wouldn't it be easier to issue me with some sort of parking validation rather than go through this every single time?'

'No,' said Varma, lowering her gun. 'Why have you come back? Where is Officer Farrell?'

'I bring information and a plan.' She passed over a slip of paper.

'What are these?'

'Coordinates I think the Time Police will find useful.'

'Why can't you just bring a bottle of crap wine like everyone else? Where are you going?'

Max paused, half in and half out of her pod. 'Back to sort things out. There's a pod and three men who were so terrified they wouldn't even stop for me and my blaster. Something frightened the living shit out of them. And I think Matthew might be there as well, so I thought I'd nip off and make a bad situation considerably worse.'

She took another step backwards into the pod.

Varma shook her head. 'Wait, I need to consult with Commander Hay about this.'

'Sorry – can't wait.'

'I forbid you to . . .'

'Varma, I'm going to check out these coordinates. Now. You coming?'

'Of course not. We don't just jump on a whim. We're not bloody St Mary's.'

'See you later, then.'

Max stepped inside the pod and reached up for the door control.

'Max – wait.'

The words 'no time' drifted out of the door.

Varma made what she later described as an executive decision. 'Harvey – give me your blaster. No – the big one. Don't argue. Just hand it over. Make sure Hay gets these coordinates and tell her it sounds like a job for at least one team and possibly a clean-up crew.'

Seizing the blaster, she followed Max into the pod, shouting, 'And someone tell Major Ellis.'

A second later, the pod was gone.

17

In another part of the building, Jane was still staring out of the window. She was doing that a lot today. Her future, so well mapped out this time yesterday, was now completely derailed. It was all very well Luke Parrish saying he wouldn't work with her; now she didn't see how she could possibly work with *him*. Not after what his father had done. North had given her the bare facts, placed a sympathetic hand on her shoulder and left her to think it over. And now alarms were going off, and there were people running past her door, shouting to each other as they went. Jane was very familiar with feeling that the exciting things were always occurring without her. That just about summed up her life. Until these last few years, anyway. Well, it had been fun while it lasted.

In an attempt to cheer herself up, Jane turned her thoughts to her last conversation with Grint. He, at least, showed no signs of wanting her out of his life. On the contrary, he was proposing . . . yes, just what was he proposing?

That they go away. Together. On a holiday. Or something more. But what exactly? What did he want? Come to think of it – what did *she* want?

207

'Oh, sweetie,' sighed Bolshy Jane. 'He wants to shower you with rose petals and roger you senseless in the moonlight.'

'Are you sure?' enquired Jane, quite startled at the picture currently forming in her mind.

'Well, it's Grint, so substitute copies of *Bombs and Blasters* for rose petals and napalm fire for moonlight, but yeah, rogering . . . massive rogering . . . definitely.'

Jane felt the blush spread across her face. Great – now she even blushed when there was no one else around. Even her ears were hot. She wondered what would happen if the two sides met around the back of her head in one huge, all-enveloping tide of crimson. Probably her head would explode. Like in that old film Matthew had made her watch, saying it was a classic. She'd been quite surprised at how spectacularly high the blood had spurted, and glanced up apprehensively at her own ceiling.

'Sweetie, will you concentrate?' said Bolshy Jane.

Jane was only too happy to comply, and sat down to consider possible destinations and completely not in any way thinking about what they would do when they got there.

Somewhere in the recesses of her mind, Bolshy Jane prayed for strength.

Someone knocked at the door. Grateful for the distraction, Jane opened up to see Lt Grint once again.

'Oh, hello.' She held the door open further. He declined to enter, however, shuffling uncomfortably on the threshold.

'The thing is, Jane . . . they've said . . . I've been ordered . . . Ellis told me . . . I have to get out of the building for a few days. Some sort of . . .' he thrust his hands in his pockets, out of sight, 'misunderstanding about something. You know . . .'

Almost equally bereft of speech herself, Jane nodded.

'So back to my original question – if we decide to go away . . . together . . . where would you . . . ?'

'I don't honestly know,' said Jane. 'I haven't really ever been anywhere. There were a few school trips to Wales . . . and France, I think, but my grandmother wouldn't pay so I couldn't go. It wasn't just me,' she added, hastily. 'There was a boy who had a medical condition and he didn't go either, so we just sort of hung around together until the class came back. I don't think he liked me much so we didn't . . . you know . . . do anything much. And when everyone returned, all the lessons were about the trip and what they'd learned, and essays and things which we couldn't do, so . . . you know . . . I don't really know where I want to go. Sorry.'

She hung her head and waited for Grint to depart exasperated. He didn't, so she looked out of the window rather than meet his gaze. 'What about you?'

'Um . . .' Grint pulled himself together because at this rate they'd never get out of TPHQ. For someone who made command decisions on an almost hourly basis, this was proving unexpectedly difficult. He rather suspected that by now Luke Parrish would have bundled Jane out of the building, miraculously transported her to some romantic hideaway – of which he no doubt had several scattered around the world – showered her in champagne . . . and melted chocolate and . . .

He pulled himself together and remembered Jane liked history.

'Well, it would be nice to get away from whatever's going on here. Out of London completely, in fact.'

Jane nodded. 'Yes, good idea.'

'How about somewhere with history?' He racked his brains. 'Salisbury? Rushford? Shrewsbury? Cardiff?'

Jane's eyes lit up. 'Oh yes – any of those. We could go by train. I know it's not very comfortable – unless we could afford the hyperloop, of course. We could explore the town, have a picnic perhaps, find a nice hotel . . .'

The word *hotel* brought them both up short, raising, as it did, the dread question – one room or two?

One room dredged up all sorts of implications too complex for either of them to get their heads around at this precise moment. *Two* rooms, however . . . even worse.

At that moment Grint's com chirped. He pulled it out and read the message, frowning slightly.

'Jane, I'm sorry – Farenden wants me in his office. And you're to put yourself on standby, as well. They might have a job for us.'

'Has something else happened?'

'Looks like it.'

Jane watched him disappear off down the corridor. The Time Police were a wonderful organisation, but when they put their minds to it, they could really bugger up a person's love life.

'Yes,' sighed Bolshy Jane. 'We're never going to get any at this rate, are we?'

18

Normally, Luke would have walked to St James's Square. The two-mile stroll was usually very pleasant. Today, however, he took a water taxi to Whitehall, carefully disembarked and, trying not to hobble, made his way through St James's Park. Since he was officially on leave, he was unarmed and wearing civilian clothing. Donning a pair of sunglasses had done very little to conceal his colourful facial injuries. The water-taxi driver had gone so far as to ask him if he was all right, mate.

On reaching the headquarters of Parrish Industries, he took the steps slightly more slowly than usual, pushed his way through the doors and addressed the first receptionist who caught his eye.

'Please inform Mr Parrish that Officer Parrish from the Time Police is on his way up.'

Without waiting for a response, he limped towards the lift.

The ride took only a few moments, although for some reason his fellow passengers all got out at the next floor. He carried on to the penthouse alone.

Ms Steel was waiting at the receptionist's station. She raised her eyebrows at his bruises but made no comment. 'Mr Parrish will . . .'

'. . . see me now,' said Luke, opening the door.

Raymond Parrish was writing at his desk.

'Hands on the desk, please,' said Luke. 'Keep them where I can see them.'

Raymond Parrish remained calm. 'May I ask . . .'

'No, you may not. I'm the one asking the questions and you're the one answering them. Thank you, Ms Steel. Your services will not be required.'

She looked at Raymond Parrish. 'Shall I call security?'

'No,' said Luke. 'I don't want to have to shoot anyone today but I will should I find it necessary. I am here on official Time Police business . . .'

Ms Steel stood her ground. 'If that were so, Officer Parrish, then you would be armed, in uniform, and there would be a squad of you.'

Luke shrugged. Quite painfully. 'You're absolutely right, Ms Steel. I am completely alone at the moment. I have no squad. My recent behaviour has caused my team to abandon me. I have no back-up. In fact, I have, as you have so many times predicted, made a complete balls-up of everything, and should you wish to complain to Hay, she will almost certainly seize upon the opportunity to boot me out of her organisation for good. Not a single person at TPHQ would mourn my passing. You've called my bluff, Dad. You have only to pick up the phone and all this goes away. Including me. To enjoy a short spell inside, probably, for gross misconduct in a public office. So – what are you waiting for?'

'I am waiting for you to close the door behind you.'

Luke ignored this. 'This is your last chance, Dad. I'm sorry, but the net is closing around you. Yes, at the moment it's only me, but you can't rely on that happy state of affairs continuing for very much longer. It really would be much better for both of us if you were to answer my questions voluntarily instead of waiting until they come for you. And believe me, they will be coming for you.'

Raymond Parrish put down his pen. 'I trust you have received the appropriate medical treatment for those injuries.'

A week ago, Luke might have impatiently brushed this aside. Today, he took a more measured approach. 'Your concern is appreciated. Please be very careful with your hands. And before you say something conventional such as, "You surely wouldn't attack your own father," may I suggest you take a moment to reflect.'

'On what?'

'Anything you like. But please keep your hands in sight at all times.'

'Mr Parrish?' said Ms Steel, again.

Luke never took his eyes off his father. 'Perhaps you should take a moment to go and reassure your security people, Ms Steel. This isn't official Time Police business – yet – but it will be in a very short time. My concern was to spare Parrish Industries the embarrassment of its chairman, managing director and principle shareholder being dragged from the building in handcuffs. And the possible damage to your share prices after the scandal of Site X, of course – but you must do as you think best.'

He stepped back and waited.

'It's all right, Lucinda,' said Raymond Parrish, quietly. 'Thank you.'

Ms Steel paused a moment as if to argue and then left the room, closing the door behind her.

'I have some questions,' said Luke, as soon as the door had closed. 'Please answer carefully and concisely.'

Raymond Parrish inclined his head.

'Who is Helen Portman?'

Raymond Parrish frowned for a moment. 'To the best of my recollection, she was a very distant cousin of yours. I'm afraid I can't give you the exact relationship, but it is very remote.'

'Did you know she married an Aaron Lockland?'

'No. I have never before heard that name. Is he any relation to . . . ?'

'What is your relationship with his mother? Mrs Lockland of Lacey Gardens?'

'As far as I know – none.'

'Please take some time to review your last answer very carefully.'

'I don't need to. I'll say it again – I have never heard of her.'

'You aren't asking what all this is about?'

'You have made it very clear that I am to answer questions, not ask them.'

'Have you ever informed on anyone to the Time Police?'

'No. Never.'

'You are quite certain of that? Never informed on Portman and Webber?'

'No.'

'Or the Locklands?'

'No. Is this to do with Officer Lockland in some way?'

'An accusation has been made.'

'Concerning me?'

'That you were behind a successful attempt to lay information

214

against Jane's parents with the Time Police. That the Time Police acted on this and both Locklands died.'

'I can assure you, Luke – I have never done any such thing.'

'The witness was very certain. And had no reason to lie.'

'Neither do I. Again – I have never done any such thing.'

'The witness was also very afraid.'

'That might be because the witness is lying.'

'She said you threatened to hurt her if she ever divulged who had given her the information in the first place.'

'You are saying that I told her and she told the Time Police?'

'I am. Fortunately the witness was more terrified of the Time Police than she was of you. Perhaps you're slipping.'

'I can assure you I retain my full faculties. I do confess to some bewilderment though. Is it possible your witness has confused me with someone else?'

'The witness referred to you by name.'

Raymond Parrish stiffened.

'What name?'

'Your name.'

'Raymond Parrish?'

'That is your name, is it not?'

There was a long silence. 'It is also the name of your grandfather. Raymond is a family name. Your mother had quite a struggle to have you named Luke.'

Luke stared at his father, his thoughts suddenly in turmoil.

Raymond Parrish leaned back in his chair and looked out of the window.

Neither man spoke until Luke said, 'You're saying you think it was my grandfather?'

'Well, I know it wasn't me and he's the only other Raymond Parrish I've ever known.'

Luke sat down rather suddenly, saying quietly, 'Why would he do that?'

Raymond Parrish was a vigorous man who had aged well. Until this moment. Now, for some reason, the lines on his face had deepened.

'You said it yourself, Luke. Helen Portman.'

'You mean – revenge?'

'On the Portmans, yes. An attempt to embarrass them publicly, perhaps. He probably hoped that the scandal would weaken them.'

'It didn't weaken the Locklands – it killed them.'

There was a moment's silence and then Raymond Parrish said, 'Your grandfather didn't pull the trigger, Luke. The Time Police did that.'

Luke's voice cracked. 'What did he think would happen to them?'

'I suspect he thought that after the Portmans had made a major donation to the Time Police, the Locklands' offences would have been found to be comparatively minor. A very short prison sentence – if that – and that would have been the end of the matter.'

Luke was almost beside himself with rage. 'And how did that work out for everyone?'

Raymond Parrish studied his son closely, taking a moment to reply. 'Luke, you are angry with me.'

'I'm always angry with you.'

'And you're angry with Jane Lockland.'

'Well, of course I am. She's half Portman.'

'As are you. Something for which neither of you can blame yourselves. Or each other. Let me ask you this again – why are you so angry at Jane?'

'Isn't it obvious? Because . . .'

The thought came from nowhere, slamming into place. Or rather, had always been there and he'd only just seen it. Because . . . Grint. Nothing to do with the Portmans. Well, a little bit, perhaps, and yes, he'd felt shock and astonishment at Costello's bombshell – all perfectly natural – but he'd lashed out at Jane. Who never hurt anyone and who must easily have been as shocked as he was himself. Devastated, in fact.

An image flashed across his mind. Jane holding him up as they struggled through the snow. Desperately scrabbling around looking for his glove. Losing her own valuable body heat even though, for two of his fingers, it was already too late.

And Matthew – what he'd said to Matthew had ended his life in Team 236. The life he'd actually quite enjoyed. He'd been given a second chance with the Time Police and he'd torn it all down with his own hands *because that was what he always did*.

Just for a moment, his world swayed. Because of his injuries, obviously. He struggled to focus because his father was speaking again.

'And you are angry with the Time Police.'

Luke struggled to find his former rage. 'Of course I am. They killed Jane's parents. What did you expect?'

'But mostly, you are angry at yourself.'

There was a long silence. Luke found himself with nothing to say.

Raymond Parrish gestured at his face. 'Luke, who did this to you?'

217

'That's not important.'

'I see from the stitches that you have received treatment, but should you actually be out of bed?'

Luke struggled to bring order to his thoughts, saying, 'I have to find out what happened to Jane's parents. And why.'

'I have told you what happened. Luke, I know I never speak of him – but your grandfather could sometimes be . . . My relationship with him was sometimes very similar to that of yours with me. I know *I* didn't inform on the Locklands. If indeed the witness is telling the truth, then it can only have been him.'

There was more silence.

'We have a nurse on the staff here. I feel I should send for him.'

'No, I'm fine.' Luke jerked himself to his feet, ignored his swimming head and began to pace. 'You really think he did this?'

'Well, obviously I don't know for certain, but knowing *him* . . . yes, I could imagine that happening.'

Luke sighed. 'Good job he's dead, isn't it?'

'Yes.'

'And yet still reaching out to destroy people's lives. I admit I haven't handled any part of today particularly well, but his actions have cost me my team. The only people who . . . well, never mind that now.' Luke squinted through his still-swollen eyes. 'Jane . . . I said some things. When I found out she was a Portman.' He gestured at his face. 'Someone who values her properly did this. I might have deserved it.'

Raymond Parrish said nothing.

'I was . . . I was their team leader. I liked what I was doing. I was actually awarded a commendation . . .'

'I know,' said Raymond Parrish quietly. 'I was there to see it.'

Luke struggled to keep his voice steady. 'It's all gone, Dad. I've thrown it all away.'

'Well, I don't think you can take all the credit – your grandfather certainly played a large part.'

'Sorry, Dad. You gave me a chance and I squandered it.'

'I see no squandering.'

Luke shook his head, staring at the floor.

'I think,' said his father, gently, 'that this last year has not been easy for you. You have learned some hard lessons, Luke. Yes, I know you are now financially supporting the Tannhausers after their son died. That is an honourable thing to do. I know what you did at Site X. You handled yourself well and kept your head. I also know that if your grandfather were alive today then I would probably strangle him with my bare hands.' He smiled. 'You see now from whom you get your . . . impulsive nature.'

'Well,' said Luke hoarsely, 'that's one way to describe it.'

'Are you on any medication?'

'Why?'

Raymond Parrish touched an area of the panelling which sprang open to reveal a decanter and glasses.

Luke fished in his pocket, finally locating a small blister pack which he threw in the bin. 'Not any longer.'

Raymond Parrish smiled. 'Good.'

Half an hour later, the atmosphere was calmer. No personal issues had actually been debated. Most of the conversation had revolved around football, Parrish senior's plans for a second roof garden, and some scandal involving mutual acquaintances and a police raid at exactly the *wrong* moment – although exactly the *right* moment for the police once they'd managed to stop laughing, but somehow, in true masculine fashion, a tentative understanding had been reached.

Luke set down his glass. 'Thank you for that. Better than painkillers. However, I must get back to TPHQ. They've only given me a couple of hours.'

Raymond Parrish also stood up. 'I can offer you a lift back.'

'That's kind, Dad, but I think I'll walk. I'd like to be on my own for a bit. Lots of thinking to do.'

'I understand.'

'I think, after I report back to HQ, I'll ask permission to go back to my old apartment for a while. Spend some time reviewing things. My future. It'll be interesting to see if Hay makes any attempt to get me to stay.'

'Oh, I think she will. She sees something in you.'

'Saw something, Dad. That's not there any longer. Add her to the list of people I've let down.'

'I think, Luke, we would both benefit from a change of scenery. Would you care for a quiet drink somewhere else? There's a very good little place around the corner. We can bundle you into a water taxi afterwards to get you back in time.'

Luke considered this. 'Good plan, Dad. On you, I'm assuming.'

Raymond Parrish was straightening his tie. 'Well, that hadn't been my original plan . . .'

'I doubt my Time Police wages will stretch to your smart "little place around the corner", but perhaps there's a whelk and jellied eel stand out on the pavement.'

Raymond Parrish smiled. 'Almost, I am tempted. If only for the treat of seeing you force down a jellied eel. Shall we go?'

220

Ms Steel was discreetly loitering in the reception area.

'Ah, Lucinda, I'm going out for a few minutes.'

Her hand strayed towards the phone.

'No, it's all right – I shan't be needing my team.'

'Sir . . .'

'About an hour, I think. Certainly no longer. Ready, Luke?'

Some moments later, they emerged from Parrish Industries HQ and started down the steps.

A long black car drew up beside them.

19

Although Matthew was expecting it from this battered pod, the jump was even rougher than he had anticipated. He suspected a combination of ancient pod and inexperienced pilot. He hadn't had time to catch more than a glimpse of the exterior, but the interior, although showing definite signs of wear and tear – one of the seats had split and the stuffing was coming out – was clean enough. There was a faint smell of bleach so someone must have mopped it down recently. A switch under the console clunked loudly as something electrical kept turning itself off and then back on again. There was also an ominous rising whine that seemed to come from everywhere.

Matthew was unused to a noisy pod. Apart from the occupants, of course. Both Time Police and St Mary's pods frequently resounded to the sounds of swearing, moaning in pain, Luke arguing with the AI and so forth. The sudden, jagged flash of homesickness for Team 236 was almost painful. He remembered Luke's incessant complaining. Jane's calm good sense. The way she blushed whenever she spoke and then blushed again when she realised she was blushing. He really thought they'd had something, the three of them. Weirdos with their own way of doing things. They'd belonged together and yet – in an hour, a minute even – their whole world had collapsed. Whether there was any chance of it ever being rebuilt . . . Would that even be wise? Teams did fall apart occasionally, and their members either found themselves another team or left altogether. How could Team 236 come back from something like this? Were those days gone forever?

The landing wasn't quite bone-shattering, but Matthew took care to stagger sideways anyway.

The other man laughed. 'First time in a pod?'

'No,' said Matthew defensively.

He watched the man shut things down, all the time making careful mental notes for possible future use. This was a primitive pod. Even more primitive than the one he'd once found in Henry Plimpton's back garden. Under cover of pulling himself back together again, he took a surreptitious look around. A basic camera. No decontamination lamps. The locker had taken a hit at some point – the metal door was buckled and wouldn't close properly. Torn seat. Scuffs and stains on the walls and floor. But things could be worse. At least he was still alive.

The man turned his head to address Matthew. 'What happened to Broom?'

He could only assume that Broom was Blue Coat. 'He was attacked.'

The man straightened up, no longer as friendly as he had been. 'By you?'

'What? No.'

'What's your name?'

Matthew thought quickly. 'Adrian Meiklejohn.'

If this man had heard of Adrian, then this might be a way in. On the other hand, if he'd actually met the real Adrian – tall and chatty Adrian as opposed to short and taciturn Matthew – then he'd be in a lot of trouble, but it was too late to take the words back now. 'Broom said I could get a job. I'm not bad with these things.' He gestured around at the pod.

The man nodded. 'Name's Jim. What were you doing back there?'

'Broom was going around telling everyone it was the Time Police that shot those people. He told me to back him up.'

'What went wrong?'

'Nothing. Everything was fine. We hid round the corner, and then when it was all over, we went in and told people the Time Police did it. As instructed. Then we legged it before the police got there. Just as we got to the end of the alley, some bloke jumped out at him. Broom, I mean. No idea who he was. Broom shouted to run so I did. Don't know what happened to him. Should we go back to look?'

'For Christ's sake, we're not the bloody cavalry. Course not.' He looked at Matthew. 'I suppose I'd better let the boss take a look at you.'

The door opened and cool, fresh air flooded in.

'Is he here?' said Matthew, suddenly anxious. Had Henry Plimpton landed here before him? And if he had – would he recognise Matthew? Were these events in Henry's life taking place before or after Team 236 met him in the 20th century? He had no way of knowing.

And a further complication – just because the events in Lacey Gardens had occurred some fifteen years ago did not mean Henry Plimpton had perpetrated them fifteen years ago. He might kill Jane's parents in his future. It would be a huge mistake to assume his Timeline was running in conjunction

224

with Matthew's. Because Matthew had met Henry Plimpton last year did not mean Henry Plimpton had met Matthew last year. Even Matthew had difficulty with this concept, and some academics had actually gone mad trying to get their heads around it. Of course, there was always the argument that most of them had been pretty barking to begin with.

And an even further complication – Matthew had no idea where Plimpton had gone after Lacey Gardens. He could be anywhere. And what had he done with John Costello's pod?

He thrust these thoughts aside. As his mother would say – always concentrate on the now. Everything else then usually takes care of itself.

He looked up at Jim. 'Mr P, you mean? Can I meet him?'

'No. He's got a lot on at the moment. Might be a couple of days before he turns up. We're still setting things up here. Nothing's finished yet.'

'Well – how can I get a job if I can't . . .'

'See Tucker. He hires and fires.'

'OK,' said Matthew, filing all this away for his future report. The one he hoped he'd live long enough to write.

Intentionally or otherwise, the man still remained between Matthew and the door. 'So how d'you know Broom, then?'

Matthew shuffled his feet. 'He's friends with my sister,' and crossed his fingers he shouldn't have said, 'He's friends with my brother.'

The man gave a crack of laughter. 'Yeah, that sounds like Broom,' and Matthew gave a silent sigh of relief.

'Come on, then. Can't hang around here all day.' Jim stepped out of the door, motioning for Matthew to follow him.

Matthew hung back with very realistic reluctance. 'Where are we?'

'Here. Come on.'

Matthew took a deep breath. Standing on the threshold, he peered cautiously at the world outside.

The air was cool and moist and had a bite to it. There was a faint smell of earth and grass and water. The sky above was a brilliant royal blue, and as he looked up, a long, straggly V-shaped line of birds flew high overhead. He couldn't see it, but rather thought he could smell the sea. The sun shone but summer was obviously long past. He shivered in his hoodie.

'Yeah,' said Jim. 'Winter is coming. Come on.'

Matthew didn't move, obviously reluctant to step away from the illusory safety of the pod.

The man laughed again. 'It *is* your first time, isn't it?'

'No,' said Matthew again, wondering if he should take care to sound a little less certain this time. Just a teenage boy trying to make himself look good. Still apparently too nervous to venture too far from the security of the pod, he used the time to take a good look around.

He appeared to be looking at some kind of fort. Hey – how cool was that? An actual fort. Tall, roughly hewn logs surrounded a circular area dotted with a strange mixture of structures both ancient and modern. There were a number of wooden huts made of weathered grey planks, horizontally laid. All the huts were of a similar size and rectangular, but with strangely curved roofs, almost like Dutch barns. Each hut was surrounded by what had once been a small garden, enclosed by a rough picket fence. There was a strange, forlorn air about the huts. No smoke rose from the chimneys and the gardens were

226

massively overgrown, with the leaves and long, coarse grass beginning to turn brown as winter approached. Both the huts and the surrounding walls had been here some time, though. The timbers had weathered in, there were no raw cut marks in the wood, and no fresh earth where the logs had been sunk into the ground.

In contrast, a cluster of modern buildings were grouped together in the centre of the enclosure. He could see what looked like a forge standing next to a modern prefabricated workshop of some kind. On the other side of the forge stood another modern structure. Smoke trailed from a thin metal chimney and Matthew was certain he smelled cooking. A mess hut? That would make sense.

He looked around again. As far as he could see, there was only one way in or out of this compound. A small gate had been cut into the palisade. It was very narrow – it couldn't possibly accommodate more than one person at a time, and even then, a big man would have to turn sideways. A sensible precaution. The gate itself was closed, held firmly shut by a sturdy crossbar.

The walls were too high to see over and he couldn't help wondering what lay on the other side. A walkway ran around the palisade, presumably accessed by rough ladders, although these lay on the ground at the moment, half buried in the long grass. If he could manage to get up there, what would he see on the other side?

Matthew shivered, suddenly uneasy. There was a desolate and lonely air about this place that was unnerving. And there was something else . . . He turned his head, trying to locate . . . what? What was it about this place? He suddenly found himself extremely reluctant to leave the pod. As if stepping outside . . .

actually setting foot in this place . . . would somehow expose him to . . . what?

The thought flashed through his mind that there are places in the world where people are not meant to be. Places that keep themselves apart. Separate. Secret. He looked down. His forearm was covered in goosebumps. 'We should leave.'

Suddenly unnerved, Jim jerked around to look at him. The kid's eyes looked weird. 'Did you say something?'

Matthew blinked himself back again. 'No.'

Taking a deep breath, he stepped outside into this new world.

Another pod stood alongside, as shabby and battered as the one in which he had arrived. Not John Costello's pod, he was pleased to see. The door was open and he could hear a voice inside droning on and on without a break. A long, long monologue. Either a prayer or a curse, he decided. The two were often very similar.

A long, low, open wooden shed stood opposite the pods. A former stable or animal shelter, possibly, since it looked to be of a similar age to the huts. Two-thirds of it was stacked full of freshly hewn logs. Ready for winter, he guessed.

Half a dozen generators occupied the rest of the stable, their thick black cables snaking through the grass. He looked around for the fuel store. Yes – over there. As close as possible but still a safe distance away from the forge. In case of an accident. Because if the fuel went up . . .

Solar panels had been laid out where they would catch the most sun. Sensible not to be dependent on only one power source. Solar for when the sun shone – generators for when it didn't. And wood for when all other options were exhausted.

Matthew had several times visited St Mary's remote site – their

228

secondary site to which they could retreat whenever threatened – and this set-up looked very similar. Even down to the freshly turned areas near the mess hut. Whoever these people were, they'd been supplementing rations with an occasional salad crop or a few fresh vegetables. He wondered if they hunted and fished as well. He was certain he could smell the sea.

He nodded to himself. This was Henry Plimpton's remote site. It had to be. He wondered again where Henry was now. Not here, anyway, which Matthew was inclined to consider a Good Thing. The news that it might be a couple of days before he turned up was very welcome. Matthew definitely did not intend to be here in a couple of days. Or even a couple of hours if at all possible.

He looked down. The ground beneath his feet was wet and spongy. They'd need duckboards in the winter. If not sooner.

He tilted his head, listening. There was no hum of equipment or machinery. No birds sang. Just the sad wind sighing in the trees.

'Come on,' said Jim, giving him a small push. 'Let's find Tucker.'

'Will he give me a job?' said Matthew apprehensively.

'You'd better pray he does,' was the cheerful response.

'Why?'

'Well, we don't usually bother with a polite letter thanking people for their application but regretting that on this occasion they have been unsuccessful.'

'Oh,' said Matthew in a small voice.

'And here he is,' said Jim. He raised his voice. 'Tucker!'

A large man had exited the other pod and was staring at them. 'Where's Broom?'

'Didn't make it back. This one did. Looking for a job.'

Tucker stared. 'Who're you?'

Matthew took a deep breath. 'Adrian Meiklejohn.'

'What the fuck sort of name is that?'

'My name,' whispered Matthew.

'Well, Adrian Meiklejohn, and why should I give you a job?'

'Broom recommended him,' said Jim.

'Broom's an idiot.'

Jim appeared to consider this. 'Well, yeah, but . . .'

Tucker ignored him. 'What can you do, Adrian Meiklejohn?'

'Well, I'm pretty good with pods.'

'How good?'

'Bloody brilliant actually. I was being modest.'

Tucker stared for a moment. 'Suppose I've got a pod that's drifting badly. What should I do?'

'Confirm its current position. As accurately as you can. Use a sextant. When the pod knows where and when, then you can use those coordinates to recalibrate its guidance system. Usually takes about half a day. Check the chronometer while you've got the boards out. Saves doing it later. Programme in some known coordinates and make a test jump, preferably taking another pod in case some pillock hasn't put things together properly. It can happen. Make two or three more jumps, all to known and verifiable coordinates, refining the system each time, and you should have an accurate pod at the end of it. If not, look for an underlying cause. Faulty guidance system perhaps, or – and this is very likely – operator error. Incorrectly calculated coordinates maybe. In fact, always check the human element first. Pods are quite bright. Most people aren't.'

Tucker stared at him for a moment. 'How do you know all this?'

'Built my own pod.'

'You?'

'Well, not just me. I usually just do the theory. My sister did most of the work.'

'Your *sister*?'

'My little sister.'

'With her baby doll and her glitter pen.'

'Not that I saw,' said Matthew, on whom sarcasm rarely worked. 'Although she is very innovative. She once installed an entire surveillance system using an old TV monitor, ten feet of cabling and a breadknife.'

Tucker loomed ominously. 'You taking the piss?'

'Strangely, that was what the Time Police said. Just before we jumped away and left them standing.'

A low rumbling indicated either that Tucker was amused or that a small earthquake was in progress. He addressed Jim. 'Take him in to Clore. Bastard pod's playing up again.' He turned to Matthew. 'It's never been right. Not since the day we ... acquired it.' Tucker seemed quite aggrieved that the former owners hadn't given the pod a quick service just prior to having it stolen from them. 'See what you can do and I'll consider letting you live.'

He walked away and Jim ushered Matthew into the second pod.

Clore proved to be a heavy, thickset man with heavy, thickset fingers. Matthew had no clear idea what he looked like since about sixty per cent of him was under the console. Dismantled boards and discarded tools lay scattered around him. He was

231

cursing in a long, slow, continuous mutter that showed no signs of ever running down.

Jim kicked his ankle. 'Hoi. Got you an assistant.'

For a moment Matthew thought Clore was experiencing some sort of convulsion but this turned out to be the complicated manoeuvres necessary for a very large man to extricate himself from a very small space.

Clore squinted up into the light. 'Who the fuck are you?'

Correctly divining this question was directed at him, Matthew said brightly, 'Adrian.'

'What sort of name is that?'

'My name,' said Matthew, making a mental note to be kinder to Adrian when they next met.

'Tucker sent him to have a look,' said Jim.

'Well, thank Christ for that,' said Clore, heaving himself to his feet. 'This is killing my eyes.' He looked Matthew up and down. 'Where are your tools?'

'Didn't get a chance to bring them,' said Matthew, very carefully not looking at Clore's. He'd once been in the Pod Bay when someone, either deliberately or otherwise, had picked up someone else's tools and like everyone else, he'd backed away from the ensuing . . . *dialogue*, was a good word. He certainly wasn't going to ask Clore if he could borrow his. You didn't do that. People had their own tools, familiar, worn to the shape of their hands, more precious than members of their own family in some cases. All the techies at St Mary's and the mechs at TPHQ had their own toolbelts which anyone else touched at their peril.

Clore nodded at the tools. 'Don't use the ones with the blue handles.'

'Understood,' said Matthew, dropping to his knees and crawling under the console. 'Any chance of more light?'

Clore pulled off his headtorch and passed it over. Matthew called down silent blessings on long hours in Hawking with both his father and Mikey, rolled on to his back and got stuck in.

Time passed. Matthew, hard at work, was almost completely oblivious to the outside world, until the outside world intruded on him.

'Hoi,' said Jim, sticking his head through the door. 'Pack up now.'

'I haven't quite finished.'

'No one works after dark.'

Matthew remembered the generators. 'Why not? You've got plenty of power.'

'Kept for emergencies. We only light the mess hut. Can't afford to waste power here.'

Matthew, careful to keep his attention on wiping down and replacing Clore's tools, enquired casually, 'Where's here?'

'Here,' said Jim again, as unhelpful as ever.

'Why can't you afford to waste power?'

'We keep the gate lit and there's power to the mess hut and that's it. Oh – if you're still alive after supper – no wandering about after dark. Not for any reason.'

Even Matthew dared not ask why not. Not again. 'What if I want to pee?'

'Buckets in the huts.'

'Do I have a bed?'

'Dunno. Up to Tucker. You done here?'

'Nearly. Some refinements tomorrow and I think it'll be good to go.'

'You'd better be sure cos you'll be the one making the test jump.'

'OK,' said Matthew carelessly. 'Have I earned supper? I'm starving.'

'Yeah,' said Jim, suddenly friendly. 'Come on.'

The atmosphere outside had changed. It wasn't just that the temperature had dropped – although it had – it was more that the walls, for some reason, seemed suddenly taller. Closer. Darker. Threatening.

Matthew stopped. 'Are we safe here?'

Jim, master of the evasive answer, didn't even bother to try.

Compared to the gathering dusk outside, and even though it was lit only by a solitary lantern on the counter, the interior of the mess hut seemed bright and cheerful. Work lights had been hung from the ceiling and a heavy-duty portable field cooker stood at one end. Three lanterns and a row of sand buckets were ranged against one wall with no less than three fire extinguishers within easy reach. Matthew was impressed, despite himself. It would appear that Mr Tucker ran a tight ship.

The atmosphere was warm and a little steamy, but somehow cosy. Rough hangings at the window shut out the cold night.

A counter divided the hut in half. Cooking took place at one end and eating at the other. Thick white plates were stacked on the counter, together with a tray of cutlery and a rough basket piled high with bread rolls. There were four tables, each with four chairs. Seating for sixteen people. But there weren't sixteen people present. Had there once been? Did people come

234

and go? Like Plimpton and his team. Bringing back stolen pods. Yes, that would work. Henry Plimpton would steal any pod he could get his hands on and then bring it back here for repairs or reprogramming. Was he building a fleet? Was this his main base of operations? Unlikely. This was a depot, perhaps. Again, Matthew wondered where and when he was. And Henry Plimpton. Where and when was *he*?

The mess hut was sturdily built with its floor and walls made of some modern material. For ease of transportation and erection, obviously. There were two windows set in opposite walls and that was it. No books, music, holo streamers, nothing. Unless people had personal effects in their huts, of course. Although hadn't Jim said there was no power to the other huts?

At that moment, he heard the generators start up. The overhead lights flickered. Jim looked at his watch. 'Six o'clock. Bang on.' A few lights came on outside, mostly around the gate area. He could hear men calling to each other. Clearing things away for the night. They entered in groups of two or three, rubbing their hands against the chill.

Something smelled good. Matthew forgot to be curious and sniffed appreciatively. 'What is that?'

Jim shrugged. 'Stew. A bit of this and that. We all take it in turns to cook. As will you. If Tucker lets you live. And just a word of warning – we like our food here. If you can't already, learn to cook, or the boys'll kill you deader than even Tucker could manage.'

'I saw the veg beds,' said Matthew, changing the subject from his possibly imminent demise. 'Do you hunt? Is there fresh meat? Or fish?'

'No,' said Jim shortly. 'Not any longer.'

An ambiguous reply if ever there was one. Why did they not go hunting any longer? Was there no longer a supply of fresh game to hunt? Or was there some other reason?

'Stand still, everyone,' said Tucker, coming in and closing the door behind him. He seemed to be performing some sort of headcount. 'Nine, plus Andy checking the gate. Ten.'

'Eh?' said someone. 'That's one more than yesterday.'

'Would you rather it was one less?'

The man seemed to draw into himself. 'No.' He stared at Matthew. 'Who's this?'

'New boy,' said Jim, gesturing to Matthew. 'His name's Adrian.' Someone sniggered. No one else introduced themselves.

Matthew reflected briefly. This wasn't the first time he'd pitchforked himself into a situation with no thought as to how he'd get himself out. Yes, he was currently alive, but that could change at any moment. He sighed. Well, at least the situation couldn't get any worse.

About which he was completely wrong.

'We serve ourselves here,' said Jim, making his way to the counter and taking a plate. Matthew stayed close to him but there was no pushing or shoving. Today's cook heaved a vast cauldron of steaming stew on to the counter and doled out generous portions. They helped themselves to a couple of bread rolls and took it all back to the tables. Matthew found himself sitting with – or possibly sandwiched between – Clore, Jim and Tucker.

So, including himself, there were nine men altogether. Ten, if you counted the absent Andy. No one spoke as they sat down to eat. Matthew found himself wondering about the position of the tables. There was plenty of room in the mess hut and yet the tables were almost huddled together in the centre of the room.

These were big, tough men. Surely they weren't intimidated by their surroundings?

'How'd he do?' said Tucker, picking up his fork and not even looking at Matthew.

Before either Clore or Jim could answer, someone from the next table got up and switched on the coffee machine. The hut was suddenly full of the smell of coffee and Matthew was instantly transported back to the illegal coffee machine in their office. And Luke and Jane. And North and Ellis negotiating their daily dose. And Team 235. All of which seemed a very long time ago now. For a moment he had to work very hard at not wondering if he'd ever see them again. And this certainly wasn't the moment to think about Mikey.

It was Jim who answered. 'Pretty good. Seems to know what he's doing.'

'Clore, give it a good going-over tomorrow, first thing.' Tucker stared stonily at Matthew. 'I'll decide about you then.'

'Tools?' said Clore, seated on Matthew's right hand.

'All put away,' said Matthew, careful to concentrate on his stew.

'Cleaned?'

'Of course.'

Clore nodded. No more was said.

The meal was simple but good. Matthew recognised standard compo rations, tarted up with some fresh herbs and onions. There was no alcohol. Matthew suspected another Tucker rule.

They'd been eating for a few minutes when suddenly someone looked around and said, 'Andy's not back yet?'

The room went very still.

'Told you,' said Tucker, his tone casual but his shoulders tense. 'He's checking the gate.'

'That was more than five minutes ago. He should be back by now.'

The atmosphere had changed completely. Suddenly this was no longer the warm, bright, slightly steamy mess hut. Everyone stopped eating and looked around as if Andy might be discovered hiding unnoticed in a corner.

Someone sucked in their breath. 'Not again.'

'Shut up,' said Tucker. Pushing his plate aside, he stood up. 'Jim, Clore, Otto – with me. Everyone else stay here.'

He crossed to a metal locker in the corner and unlocked it with a key from his belt. Four smallish blasters were stacked inside. Tucker took them down and handed them out, saying, 'Lock the door behind us. Don't open it for anyone without the safe word. Geranium. That's an order. Lights.'

Matthew, nearest to the switch, turned out the lights, leaving just the dim lantern standing on the counter where the men had queued for their food.

Tucker eased open the door and the four men disappeared into the night. Only the gate was lit up, which made the rest of the compound seem even darker. Matthew could see the beams from their torches criss-crossing the night. Someone shut the door behind them and dropped a crossbar into place. Two more men crossed the room – one to each window – pulled aside the hangings and peered outside.

Matthew was bursting to ask what was happening – and where the hell they were – but no one would have answered. Every single man was rigidly still, his head cocked to one side.

Listening.

Listening to the silence.

238

20

In Briefing Room 3, what had become known as Team Tesla were assembling for their briefing. Lt North would lead. Officers Rossi, Socko and Hansen were to accompany her, together with Amelia Meiklejohn – the technical consultant, as she had designated herself.

Major Ellis entered the briefing room.

'Good afternoon, everyone. Sit down, please. You all know why you're here.

'One – Nikola Tesla, personal papers for the retrieving of.

'Two – Henry Plimpton, for the possible apprehension of.

'A word before we begin. We will be operating in mid-20th-century New York. Yes – I am aware that's in America. Yes – I am aware there is a treaty. Yes – I am aware we will be contravening said treaty in many, many ways. And you – all of you – should be aware that if anything goes wrong, the Time Police may not be able to retrieve you successfully. Or even at all. You will, therefore, oblige me by making certain nothing – absolutely nothing – goes wrong with this mission. Is that clearly understood?'

Heads nodded around the room.

'However, before you panic utterly – we leave that sort of

thing to St Mary's – America in 1943 is not yet reduced to the condition in which she finds herself today. The southern states are habitable. California is still attached, and radiation, pollution, corruption and civil war have not yet taken hold. The Statue of Liberty still stands. At this point in their history, America is a young, strong, vibrant, optimistic country, taking its place in the world and eager to do so. For everyone's sake, you will keep all interaction with contemporaries to a minimum, and any discussions as to their future are strictly forbidden. There is to be no contamination of any kind. Even if it means your lives. Is that clearly understood?'

Heads nodded again.

'Good. This briefing will be presented by Lt North. When you're ready, Lieutenant.'

North stood up and faced the room. 'Thank you, sir.' She flashed a face on the screen. 'Nikola Tesla. Born 10th July 1856 in Smiljan, Croatia. Died in New York, 7th January 1943. His legacy is sometimes overshadowed by his former employer, Thomas Edison, but Tesla was a prolific and imaginative inventor. Sadly, at the end of his life, he fell on hard times, and for the last ten years, his circumstances forced him to live in two rooms at the New Yorker Hotel.'

She brought up an image of the hotel – a massive, art-deco-style building.

'He can't afford to pay his bills and is living on the promise of something extraordinary, the notes about which he has been keeping in his safe. He suffers from OCD, sleeps badly, compulsively polishes his cutlery and has a phobia about touching hair. There's also a rumour he fell in love with a pigeon.'

She smiled slightly. 'For those of you who think he's just a broken and bonkers old man – he wasn't always so. In 1893 he built the world's first hydroelectric plant at Niagara Falls. He constructed a twenty-storey tower in Colorado that could build up huge electrical charges. There were rumours it could shoot lightning bolts one hundred and thirty-five feet long. He discovered alternating current. He was also very concerned at the rate with which the world's resources were being used up. About which, as we now know, he was absolutely correct. At least two of his projects, however, caused significant concern. He was working on a method of providing wireless electricity – something that would have been years and years ahead of its time had he been successful – and also . . .'

North paused significantly, closed her eyes, and with the air of one taking a bull by the horns, said, 'He claims to have invented what newspapers at the time referred to as – and please excuse the capital letters – a Death Ray.'

A stir of excitement ran around the room. It was immediately apparent that, like it or not, the capital letters were there to stay.

'What?' said Socko, sitting bolt upright. 'You're kidding. An actual Death Ray. How cool is that?'

'Seriously?' said Rossi. 'Does it work? Can we try it out?'

'Tesla himself didn't actually think of it as a Death Ray. He called it his teleforce weapon, the purpose of which was to knock enemy aircraft out of the sky so no country could ever be invaded again.'

'Yeah,' said Rossi, sourly. 'And how do we all think *that* would have worked out?'

North sighed. 'I shall assume your questions are rhetorical, officers. If I might continue . . .'

Team 235 subsided.

'On 8th January 1943, a maid will ignore the *Do Not Disturb* notice which has been hanging off his door for several days and find Nikola Tesla lying dead on the floor. A sad end to an extraordinary life, but, from our point of view, this is where the fun really starts.'

Rossi was tapping at his scratchpad. 'Do we know how he died?'

'In 1937 he was hit by a taxi and quite severely injured, although he refused medical treatment. That won't have done him any good and he never recovered fully, but the official cause of death was coronary thrombosis.

'Once his body is discovered, everything will happen very quickly. The hotel notifies his nearest relative – a nephew – Sava Kosanoviç, a Serbian politician and diplomat living in New York as a member of his country's government-in-exile.

'When Kosanoviç opens the safe, he examines the contents, and removes a 75th birthday memorial book. A personal memento. He then changes the combination of the safe and departs. All of which he, as Tesla's heir, is perfectly entitled to do.

'The next people to turn up are slightly less legal. The Department of Justice Office of Alien Property Custodians immediately begin to remove trunks full of papers, records and belongings. They're acting outside their jurisdiction since Tesla was, in fact, a US citizen. However, no one stops them and most of Tesla's papers are removed.

'What is not there, however, is Tesla's notebook. According to his nephew, Tesla kept a black notebook detailing his inventions and with specific pages marked "Government". This notebook disappeared – no one knows how or when – and has never been seen since.

'So, as you see – we have a very narrow window of accessibility. Attempting to remove Tesla's papers *after* his death leaves us with no time in hand before the nephew and then the Department of Justice arrive. We don't know the exact moment he dies on the 7th and it's very possible he might not feel well enough to go out on his daily walk on the 6th, so our initial attempt will be made on Monday the 4th. Which, should we be unsuccessful, will still leave us Tuesday the 5th for a second go.

'Fortunately for us, Nikola Tesla is a man of regular habits. Every day he walks to Bryant Park to feed the pigeons and call in at the New York Public Library, after which he returns to the hotel. It's his daily routine and he never deviates from it.'

Ellis stirred. 'It seems odd – and sad – given the vast expanse of his mind, that his physical world should be so very small at the end of his life.'

'Yes,' said North. 'He dies alone and forgotten. In 1994, however, in belated recognition of his genius, I believe they named a street corner after him – Nikola Tesla Corner, situated at West 40th Street and 6th Avenue, Manhattan.'

Her audience regarded her blankly.

'What?' said Rossi.

North heaved a sigh that just about skirted the borders of irritation but managed to convey an ocean of unexpressed exasperation, nonetheless.

'In the not unlikely event of any of you becoming lost, in Manhattan, streets run east to west and are numbered. The further north you go, the higher the number. For example, the most southern street is East 1st Street. The most northerly is 220th Street. Simple.'

Her audience continued to regard her blankly.

'Please bear in mind that most streets begin with either East or West. This will tell you whether you are east or west of 5th Avenue. Odd-numbered streets run west – even-numbered streets run east. Odd-numbered buildings are on the north side of the street – even on the south.'

North paused. Lightly stunned, her audience stared back at her. Major Ellis concentrated on his boots.

'*Avenues*, however, run north to south and their numbers ascend from east to west. With the exception of Broadway, which bucks the trend completely and runs diagonally.'

She made the mistake of pausing again.

'Why?' enquired Rossi, eyes big and innocent.

He should have known better.

'Because it follows the ancient Wickquasgeck trail made by the original Native American inhabitants. It was necessary for the trail to find its way around all the swamps, streams and rocks littering the area at the time.'

She looked up from her notes. 'Any follow-up questions? No? How disappointing. I had a shedload of background detail prepared, which I will, nevertheless, flash to your scratchpads. Whether you like it or not.'

'Now look what you've done,' muttered Socko to Rossi. 'And we'll have to read it because she's bound to ask questions later.'

'If she doesn't shoot us first,' said Hansen.

Behind them, Ellis cleared his throat and they fell silent.

North continued. 'Tesla's route is well known. Hotel, park, pigeons, library and back to the hotel. Monitoring him should not be an issue.'

'Do we know what happened to the papers the government took away?' enquired Hansen, flicking through his scratchpad.

North consulted her notes once more. 'Once in the US government's possession, Tesla's papers were examined by one John Trump, a scientist from the now defunct but highly regarded at the time Massachusetts Institute of Technology. After collaboration with several Naval Intelligence officers, Trump categorically stated the papers contained no new info that could "constitute a hazard in enemy hands". Based on the papers he had seen, Trump concluded that even if there was a Death Ray, and it did work, it would be of only very limited power. John Trump was a respected scientist and given that, even during the years when their situation was so critical, America significantly failed to develop a Death Ray, I think we can assume he was telling the truth.'

Rossi stirred. 'So, if there *was* anything important or dangerous in Tesla's papers . . .'

'If there was, it was almost certainly removed before the American officials turned up – possibly even before his nephew turned up – and yes, given that Henry Plimpton has expressed an interest, I think we can all guess by whom.'

'Are we so certain anything was stolen?'

'Tesla's nephew always maintained that the important stuff had been removed – including Tesla's famous black notebook.'

Socko lifted his hand. 'But if Tesla died poor and alone, doesn't that mean that this Death Ray never existed after all? That it was only a figment of his imagination. Perhaps Tesla was a little confused towards the end of his life.'

North nodded. 'That is certainly a possibility, but in 1935 Tesla received $25,000 from a Mr Bartanian of the Amtorg

245

Trading Corp – an American–Soviet trading organisation – to supply plans and specs for an apparatus that could project particles to a distance of one hundred miles at speeds of anything up to three hundred and fifty miles per second, so someone obviously believed he was on to something.'

'Gotta say, that sounds like a Death Ray to me,' said Socko, happily.

'Amtorg continued to exist during the so-called Cold War, but was wound up after the Soviet collapse in 1998. However, some people were convinced that by then – possibly via Kosanoviç – the Soviets were already in possession of Tesla's secrets.'

'But they also have significantly failed to develop a Death Ray,' said Socko.

North nodded. 'That is correct. So, either it doesn't work or they never had the relevant information in the first place.'

'Because someone else has it. A private individual rather than a state, perhaps?'

Hansen shifted on his seat. 'I don't know,' he said dubiously. 'A Death Ray? I mean – yeah – super cool – but did people actually think . . . ?'

'Do not underestimate the paranoia of those times,' said North. 'And when one considers subsequent events within the US itself, I think it fair to say that if they'd had even a sniff of a Death Ray, then things could have been even more catastrophic. If that's even possible. However, before we are all overcome by the plot of a very third-rate science fiction novel, please bear in mind that this supposed Death Ray wasn't the only thing Tesla was working on. Another of his projects – and equally valuable in its own way – was wireless electricity. The supply of electricity without any wiring was considered to be almost miraculous and aroused great feelings – good and bad – at the time. J. P. Morgan – one of Tesla's backers – withdrew his funding immediately. Hardly surprising since free electricity would put him out of business. It is probably safe to say that that invention wouldn't have been any more popular than the Death Ray. Slightly less, in fact.'

'So the Death Ray business might be just a red herring,' said Rossi, thoughtfully, 'and it was the secrets of wireless electricity that were so important.'

'That is certainly a possibility to be considered.' North shut down the screen. 'Whatever the contents of Tesla's papers, however, we cannot risk them falling into the hands of Henry Plimpton. Or anyone other than us.' She began to gather her notes together. 'Major Ellis, sir.'

'Thank you, Lieutenant,' said Ellis, getting to his feet again. 'As stated, our priority is to secure Tesla's papers. They have the potential for disaster in *anyone's* hands so the apprehension of Henry Plimpton is, today, second on our list of priorities. Obviously, I'd like both, but if you have to make the choice between one or the other, then it's Tesla's papers. Be very clear on that.'

They nodded.

'Will we actually be able to speak to Tesla?' enquired Mikey. 'There's so much I want to . . .'

'Not under any circumstances,' said North, in a voice that brooked no argument. 'The possible consequences of someone like Nikola Tesla being granted an insight into future scientific developments is too horrific even to contemplate. American history is far too fragile to withstand any contamination – no matter how well intentioned.'

247

'Yes, but . . .' began Mikey and, given the determination of both protagonists to have their own way in all things, Ellis thought it prudent to intervene.

'Right, then – under the leadership of Lt North, there will be two teams. The first will consist of Lt North, Officer Rossi and Miss Meiklejohn. Their objective will be the hotel itself, the New Yorker. They will wait for Tesla to depart on his daily walk, after which they will gain access to Tesla's rooms and the safe therein.'

'Are they just going to pick it up and walk off with it?' enquired Socko.

'No,' said Ellis, calmly. 'The safe will be accessed by – and please hold your indignation in check – Mr John Costello, who has a certain expertise in this area.'

Hansen raised his hand. 'Um . . . why?'

'Mr Costello is a man of many talents – one of which is safe-breaking. I've spoken to him and he does not anticipate that a simple mid-20th-century hotel safe will cause him any great difficulties.'

Silence greeted this remark.

'Assuming your silence means your unqualified approval of my decision, I shall proceed with the rest of the briefing. Everyone else is to monitor Nikola Tesla as he feeds the pigeons in Bryant Park. Just in case Plimpton has any intentions towards the man himself.'

Ellis brought up an old black and white image of a space crammed full of bushes and trees. 'You will set down in Bryant Park itself. As you can see, this is not a modern park full of open spaces. Pathways are overhung by dense trees. There's undergrowth and thick shrubbery everywhere. Large areas of

248

the park are not visible from more than twenty feet away. This will work both in your favour and against it. Be aware of your surroundings at all times.'

'Are we sure Henry Plimpton will turn up?' enquired Socko.

'Such information as we have leads us to believe he will make an attempt. Either on the papers or the man himself. And even if he doesn't, Nikola Tesla's private papers *must* be retrieved with all speed. Death Rays and wireless electricity might only be the tip of the iceberg. Heaven knows what other world-changing ideas might have been knocking around in that genius head of his.'

He switched off the screen. 'Now – I know we don't normally bother, but given the sensitivity of the location, very nearly accurate costumes have been procured for you. At great expense so don't go bleeding on them. World War Two is in full swing and all foreigners will be regarded with great suspicion. Keep any interactions to a minimum. In fact, Officers Kohl and Rossi are forbidden to speak in public. My apologies, gentlemen. Please make sure none of you get yourselves arrested because, given the treaty and its terms as they relate to America, I really don't know what we could do about it, so if they don't shoot you on the spot, you'll probably spend the rest of your lives in an internment camp.'

Ellis hesitated. 'Remember also – segregation. There are separate entrances for separate races. Establishments exist that only serve one race to the exclusion of others. Walking into the wrong one will cause comment – if not actual arrest. And above all else – please remember that America has not yet begun to turn on itself and as Lt North has reminded you, it is vitally important no one does anything either to precipitate or delay events that must happen. Any questions?'

Officers shook their heads.

'Good luck, everyone. Dismissed.'

21

Ask anyone – either at St Mary's or TPHQ – about Matthew Farrell's legendary appetite.

'A black hole for food,' as someone once described him.

It was a constant mystery how one person could pack away so much food and yet still remain so small and scrawny. Officer Farrell himself frequently described it as a gift.

The stark experiences of his early years meant he never wasted food and he wasn't wasting it now. He too watched and listened but he also continued to eat his stew. Yes, all right, he might be alone in an unknown time and place with unknown dangers threatening at every turn, but you never knew when the next meal would turn up. Or even *whether* the next meal would turn up.

Apart from the occasional glooping noise from the coffee machine there was only silence. Finishing his stew, he quietly laid down his cutlery, reached for the remains of his bread roll and began to mop up the gravy. After all, this might be his last ever meal.

'How long have they been gone?' asked someone. A tall, lanky man with hair like Sideshow Bob. Except his was black.

'Too long,' said one of the men at the windows, turning his head to peer out.

'See anything?'

As he spoke, all the outside lights came on. Bright, white, dazzling lights. Shadows fled.

'Yeah,' said the first man at the window. 'I can see them. They've split up. Jim and Clore are checking the generators and the control room. Tucker and Otto are heading for the gate. Looking for Andy, I suppose. No one else out there that I can see. Fisher – get on the door in case they need to get back in a hurry. Don't forget the safe word.'

Matthew chewed his last mouthful and swallowed. 'Why would they need to get back in a hurry? Are we under attack? Are there locals here? Are they hostile? Can they get in? What's going on?'

For a long time, he thought no one would answer and then the tall man with the wild hair came to sit opposite him.

'It comes in the dark.'

'Shut up, Trip. No point in frightening the lad to death.'

'Oh, it's far too late for that,' said Matthew, conscious of his heart beginning to race. His mind went back to that moment just outside Jim's pod. That sense of . . . was there such a word as unwelcomeness? Hostility? Resentment? 'This lad's already scared shitless. What comes in the dark?'

'There's something out there,' said Trip. 'A bear, perhaps. Or a lion. Or maybe a wild boar. Something big, anyway. In the forest. It comes out of the dark and . . . attacks . . . people. We've lost two men so far.'

'When you say "attacks people" . . . ?' said Matthew, and waited.

Trip remained silent.

'He means it takes people,' said a man from another table.

'Johnson first. Then Li. Johnson was there one minute . . . and gone the next. No sound. No struggle. No trace. Just . . . gone.'

'And Li?'

Someone else spoke, staring down at the table. 'We were on our way to supper. It was dark. He was ahead of me. He walked around a hut. I was about ten paces behind but when I came round the other side he wasn't there.' He sounded bewildered. 'He wasn't anywhere.'

'Didn't you see anything? Hear anything?'

The man shook his head. 'Not a thing. At the time I thought he'd somehow got to the mess hut ahead of me. But he hadn't.'

'How do they get in if the gate's . . . ?'

'Not they. It.'

'Shut up, Fisher.' Trip stood up and went to the window by the door, easing the other man aside. 'They're coming back. I can see Jim and Clore heading this way. Tucker and Otto are doing a final sweep. Looks like they're leaving all the lights on tonight.'

'And Andy?'

Trip hesitated and then said quietly, 'No sign.'

Matthew got up, poured a mug of coffee and took it to Trip. 'Here.'

'Cheers, kid.'

In this situation, Matthew had absolutely no objection to being called kid. They could call him anything they liked. Other than officer, of course. He took the opportunity to peer out into the floodlit compound. Jim and Clore were some twenty yards away, heading back towards the mess hut. Jim was in front with Clore watching his rear. Tucker was checking the door to the workroom next to the forge. He had his back to Matthew.

253

Otto, his blaster moving from left to right, was covering him as he did so. Everything was quiet and professional – these men obviously knew what they were doing.

Trip turned aside, looked for somewhere to put down his coffee, found nowhere, and turned back to the window.

'Holy fuck!'

Matthew leaped back as Trip's steaming coffee went everywhere. Mostly over Trip himself. Who barely seemed to notice. Behind him, chairs scraped across the wooden floor as the remaining men leaped to their feet. They crowded around the window.

'What?'

'What did you see?'

'What happened?'

Trip seemed unable to speak for a moment. He was craning his neck to see out of the window. Up. Down. Left. Right. His mouth opened and closed. Shock. Astonishment. Disbelief. When he eventually managed to get the words out, his voice was high with fear.

'The gate's open.'

'What?'

Men crowded around.

'You said it was shut.'

'It was. I saw it.'

'Me too,' said Matthew, nodding. 'It was definitely closed.'

'It's always closed,' said someone. 'Tucker told us to keep it shut. After . . .' He tailed away. And then, suddenly, 'Where's Otto?'

Matthew was pressed hard against the wall as men crowded around the window.

'I can't see him anywhere,' said Trip, still frantically craning his neck around. 'He's gone. Where . . . ? . . . the fuck? He was there. I saw him. Where's he gone?'

'He's taking a whizz somewhere,' said someone, hopefully.

'I can't see him.'

'Well, he's not going to do it in front of everyone, is he? He'll be behind a hut.'

'Who's gone?' demanded Matthew, pushing men away to give himself a little room. 'Who's disappeared? Tucker?'

Trip swallowed. 'Otto.'

Hot coffee dripped unheeded. The silence was so complete that Matthew could actually hear each individual drip splatting to the floor. Trip was shaking all over. Shock, Matthew decided – although whether from his scalded hand or Otto's disappearance was unclear.

'Hey,' he said softly. 'You should have that looked at.'

'Kit under the counter,' said Fisher, apparently unwilling to move from his safe spot against the wall.

Matthew pulled Trip away from the window. Two men moved up to take his place.

It's always good to have something to do in a crisis. Matthew concentrated on gently placing Trip's hand in a bowl of cold water.

'Yeah, don't shove it under running water,' said Trip faintly as Matthew rummaged for the first-aid kit. 'No one's going outside to pump some more. Not tonight.' He turned at the sudden sound of the door being unbarred. 'What's happening?'

'I think they're going to look for Otto.'

If possible, Trip turned an even whiter shade of pale. 'No,' he said, surprisingly strongly. 'Keep that door closed. You heard what Tucker said. Don't open the door.'

'What about Otto?' shouted a man.

'They won't find him. Otto's gone.'

'You don't know that.'

An older man raised his voice. 'We never found Johnson. Or Li. I tell you, man, this place is evil.'

Trip turned on him in sudden temper. 'Shut the fuck up, will you?' He took several deep breaths. 'What's going on out there now?'

'They're all together. Tucker's closing the gate. Again.'

'Do not take your eyes off him. Any of them.'

'They're coming back,' said Fisher. 'Fast. Get the door open.'

Someone heaved the door open and the next moment, three men burst into the hut and halted, getting their breath back.

Tucker laid his gun carefully on the table, checked the door had been secured properly behind him, wheeled about and decked the man who had opened it. Not a huge blow – more a slap. Matthew thought the man might have fallen over out of sheer surprise.

He sat up, hand to his face. 'What the fuck . . . ?'

Tucker loomed. 'What did I tell you about opening the door?'

'It was you. I saw it was you.'

'Did I give the safe word? Did you ask for it? No – you just opened the door like an idiot. You could have let anything in.' He picked up his gun again. 'Listen up, all of you. *No one* comes in without the safe word. No matter what they say or who you think it is. Got it?'

Heads nodded.

'It got Otto,' said someone, still peering out of the window.

'He,' said Tucker firmly. 'There's no *it*. We talked about this. It's some of the locals. They've found a way of opening the gate that we don't know about. Or, more likely, they're getting over the wall somehow.'

'So, where's Otto, then?'

'They took him. Two or three of them will have struck out of the dark and dragged him out through the gate before he knew what was happening. This is why I said no one goes anywhere alone. They strike from the shadows and then vanish, but they're just men. Understood?'

Their expressions indicated that every man understood but disagreed.

Matthew, busy spraying Trip's hand with medical plastic, listened to the raised voices. He could make out Tucker's. And Jim's. Everyone else was just a jumble. It would seem there were two factions. One wanted to grab a pod and go. Now. Never mind what the boss said. He wasn't here, was he? The speaker wasn't going to hang around to be picked off at leisure. He was out of here now. And anyone who had any sense would come with him.

The other faction maintained they were being well paid for this. They had only to wait until the next shift turned up and then they could all go home and be rich for a while.

The first faction was of the opinion no one was going to live that long. The next shift was already late. Suppose they never arrived at all?

Someone demanded to know why not. 'Why wouldn't the next shift arrive?'

'Because they're not coming,' said another voice. 'We've been abandoned. There's nothing here of any great value. Just two shit pods that don't work properly and never have, and a handful of expendables. The boss has changed his mind and set up elsewhere. Or maybe the Time Police have got him.'

Matthew kept his attention on Trip's hand. That was actually a very valid point. Suppose his mother had alerted the Time Police and the Time Police had tracked down Henry Plimpton and he and the rest of his team were already in custody. If no one talked – and Henry Plimpton did seem to have the knack of inspiring fear among his workforce – then the men on site might never be relieved. Because no one would ever know they were here.

On the other hand, from Matthew's point of view, Henry Plimpton not turning up here would be good. It would certainly solve all the problems about where he and Matthew were in each other's Timelines. He was certain Tucker would make him personally test the pod he'd been working on as soon as it was light, which was all to the good. He could jump out of here and never come back. It wouldn't be that easy, of course. They wouldn't allow him to handle the pod alone – Tucker and Clore would certainly be with him – but he'd think of something. Avoiding a meeting with Henry Plimpton was a top priority. As was reporting back to TPHQ.

In the meantime, however . . . there was this to deal with.

'Maybe there's no one left to come back for us,' Fisher was saying. 'Our relief should have been here last week. I tell you, we're all going to die here if we don't get out now – this instant.'

There was another babble of voices.

Tucker thumped the table for silence. 'Precise dates are difficult. You know that as well as me. That's why we allow a fortnight either side. They'll be here. We've got at least another week before we need to start worrying.'

Fisher wasn't going down without a fight. 'We're expendable. Why isn't the boss here? And what about all the new equipment we were promised? And the relief team? Where are they? Has anyone actually seen any of this wonderful pay we're supposed to be getting? I keep telling you – we've been abandoned here.' He gestured angrily. 'These secret locations are all very well, but we've been dumped. The boss has cut his losses and they're never coming back for us.'

The mess hut rang with the clamour of heated discussion.

Presumably fed up with using his hand, Tucker banged a mug on the table. 'Shut the fuck up, all of you.'

They shut the fuck up.

A good man, thought Matthew. Well, no, not a *good* man – not by Time Police standards, anyway. But definitely the sort of man needed at this moment. The mood was dangerous. These men were only one step away from flat-out panic. Not that he blamed them. Four members of their team had vanished without trace. Two of them in the last half-hour. And right under their very noses.

'No one's going anywhere at the moment . . .' began Tucker.

'You can't keep us here,' said the argumentative man. 'You can't make us stay.'

Tucker nodded. 'You're right, Fisher – I can't. Clore, open the door and push him out, will you?' He looked back at Fisher. 'If whatever's out there will let you get to a pod, then you're welcome to take one.'

'Take the one on the right,' said Clore. 'The kid's been

259

working on it and I haven't had a chance to check it over yet. If it's going to go bang, it might as well go bang all over you.'

'Actually, the other one's not that brilliant, either,' said Jim. 'It's doing that funny whining, clunking thing again.'

'There you go,' said Tucker. 'Neither's very safe. Are you so hell-bent on fucking off to save yourself that you'll risk a dodgy pod? Dunno about the rest of you, but I reckon I'm better off here. Even if there is something wandering around out there. Which there isn't. And, Fisher,' he loomed suddenly, 'you might want to think twice about leaving your mates behind. Cos I'll tell you this for nothing – should we ever meet again, I'll give you such a kicking you'll wish you'd died here. Still – time's a'wasting. You'll be wanting to be off.'

He seized Fisher and began to drag him, struggling, to the door.

'Fuck you, Tucker.' Fisher wrenched himself free. 'I'm not going out there alone.'

'No one's going out there,' said Tucker, pushing him into a seat. 'Not while it's dark. Forget your own huts – we all sleep here tonight. Tomorrow – when the sun shines – we'll discuss our options.'

Silence.

Matthew pulled a flexi-glove from its sterile wrapping.

Tucker nodded to Trip's hand. 'What happened there?'

'Spilled my coffee.' He winced as Matthew began to encase his scalded hand.

'Clumsy bugger.'

Trip nodded. 'Yeah.' He looked at Matthew. 'Cheers, kid.'

Matthew began to clear away the wipes and repack the med kit. Slowly, the mood calmed. Men returned to their tables and sat down. Taking advantage of the cooler atmosphere, he said, 'Can I ask a question?'

Tucker accepted a cup of coffee from Jim and sat down. 'Might as well.'

Fisher muttered something along the lines of hoping Matthew lived long enough to hear the answer.

'Where are we? What is this place?'

'Well,' said Tucker, 'we don't tend to bandy the name about because we're not supposed to be here.'

'You mean because you're – we're – illegal Time travellers? Illegals.'

'Not that – although we are – but it's more a *geographical* than a temporal crime.'

Matthew's head shot up. 'Shit. We're not . . . Surely not . . . We're not in *America*, are we?'

'Give the kid a biscuit.'

Matthew, taking this literally, opened the biscuit tin and helped himself to more than one.

'So,' he said, spraying a few crumbs, 'it's quite a big country. Where exactly in America?'

'A little place. Well, it's an island, actually. Tucked away. Isolated. Marshland and pine woods. Some indigenous people. You've probably never heard of it. I certainly hadn't.'

Clore and Fisher were shaking their heads. 'Nor me.'

'Well, try me. Where is this place and what are we doing here?'

Tucker drained his mug and set it down.

'Roanoke.'

22

Matthew stopped chewing. Sadly, no one who knew him well was around to witness this phenomenon.

He stared. 'Oh my God.'

'You've heard of it?'

'Well, yeah – haven't you?'

'Not before I got here. How do you know about it?'

Matthew decided not to mention that the intriguing history of Roanoke and the ultimate and possibly grisly fate of its vanished inhabitants had proved so irresistible a temptation to Adrian and Mikey that it had taken the combined might of his mother, his father, and Uncles Peterson and Markham to dissuade them from embarking on a 'fact-finding tour' from which, especially given the events of this evening, it was very possible they might never have returned.

'Heard about it in college,' he said briefly.

Tucker blinked. 'You went to college?'

Matthew began to embroider his past. Not something he'd ever had to do before. The real version was usually colourful enough. 'Not for very long. They kept expecting me to get up in the morning and attend lectures. And then they expected me to spend my evenings writing essays.' He shook his head. 'That was never going to happen.'

'They kicked you out?'

'They invited me to vacate the premises,' said Matthew with dignity. He saw talkative Jim open his mouth to ask another question – or possibly another half-dozen questions – and changed the subject.

'So what year is this? When are we?'

Jim shrugged. 'Precisely? No idea. Is it important?'

Matthew tried to think this through. After the final abandonment presumably, but before more permanent settlement around the early 18th century. He shook his head. Not important at this moment.

'This choice of site,' he said carefully. 'Who made it?'

Tucker shrugged. 'The boss, as far as I know. Why? What do you know?'

'I don't know anything that isn't known generally,' said Matthew quickly, wanting to avoid being thought a smart arse. 'Although apparently not by everyone. I wonder if that was why you were chosen.'

'I was chosen,' said Tucker evenly, 'because I'm good at my job and my crew are top-notch.'

His voice was just loud enough to be heard by his top-notch crew. Matthew began to suspect that Tucker was actually a very clever man, even if he and his team did know nothing of the time and place in which they'd been dropped. He paused to collect his thoughts and to choose his words carefully.

'From what I've read,' he said, trying to remember that not everyone had been brought up on a diet of historical calamity and catastrophe, 'a colony was set up by a bloke called Raleigh in fifteen something or other.'

'Good Queen Bess,' said Tucker, unexpectedly.

'Yes, I think so,' said Matthew, vaguely. 'Anyway, they were unlucky right from the word go.' He gestured around. 'The leader of the first colony, Ralph ... Lane, I think, probably built this compound. He also managed to alienate the Native Americans – and without their help, the colonists were all in danger of starving to death. Anyway, just in time, they were rescued, I think by Francis Drake, and taken back to England.'

'I've heard of him,' said Clore. 'He won the Armada.'

Matthew decided that was close enough. His mother wouldn't have been able to let the comment go but he had more important fish to fry at the moment.

He nodded. 'Anyway, they all pushed off back to England before they starved. With the sort of bad luck that would dog the colony at every turn, the supply ship arrived only a week later.'

'Bit of a bugger,' said Clore, helping himself to more coffee.

'The supply ship left fifteen men here,' said Matthew.

Tucker frowned. 'Why?'

'Something to do with retaining legal possession, I think.' Matthew hesitated. 'Preventing the French from taking over the claim. Or the Spanish. Whoever.'

'What happened to the fifteen men?' demanded Fisher.

'No one's quite sure,' said Matthew feeling, on balance, that this was a slightly more acceptable answer than *no one ever saw them again and their fate remains a mystery to this day*. 'Anyway, Raleigh wasn't prepared to give up on his colony so they had another go. But the second bunch of colonists arrived

264

too late in the year for planting and harvesting, and before very long, they too began to run out of food.'

'Bloody hell,' said Clore, returning with his coffee.

Matthew thought it would be wise to seem a little hazy on detail. 'Their leader – um . . . White . . . John White? . . . Yes, John White – sailed back to England promising to return with more equipment and supplies.'

He stopped.

'And did he?' enquired Tucker.

'Only after it was too late. Not his fault. He encountered a great many obstacles, not least the war with Spain and all English ships being commandeered to fight them off. It took him several years to get back here, and when he did, there were no signs of any of the colonists anywhere. Like the fifteen men, every single one of them had disappeared and the site was completely deserted. The only clue as to where they'd gone was the word *CROATOAN*, carved on a palisade timber near the gate.'

'I've seen that,' said Trip, sitting up with a jerk. 'It's still there. What does it mean?'

'It's thought they might have gone off to nearby Croatoan Island and lived with the Croatoans there.'

'And that's definite?' said Jim, who had been very quiet. For him.

'No,' said Matthew quietly. 'It's just guesswork.'

'There's another carving,' said Jim, quietly. *'CRO.'*

'CRO?' said Matthew, apparently astonished and intrigued.

'Yeah,' said Fisher. 'Just *CRO*.' He stared at Tucker. 'As if someone never lived long enough to finish the message.'

Matthew shook himself. 'Anyway, no one knows what

265

happened to the colonists. Or the men left behind to safeguard the claim. Or why everything always seemed to go wrong for anyone who tried to live here.' He sipped his coffee. 'Sadly, their bad luck wasn't finished. When White tried to sail to Croatoan Island to look for the missing colonists there, his boat was beaten back by bad weather. After that had blown over, he couldn't persuade the sailors to make another attempt. He never saw any of his colonists again and was forced to return to England, a broken man.'

'Did the colonists make it to the island?'

Matthew shrugged. 'No one knows.'

'The bloody place is cursed,' said Fisher, leaping to his feet to look out of the window again. 'We need to get out of here now. While we still can.'

He headed towards the door and was intercepted by Tucker. As soft and fluffy as a monolith. 'Sit down.'

'But . . .'

'I said, *sit down*.'

His tone was gentle but there was no mistaking that this was a command. Fisher tried to hold his gaze, failed, and sat back down.

'We could leave now,' said Jim, quietly. 'My pod's working. It's not brilliant . . . But it would get us out of here.'

'We could,' said Tucker, pleasantly. 'We could risk walking out of that door and straight into the arms of whatev— whoever is out there – or we could wait until daylight before making any decisions.'

Clore shifted. The chair creaked under his weight. 'We ain't been paid yet.'

'Nor will we be if we don't complete the shift,' said Tucker, nodding. 'We'll have spent six weeks in this shithole with not a penny to show for it. Plus, we probably won't ever work again. Not for the boss, anyway. And don't tell me he wouldn't put the word out.'

Wisely, he said no more, leaving his colleagues to contemplate this statement.

'We're getting low on supplies,' said the man who had been their chef for the evening. 'And there's not much fuel left for the generators. And then we'll have no lights at all.'

'The relief team will arrive any day now,' said Tucker. 'We go back in their pod, pick up our pay and . . .'

Matthew had been thinking hard. 'Can I ask another question?'

Tucker looked at him. 'What?'

'Well, I've only been here a few hours, but a couple of things have struck me.'

'Such as?'

'Well, I gather you're some sort of depot site?'

'We are. Spare pods, supplies, equipment, pod maintenance – all that sort of thing.'

'And you alternate with another crew?'

'Yeah.'

'Has this happened to them?'

'Dunno,' said Tucker. 'New site. We're the first crew in.'

'How long have you been here?'

'Like I said – just over six weeks.'

'When are you due to be relieved?'

'Last week,' said Fisher, loudly.

'OK,' said Matthew, bracing himself. 'Are you so sure they will turn up? And what plans have you made for if they don't? Turn up, I mean.'

The coffee machine glooped again in the silence.

Tucker scowled at him. 'What are you saying, kid?'

'I'm not sure,' said Matthew, feeling his way. 'I mean – suppose, for a reason we don't know about, and not necessarily bad – suppose they don't turn up. What then?' He sat back to watch the result.

Tucker scoffed. 'Why wouldn't they?'

'Two old pods, a few supplies, a bit of old equipment. There's nothing really valuable here, is there?'

'There's us,' said Tucker, meaningfully.

'You're all Mr Plimpton's men?'

'No. Just me. I recruited the boys here.'

'So you're not actually Mr Plimpton's men at all.'

There was a short silence. Men looked uneasily at one another.

Matthew made haste to pursue his advantage. 'Exactly why are you here?'

'Told you. Setting up the site. A place for the boss to operate from safely. In America, where even the Time Police don't go. Why do you ask?'

'Well,' said Matthew hesitantly, 'you've been here for six weeks. How many men have you lost altogether? Four? More? At this rate . . .'

There was a long pause. Matthew could practically hear their minds working. If he could build on their fears, undermine their confidence, they might decide to pull out early – pay or no pay. Half of them had one foot out of the door already. And if he could get them to leave, he could . . .

What? What could he do? Would they allow him to set the coordinates? Pilot a pod? No, of course not. The best he could hope for was that they returned him whence he came. But that in itself would be a result. He could rendezvous with his mother and take what he knew back to TPHQ. Yes – he could work with that. All he had to do was undermine their resolve, panic them into doing something stupid and then capitalise on the situation. Somehow. And definitely before Henry Plimpton turned up with his relief crew. He wished now he'd made more of the colonists' mysterious fate.

Shifting in his seat, he said carefully, 'When you arrived here – did you find any clues as to what happened to the previous colonists? Did they leave anything behind?'

His comment seemed to have struck gold. Tucker gave him an evil look but said nothing.

'There were a few things in the huts,' said Jim, always happy to shove his oar in. 'Boots. Gloves. A Bible. A shirt. Some women's stuff. Bits and pieces.'

Matthew frowned. 'Who would leave behind a good pair of boots? And definitely who would leave behind their Bible?'

A few men shifted uneasily.

'Yeah,' said someone. 'Maybe people who had to leave in a hurry. People who had to run for their lives, perhaps.'

'Shit,' shouted Fisher, from the window. 'The gate's open again.'

It was at exactly that moment that the generators died and the compound lights went out.

23

Team Tesla's pod landed softly near a path close to the perimeter wall of Bryant Park. The area was comparatively thicket-free.

'Just as well,' said Mikey, checking the screen. 'If we'd landed in that tangle over there, I'd have had to be carried to the path.'

Socko raised his eyebrows.

'Nylons,' said Mikey, seemingly thinking that explained all.

Socko looked around helplessly.

North patted his shoulder. 'Never mind.'

She turned to the rest of her team. 'Final clothing check.'

All the men, including John Costello, wore soft hats, dark overcoats and woollen scarves. There were no frills. This was wartime fashion. Every garment was cut using the minimum amount of material and using the minimum number of buttons. No cuffs, no belts, no embellishments of any kind.

North and Mikey both wore similar navy-blue coats and sturdy shoes. Mikey sported a grey beret rakishly pulled so far to one side of her head that Rossi had accused her of walking alongside it. North wore a very dashing Robin Hood–style hat – complete with a feather, but only a very small one.

She addressed her team. 'It doesn't matter that our clothing

270

is slightly old-fashioned or ten years old. These days people are making-do and mending. We look just smart enough not to be turned away at the door and not smart enough for people to suspect we've bought our clothes on the black market.

'Rossi, Meiklejohn, Costello and I will go straight to the New Yorker Hotel. Once inside we'll split up, find ourselves somewhere to sit where we can monitor the lifts and entrance closest to the park, and stay there until we spot Tesla leaving. Just a friendly word of warning, Mr Costello – you are tagged. Your every move will be closely monitored by Team Two-Three-Five. In the event of you causing any trouble, I will shoot you myself, step over your body and continue with the mission. On the other hand, cooperate with us and your troubles will melt away. Not a difficult choice, I would have thought, but it's up to you.'

Costello nodded. Gone was the haggard patient from MedCen. After a nap and a good meal, an armful of something stimulating, and with a smart new hairstyle, brown overcoat and antique leather briefcase, he looked very nearly respectable.

'Open the door, please,' said North. The door hissed open. America lay before them. She stood very still. No one said anything, but all of them were conscious of a very definite reluctance to cross the threshold.

'When did the Time Police last land in America?' whispered Rossi.

'They aren't landing here today,' said North. 'This never happened. Good luck, everyone,' and stepped out into America.

One by one the others followed her outside.

The park was old-fashioned in layout but perfect for their purpose. There were no wide-open grassy spaces or long views.

271

The planting was tightly packed, neglected and unkempt. Curving paths were hemmed in by old, overgrown shrubs and trees, and the whole park was encircled by a high perimeter wall. A weak sun was shining, but so dense was the planting that, even with the trees bare, all the paths were deeply shadowed.

'Built themselves a nice little crime trap here,' said Hansen cheerfully, watching his breath puff in the cold morning air. 'God knows what happens here after dark. Or even before dark.'

'As long as it doesn't happen to us,' said North. She turned to Hansen and Kohl. 'We'll advise as soon as Tesla leaves the hotel. Rossi, you'll stick with Tesla. We know his routine so take care to stay out of sight. Report any unusual occurrences – any approach by anyone – you know the drill. Use your coms but discreetly.'

Heads nodded. No one spoke. There was an air of apprehension. Hansen swallowed, loud in the silence.

North lowered her voice. 'I know we're not supposed to be here. The treaty clearly states no one jumps into America in return for them not jumping at all. If we're caught, the consequences will be more than serious. However, think about this: if we fail today, then we could be in for a world of trouble. Everyone could be. But we're the Time Police and we can handle this. Stay calm, do your jobs and everything will be fine.'

She, Rossi, Mikey and John Costello set off at a brisk walk. 'Before we freeze to death,' said Mikey, shoving gloved hands deep into her pockets. 'We don't get winters like this these days, do we?'

No one replied.

The morning was icy cold. Mikey could see their breath frosting ahead of them as they walked. She could hear a faint hum of traffic from the other side of the wall, until they exited the park and suddenly found themselves face to face with a wall of noise.

'Wow,' said Mikey, in well-simulated amazement.

North eyed her. 'Yes – because you've never been here before, have you?'

Mikey grinned. 'Well, not here exactly, but . . .'

'*Don't* tell me.'

'Wasn't going to. Still not convinced you're not going to shoot me.'

'And here would be an excellent place to do it,' said North.

'I find it interesting the thought has crossed your mind.'

'Not crossed,' said North. 'It lives there permanently. But until that happy day, shall we get cracking?'

She and Rossi led the way, with Mikey and Costello a few yards behind. Mikey was bright-eyed and interested, peering into shop windows and stopping to read posters exhorting citizens to remember there was a war on. A ferociously be-whiskered man in a top hat pointed directly at her. Apparently, the US Army wanted her. Mikey grinned. Not as much as the US police, probably, but let's not go there.

American flags fluttered everywhere. From public buildings, shops, public parks, offices – everywhere. Only forty-eight stars, she noticed, which would increase to forty-nine, then up to fifty, then fifty-two, then forty-nine again, then forty-six, and then the states would go down like skittles. She couldn't remember how things stood in her own time. Or what was currently her own time. Alongside her, John Costello pulled down his hat and kept his eyes on the pavement.

There was a strong smell of exhaust fumes, hot metal, hot tar, even coffee. And it was noisy. The sound of traffic was deafening, with horns, engines and clanging streetcar bells.

'Wasn't there supposed to be a petrol shortage?' enquired Rossi of North. 'And tyres?'

She shrugged. 'People still need to travel to and from work, I suppose. Factories are running twenty-four hours a day.'

Mikey surveyed the busy scene. 'It's all go, isn't it?'

It was indeed all go. Around them was the clatter of shop-keepers putting up their shutters. Newspaper vendors shouted the headlines. There was even the clopping of an occasional horse-drawn vehicle.

'This is so cool,' said Mikey, surveying the traffic roaring past. Buses, taxis, cars – large, clumsy-looking cars with knobbly headlights and running boards – bicycles and pedes-trians milled around in all directions.

'Remember,' said North, over her shoulder, 'they drive on the wrong side of the road here.'

'I know that,' said Mikey and immediately wished she hadn't.

North eyed her speculatively. 'Do you indeed?'

'Read it in a book,' said Mikey, improbably, and quickened her pace, wrinkling her nose at the strong smells around her.

There were a lot of uniforms about. Most men and a sur-prising number of women wore a uniform of some kind. Drab olive, dark blue, the famous pinks and greens – the only flashes of colour were the medal ribbons. Civilian dress was equally sombre – all dark browns and greys. And utilitarian. Most people wore a hat of some kind. Heads down, muffled against the cold, they hurried along the pavements – sorry, sidewalks – in a great hurry to get wherever they were going.

As an ex-illegal Time traveller, Mikey had knocked around the Timeline and was no stranger to tall buildings, but these buildings were really tall. It was like walking along the bottom of a narrow canyon. The sky seemed a very long way up. She was particularly fascinated by the diagonal metal stairways zigzagging up and down the outside walls.

She was enjoying the walk. It was good to get out. She'd forgotten how much fun this sort of thing could be. Rocketing up and down the Timeline with Adrian, having adventures, defying the Time Police. Sadly, those days were done. For the time being, anyway.

They had the address – 481 8th Avenue – but the New Yorker wasn't hard to find. Massive and monumental, it reared above them. Mikey tilted her head back and looked up. A long way up.

North sighed. 'Try to look less like a tourist, please.'

'I'd rather they despise me as a tourist than shoot me as a spy.'

North conceded the point. 'As agreed, we'll split up and go in separately. In case of trouble. If anything happens to me, then take your instructions from Rossi. The mission comes first. Everyone set?'

Mikey and Costello nodded and watched Rossi escort North through the doors. They waited. There was no gunfire, screaming or shouting.

'Now us,' said Mikey. John Costello offered her his arm and together they made their way inside.

After the bitterly cold day outside, the heat smacked them in the face. It was obvious that Americans really, really believed in central heating.

'You all right with this, Jakey?' said Mikey as he carefully removed his hat and smoothed his hair over the now much more discreet wound dressing.

'Yeah,' he said, his eyes darting everywhere. 'New start. It's all good.'

She pulled off her gloves and stuffed them into her pocket. 'You're nervous.'

'I'm shit-scared,' he said in an undertone.

'Don't worry – the Time Police keep their word.'

'Not them. It's that bastard Plimpton I'm worried about. If he sees me here, my card's marked for life.'

'He won't. Let's find somewhere to sit down and blend in.'

Costello looked at their opulent surroundings. 'Yeah – good luck with that.'

The New Yorker's foyer was magnificent.

'Lobby,' said Mikey.

'What?'

'They call it a lobby.'

'Still pretty cool, though.'

The lobby was indeed pretty cool. Two storeys high and vast. A wrought-iron and wooden balcony ran around the room at first-floor height, supported by square marble pillars running from floor to the ceiling high overhead. Subdued lighting in the art deco style shone softly down upon them.

Downstairs, at ground-floor level, the layout was formal with a patterned carpet in deep, muted colours. High-backed chairs were placed at rigidly precise intervals around the walls. Mikey had visions of an unfortunate member of staff tasked with a measuring stick every morning.

Deep leather armchairs were grouped around coffee tables

also set at militarily precise distances from each other. Table lamps sent out more gentle light. For ambiance, presumably, rather than actually providing illumination.

It was all very grand, but not particularly homely or welcoming, and there was a whole forest of potted palms on both levels. Perhaps the hotel had been able to secure a job lot.

Huge murals decorated the walls. Mikey recognised a dramatic depiction of the Manhattan skyline. And what looked like the early settlement of New Amsterdam by the Dutch. There were even more murals on the ceiling, set against a glowing golden background. The whole lobby smelled strongly of old-fashioned wax polish, damp wool and cigar smoke. This huge area, designed to hold many people, was, at this moment, comparatively deserted. Whether because of the war or the earliness of the hour was not clear.

'Here,' said Costello, and he and Mikey found themselves two seats against the wall. Mikey could see North and Rossi occupying a similar position behind a marble pillar on the other side of the foy— lobby.

'These seats are very uncomfortable,' complained Costello, laying his hat on the coffee table.

'I think they're designed to persuade you to wait in the bar instead,' whispered Mikey.

John Costello brightened. 'An excellent idea. Shall we go?'

'Don't tempt me.'

To their right, a long, gleaming wooden counter ran almost the length of one wall. Row upon row of pigeonholes stood behind it. The counter was obviously designed to cope with hordes of guests simultaneously, with what looked like positions for twenty receptionists.

'Desk clerks,' said Costello.

At the moment, however, there were only two – both men and both elderly.

'The regular staff have been called up to the war, I expect,' said Mikey.

A desk clerk pinged a bell and immediately, from nowhere, a uniformed boy appeared.

'A bellhop,' whispered Mikey in delight.

'A what?'

'A porter. Carries the luggage.'

'I usually have to carry my own,' said Costello, gloomily. 'When I have any.'

They sat in silence for a while.

'The Brooklyn Dodgers stayed here a couple of years ago,' said Costello, reading a plaque on the wall.

'And now the Time Police Dodgers are here,' said Mikey and they looked at each other.

Costello said suddenly, 'What are you doing here, Mikey?'

Mikey chose to misunderstand him. 'You know why. Tesla's papers. And to grab Henry Plimpton if possible.'

Costello sighed. 'You won't. No one ever does. He gets away every time.'

'Hush,' said Mikey. An elderly waitress was approaching, neatly attired in an old-fashioned black dress and white apron, and carrying a tray with the letters NY emblazoned in silver.

'Can I get you folks anything?'

'We're just waiting for our friend,' said Mikey, swiftly. 'Who has probably overslept. But thank you.'

'Would you like a coffee while you wait?'

'How very kind,' said Mikey, not panicking in any way, because none of them had any money. 'But we've already changed our money back into sterling.'

'On the house,' said the waitress, unnecessarily wiping down the already immaculately gleaming table. Mikey had the impression she was grateful for something to do. 'Compliments of the New Yorker, ma'am.'

'Well, in that case,' said Costello, 'thank you very much. That would be most welcome.'

The waitress moved away.

'Lovely,' said Mikey cheerfully. 'A very welcome cup of coffee – on the house – and it'll annoy the hell out of North. As Luke would say – no downside.'

Their coffee came very quickly – in a large pot with gener-ously sized white cups and saucers, all with the New Yorker emblem emblazoned in silver on every piece. The hotel obvi-ously spared no effort when it came to self-publicity. Mikey caught Costello eyeing up the teaspoons.

'Don't even think about it. If you get caught, the Time Police will, literally, abandon you to your fate. Shot as a spy. Impris-oned as a thief. Snatched by Henry Plimpton. Your choice.'

Costello sighed and sipped. 'Mm – good coffee. Better than that evil stuff you get at TPHQ anyway.' He looked at Mikey. 'Don't you ever long for a decent cup of tea?'

'Oh God,' said Mikey. 'So much.' She paused. 'I wonder . . .'

'What?'

'I wonder if I could manufacture a tea substitute. Indistin-guishable from the real thing but not the real thing.'

'Oh my God,' said Costello, suddenly enthusiastic. 'We could make an absolute bomb.'

'We?'

'I gave you the idea. I deserve a cut.'

'Well, let's hope we both live long enough to give it a try. Meiklejohn and Costello – Purveyors of Quality Tea Substitute.'

'Costello and Meiklejohn, you mean.'

'No, I'm pretty sure I don't.'

'How about C&M? Much snappier.'

'How about "M&C – Quality Tea"?'

'Perfect.' He grinned at Mikey. 'This time next year we could be millionaires.'

The lobby was coming to life. People pushed their way through the street doors. A short queue had formed at the reception desk. A telephone rang somewhere. Bellhops ran hither and thither, pushing luggage trolleys in and out of the lifts.

'There are twenty-three lifts in this building,' said Mikey, apropos of nothing.

'Good heavens,' said Costello vaguely, reaching for the pot again. 'More coffee?'

The morning wore on. North and Rossi sat serenely in their corner, exchanging a word every now and then and apparently completely unconcerned at the non-appearance of Nikola Tesla. Mikey, however, was becoming uneasy. They'd been here over an hour now. The coffee was gone. Their cups cleared away. The morning rush was subsiding. Guests had breakfasted and were departing for the day, to be replaced by new arrivals pouring through the doors. Every now and then there would be a surge of people as they emerged from the hotel's own private subway station. Despite all this activity, however, she had a nasty feeling that sooner or later, someone would come over and ask if they could be of any assistance in that *particular* tone of voice. The one that says, 'Push off before I call the cops.'

Being moved on wouldn't be a complete disaster. There were other entrances and other lifts, too, but these were the doors closest to the park. It seemed logical that Tesla would use the most direct route.

Hansen's voice spoke in her ear. 'Anything?'

It had been agreed North would speak for them all. 'No. Nothing yet.'

He grunted and closed the link.

A huge clock hung on the wall above the desk. Its hands pointed to ten fifteen. How much longer would they have to wait? How much longer would they be permitted to wait?

And then – just as Mikey was beginning to wonder if she'd been too clever for her own good, that somehow she'd got it wrong and they were all wasting their time – Hansen spoke again.

'Ma'am, we have a pod signature. One hundred yards away to our north. Heads up, people. Looks like Henry Plimpton is here at last.'

24

They barely had time to react when the lift chimed pleasantly. The doors parted to reveal an elderly couple, both warmly – and unusually, given all this wartime austerity – dressed in furs. They headed towards the reception desk. Behind them shuffled a single gentleman who leaned heavily on a walking stick. He was dressed for the outdoors in a vast dark overcoat and a lemon-yellow scarf. The small part of his face visible between hat and scarf looked vaguely familiar.

'I think that's him,' whispered Costello.

Across the lobby, North tapped her wrist significantly, as if she couldn't be bothered to wait any longer. She and Rossi rose to their feet, exchanged a few words and shook hands. Rossi waited as Tesla passed him and then followed him out into the street.

John Costello picked up his hat and again offered Mikey his arm. They made their way quietly towards the row of lifts.

'Elevator,' said Mikey quietly. 'They're elevators. And don't forget that in America it's ma'am as in jam and not ma'am as in harm.'

The lift doors opened.

'Wait,' said Mikey softly. 'Let North go first.'

'That's a very good idea,' said John Costello, who appeared to be in the grip of second, third and fourth thoughts. 'In fact, let's not go at all.'

'Now, Jakey . . .'

'Fire truck off, Mikey – as you people are so fond of saying. This is just asking for trouble. If Plimpton turns up . . .'

'Then we'll deal with him,' said Mikey crisply. The lift doors closed and North disappeared from sight. 'But with luck, we'll be in and out before Plimpton even gets here.'

The doors to the right-hand lift opened. 'This one,' said Mikey, guiding him in, because once the door closed, John Costello wasn't going anywhere other than upwards.

She smiled at the operator. 'Thirty-third floor, please.'

The lift was both fast and smooth. As opposed to the cranky affairs at TPHQ which were neither. And had a mind of their own when it came to delivering passengers to their requested destinations.

'You're English?' said the operator, a grizzled old man with medal ribbons proudly displayed across his chest.

Mikey beamed at him. 'We are. And greatly enjoying our trip to your lovely country.'

She nudged Costello, who nodded.

The operator regarded the civilian-dressed John Costello suspiciously.

Mikey assumed an expression of great concern. 'How's your leg, Uncle Jake? Still giving you trouble?'

Mr Costello nodded bravely. 'It's nothing. But I shall be pleased to sit down.'

Mikey patted his arm, every inch the solicitous . . . niece?

283

Daughter? Nurse? Good-time girl? They really should have worked this out before embarking on this jump. 'Not long now, Uncle.'

'No indeed,' said the lift operator. 'Our elevators travel at a speed of eight hundred feet per minute.'

'Goodness gracious,' said Mikey, taking care to look impressed. 'Are you taking us to the moon?'

The lift came to a smooth halt. 'And here we are, ma'am.'

He touched his cap as they exited the lift.

'What a nice man,' said Mikey, as the lift doors closed and it shot off somewhere else. Still at eight hundred feet per minute, presumably.

'He just wanted a nice tip,' said John Costello.

'Never mix your lights with your darks,' said Mikey vaguely, scanning the list of rooms. 'Three-three-two-seven and three-three-two-eight – this way. Come on.'

North was waiting for them and the three of them followed the corridor.

Hansen's voice sounded in their ears. 'Plimpton and two others have exited the pod. Assuming they're heading your way.'

'Are you able to intercept?'

'Negative. People everywhere. Do we follow?'

North paused for thought. It was tempting . . . but if they all missed each other . . . or had to make a quick getaway . . . No. This was not a time for improvisation.

'No. Stick to the original plan. You should have eyes on Tesla any moment now. He is your priority.'

'Copy that.'

North turned to John Costello. 'We have to move quickly. We might have only minutes.'

Silence was all around them. The only sign of life was a maid in a smart blue and white uniform taking a pile of towels from her trolley and disappearing into one of the rooms at the far end of the hall. Otherwise, the corridor was deserted. No sound of voices or opening and closing doors. Instinctively, they trod quietly although there was no need. The thick, heavily patterned carpet deadened all sound. The geometrically patterned wallpaper distracted the eye. There were no windows, and light was provided by soft uplighters near the ceiling and by tall table lamps on narrow console tables.

'It's like a well-carpeted morgue,' whispered Mikey.

Room 3327 was directly ahead of them at the end of the corridor with 3328 alongside. North stepped aside to make room. 'Off you go, Mr Costello.'

Other than the maid, they hadn't met a soul and nor did they expect to now, but nevertheless North and Mikey arranged themselves in such a way as to conceal him from any chance-met guest. They stared at the wall, apparently enraptured by the pattern on the wallpaper as he went about his work.

Time passed. Rather too quickly for their taste.

'How's it going?' whispered Mikey.

There was no reply.

They turned to see the door standing ajar and no sign of John Costello anywhere.

'Smart arse,' muttered North, stepping inside.

Mikey halted on the threshold. 'Dear God, what a hideous room.'

It was indeed a hideous room. Very hot and stuffy, with a claustrophobic flower-print wallpaper in varying shades of

285

brown. The carpet was covered in brown swirls. The paintwork continued the theme, being a shiny conker brown.

This room appeared to be Tesla's living quarters. There was a neatly made bed with a hefty wardrobe standing opposite. A matching bedside cabinet – 'Nightstand,' said Mikey – was positioned to the left of the bed. All the furniture was made of dark, heavy wood. An armchair had been placed by the window, which offered a magnificent view of the New York skyline.

Mikey looked around. Given that Tesla had been living here for ten years, there was a sad lack of personal possessions but, on the plus side, everything was neat and tidy and in its place. A pleasant smell of polish hung in the air.

'Good,' said North. 'The maid's been. We should be undisturbed.'

'Until Henry Plimpton turns up,' said John Costello, gloomily, looking over her shoulder.

'Then get on with it, please, Mr Costello.'

She opened her com. 'Hansen, we're in.'

'Copy that.'

John Costello was already looking around. 'This is his bedroom. The safe must be in the other room next door.'

'Connecting door,' said Mikey, opening it carefully and peering through. 'We don't have to break in again. Let's go.'

In addition to the same depressing colour scheme, the second room contained a desk, two filing cabinets, a lot of shelving, cupboards and, in the corner, a substantial-looking metal safe.

'Wow,' said Mikey. 'Look at the size of that thing.'

'I hear that all the time, said Costello, 'but in this instance, I'm assuming you mean the safe.'

He knelt, pulled out a leather roll secured with string, laid it on the carpet in front of him and began, carefully, to unroll it. 'Can you two push off and give me a bit of peace? I need silence.'

'Not a chance,' said North.

'The windows won't open and the outer door's locked,' said Mikey, who had checked. Always being aware of your exits was the number one rule for illegal Time travellers. And quite often for legal ones, as well. 'He's not going anywhere. Relax.'

'Done,' called Costello.

'Told you he was good,' Mikey said, smirking, as the heavy door swung open.

The safe was stuffed full of files, folders and loose papers. Alone, on the top shelf, rested an A4 notebook with a soft black cover.

'Eureka,' said North.

'Bingo,' said Mikey.

Costello began to stuff papers into his briefcase, his hands shaking with nervousness.

'Make sure you get the notebook,' instructed North.

He scowled. 'Already done. Get off my back.'

'Now what?' said Mikey.

'We'll have to destroy them. Can't take them back with us.'

'Where?'

'In the park somewhere. Shouldn't be a problem – there's plenty of cover there.'

Mikey frowned. 'Aren't you at least going to copy them? Take photos? We can't destroy them completely, surely?'

'Yes, we can. And before you start, you know why not. These papers go missing after Tesla's death and have to stay that way. Go and check the other room. Make sure there isn't anything in the bedside cabinet or dressing table.'

Mikey scowled at her but disappeared.

'Nearly finished,' said Costello, reaching for the last of the papers in the safe.

North turned back to him and allowed herself a brief moment of satisfaction. Quick and easy and without a hitch. This was how all missions should be.

At exactly that moment there was the sound of a key in the lock. Before anyone had time to move, the door swung open to reveal a respectably hatted and coated figure. For one heart-stopping moment, North thought Nikola Tesla had returned and caught them. In a second heart-stopping moment, she realised it was Henry Plimpton. Short, plump, bespectacled, neatly dressed, mass-murdering Henry Plimpton.

He smiled pleasantly.

'We meet again, Jake. I always knew we would one day.' He held out his hand. 'And how kind of you to have everything ready for me. I'll take that, if I may.'

25

This was not Lt North's first meeting with Henry Plimpton. She and Major Ellis had been Team 236's supervising officers during their training. She'd monitored the sad shambles that had been 236's first proper assignment – when Henry Plimpton had pulled the wool over all their eyes. Like every other officer, Lt North had vowed revenge. She was not about to let Tesla's papers go. Not without a fight, anyway. Except, of course, her hands were tied. This was America and their instructions were to keep a low profile. Quick and quiet. Don't get caught. Hay had been very explicit on the subject of not getting caught.

That still didn't mean Plimpton was getting the papers.

She said sharply, 'Don't move, Costello. Stay exactly where you are.'

Costello remained motionless – more through terror, she suspected, than obedience to her instructions.

Henry Plimpton smiled. 'You should know better than to listen to the Time Police, Jake. At least I'm assuming she's Time Police. A face like a slapped arse, so who else would she be? Hand over the papers and I'll consider letting you live. And before our heroic Time Police officer contemplates anything silly – several of my colleagues are out in the hallway and others are scattered at strategic points around the building. Oh – and, of course, I'm armed.'

A small, silenced weapon miraculously appeared in his hand, seemingly from nowhere. Or so it seemed to North.

Henry Plimpton's smile took on a taunting quality. 'And you won't be, officer, will you? Armed, I mean. And just to rub your nose in it, I don't care if I kill a whole truckload of contemporaries. I don't care if I start a major political and temporal incident. I don't care if I bring this building down around your ears. Let me assure you – the phrase *massive loss of life* means nothing to me. It used to mean nothing to the Time Police, either, but you've rather had your claws clipped these days, haven't you? Definitely not the organisation you used to be.'

He looked down at John Costello again. 'Last chance, Jake. Hand over the papers.'

For a long time, nothing happened. There was complete silence in this overheated, over-patterned room and then, very slowly and deliberately, John Costello looked at the papers in his hand, then placed them inside the briefcase and fastened the leather straps, carefully making sure all was secure. He seemed completely engrossed in what he was doing. The silence went on and on.

North was already formulating plans to overpower Henry Plimpton and retrieve the briefcase. An action she did not expect to survive. Her best hope was that Meiklejohn would have the sense to stay quiet and out of the way in the other room. Meiklejohn could alert Team 235 and pass the problem on to them while North and John Costello watched their own blood seep slowly into the carpet. Unless, of course, Kohl and

Hansen were no longer in the picture. Nor Rossi. Given the ruthlessness of Henry Plimpton, it was perfectly possible that 235 were already dead. She might be the only officer remaining, and to let Henry Plimpton get away without doing everything in her power to prevent it was unthinkable to North. It was her duty to prevent his escape and to always do one's duty was the code of the Norths.

Unconsciously, she tensed her muscles. Should she go for Henry Plimpton or the briefcase? Plimpton, obviously. At this moment, Costello still retained possession of the briefcase. Without North, the chances of Meiklejohn somehow getting him and it out of the hotel were worse than zero, but perhaps they could somehow barricade themselves in the other room. If they were still alive, what were the chances 235 could get here in time? Again, worse than zero. Perhaps she should allow Costello to hand over the case and trust that 235 were still alive and could somehow intercept Plimpton as he attempted to return to his pod. She, Meiklejohn and Costello would be dead but, with luck, the mission could still succeed.

It was not to be. Other than Hunters, very few Time Police officers work alone. For them, teamwork was always the way forwards. Sadly, John Costello was not part of the team. He had never worked with North. Barely knew her, in fact. Had certainly never heard of the code of the Norths.

He began to offer up the briefcase.

'Don't you dare,' warned North.

Plimpton reached out. 'Give it to me, Jake, or I'll shoot you both and take it anyway. In fact . . .'

He raised the gun and aimed it at Costello.

North tensed, ready to move.

'No,' shouted Costello. 'Here. You can have it. No need to shoot anyone. Least of all me.'

Kneeling up, he cautiously handed the briefcase to Plimpton, who tucked it carefully under one arm, politely said thank you, and shot him anyway. North, who had been expecting something like this, threw herself to the floor. The shot took John Costello in the shoulder. As he toppled slowly on to his side, Henry Plimpton disappeared out of the door, slamming it shut behind him.

Mikey raced back into the room. She threw herself to her knees, gently turned Costello on to his back and began to unbutton his clothing. 'Jake? Can you hear me? Jakey – don't die.'

Pulling off her beret, she folded it into a pad and stuffed it under his shirt.

North was already heading for the same door through which Henry Plimpton had escaped. Costello reached up painfully and grabbed her ankle.

She pulled free, but gently. 'He's got the papers.'

'No, he hasn't.'

'I saw you put them in the briefcase.'

'Yeah, you did. But you didn't see this, did you?'

Awkwardly, he reached inside his coat, partially revealing the black notebook concealed beneath. 'We can't hang around here. Any moment now he's going to discover he hasn't got the really important stuff.'

'Mr Costello,' said North, taking his good arm and, with Mikey, carefully helping him up, 'I personally will see to it that your resettlement grant is a generous one.'

'Jolly good,' said Costello faintly, swaying in a non-existent breeze.

'Can you walk?'

'I have to.'

North arranged his scarf to hide the bullet hole. They straightened his coat, handed him his hat, took an arm each, and set off down the still-silent hall, heading back towards the bank of lifts. There was no sign of Plimpton and his men anywhere, although how long that could be expected to last . . . Plimpton would surely seize the first opportunity to inspect the papers and realise the notebook was missing.

'Remember,' said North, pressing the call lift button, 'old and frail.'

'No problems there,' grunted John Costello.

'There's another lift coming up,' said Mikey, watching the floor indicator. 'What if it's Plimpton coming back already?'

One lift was climbing towards them. The other – the one they'd summoned – was descending. Which would arrive first? North looked over her shoulder for somewhere to hide. Mikey was repeatedly stabbing the button.

'That won't make it come any faster,' said North in exasperation.

The descending lift arrived and the doors pinged open. 'Want to bet?' said Mikey, smugly.

They stepped inside just as the second lift arrived. Their doors closed as the other doors opened. North released the breath she hadn't realised she'd been holding.

Eight hundred feet a minute didn't seem anything like fast enough.

Mikey patted Costello's arm. 'How are you feeling, Uncle Jake?'

'Very good. Very good, thank you.'

North was addressing the elevator operator. 'Sir, can you tell me where the entrance to the subway is situated, please?'

'From the ground floor, out of the elevator and turn left, ma'am. Straight ahead of you and then follow the signs. You can't miss it.'

'Thank you.'

The lift doors pinged open and they turned right into the now very crowded and noisy lobby. An air of busyness prevailed. People moved hither and thither, registering, checking out, greeting friends . . . Bellboys were manoeuvring trollies piled high with luggage.

'Wait,' said John Costello. 'He said left.'

'Neat,' said Mikey. 'The first thing Plimpton will do is check the room and find neither we nor the papers are there. He might already be on his way back down again. We can't outrun him. With luck, he'll question the operators and head off towards the subway.'

'Over here,' said North. Blessing the discreet lighting, she nudged them behind one of the pillars. They found John Costello a seat and he sank down with a sigh of relief. Mikey leaned over him and carefully tucked in a tiny corner of blood-stained scarf.

North had opened her com. 'Hansen – can you hear me?'

'Loud and clear. You all right, ma'am?'

'Plimpton has the papers. He will certainly return to his pod at some point. I want those papers back. And don't forget to keep a watch on Tesla. We're on our way back. Costello is wounded but walking.'

'Do you require assistance?'

'Not at the moment. Retrieving the briefcase is your priority.

We have the notebook but the papers are in Plimpton's possession. Keep your coms open.'

North's speculations as to Plimpton's next move had been spot on. Another lift door pinged open. Henry Plimpton stepped out, followed by two men, each with their hands in their pockets. They stood still and surveyed the crowded lobby, taking their time. Partially concealed behind the pillar, North, Costello and Mikey remained absolutely still.

They watched their former lift operator step out of the lift and point to the left. Henry Plimpton nodded politely and the three men set off towards the subway, to be swallowed up in the crowd.

'We go the other way,' said North. 'All right, Mr Costello?'

Costello nodded. 'Not the first time that bastard's shot me. Different shoulder but just as painful.'

The air outside was bitingly cold. An icy wind had sprung up. Great grey clouds swirled overhead. The sun had completely disappeared.

'Don't like the look of this,' said Mikey. 'They got a lot more snow in these days.'

They set off towards Bryant Park. The wind blew directly into their faces. John Costello walked slowly but quite strongly.

'We need to destroy this notebook,' said North. 'Soon as possible. We can't run the risk of Plimpton finding us and getting his hands on it.'

'Down there,' said Mikey, indicating a gap between two enormously tall buildings. 'There's an alleyway.'

They veered off to find themselves hemmed in by damp, dirty brickwork. As is frequently the case, the backs of the buildings were nowhere near as smart as their fronts. Only a very thin strip of sky was visible and that a long way above them. Rusting metal fire escapes zigzagged up and down the walls. The wind seemed even stronger in this narrow space and cut through them all like a knife. Various bits of garbage swirled around their feet and sheets of newspaper blew in circles on the wind.

'Here,' said Mikey, 'behind these dustbins.'

'Trash cans,' said Costello.

'That's my boy,' said Mikey, and they grinned at each other.

They eased him into a doorway between the wall and the dustbins, suddenly out of the wind. 'You start tearing up the notebook,' said Mikey. 'I'll be back in a minute.'

'Where are you going?' said North, suspiciously.

'Do you smoke?'

'Of course not.'

'Neither do I, so I don't have any matches. Do you?'

'I swear, Meiklejohn, one day I'll swing for you.'

'I look forward to it,' said Mikey and disappeared.

Instructing John Costello to keep watch, North began to tear pages out of the notebook and stuffed them into her pocket to stop them blowing away in the wind.

Mikey appeared, red-cheeked and windswept, rattling an old-fashioned box of matches.

'Let's get this done,' said North. 'Before we all freeze to death.'

'Shit,' said Mikey, opening the box.

'What?'

'There's only three matches. We'll have to make every one count.'

Regardless of their clothing, she and North knelt on the damp and dirty paving, trying to build a small heap of scrunched-up papers.

'It's paper,' said North. 'It should burn easily enough.'

'If we can strike a match in all this wind.'

Cupping her hands, North struck a match. The flame flared briefly, steadied and then began to burn. Carefully, she applied it to a corner. Mikey picked up another crumpled ball, and held that to the flame as well.

A sudden, savage gust of wind came out of nowhere and the flame went out. The paper glowed briefly and then turned black.

'Shit,' said North. 'Where's Maxwell when you need her? That woman could set fire to snow.' Very carefully, she struck another match.

'Try the less bloodied sheets first,' urged Mikey.

This was more successful. One page began to burn. Then another. Then another, slowly uncurling as it blazed.

'Good,' said North. 'More. Faster.'

Mikey unscrumpled a sheet, carefully holding a corner to catch the flame. The wind gusted again and the tiny flame flickered wildly.

'Don't let the fire go out,' said North. 'We've only one match left.'

She pulled open her coat and held it wide in an effort to shield the fragile flames from the wind. It worked. The flames took hold, yellow and blue. The pages curled, blackened and then blazed.

'This is working,' said Mikey.

'Shit,' said John Costello, still leaning against the wall.

Their luck had run out. Henry Plimpton appeared at the entrance and began to stride down the alleyway.

'Stay out of sight,' said John Costello, pushing himself away from the wall. 'Make sure he doesn't see you. Good luck.'

He edged carefully around the trash cans and, without any attempt at concealment, began to run down the alleyway.

Mikey made a grab for him, as if to prevent him somehow, but she was too late. He managed to run perhaps six or seven yards before a single shot rang out, loud in this enclosed space. He lurched but continued to stagger onwards. Another shot and John Costello dropped like a stone, rolled over once and lay very still.

North shoved Mikey even further back behind the bins. Mikey fell on her bottom – out of sight – while North frantically ripped the last pages out of the notebook. The flames blazed higher. Black paper curled and blew through the air.

'Put it out,' hissed Mikey. 'He'll see the flames.' She shoved the last pages into her pocket as North began to stamp on the burning pages, grinding the paper into ashes, ensuring none of it could possibly be read afterwards. Together they scuffled the remains into nothing.

The running footsteps drew closer. Mikey tugged at North's coat. 'Get down.'

North crouched, just as Henry Plimpton, leading two other men, ran past at full pelt. Already in the distance she could hear shouts and possibly a police bell. The shots had not gone unreported.

Henry Plimpton paused over John Costello's body. The two men with him rummaged in Costello's pockets, yanked open his coat, even pulled off his hat in case the notebook was hidden there. Finding nothing, they dropped the body back on to the greasy stones in disgust.

Henry Plimpton peered up and down the alleyway. If he took only a few paces to his right, he would see them, easy prey, trapped between the trash cans and the wall. He remained perfectly still, peering about him. Mikey knew he knew they were here somewhere.

The bells were drawing closer. A small group of people had gathered at the entrance, shouting and pointing. One of Plimpton's men raised his gun and fired over their heads. They scattered. The other man shouted something urgently, then the three of them wheeled about and continued on down the alleyway. Turning a corner, they passed out of sight.

'Come on,' said North, squeezing out from behind the trash cans. 'This place will be crawling in a moment. We mustn't be caught here.'

Mikey was crying.

North pulled her out from behind the trash cans, but not ungently, and they ran towards John Costello.

His eyes flickered open as Mikey crouched at his side. 'You have to go.' He coughed red blood. 'Leave . . . me.' His eyes were clouding over. 'Tell Jane . . . sorry . . . Tried to save . . .'

Mikey clutched at him urgently. 'Jakey, listen. I've had a brilliant idea about artificial tea. I'm certain I can make it work. You're going to be stinking rich. All you have to do is just hold on. Please.'

John Costello, sometimes James Costello, occasionally Jake Costello, currently Prisoner Costello, closed his eyes.

North hesitated for a moment and then said quietly, 'He's gone, Mikey. I'm sorry.'

Mikey made no response.

North seized Mikey's arm, hauled her to her feet and they

walked quickly down the alleyway. The sound of squealing tyres was very close.

'He gave his life for a worthy cause,' said North, as they turned into the street. 'Don't look behind you.'

'Yeah,' said Mikey bitterly. 'The Time Police are telling me how to escape the forces of law and order.'

'Just keep walking.'

Mikey had discovered the last pages still in her pocket. She leafed through them as they walked, staring from one page to another and then back again. Suddenly, she stopped. Clenching the pages in her fist, she thrust them at North and laughed, bitterly. 'Jake gave his life for nothing. Look.'

North stared. 'What am I looking at?'

Mikey held out the crumpled pages. 'It's gibberish. Rubbish. Useless. Everything we've done today has been a complete waste of time and Jake's dead because of it. I led him to his death.'

North took the sheets off her and urged her onwards, scanning them as they walked. 'This is just . . .'

'Notes on his beloved pigeons? His lunch that day? Random words? Yeah. And thanks to me, Jake's dead.'

North shook her head. 'I don't agree. You weren't to know. You were right about everything else. And John Costello made his own choice. He did his duty. Now we must do ours.'

'He died for nothing and far from home.'

'As will we all one day. Keep walking. I want to be back in the pod before dimout begins.'

Heads down, they battled their way through the crowds. Despite the icy weather, the streets had become busier as the day had progressed. The traffic noise was such they could hardly hear themselves speak.

'Crowds are good,' said North. 'Plimpton will have to be right on top of us to find us.'

'Works both ways,' said Mikey. 'We won't see him until we fall over him.'

North quickened her pace until they were nearly running. 'I'm betting he's not looking for us. He'll cut his losses and go straight for Tesla.'

Mikey shivered.

North had opened her com. 'Two-Three-Five – anything?'

Hansen answered, 'Not yet. I have eyes on Tesla at this moment. He's feeding the pigeons. Rossi's sitting at the other end of the bench reading a newspaper he found. I'm standing on the corner opposite and Socko's keeping an eye on their pod. You?'

'The notebook's destroyed. Plimpton has the files and papers. We're on our way back.' She paused. 'Costello didn't make it.'

There was silence and then he said, 'That's a shame.'

'Yes. Stay sharp.'

'Copy that.'

Around twenty minutes later, windswept and shivering, North and Mikey entered Bryant Park.

'I can see you,' reported Socko.

'Any sign of Plimpton?'

'I'm watching his pod on the grounds he has to turn up here sooner or later, but no sign yet.'

'Stay alert,' whispered North. 'He'll be here somewhere waiting for us as we're waiting for him. We all know what to do.'

She and Mikey picked their way cautiously along narrow

paths thick with frozen, fallen leaves, pushing aside the occasional overhanging branch. The bustle of the city had faded away again. There was just their own hurried breathing and muffled footsteps.

Until . . .

Two thick holly bushes parted as Henry Plimpton and his two men stepped out from between them.

Without hesitation, North jumped sideways into a clump of mountain laurels, dragging Mikey with her and shouting, 'Now.'

Before Plimpton and his men could raise their weapons, Hansen and Socko crashed out of the bushes. None of this sissy 'sticking to the paths' for the Time Police. They crashed, roaring, out of the undergrowth, batons raised, leaving no one in any doubt as to their hostile intentions. Everyone was now very clear that the Time Police were here and that said Time Police were cold, pissed off and very anxious to return to a more civilised time and place as soon as possible, and anyone foolish enough to get in their way would very soon regret it.

One of Plimpton's minions wheeled towards Hansen, his gun raised, but this optimism proved misplaced as Hansen's baton smashed across his wrist. They all heard a bone crack and his gun flew across the path. Baton swinging, Hansen waded in.

Socko hadn't bothered with such niminy-piminy tactics, body-charging his unfortunate target, who staggered sideways and smacked his head against a tree. He fell to his knees, and Mikey, rearing up from the greenery like a small, cold Fury, kicked the gun out of harm's way and then, finding this had been insufficient to alleviate her feelings over Jake's death, kicked the gun's former owner as well. Several times.

Hansen, attempting to pull her off, tripped over a fallen branch and fell across both Mikey and her victim. Or, as he more accurately phrased it in his report later, the former illegal and the current illegal.

Not to be left out, North leaped from the laurels, fully intending to apprehend both Henry Plimpton and the briefcase. Snatching up Hansen's baton, she bore down on her target. Alas, she was hindered by the number of people currently rolling about on the ground in an indistinguishable heap. Henry Plimpton, obviously disinclined to hang around for something as trivial as rescuing his own people, took to his heels. Minion One somehow tore himself free and staggered wonkily after him.

Unable to see any way around the scrum on the ground, North scrambled straight over the top of them, which took longer than she would have liked, and when she eventually pulled herself free, their target was almost at his pod. And there were people around. North cursed the dedication of New Yorkers hardy enough to visit the park and the library in this weather.

Very, very bad language rent the air as, slowly, everyone sorted themselves out. Hansen was first on his feet, followed by Socko, both of them looking around for their target.

'Let them go,' said North, handing Hansen back his baton, and for a while there was only the sound of panting as everyone got their breath back. She looked around. Those bystanders who had been standing by were now backing away before taking to their heels. It was surely only a matter of time until the police – sorry, the cops – showed up. Again.

'Everyone all right?' enquired North as Socko inspected a cut on his knuckles.

Astonishingly, everyone was.

'Except for him,' said Mikey, aiming another kick at the dazed minion still on the ground.

Socko hauled him to his feet. 'What do you want me to do with this one, ma'am?'

North had no chance to reply. The man, obviously not as groggy as everyone had supposed, tore himself from Socko's grasp and set off down the path at a very stumbling run. They watched him slip on the leaves, very nearly fall, right himself and stagger off again. In a different direction this time.

North cursed. Truly, the Fates were against them this afternoon.

'It's too late,' she said. 'We've no chance at those papers now and my instinct is to get out of here before the police realise we're the ones responsible for their busy afternoon. Including the body in the alleyway. Still, to keep things tidy, I think we'd better make sure Henry Plimpton does actually depart the scene.'

They followed the path under the trees and out the other side. Henry Plimpton's pod – the same one he'd used in Lacey Gardens – was parked in a dark corner, looking for all the world like a groundskeeper's hut. By now, the bright sunshine had completely disappeared and already it was growing dark. They could catch glimpses of the New York Public Library lights through the trees. A few snowflakes drifted down. Mikey shivered again.

They watched the illegal stumble towards his pod. The door was firmly shut. And remained so.

He hammered on the door. 'Hey. It's me – Webb. They've gone. Let me in.'

Nothing happened. The door remained closed.

He thumped again. 'Hey. Hey. Let me in.'

Hansen frowned. 'I don't think they're going to open the door.'

'Is it a punishment?' said Socko, puzzled. 'Could they think he's grassed them up? We didn't have him long enough for him to say anything important.'

'No,' said North, slowly. 'I think this is what Henry Plimpton does. In this way, he's not burdened with an injured man. He doesn't have to halt jump preparations and risk his pod being disabled and captured. For all he knows, we could be lining up an EMP at this very moment. And it sends a message – he doesn't wait for stragglers. And that he doesn't like failure.'

'What a bastard,' said Hansen.

'He is,' said Mikey, who had met Henry Plimpton.

'Poor sod,' said Rossi, watching Webb pound on the door. 'No identity, no papers, no money . . .'

'They'll arrest him as a spy,' said North. 'His future is not bright. We'll pick him up after Plimpton's gone. He might be able to tell us something.'

'Never mind that, he needs to step back,' said Socko, suddenly. 'He's too close.'

Whether the illegal was too dazed or too panicked to work this out, they never knew. He was still kicking at the door, screaming to be let in.

'Hey,' shouted Hansen, stepping out on to the path. 'You. Webb. Whatever your name is. You're too close. You need to get out of the way, mate.' He went to run towards the illegal, who was now clawing at the door with both hands, his voice rising to a scream.

'Don't leave me. You can't leave me here. I've got a family. Open this door. Open the door, for God's sake. You can't lea—'

The pod blinked out of existence.

There was a moment of whirling man. A turmoil of arms and legs. All distorted and all in the wrong place. Something red and wet arced through the air, spraying fresh blood across the frosty ground, shockingly bright in this dull landscape.

Hansen froze in mid-stride, staring in disbelief.

Socko swallowed. 'Poor sod.' He looked down at Mikey. 'You all right, kid?'

Mikey nodded numbly, her eyes huge and shocked. Something similar had once nearly happened to her.

'Hey,' he said, not unkindly. 'Try not to dwell on it. Think ahead – not back.'

Mikey nodded again and took a few paces to the side, wiping her eyes.

North was already calling up Rossi, who reported Tesla was still communing with the pigeons.

'Stay there. We'll find you.'

'Copy that.' He shut down his com.

Hansen nodded at what was left of Webb. 'Should we . . . ?'

'I don't think so,' said North. 'We've done rather a lot to bring ourselves to the attention of New York's finest. The last thing we need is to be caught with unidentified body parts. And it's not as if we can do anything for him.'

She pointed down the path. 'This way, I think.'

They began to retrace their steps, striding briskly. Until North stopped dead. No one concertinaed into anyone else – because they weren't St Mary's, after all – but there was a certain amount of confusion.

'I don't believe it,' said North, staring wildly around. 'Where's Meiklejohn?'

They looked around. No Meiklejohn. Anywhere.

'I don't believe it, either,' said Hansen, also staring around. 'Where the fire-trucking hell could she possibly have gone?'

'Almost anywhere, I should think,' said Socko. 'I mean – look at this place, you could hide an army in here. Has she finally legged it, do you think? I always said she would one day.'

'She might be hurt,' said Rossi, looking around.

Socko shook his head. 'Only just now she was kicking the living shit out of that poor bloke. Such a little thing, too.'

'Was he? He looked pretty big to me.'

'I meant her, you dipshit. *She's* such a little thing.'

North regarded them in exasperation. 'This team gets more like Two-Three-Six every day.'

Which shut them all up.

Having a fair idea of where Meiklejohn would be, she ignored their indignation at this grossly unfair comparison with that bunch of weirdos, and set off back down the path. Around them, finally, soft snow began to fall.

Mikey was exactly where North had suspected she would be. Ignoring orders to keep interactions with contemporaries to a minimum, she was sitting next to Nikola Tesla. North sighed. The last thing an already battered Timeline needed was these two swapping what, no doubt, they would both regard as Brilliant Ideas.

Rossi, unsure whether he should intervene or not, was hovering at the other end of the bench. 'Ma'am?'

'It's all right,' said North quietly, as they approached. 'He's tired and poor and at the end of his life. In only a few days he'll be dead.'

Mikey had parked herself alongside. 'It's Mr Tesla, isn't it?'

Snow was falling on his hat and shoulders but his tired old face lit up. 'It is.'

Mikey pulled off her glove and held out her hand. 'I'm so happy to have this opportunity to shake your hand, sir, and to congratulate you on your many magnificent achievements.'

'Well, thank you, my dear.'

They shook hands.

'You will go down in history as a great man.'

He smiled, gently. 'Will I? You are too kind.'

And then his gaze sharpened. A little of the old Tesla, perhaps. He blinked at her, squinting through the gently falling snow.

Mikey continued to hold his hand, saying softly, 'You may be sure of it, sir.'

They held each other's gaze for a few seconds and then he said, 'I think you are a very unusual young woman.'

North intervened. 'Unusual enough to ask you to remain in your room for the next few days, sir.'

He looked up at her.

'You're English. Both of you.'

North nodded. 'I am Lady Celia North. My mother works for His Majesty's government. We are here to keep you safe, sir. These gentlemen will escort you back to your hotel. For your own safety, please remain there for the next few days. If you must leave your room, then try to have someone with you at all times. Please be very careful to whom you answer the door.'

'But why? Why should I do that?'

A combination of cold and urgency sharpened North's voice.

'Sir, I represent an organisation dedicated to ensuring Time flows as it should. Your work has brought you to the attention of someone who has other ideas. For your own safety, please do not leave the hotel.'

He struggled to his feet, suddenly agitated. 'My papers.'

'Are safe, sir, and will be returned to you when all danger is passed.'

'But . . .'

'Please, sir – your safety is paramount. The British and American governments . . . but I mustn't say any more.'

'Oh.' Suddenly there was hope in his eyes. 'Is it possible that finally . . . ?'

'It is very possible, sir. You understand I cannot say more at this stage.'

'No, no, I understand. This is . . . At last . . . I must return at once.'

'Thank you, sir. These gentlemen will escort you home. And don't worry about your papers. They're perfectly safe and will be returned to you for full discussion. Sometime next week, perhaps. Shall we say – seven days from today?'

Rossi, who had been looking around, interrupted. 'Er . . . Lady Celia, ma'am . . .'

'Yes. We must be going. Good day, sir.'

He raised his hat. 'I . . . Good day. I am so happy to have met you.'

'And I you, sir. It's been an honour and a privilege.'

The last they saw of Nikola Tesla was a dark, muffled figure, slowly disappearing back into the snow with Hansen on one side and Socko on the other.

'That was kind,' said Mikey, watching them go. 'His last days will be filled with a happy glow of anticipation. Thanks to you.'

'Nonsense,' said North, sharply. 'I simply wanted to prevent him raising the alarm when he found his papers had been stolen.'

'Yeah, right,' said Mikey.

They made their way back to the pod. Rossi seated himself and checked over the console. 'Not that there was any doubt, but I can confirm Plimpton's pod signature has disappeared. He's definitely gone.'

'I wonder where he's gone to,' said Mikey.

'And when,' said Rossi.

'Don't know,' said North, grimly, 'but it will mean trouble for someone, I'm certain of that.'

26

Matthew's world had been plunged into darkness. All the lights had gone out – both internal and external. The compound, the gate, the mess hut. Night rushed in. The suddenness took him completely by surprise. Along with everyone else, presumably. For a very long moment, there was no movement of any kind. Shock, surprise, waiting for their eyes to become accustomed to the sudden darkness – whatever the reason why, no one moved.

And then the spell broke. Someone bumped into a chair which toppled over with a clatter. Someone else fell over the chair and cursed. There was pushing and shoving. A dish or a mug was knocked to the floor. The room was full of angry voices and panic was in the air.

Tucker's voice came out of the dark. 'Stand still. Stand still, all of you. Find a chair and sit down. Someone turn up that lantern.'

Matthew, finding himself nearest to the counter, turned up the wick. The lantern hissed as the flame rose higher.

Fisher made a move towards the other three lanterns stacked against the wall with the sand buckets.

'Leave them,' said Tucker, quickly. 'We've enough light to see each other. Save the fuel. We might need it later.'

'We're staying here, then?' demanded Fisher. His voice was truculent, edged with fear. 'Trapped?'

'With food, water, light and heat,' said Tucker. 'Yeah, I'm happy to be trapped here until morning. Given the alternative.'

'We could make a break for it. It's not that far to the pods. We've got lanterns, and if we all go at the same time – it can't get all of us.'

'We could,' said Tucker, calmly, 'and you're right, it might not get all of us, but trust me, if it gets anyone, it will be you if I have to hand you over myself. Now sit down and shut up.'

Fisher threw himself into a chair and folded his arms. Silence filled the hut. Matthew had no watch, but he was prepared to bet it was going to be a long, long night. Tucker was wise to hold them all inside. But for how long could he keep them here?

Having considered the situation, Matthew had made up his mind. Whatever Fisher and some of the others decided, Tucker was his best chance of survival, and with Tucker he would stick. Looking around, he reckoned Clore, Jim and probably Trip would as well. Which left Fisher, and two others. Three against five. And Tucker, Jim and Clore were armed.

From the point of view of a Time Police officer, this couldn't have worked out better. After a night spent in this dimly lit hut, jumping at every sound, constantly imagining the worst, these men would be desperate to get out of here. To jump as soon as possible. Never mind where to. Anywhere that wasn't here would do. Tucker would hold them together through the night but he'd be as happy to get away as the rest of them. They'd jump away. Matthew had no idea where or when they'd go, but for him, that was unimportant. At some point, there would be an opportunity for him to exploit and he could take it from there.

In the meantime, however, there was this night to get through. He'd been here for what – three or four hours? – and during that time, two men had disappeared. Almost certainly dead. And they hadn't been the first – at least another two had vanished an unknown number of days ago. No one knew who was responsible or how it had happened. Or if they did, they weren't saying.

He stared at the counter, absent-mindedly helping himself to another biscuit. Think about it for a moment: how likely was it that some strange supernatural monster stalked the night, vanishing people without a trace? If it had been any other location than this, his first thought – everyone's first thought – would be that one of them was responsible. It was only logical. Had the Roanoke legend derailed common sense? On the other hand, Plimpton's men had seemed unaware of the history of this place until Matthew had turned up this afternoon, which rather knocked that theory on the head. On top of that was the mystery of the continually opening gate. He'd seen it himself. Firmly closed and with the crossbar in place one minute – wide open the next. And every time the gate was opened, who knew what came through? A chilling thought. Was that where Otto had gone? And Andy? Swiftly and silently dragged out through the gate? And taken where? Into the dark forest that surrounded them? For what purpose? Had they still been alive when taken? What was going on here? After all, supernatural entities didn't usually go around knocking out generators. He shook himself. Speculation was all very well, but survival should be their first priority. He was certain it would be Tucker's.

Unfortunately, Matthew wasn't the only one doing some careful thinking. Fisher swivelled in his chair to look at him. 'What about the kid?'

'What about me?' squeaked Matthew, channelling harmless teenager as hard as he could. Not looking your age was a bugger when buying alcohol but it did have some advantages.

'You turn up,' said Fisher, 'and two men disappear.'

'He wasn't here when Li went missing,' said Tucker. 'Or Johnson. Leave him alone.'

'He says he wasn't,' said Fisher. 'But who knows who was hiding in the forests outside the compound?'

'Not me,' said Matthew.

'Well, you would say that, wouldn't you?'

Shadows clung to the corners of the room but Matthew could make out at least one man nodding. Shit – this wasn't looking good. Fisher didn't really suspect him – he was convinced of that – he was only looking for someone to blame. How reassuring to be able to pin these events on something non-supernatural. And Matthew was a complete stranger, too. Not even one of the team. Blame the kid. Push him outside to take his chances. Problem solved. Although not for Matthew, of course.

Fortunately, Tucker wasn't having any of that crap.

'Of course he'd say that. As would I. Along with everyone else in here with more than one brain cell. Jesus, Fisher, if you're looking for someone to blame, at least think it through first. Yeah – the kid's been living in the woods all this time. He spots an opportunity to take out Johnson – who was built like a brick shithouse, but never mind that inconvenient fact. He overcomes Johnson so completely that Johnson vanishes without trace. Encouraged by this, he comes back again and

314

has a go at Li. More success. In fact, so good is he at this that he manages to dispose of Andy and Otto at exactly the same time he's in here enjoying his supper.'

'Yeah,' said Fisher, in no way daunted by this. 'You're right. It must have been one of *you*.' He gestured towards Tucker, Clore and Jim. 'You were the only ones out there at the time.'

'Well, I know it wasn't me,' said Jim. 'And it wasn't Clore because he was with me.' He grinned at Tucker. 'That leaves you, boss.'

Tucker stretched. 'It does, doesn't it?' He laid a meaningful hand on his blaster, still on the table in front of him. 'Anyone want to have a go at me?'

The lantern hissed in the silence.

'You say that,' began Fisher, and then jumped a mile in his seat. 'Jesus. What's that?'

Everyone turned to look at the window.

'What's what?' said Jim, craning his neck.

Fisher made no response and when they turned back, he was pointing Jim's gun at Tucker.

'Bollocks,' said Jim, crestfallen. 'Sorry, boss.'

Tucker sighed. 'You're as big a moron as Fisher.'

'Yeah. Sorry.'

'Shut up,' said Fisher, getting to his feet. 'You . . .' He gestured at a man Matthew didn't know. 'Toss their weapons over the counter. Out of reach. I'm not hanging around any longer. I don't know what's going on here and I don't want to.'

'What about your pay?' said Tucker. 'You've six weeks money coming to you. Plus the completion bonus.'

'Don't care. I reckon none of us will live long enough to see it anyway.'

315

Jim looked at Fisher. 'In that case, boss, can I have his?'

Fisher ignored him, edging around the wall towards the door. 'Anyone with me?'

'Yeah,' said one man, scraping his chair across the floor as he stood up.

'If you want my advice, Judd,' began Tucker.

'He doesn't,' said Fisher.

Another man looked from Fisher to Tucker, undecided.

Matthew's eyes glowed golden in the dim light. Something which, had his mother been present, would have caused her to listen very carefully. 'Don't go out there. Any of you. Wait until morning.'

Judd turned his head. 'Why?'

Matthew blinked. 'Sorry? Why what?'

'Why did you say to wait till morning?'

'Did I?'

Judd stared at him. 'Why should we wait?'

Matthew drew a breath. 'This is not a good place. Not one person who has come here has thrived. Most haven't even survived. Think of all the people who have disappeared. No one knows why. I certainly don't. I don't have any more info than anyone else, and believe me, some big brains have worked on the Roanoke mystery for centuries. Unless one of you is going around quietly picking off his mates – and that's always a possibility – then there's something nasty out there and going out to face it alone, in the dark, is not a good idea.'

He paused after what was, for him, quite a long speech.

One man sat back down again.

'Good man,' said Tucker. He looked at Fisher. 'Just the two of you, then. Off you go. Clore, make sure we're secured as

316

soon as they leave. Be very aware, Fisher – once you and your mate are on the other side of that door, you're on your own. There is no way we're opening it to let you back in again.' He paused. 'No matter how loudly you scream.'

There was a very nasty silence. No one was in any doubt that Tucker meant every word of it.

Matthew sat quietly. If the two of them made it safely to the pods, then they'd take Jim's. The one Matthew had arrived in. The other wasn't fully functional yet. He and Clore between them could get it going – he hoped – but if Fisher took the last working pod, then there would be no quick getaway for everyone else. He hoped he didn't look as worried as he felt.

Fisher flourished his weapon. 'Hand over the key.'

Tucker simply laughed. 'I don't have it.'

'I know that. Trip does. Hand it over.'

'No,' said Trip.

'Do it,' said Tucker.

'What?'

'Just do it.'

Reluctantly, Trip pulled out a key ring.

Matthew had no doubt separate keyholders was another of Tucker's policies. Really, he was wasted here.

Trip scowled. 'What do you want it for?'

'To lock you in here, of course. Stop stalling and put it down on the table.'

Trip sighed very heavily and looked at Tucker, who nodded. Either he was happy to be locked in all night or there was a duplicate key stashed somewhere.

Fisher gestured to his would-be follower. 'Pick up the key and get to the door.'

Tucker turned cold eyes upon him. 'Make sure you lock that door the second you cross the threshold. Clore – I want that crossbar up soonest. Be aware, everyone, this door won't open again tonight.'

Matthew's respect for Tucker, already high, rose even further. Fisher's accomplice was looking worried and even Fisher himself looked as if he might be having second thoughts. If Tucker had tried to stop them, the already jumpy Fisher would have attempted to force his way out and people would have been hurt. Allowing anyone who wanted to leave to depart in peace was a smart move.

Clore stood up slowly. Fisher's gun pointed his way but Clore never even looked at it.

'OK,' he said. 'Here's how we're going to do this. I'm on the door. You two idiots line up. I'll whip the door open. You have two seconds to get out. I slam the door closed behind you. You take very good care to lock it and then you can push off to enjoy the last five or ten seconds of your life. Ready?'

'Um,' said Fisher's follower, visibly wavering.

'Too late,' said Clore, removing the crossbar. 'I'm on my feet now. On three . . .'

The man grabbed at Clore's arm. 'Wait.'

Clore looked over at Tucker, who remained motionless. Seconds ticked by. Tucker's face was set in stone. There was complete silence in the hut. Tucker and Fisher stared at each other like a couple of cats. Everyone waited to see what would happen next.

What happened next was that the lights came back on.

Everything happened at once. As, in Matthew's experience, it frequently did.

Fisher shoved Clore roughly out of the way and wrenched the door open, the second man hot on his heels. The third made a last-minute decision and leaped to his feet. His chair clattered backwards, getting in the way of Jim as he made a grab for him. Jim fell over the chair with a curse.

Clore struggled to get out from behind the door, kicking it out of his way as the two men raced through the open door.

'Let them go,' said Tucker. He looked at the third man, still hovering indecisively. 'All of them.'

Clore just managed to get out of the way as this man also disappeared through the door, shouting, 'Wait for me.'

As per his instructions, Clore pushed the door to and rammed home the crossbar. They heard the key turn in the lock – Fisher, presumably. The click was very loud in the silent night. For a moment there was only the sound of heavy breathing. Matthew reached out and turned down the lantern. The lights were back on but they might need the fuel later.

'Well,' said Jim, righting the chair. 'What was that all about? Who turned the lights on?'

'Same person who turned them off, I expect,' said Tucker.

Matthew looked around, saying, 'And then there were five,' quite forgetting he'd several times been informed that no one found that sort of remark particularly helpful.

The five of them looked at each other.

'What now?' asked Matthew.

'We wait for morning,' said Tucker.

27

The night was cold and clear. Overhead, the Milky Way stretched across the sky like the backbone of some giant sky god. One of the Titans. Uranus, perhaps. The air was still. And silent. No sounds from the forest. No nightly insects, no birds, no predators. No – that wasn't strictly true. Something stirred, predator-like, in the shadows.

'I've got pins and needles in my bum.'

'Shut up.'

'Just saying.'

'Shut up or I'll shoot you.'

Crouched behind the generators, two pairs of eyes watched the three shouting, running men slip, slither and trip their way towards the nearest pod. If they'd simply walked briskly from A to B, their journey would have been considerably easier and quicker, but their frantic efforts to check all around them, stay together, and get over the rough ground as quickly as possible without properly looking where they were going led to a number of falls. At one point, the leading man stumbled to his knees and the other two ran into him. Their curses echoed through the no longer silent night as they thrashed around, struggling to get to their feet again. No one helped anyone else. Each trampled the others. It was, literally, a case of every man for himself.

'Miracle they haven't all shot each other,' whispered Varma. 'What's going on there, do you think?'

The compound was bright with strong white light and the men's long black shadows jumped and jerked around their feet as they ran. Eventually, they reached the pods, running from one to the other.

'This one, this one,' shouted the first man.

'Are you sure?'

'Yes, yes, this one. Inside or I'll go without you.'

The threat was enough. All the men tumbled inside. The door closed behind them and a minute or two later, the pod disappeared.

'And there they go,' said Max, trying to flex her right leg. 'Straight into my waiting arms.'

'My trigger finger was twitching all the way,' said Varma.

Max shrugged. 'We had to let them go. If they hadn't got away, we wouldn't be here.' She turned to Varma. 'Always nice to close the circle, don't you think? Well, that's them safely out of the way. What shall we do now?'

'We wait,' said Varma, adding pointedly, 'In silence.'

Max managed this for nearly four seconds. 'Actually . . .'

'No.'

'But . . .'

'No.'

'But I ran the coordinates and it's *Roanoke*.'

'I don't care.'

'We could take a quick look around.'

'No.'

'Don't you want to find out what happened to the colonists?'

'No.'

'Just a very quick . . .'

'No.'

'Because no one ever . . .'

'No.'

'But . . .'

It's difficult to scream in a whisper but Varma made it look easy. 'Shit on a stick, Maxwell – which part of "no" do you not understand?'

'Is that a genuine question?'

'No.'

Crouching uncomfortably behind a generator, Max shifted her weight again. 'How long do we wait, then? Suppose Henry Plimpton turns up. Or anyone. And I very much hope that Matthew is around somewhere. Because if he isn't . . .'

She tailed away. If Matthew wasn't here, neither of them had any idea of his whereabouts. Or his whenabouts, either.

Varma drew back deeper into the shadows. 'Time Police reinforcements will arrive at any moment. We should wait.'

'And they might not. Suppose the people in the hut decide to investigate why the generators keep stopping and starting. Let's just go over there and arrest the lot of them. For me it'll be just like the old days.'

'Yeah,' said Varma. 'And we all know how they turned out.'

'Oh, come on. Remember when I was a bounty hunter?'

'*Everyone* remembers when you were a bounty hunter.'

Max said nothing. In the way that only she could.

Varma sighed heavily. 'Oh, for fire truck's sake. All right. Ready?'

Max fired up her not as big as she would have wished but still quite hefty blaster. 'Locked and loaded.'

'You do know no one says that in real life, don't you? A simple *ready* is sufficient.'

'I could make a really funny remark about Time Police killjoys.'

'And I could just shoot you dead and go home.'

'Oh, come on – where's the fun in that?'

'I would happily sacrifice fun for job satisfaction.'

'Are we going to argue all night or actually do something useful?'

Varma scowled. 'I'll go in first. You stay just outside and watch our rear. If things go badly, your priority is to get back to TPHQ and bring help.' She considered the nearest generator. 'And I think we'll have the lights off again.'

'Roger Dodger.'

Varma sighed. 'God give me strength.'

The lights went out again.

They zigzagged across the compound, approaching the mess hut from an oblique angle.

'Just a thought,' whispered Max as they dodged from hut to hut. 'We've spent the evening putting the fear of God into them, so they're hardly going to just let us in, are they?'

'The Time Police are always polite. We will knock and then proceed accordingly.'

'I just saw a curtain move at the window. They've seen us.'

'Good. That'll save a lot of tiresome explanations. Remember, there are another thirty of us scattered around the place watching their every move.'

They arrived at the hut and arranged themselves either side

of the door. Varma rapped a polite shave-and-a-haircut knock. 'Always go for a jaunty note. Lessens the tension.' She raised her voice. 'Good evening. This is the Time Police. May we come in, please?'

The voice was muffled but apologetic. 'No. Sorry.'

Max frowned. 'They're very polite for illegals. Much more polite than the Time Police.'

Varma sighed. This was turning out to be a very long day. She raised her voice. 'That was my polite-person warning. Now let me in or die horribly in the next five seconds. Your choice.'

'We can't.'

'Lost the key, have you?'

'Yes.'

There was a long pause and then Varma said, 'Seriously?'

'Yes. Our colleagues have locked us in. A friendly word of warning since you were so polite – there's something out there. Find yourself some cover and lock yourself in. We can discuss this in the morning over breakfast.'

Varma hefted her blaster. 'Listen, buster, I wasn't in a good mood when I got here. Open this fire-trucking door and let me come in.'

'By the hair on her chinny-chin-chin,' added Max, always helpful in a crisis. 'Or she'll huff and she'll puff and she'll blow your house down.'

There was silence from the hut.

Varma stepped back and turned to Max. 'Do you think they're having a calm and rational discussion about their next course of action?'

Max shook her head. 'No, I think they're arming themselves ready to blow us off the face of the planet.'

'Surely not.' Varma addressed the hut again. 'In ten seconds, we will blow this door off its hinges and annihilate every living thing inside. Just saying.'

'I told you – we can't.'

'Ten seconds. Seven. Four.'

'What happened to nine, eight, six and five?'

'I failed maths. Stand back in there.'

'Oh, let me,' begged Max. 'Please. Pleeeeeeeeease.'

Varma sighed. 'Go on, then. *Minimum* setting.'

Max raised her blaster and fired. Having achieved her life's ambition, she fell arse over tit.

'Oh dear. Did I forget to warn you about the recoil?' said Varma, grinning. 'So sorry.'

Max climbed to her feet and they flapped their arms, waiting for the smoke to disperse. To reveal . . .

'Wow,' said Max, awed. 'Did I do that?'

The door had gone. Half the wall had gone. Taking the window with it. And some of the roof. Flames licked around a hole large enough to imperil the hut's structural integrity. Lumps of burning wood covered a remarkably large area. Inside the hut, five men were on their backs.

Varma turned to Dr Maxwell. 'You were only supposed to blow the bloody door off.'

'Sorry.'

Cautiously, blasters whining, they stood outside the former doorway and peered in.

A small figure rolled out from under a table, coughed and then sat up.

Mother and son looked at each other for a moment and then

Matthew quavered, 'Please don't shoot me. I only wanted a job. I didn't mean any harm.'

There was a short silence during which enlightenment occurred.

'OK, sonny,' said Varma. 'Hands on your head. Is this all of you?'

'Yes. Please don't shoot us.'

'No one in any of the other huts?'

'No.'

'Weapons?'

'Not on us.'

'I'm coming in. Please don't any of you do anything stupid.'

'No, no. We won't.'

Slowly, Varma first and Max bringing up the rear, they moved inside the hut. Although *inside* was now a relative term. Four men were slowly picking themselves up and, without being told, went to stand against the far wall, their hands on their heads. Varma nodded approval. It was always good to work with professionals who knew the drill. A quick look around told her there was no one else in the hut.

'Max, stay outside and keep watch.'

'No,' said a big man, suddenly. 'You don't leave anyone alone out there. We need to stay together.'

Varma looked at Matthew, who nodded. 'There's something weird out there.'

'Yes,' said Varma. 'The Time Police. Six teams currently watching your every move.'

The big man spoke again. 'Worse than the Time Police.'

Varma scoffed. 'Unlikely.'

'No,' said Matthew. 'He might be right.'

'If you're referring to the lights going on and off – that was us. Nothing weird at all. Just us and the trip switch.'

Matthew shook his head. 'Is the gate open?'

Max peered across the compound. 'Yes. Is that significant?'

'Might be.'

One of the men spoke. 'Was it you? Opened the gate?'

Varma shook her head. 'No. Why?'

'Shit.'

Max and Varma exchanged glances and then moved to stand closer together. Both sides looked at each other.

'Let's get the formalities over with, shall we?' said Varma. 'I am Officer Varma and you are all under arrest for Time crimes later to be determined. And you are . . . ?'

'Tucker,' said Tucker. 'Clore,' he pointed to the big man. 'Jim and Trip. The kid's Adrian. Now, can we go?'

'*You're* Adrian Meiklejohn?' said Max, grinning.

'Yeah,' said Matthew.

Max turned to Varma. 'Big price on this one's head. There'll be a promotion for us.'

'Stop padding your part.'

Max grinned.

'Listen,' said Varma. 'The five of you are valuable to us. I'm empowered to offer you partial amnesty if you cooperate. It's not you we're after. What's in the locker over there?'

'Armoury,' said Tucker. 'But empty at the moment. Key on my belt.'

'Hand it over. Carefully.'

Tucker laid it on the table.

Varma gestured to Matthew. 'Bring it to me. Carefully.'

Matthew obeyed. 'Please – we have to leave. It's not good here.'

Tucker interrupted. 'How did you know we were here?'

'Your three friends were very helpful to us,' said Max, past master at making statements that were very nearly adjacent to the truth.

Tucker swore under his breath.

'Yeah – if you're going to spread rumours about the Time Police murdering civilians, don't be surprised if the Time Police actually turn up to check it out. We were investigating when your friends ran straight into our arms.'

Tucker swore again.

'Never mind,' said Varma, comfortingly. 'We've come to take you away from all this.'

'Just you two?'

'Our colleagues are awaiting the main event. When is Henry Plimpton due?'

Tucker shook his head. 'No idea. He doesn't visit often.'

'But the relief team's due any moment,' said Matthew helpfully.

'Shut up, kid,' said Tucker.

'Sorry.'

'Trust me,' said Varma, 'you are small fry. Our task is to remove you to safety before the shit hits the fan.'

Clore rallied. 'Suppose we won't go.'

Varma brought up her blaster. 'Then we'll shoot you, rejoin our colleagues, wait to see who turns up next and shoot them dead, too. I'm not hanging around over this one – the inter-departmental boxing championships are coming up and I aim to win. Again. So – cooperate or die. As long as I'm back for my training session tonight, I don't care which.'

Max dialled up her blaster. Maximum setting. The whining note increased. Otherwise – not a sound.

Tucker narrowed his eyes. 'What's in it for us?'

'Well, we already have Mr Costello in custody – yes, I can see that name rings a bell – and he's been offered and accepted amnesty. Depending on what you have to say, the same deal could be offered to you. You won't get away scot-free, of course – someone has to answer for the murder of Aaron and Helen Lockland – yes, we know all about that – but allowances will be made for cooperation. Not meaning to be unkind, but it's not you we really want.'

Still silence.

'Or,' said Max, muscling in on the role of Bad Cop, 'we could just disable your remaining pod and leave you here to take your chances. See – lots of options for you to consider, courtesy of the warm-hearted Time Police.'

Varma eyed her. 'Shut up or I'll shoot you, too.'

'As you can see,' said Max, 'my colleague is not her usual warm and fuzzy self. I'd accept her kind offer if I were you.'

There was even more silence in the hut. Max waited quietly, hoping her face gave no clue to her thoughts. Because she and Varma weren't going to get away with this. Four illegals against three angels. Not bad odds – especially since two of the three were heavily armed, but time might not be on their side. Matthew had told them the relief crew was on the way. Even Henry Plimpton himself might turn up at any moment. These men needed their minds making up for them.

Max turned, aimed, and blew out part of another wall.

Structural integrity failed and more of the roof came down around their ears.

'Will you stop doing that,' shouted Varma.

'Sorry. I didn't know that would happen.'

'That's because you've got it on the wrong setting, you moron.'

'Oh. Sorry. Shall I have another go? How about that other bit of wall there? Stand aside, Mr Tucker.'

Matthew was watching Tucker and his men. These were the more thoughtful members of Henry Plimpton's team. He had no idea what Tucker was thinking. Jim and Clore were staring at Tucker. Trip was staring at the floor. Time was ticking on. And now none of them had any defence at all against whatever might be out there. Perhaps they needed another nudge.

'Yes,' he said, suddenly. 'I'll submit to arrest.' He turned to his former colleagues. 'I'm sorry, but I just want to get out of here. I reckon my choice is between them . . .' he nodded at Officer Varma and her overenthusiastic assistant, 'or whatever's out there, and I choose *them*. And even if Mr P does turn up, I don't think he's going to be very happy with us when he finds out what's been happening here.'

'Good lad,' said Varma, because he was. Matthew, she hoped, was the pebble that heralded a landslide. Between the wrecked hut and Matthew breaking ranks, the four men had suddenly realised their position was not as strong as it had been a few minutes ago. And although they were plainly dubious, there was always the possibility the area was indeed crawling with Time Police officers.

'And,' said Matthew, abandoning his nervous-teenager persona, 'we really do need to get out of here.'

'Why?' said Varma, sharply.

Clore shifted his weight. 'We told you. There's something out there. We've lost two men tonight.'

Varma grinned. 'To say nothing of the other three we met earlier today. And their pod. Good luck accounting for all that to Henry Plimpton. Nice, sympathetic Mr Plimpton who handles failure so well. My suggestion is that we take you all into custody immediately and return to TPHQ. If you hang around until we take down Henry Plimpton, you'll all be lumped in with him and the charges will be considerably more severe. Murder, to begin with. Leave now and put some distance between him and you.'

Still with his hands on his head, Tucker turned to his colleagues. 'I'm inclined to accept the Time Police's kind offer.'

Reluctantly, the other three nodded.

The lights came on. For an instant everything was flooded in dazzling white light. And then went back out again.

Max's voice came out of the dark. 'This time, that wasn't us.'

The only sound in the dark hut was the hissing lantern. And breathing. Human breathing, Matthew hoped. Naturally, it was Jim who broke the silence.

'It's out there again.'

'No, it's not,' said Tucker, in exasperation. 'For God's sake, get a grip. It's only the ten-minute warning. The generator needs refuelling.'

'Well, I'm not doing it,' said Clore.

'No one is,' said Tucker calmly. 'We still have a few minutes. Easily long enough for us to get out of here. Although we shouldn't hang around.'

'Yeah,' said Jim, accusingly. 'Especially since we now have

no protection at all.' He surveyed the big hole where the door, two of the walls, the window and most of the roof had been.

'Yeah,' said Max, apologetically. 'My bad.'

'On the other hand,' said Tucker, looking Varma in the eye, 'we could always rely on all your colleagues out there to come and rescue us.'

'That might not be wise,' said Varma. 'We need to organise our getaway vehicle. What have you got? Ours is a little . . . small.'

'Ours doesn't work,' said Tucker.

There was a pause, during which a Time Police officer might have been rolling her eyes. 'Right, then,' she said, eventually. 'Everyone back to our pod.'

Max plucked at Varma's sleeve. 'Not sure we'll get them all in. Have you seen the size of those two on the end?'

'If I thought it would help, I'd leave you behind.'

Max shook her head. 'You're really not dealing well with this, are you? We need to get you back to TPHQ so you can start hitting people again. That'll cheer you up.' She turned to the others. 'I'm genuinely not sure we can get you all in. Some of you may have to lie on top of each other.'

'Let's get there first,' said Varma.

'There are two guns behind the counter,' said Tucker, suddenly. 'Give one to me. And Clore as well.'

'Hey,' said Jim.

'You lost yours,' said Tucker, heartlessly. 'Suck it up.'

Jim subsided and everyone looked at Varma.

Slightly – very slightly – Matthew nodded.

'All right,' said Varma, eventually.

Matthew scrambled behind the counter and picked up the two guns, handing them to Varma.

'Trip and Clore, you can have one each. The second either of you points one at me, I'll fry you. Max, you hand over Big Boy to Mr Tucker here. Incidentally increasing our chances of survival by one hundred per cent. You'll lead the way. Straight to your pod. No diversions to peer at anything historically interesting. Mr Tucker, I'm paying you the compliment of allowing you to lead your men. Adrian, you're at the back with me. Hands on the shoulder of the one in front. No one breaks ranks. We move as one. Torches and lightsticks ready?'

'Lantern,' said Matthew, scooping the one off the counter and handing it to his mother.

'Line up,' said Varma. 'Everyone ready? OK. Thirty seconds – forty-five tops – and we're all safe. Take it steady and stick together. Let's go, people.'

Nobody ran. Running over rough ground is never a good idea. Especially in the dark. Max picked her way towards her pod, holding her lantern high. They moved in a tight group – everyone maintaining physical contact with everyone else.

The long grass caught at their ankles. Jim stumbled and cursed. Tucker steadied him then pulled him back in line. Past the dark forge. Past the workshop. Past the woodpile. Past two of the older wooden huts.

Max paused. A wide-open space lay ahead of them. The fuel store stood in a dark corner, almost invisible in the shadows.

'Where's this bleeding pod?' whispered Jim, staring wildly around. The stars shone only a very faint light but it was easy to see there was no pod here. Max heard Tucker rumble something behind her and remembered she'd given him her blaster. Ah well – it had seemed a good idea at the time.

'It's here,' said Varma quietly. 'Just follow my colleague.'

'Oh,' said Jim. 'I know. It's got one of those things, hasn't it? What do you call them? Camouflage thingies.'

He seemed inclined to discuss the matter further.

'Stop talking,' hissed Varma. 'Move.'

They set off again.

'We're nearly there,' said Max, who had, for once, remembered to mark the position of her pod, because nothing is more difficult to find in a crisis than an invisible pod. 'All right. When the corner of that hut lines up with that broken bit of rain butt . . .'

Matthew began to entertain thoughts they might get out of this after all. That they might actually get back to TPHQ. He could imagine the luxury of a hot shower – a drink in the bar afterwards. Something to eat, and a chat with Jane. He wondered briefly how her day was going.

Better than his, certainly. He didn't know it at the time, but at exactly this moment, nearly three hundred and fifty years in the future, North was in New York and prophesying that wherever Henry Plimpton went next, it would mean trouble for someone – and she was exactly right.

Not thirty yards away a pod materialised, and at exactly the same moment, the lights flickered and came back on, effectively destroying any hope of them melting away in the darkness.

Fire-trucking fire truck.

28

Max stopped dead. To get to her pod they would have to pass this new one. The one standing between them and escape.

The door opened as a short, plump man strode out. He was rummaging in a briefcase as he walked and actually managed three or four strides across the compound before looking up and coming to an abrupt halt.

Four men appeared at his shoulder, talking among themselves and obviously not expecting any trouble. Everyone stopped dead.

Both sides eyed each other. That Henry Plimpton was as surprised as they were was very obvious.

Matthew took half a step behind Clore, whose size would easily conceal him. Would easily conceal a small house, actually. As far as he could see, Plimpton looked no different to the last time he'd seen him, although not a great deal of his face was visible between his hat and the upturned collar of his overcoat. The bit that could be seen, however, looked very, very angry. Wherever he'd been – whatever he'd been doing – it obviously hadn't ended well. For him, anyway. And probably not for anyone else, either.

Plimpton's gaze swept across the obvious Time Police

officer, Tucker and the rest. Max took a moment to be grateful for anonymous blue jumpsuits. If anyone asked, she could be a Jehovah's Witness.

'Yeah,' said Tucker to Varma. 'Now might be a good time for your thirty or so colleagues to jump out shouting, "Surprise."'

'In their own good time,' said Varma, evenly. 'If you take a moment, Mr Tucker, you'll see that we're armed and they are not.'

'For the moment.'

Henry Plimpton looked around. 'Tucker? What's happening here?'

'Evacuation,' said Varma. And said no more.

'What?' He stared in puzzlement at the wreckage of the burning hut across the compound.

Behind them, the generator coughed another warning. Red lights flickered. They needed either to refuel it or switch to another. This one was nearly finished. And then the darkness would close in, bringing whatever was out there with it, probably. And then the shooting would start.

The situation was finely balanced. On one hand stood Henry Plimpton and his men – four of them – but since none of them had been expecting trouble, no one actually had a weapon in their hands at this moment.

On the other side, stood three Time Police officers – if you counted a recently seconded historian. Two, if you discounted Officer Farrell in his current incarnation as Adrian Meiklejohn. But since the historian was famously possessed of a wandering and wayward spirit, it was probably wisest to call it just the one Time Police officer – who, yes, was armed, but had recently made the now very bad decision to arm her prisoners, as well.

So actually, it was Henry Plimpton, his four men, Tucker and his four men – including the aforementioned Adrian – versus one sadly overburdened officer and her erratic assistant.

Varma tried not to sigh. The chances of her living long enough to win the inter-departmental boxing championship for the third year running were looking increasingly slim.

She drew herself up. 'There has been . . . an issue.'

All eyes slid back to the still-smouldering mess hut.

'Tucker?' said Henry Plimpton again. Ominously. His four men began to fan out.

'Stand where you are,' said Varma sharply. 'For your own safety, stay close together.'

Tucker nodded. 'She's right, Mr Plimpton. Keep together.'

'Are we taking orders from the Time Police now?'

'Yes,' said Tucker, simply. 'People have been going missing. We've lost two men tonight. Not an hour ago.'

'Where did they go?'

'No one knows. Here one minute. Gone the next. Something opens the gate and takes them.'

Henry Plimpton laughed. Actually laughed. 'I never took you for such a fool, Tucker. They've properly pulled the wool over your eyes, haven't they? There's nothing sinister going on here. Your people deserted. That's all.'

'Andy was checking the gate and . . .'

'Andy opened the gate and pushed off.'

'Otto vanished. Almost in front of . . .'

'Otto stepped behind a hut, waited until you were looking elsewhere and then did the same. Or Andy opened the gate for him. Whatever. They've made a fool of you, Tucker.'

'Johnson . . . Li.'

337

'You've been haemorrhaging men, Tucker, and cooked up some sort of supernatural explanation for it.'

There was silence as Tucker – and everyone else – thought about this. About this all too likely explanation for the strange disappearances. It was the men themselves who opened the gate. Of course it was. Any other explanation was ridiculous. And it had been the Time Police switching the lights on and off. Imagination and nerves had done the rest. Matthew tensed. Tucker and his men were seconds from rounding on Varma and Max. What could he do?

As it turned out, he didn't have to do anything. Henry Plimpton, figuratively speaking, shot himself in the foot.

Turning to his men, he shouted, 'Kill them. Kill them all.'

'What?' said Jim, outraged. 'You bastard.'

Varma brought up her big blaster. 'Everyone stand still. You are under arrest. Move and I'll fire.'

'Ah,' said Plimpton. 'Finally. There's the Time Police we all know and love. The last one was a sad disappointment.'

Varma ignored this. 'Put your hands on your head and get down on the ground. Now.'

Plimpton ignored this. 'Tucker – shoot them.'

'Fuck off,' said Tucker. 'You just ordered us killed.'

'Shoot them and I'll let you live.'

'No, he won't,' said Max. 'You shoot us and while you're doing that – he shoots you. Simple.'

'His men are unarmed at the moment,' said Varma. 'It would appear, Mr Tucker, that you hold the balance of power. Who will you choose?'

It was slowly dawning on Henry Plimpton that this wasn't

the unquestioning obedience he expected. 'I gave you an order, Tucker.'

'You also gave your men an order. To shoot us.'

He tried for an unconvincing smile. 'I was overhasty. I regret that now.'

The lights flickered again. For longer this time.

Matthew glanced across the compound. 'Gate's still open,' he muttered to Tucker. 'I don't want to be here when the lights go out for good.'

The generator coughed. One of Plimpton's men moved. Reaching for his weapon, perhaps.

'Stand still,' shouted Tucker.

The man laughed. 'Oh, come on, Tucker, you're not going to shoot me.'

'Don't see why not,' said Tucker, not smiling in any way. 'You're going to shoot *me*.'

'I misspoke,' said Henry Plimpton, now back in control. 'Why don't we . . .'

The lights went out. One, two, three, four seconds. And then came back on again.

Henry Plimpton carried on from where he'd left off, '. . . sit down and talk about . . .'

'Mr Plimpton,' said Varma quietly. 'Have you counted your men recently?'

For a long second, Henry Plimpton stood very still. Very, very still indeed. Then he turned his head. Only three men stood alongside him.

'Don't be ridiculous. He's gone back into the pod. For weapons.'

The generator spluttered and fell silent. A second later all the lights went out.

'Move,' shouted Varma. 'And stick together. Tucker . . .'

'With you,' said Tucker.

'Already moving,' said Max, breaking into a run.

Blaster fire lit up the night sky. Tucker and Varma were laying down covering fire. With luck, Plimpton and his men would take refuge in their pod.

'This way,' shouted Max. 'Follow me.'

She smacked hard into something that didn't give an inch. Someone smacked into her. And then someone else into him. She struggled to free herself. 'Bloody bollocking hell. Get off me. Door.'

The door slid open, revealing a greenish glow because a prudent Time Police officer had instructed an historian to switch to night vision before they left.

'Inside,' shouted Max. 'Quick. Give me that.'

She wrenched Tucker's blaster back off him.

'What are you doing?' demanded Varma, still laying down fire.

'Old trick. If in doubt, blow up the fuel store.'

Tucker took back the blaster. 'Get inside and fire this thing up. I'll do it.'

'We'll both do it,' said Varma.

Jim, Clore and Matthew were already inside. Trip stood by the door. 'Come on. Hurry up.'

There were three people in there already. Max squeezed in and fought her way to the console. And there was still Varma, Tucker and Trip to get in somehow.

'Bloody hell,' said Jim, critically. 'It's a bit small.'

'It's a one-seater, you pudding,' said Max, firing up the console. 'You can always get out if you're claustrophobic.'

A mighty explosion rocked the night. And the pod. People staggered. White lights flashed as another smaller series of bangs echoed around the compound, lighting up the darkness.

'Fuel store,' said Matthew.

'Like firework night,' said Max, happily.

'We can't get in,' shouted Varma. 'There's no room. Shove up, you lot.' She was laying down covering fire all around Plimpton's pod.

There was a certain amount of rapid shuffling.

'No good,' reported Jim. 'Half of Tucker is still outside.'

'Perhaps we'd be better off taking our chances here,' said Trip, unhappily.

Tucker tried to push him inside. 'Are you insane? No.'

Outside the pod, red and orange flames leaped up to meet the stars.

'Wait,' said Max. 'Everyone stop. We have to go at this scientifically.'

'Well, get a bloody move on,' shouted Jim. 'Because we blew up the fuel store, everything's on fire and the boss won't be happy. They'll be coming after us any second now and there's still something out there. We have to go.'

Max was issuing instructions. 'Matthew – you squeeze underneath the console.'

'Matthew?' said Tucker sharply and was ignored.

'Tucker and Clore – against that wall. Trip – you fold yourself up and get into the bathroom, and then Jim and Varma can stand in front of the door.'

There was even more heaving and shuffling.

'And get that door shut.'

'Surely Henry Plimpton's too busy to bother with us,' said Varma. 'There must be stuff out there he wants to save.'

Max shook her head, unusually grim-faced. 'Never mind Henry Plimpton – get that door closed. We don't want something we can't see getting in. That happened to me, once.'

'Where would we put it?' grunted Varma, pushing against Tucker to make herself some room, but Max, who still had nightmares about a severed head opening its eyes and smiling up at her, was not inclined to mess about.

'I can't get to the console.'

'This bloody seat's in the way,' said Clore. 'Tucker – give us a hand here.' He caught hold of the seat. 'To me. To you. To me.'

Together, they yanked the seat back and forth, until finally, with a nasty metallic graunching noise, the stem snapped.

'Out of the way,' shouted Tucker, and they threw the remains out into the still quite exciting night. Max caught a glimpse of burning huts and running men and then everyone shunted up an inch or so and the door jerked shut.

Someone breathed a great sigh of relief. Not Max, obviously, whose mind was now running on what the owner of the pod was going to say about this.

'Dad's going to go apeshit,' said a voice from under the console.

'Dad?' said Tucker.

'Don't worry about that, son. With luck we'll die here and won't have to face him.'

'Yes,' said Varma, impatiently. 'Let's all look on the bright side. Can we go?'

Over their heads, something heavy thudded on to the roof.

342

Everyone froze.

'What was that?' said Jim in a tiny voice.

'No idea,' said Max. 'Could be anything. Debris from the explosion. Henry Plimpton trying to prevent us escaping . . .' She tailed away. Over their heads there came the faintest groan of overburdened pod.

Varma twisted to look at Max. 'We really need to get out of here. Now.'

'No sooner said. Everyone brace for impact. Computer – emergency extraction. *Now*.'

29

Back at St Mary's, life had very nearly returned to normal. The fire was almost under control. All that remained was the smell. In Hawking, a cautious cup of tea for everyone was being mooted when the alarms went off. There was a moment's astonishment and then every techie scattered in every direction known to man. In fact, in their haste, they might have invented several new ones.

A small pod materialised some six feet from the ground, hung for a moment, defying both narrative belief and the laws of gravity, before crashing heavily to the floor, bouncing once, skidding with an ear-bleeding shriek of metal, and finally coming to rest against the plinth for Number Five.

'Butter side up,' Mr Dieter commented, picking himself up off the floor. Occasionally a pod would land on its door and since there was only one way in or out, righting it was a matter of both urgency and a forklift.

Inside the pod, things were not quite so hunky-dory. An emergency extraction is no fun when your pod has more than exceeded its passenger capacity and three of those passengers are big men. And two of them are really big men.

'Get off me,' said Varma, tightly, crushed under the weight of an enormous illegal.

Tucker grinned down into her face. 'Make me.'

'Oooooooh,' said Max.

Varma glared. 'I have been the inter-departmental Don't Fuck With Me champion for the last two years and intend to make it three. Get off me or find my boot prints on your spleen. Your choice.'

Tucker grinned again. 'It would be so worth it.'

'Oooooooh,' said Max.

'Shut up, Max.' Varma looked at Tucker. 'Last chance.'

Some sort of seismic shift occurred as Tucker hauled himself to his feet and then, grinning, offered a hand to Varma, who looked at it for one moment – obviously contemplating ripping his arm out of its socket – before accepting his offer. People surged and staggered in a pod designed for one person and actually carrying seven. Eight and a half if you adjusted for Tucker, Clore and Matthew.

'I wonder if St Mary's is still on fire,' said Max, trying to access the screen. 'I do feel a little guilty about leaving them to cope alone.'

'Trust me,' said Varma. 'Whatever the crisis was, your absence can only have improved the situation.' She paused. 'Just out of curiosity – what was the crisis?'

'Greek fire,' said Max.

Varma considered this. 'Is it too late to go back and take our chances with whatever it was at Roanoke?'

Exiting the pod was not as easy as it sounded. Jim and Clore were the first to emerge. Like toothpaste, as Jim said. Then Matthew, squeezing between Tucker and Varma and grinning at them in a manner which made Varma wish she could get an arm free to box his ears. Then Tucker and Varma. Trip let himself out of the bathroom and finally, Max.

'It's like one of those clown cars,' murmured Dieter, standing at the head of a gaggle of techies, all armed with fire hoses and medical kits. 'They just keep on coming. Unbelievable.'

By the time the pod's passengers had all straightened their clothing and sorted themselves out, Dr Peterson had arrived in Hawking.

Max beamed. 'Dr Peterson, sir. Good afternoon.'

'Don't give me that crap,' said Peterson. 'Who the hell are all these people? Where have you been? What's going on?'

Max sniffed. 'Is the fire out yet?'

'Getting there.' He looked at Dieter. 'Tell everyone to stand down. Please inform the professor we may have a new source of urine should he need it.' He eyed the newcomers. 'Does anyone here have a full bladder?'

'Not any more,' muttered someone.

'What is this place?' demanded Tucker in disbelief.

Peterson frowned at Max. 'You haven't answered my question.'

'Which one?'

'Any of them.'

'We need a pod.'

'Why?'

'To get our prisoners back to TPHQ.'

'Oh God – you haven't taken up bounty-hunting again, have you?'

'No, of course not.'

'Only you promised.'

'I know.'

Peterson craned his neck. 'Is that Matthew?'

'It is. And I don't know if you've met Officer Varma, who is representing the Time Police this afternoon.'

Varma nodded politely.

Tucker silently caught Jim's eye. And Trip. And Clore. Surreptitiously, all four men began to edge towards the open hangar doors, through which could be glimpsed the smoky road to freedom.

'Good afternoon,' said Markham, miraculously materialising behind them and maintaining the standards so dear to his heart. 'Leaving so soon?'

'Oh God, here's Dad as well,' muttered Matthew as a smoke-streaked, soggy Chief Technical Officer appeared. 'Now you're in trouble.'

'Not me,' said Max, quickly. 'I didn't break the seat.' She turned to Tucker and Clore. 'You two are so dead.'

'What the hell is this place?' demanded Tucker, again.

'Dr Peterson,' said Varma, striving to keep things on track – because this was St Mary's, after all. 'On behalf of the Time Police, may I formally request the loan of a pod to transport my prisoners to TPHQ.'

Peterson stared at Max. 'You're under arrest? Again?'

'No, of course not,' said Max, visibly annoyed at this unjustified slur.

'I left you supervising the evacuation,' said Leon, accusingly.

'Did that,' said Max. 'Then we nipped off for a bit.'

'We?'

'Hi, Dad,' said Matthew, emerging from behind Clore.

There was a long silence from Leon who gazed stonily from his wife to his son and finally to his pod. *My pod.*

It was very apparent where his priorities lay.

'It wasn't me,' said Max, quickly, grassing up offspring, temporary colleagues and prisoners without a second thought.

'Or me,' said Matthew.

'Or me,' said Varma.

Leon sighed deeply. 'Not that anyone's interested, but the fire is finally out. Everyone can return to normal duties – not you, Max.'

'But I have to return the prisoners to . . .'

'No need,' said Varma, with completely unnecessary cheerfulness. 'Officer Farrell and I have everything in hand. Thank you for your assistance, Dr Maxwell.'

Jim blinked. 'Who's Officer Farrell?'

'We're not going anywhere,' said Tucker, obviously prepared to make a fight of it.

Varma sighed. 'You don't want to stay here, mate. Trust me, you'd be better off at Roanoke.'

'You've been to Roanoke?' demanded Peterson, rounding on Max. 'Without me?'

'Or me?' said Markham, indignantly.

Varma rubbed her forehead. 'Oh God . . .'

'Or me,' said Adrian indignantly, appearing from inside Number Three.

'Oh hi, Adrian,' said Matthew. 'Didn't see you there.' He turned to Tucker. 'Guys, can I introduce the real Adrian Meiklejohn?'

Tucker glowered. 'So who the fuck are you?'

Matthew smiled brightly. 'Officer Farrell. Of the Time Police.'

Tucker stepped back. 'The fuck you are.'

Max beamed, radiating maternal proudness. 'He's very good, isn't he?'

Varma had another go. 'Dr Peterson, I appeal to you. A pod. Please. It's been a very long day.'

Peterson looked at Leon, who sighed and said, 'Number Eight is good to go.'

'Thank you,' said Varma. 'This way, gentlemen.' She raised a mocking eyebrow. 'And Officer Farrell of the Time Police, of course.'

Matthew sighed. 'I'm never going to live that down, am I?'

'Not if you live for a million years.'

They prodded their prisoners in the direction of Number Eight.

'Not you,' said Leon, grasping the back of Max's jumpsuit.

'See you later, Mum,' called Matthew. 'Thanks for your help.'

Peterson turned to Adrian and Markham. 'Go with them, would you? If only to make sure we get our pod back.'

A scowling Leon had been inspecting the interior of his own pod. His voice drifted out of the door. 'Where's the bloody seat?'

'We had to throw it out,' called Max.

'Had to? *Had to?*'

'To get everyone in. And even then, it was a little bit on the snug side. We really had no choice. Ask them.'

She gestured to Varma, the prisoners and her offspring, all of whom were just disappearing into Number Eight, along with a grinning Markham and Adrian.

Dieter edged everyone back behind the safety line and Number Eight disappeared.

'Right, then,' said Peterson. 'I don't know about you lot, but it's been a busy afternoon and I could do with something alcoholic.'

'Very much ahead of you there,' said Chief Technical Officer Farrell. He turned to his wife. 'Drinks on you, I think.'

350

30

Back in her office at TPHQ, Commander Hay was contemplating her long-since-abandoned lunch. A half-drunk mug of cold coffee sat on her desk, alongside a stale sandwich with just one bite taken out of it. She sighed, just as Captain Farenden appeared in the doorway. 'You are wearing your bad-news face, Captain.'

'That is because I have some bad news, ma'am.'

Hay flung down her pen. 'Oh, what a shame – this day has been going so well and now you've spoiled everything.'

Farenden closed the door behind him, saying quietly, 'Ma'am – the bill has failed. We won't be getting our increased funding.'

Hay's mouth dropped open in shock. 'What? You're kidding me.'

He shook his head. 'I'm sorry, ma'am. No.'

'Fire-trucking fire truck, Charlie. Find out which of those fire-trucking bastards let us down and have them shot immediately.'

He held her gaze.

'You are wearing your even-worse-news face, Captain.'

He hesitated for a moment.

'Out with it, Charlie.'

'It was Mrs Farnborough, ma'am. She defied the government whip.'

Hay gaped at him in disbelief. 'She didn't vote for the bill? After she said she would? She made a promise. A politician's promise, obviously, but . . .' She tailed away. 'I wouldn't have believed it of her. Dammit, Charlie. How could I be so stupid? Once a politician, always a politician, I suppose.'

'Worse, ma'am. Not only did she not vote for the bill, she persuaded a number of other members not to support it, either. We lost by ten votes.'

It wasn't often that Commander Hay was completely dumbfounded, but she certainly was at this moment.

'The question is rhetorical, Charlie, but I feel obliged to ask it anyway – why?'

'I have no idea at this moment, ma'am. I've had a word with a friend of mine at Westminster and I may have something to tell you later on.'

'I'm going to ask another stupid question – are you absolutely sure about this?'

'Regretfully, ma'am – yes.'

'Can you get me Mrs Farnborough on the phone? Although God knows it's too bloody late now.'

'I've spoken to her office, ma'am. Mrs Farnborough left the Commons immediately after the vote, returned home and is not available to anyone for comment. The Whip's office is clamouring to speak to her. As is the office of the Prime Minister. No one knows what's happening, ma'am, but it's certain her political career is over.'

'Shit, Charlie. Where does this leave us?'

'Up the financial creek without a paddle, ma'am. I do feel that your complaints about my wanton and reckless expenditure over the Paris Time-Stop last month are now fully justified.'

'This is . . .' Hay appeared to be groping for the appropriate words to describe this catastrophe.

'An unmitigated disaster, ma'am.'

'We really are not having a good day, are we? The attack on Costello. The death of Mrs Lockland. This business with Lockland's parents. Breaking the treaty. We just can't do anything right today.'

Captain Farenden's com bleeped. 'This might be my friend in Westminster now, ma'am. Would you excuse me one moment, please?'

He turned away and listened. For some time. At the end, he said simply, 'Thank you,' closed his com and stood still for a moment.

'What?' said Hay, who knew her adjutant.

'Ma'am, this might be nothing, but . . . Officer Parrish failed to return at the designated time. All efforts to contact him have failed and he has been reported AWOL.'

'What?'

'He hasn't come back, ma'am.'

Hay slammed her hands on her desk. 'Seriously, Charlie? Isn't there enough going on at the moment? If he's drunk in a bar somewhere, I'll . . .'

'Or possibly his meeting with his father went badly.'

'Definitely in a bar somewhere in that case,' said Hay.

'Ma'am . . . if there was some kind of physical alterca-tion . . . he might be in gaol somewhere. Although someone would probably have let me know by now. Or possibly he has succumbed to his injuries. Substitute hospital for gaol.'

There was a pause as Commander Hay readjusted her ideas and made a conscious effort at self-control. 'That's a very good point, Charlie. If it was any other officer than Parrish, what would we be doing right now?'

'An overdue officer who cannot be reached is always cause for concern, ma'am. Normally, we'd be attempting to contact him, discreetly checking to see whether he has actually left his designated destination. Checking to see if he even *arrived* at his designated destination. And so forth.'

'What progress have we made on verifying officers' alibis?'

'For both incidents? It's slow work, ma'am. Yes, most officers are able to alibi each other, but the cross-checking takes time.'

'Send Grint and Lockland to look for Parrish. Neither of them would be my first choice to bring him in, but we know they're both in the clear. Despatch them forthwith and tell them not to come home without him. And in the case of Lt Grint – to bring him home intact.'

'Yes, ma'am. And our currently dire financial situation?'

'Ignore it, Charlie. We are the magic porridge pot. We keep going until someone specifically orders us to stop.'

'I feel it incumbent on me to point out we have no money, ma'am.'

'Never stops the government, Charlie. Full steam ahead and damn the torpedoes.'

'Er . . . yes, ma'am.'

*   *   *

Lt Grint and Officer Lockland met in Team 236's deserted office.

'This is going to be fun,' said Bolshy Jane, eyeing Lt Grint as he poured two illegal cups of coffee.

'Shut up,' said Jane.

'Is this better or worse than working with Parrish, do you think?'

'Shut up,' said Jane.

'Or even Sawney?'

'I shan't tell you again,' said Jane. 'In case you hadn't noticed, I'm not having a good day.'

'Self-pity isn't going to help, sweetie. You have a job to do. The best thing now is to focus on that.'

Any further internal dialogue was interrupted by Lt Grint putting a coffee in front of her. 'Are you up for this, Lockland?'

Jane nodded. 'I am.'

He regarded her steadily. 'You know why I had to ask?'

'I do, sir. You can rely on me. I'm both willing and able to handle this mission.'

'Good to hear. So – what do we know?'

Jane consulted her trusty notebook. 'According to his leave sheet, Officer Parrish's designated destination was Parrish Industries HQ in St James's Square.'

Grint pondered for a moment. 'I don't think we should give them any advance warning, do you? We'll enter the premises and demand possession of Officer Parrish.'

'Yes,' said Jane. 'And if they don't have him?'

'My betting is that they do. My honest but unflattering opinion of Parrish is that he's attempted to come to blows with his father, been overcome by their security people and shoved in a darkened room somewhere to cool down. They'll probably be quite relieved to see us.'

'And if that isn't the case, sir?'

'Then we look for him in the nearest bar. It's not rocket science with him, is it?'

Jane was doubtful. 'Do you think that's all it will take?'

'In my experience, things are never that easy, but we'll see.'

'Do we go armed?'

Grint grinned at her. 'Oh yeah.'

There was no need to introduce themselves at Parrish Industries. Jane would have said they were greeted almost with relief.

A grave-faced Lucinda Steel met them in reception. 'Would you come this way, please?'

Grint stood his ground in the crowded foyer. Streams of people parted around him and reformed on the other side. 'I don't think so.'

Ms Steel gestured towards the lift. 'No, this way, please.'

'Why?'

She kept her voice low. 'If you are here to investigate the unexplained disappearance of Mr Parrish, then this is not something we would want to discuss in public.'

Grint nodded but remained stationary.

Ms Steel tried to edge him towards the lift. Her desire to remove them from public view was very apparent. 'Mr Parrish's disappearance is a problem. There are security issues.'

'He was here, then?' said Jane.

'Yes, of course he was. I myself was with him.'

'How did he seem?'

'Perfectly normal.'

Jane frowned. *Perfectly normal* were not words anyone would use when considering Luke Parrish's current state of mind.

'When was he last seen?'

'Around an hour ago, when he left the building.'

'Destination?'

'Unknown. He left no word. We cannot contact him. This is unprecedented.'

Jane stared at her. If Ms Steel had been at all familiar with the concept of hand-wringing, then hand-wringing would be happening big time.

'We are not, at this moment, overly concerned,' said Jane, remembering their instructions to downplay Luke's AWOL-ness. 'There could easily be a very simple explanation.'

'I think you are guilty of a grave underestimation.'

'It is possible that he hasn't yet recovered from his recent injuries and could simply be too unwell to . . .'

'What injuries? What are you talking about?'

Jane stared. 'You didn't notice? You said you were with him.'

'Notice what?'

'Officer Parrish recently sustained . . .'

Ms Steel stared at her. 'Why are we talking about Luke?'

The three of them stared at each other and then all tried to speak at once.

Grint held up a hand the size and general shape of a coal shovel. 'Wait. Everyone be quiet.' He turned to Ms Steel. 'Somewhere private, please.'

Just the very faintest twinge of exasperation crossed Ms Steel's face. 'As I have been endeavouring to arrange, Lieutenant. This way, please.'

She led them to the lift and instructed it to take them to the penthouse floor. They walked past the empty reception desk and into Raymond Parrish's private office. This was a large room with quietly understated furnishings. A SmartDesk stood across one corner. Two long sofas ran parallel to one wall with a gleaming coffee table between them. On the other side of the room stood a long briefing table. One wall was filled with three large and six small screens, currently blank.

'Please sit down.'

They seated themselves on the long sofa opposite Ms Steel, who indicated that Grint should open the batting.

'We are investigating the disappearance of Officer Parrish, last seen heading here to speak with his father.'

Ms Steel clasped her hands in her lap. 'You think that Luke has vanished as well?'

'Yes – unofficially he is AWOL.'

'Oh dear,' said Ms Steel. 'That makes it even more serious.'

'Why? Makes it even more serious than what? What are you talking about?'

'I'm talking about Raymond Parrish. Who has simply vanished without trace.'

Jane's first – and not entirely frivolous thought – was that Luke had murdered his father and fled the country.

'Hardly,' said Bolshy Jane, scornfully. 'No lifeless body stretched out on the carpet.'

'Even Luke Parrish would know to conceal the body.'

'No bloodstains, sweetie.'

'He used a blaster.'

Bolshy Jane wasn't having any of that. 'No scorch marks.'

'He poisoned him, then.'

358

'For heaven's sake,' said Bolshy Jane. 'Pull yourself together.'

Grint, presumably not prone to such internal dialogues, was continuing more conventionally. 'Do you suspect Officer Parrish of harming his father?'

Ms Steel shook her head. 'I wasn't present for the interview, but . . . I don't think it was particularly friendly, but then they left together so . . . I don't know.'

'Luke wouldn't do that,' said Jane, loyally.

'He couldn't,' said Grint – someone with a far more realistic appreciation of Officer Parrish's abilities. 'Not on the premises, anyway. I bet every third person here is an armed security officer. And don't tell me Mr Parrish doesn't have up-to-date anti-kidnap training.'

Ms Steel nodded. 'He does.'

'And wouldn't hesitate to use it? Even against his own son?'

Ms Steel didn't answer directly. 'I've pulled the relevant CCTV footage,' she said. 'You can view it here on this screen and form your own opinion.'

One of the large screens on the wall opposite them flickered into life. A camera mounted in the foyer showed a rear view of the Parrishes – *père et fils* – exiting through Parrish Industries' imposing front doors. This switched immediately to a side view of them descending the steps together. Neither was speaking but there were no obvious signs of hostility between them.

A large black car appeared smoothly from somewhere out of shot and cruised to a halt. The rear door opened automatically. Both Parrishes climbed in and the car pulled away out of sight.

'Before you ask,' said Ms Steel, 'not one of ours.'

'I want that registration traced,' said Grint.

'My people are already on it,' said Ms Steel.

'My people are faster.'

Jane was already opening her com to pass the details to TPHQ.

'There are more cameras per square mile in this city than anywhere else in the whole world,' said Grint. 'We should be able to trace the car easily enough.'

And they did. Only a few minutes later, the response came through. The car had pulled into a nearby underground car park. And had not reappeared. Full details of ownership had been flashed to their scratchpads.

Jane looked up from her screen. 'Portman House.'

'Well,' said Grint. 'That was suspiciously easy. No attempt at concealment. Broad daylight. I don't think anything sinister is intended.'

'We don't know that,' said Ms Steel, firmly. 'I'll call for a security team to go with you.'

'Thank you,' said Grint. 'That won't be necessary.'

Ms Steel looked at the smallest and skinniest officer in the Time Police. 'If you say so.'

'I do say so,' said Grint, getting to his feet like an unfolding mountain. 'With luck, we should be able to locate and extract both Parrishes within the hour. Thank you for your assistance, Ms Steel. With me, Officer Lockland.'

31

The black car was nosing its way gently through the quiet streets. No rush. No panic. Nothing to alarm the passengers.

Luke stretched luxuriously. It was a very long time since he had last been inside a car, far less something high-end like this. 'Nice ride, Dad.'

Raymond Parrish had been looking around. 'Luke, my boy, I have no desire to alarm you, but I suspect this is not my car.'

Luke sat up in a hurry. 'What?'

He stared around for a moment, made an attempt to force open the door, and cursed the fact he hadn't been allowed to bear arms despite being a family visit.

'Hey!' He pounded on the reinforced glass partition. The driver's eyes met his briefly in the mirror and then slid away.

Luke thumped some more. 'Let us out.'

There was no response.

'No,' said Raymond Parrish, calmly. 'This is definitely not my car. The dashboard has been manufactured from mahogany. And not, I suspect, from a renewable source.'

'The villains,' said Luke, sarcastically.

'My point exactly.'

Luke fumbled for his com.

'I doubt it will work, Luke. Most cars of this type are shielded. Nothing getting in also means nothing gets out, unfortunately.'

The Thames slid past the right-hand window.

Luke regarded his father with what he felt was justifiable exasperation. 'Dad, how could you get into a car that isn't yours?'

'I followed you.'

'I thought it was your car.'

'A mahogany dashboard and leather seats? I have obviously failed in my duty as a parent.'

Luke tried the door again.

'It won't open,' said Raymond Parrish. 'We covered all this in anti-kidnap training.'

'Were you asleep during the part when they warned you about getting into strange cars?'

'I confess I did not see that eventuality ever arising.'

'Well, when you finally deigned to pay attention to what was probably the most expensive anti-kidnap training in the world – and I think you should ask Ms Steel to organise a refund – what was their advice to anyone daft enough to get themselves into this situation?'

Raymond Parrish settled back. 'Wait and see what happens next.'

'Do you know whose car this is?'

'Well, not for certain, but the unfashionable make and model, poor design and insipid colour scheme are leading me towards the inevitable conclusion that this is a Portman vehicle.'

Luke glared at his father and passed the journey tugging on door handles and fiddling with door locks.

Raymond Parrish passed the journey with a series of idle

comments on familiar landmarks encountered along the way, until Luke hurled himself back in his seat in exasperation.

'Dad, this is not a sight-seeing tour.'

'Our instructor advised us to try to remember the route. I am endeavouring to remember the route.'

Luke closed his eyes.

Not fifteen minutes later, the car turned off the road and into a small, private, underground car park.

'Really?' said Raymond Parrish, critically. 'We could have walked it more quickly. I fear the relationship our friends the Portmans have with the planet is not a happy one.'

The doors opened automatically and, after leaving an interval long enough to make it clear they were only disembarking because they had nothing better to do, both Parrishes climbed out and looked around. The car park was small and private, containing only half a dozen other cars, all parked neatly in their allocated spaces.

Luke opened his com again.

'We are underground, son.'

Luke sighed and put it away. 'Do you know where we are?'

'The bowels of Portman House, I suspect.'

'All right,' said Luke. 'Since you appear to be the fount of all knowledge – do you know *why* we are here?'

'Well, not for certain, but I have a very good idea. This is a private matter, Luke. You should go.'

Luke looked across the car park. 'I'm not leaving you, Dad, and I think leaving might be a bit of a problem anyway.'

A nearby lift door had pinged open and four black-suited men emerged. They arranged themselves either side of the lift, rather in the manner of a guard of honour, and waited, hands clasped in front of them in the traditional security stance. No words were spoken but their intent was plain.

Raymond Parrish raised his voice. 'I know why *I* am here, but I am willing to overlook the coercion part of the transaction in return for you releasing my son, who is an officer in the Time Police, as you well know, and I suspect they won't look favourably on this at all.'

No one responded in any way.

'Worth a try, I suppose,' said Raymond Parrish to Luke.

Luke fixed the driver with his special Time Police glare. 'You are so dead.'

Secure behind his bulletproof glass, the driver ignored him.

Disregarding everyone, Raymond Parrish adjusted the nearest wing mirror to a favourable angle and spent some time making sure his tie was just so. He straightened and turned to Luke. 'What do you think?'

'No, sorry, Dad,' said Luke, critically. 'Still looks a bit skew-whiff to me.'

Mr Parrish senior made a slight sound of annoyance and turned back to the mirror, saying quietly, 'What are they doing now?'

'Just waiting. Looks like they have instructions not to harm us.' He grinned at his father. 'No matter how irritating we might be.'

It took a while, but eventually Parrish senior achieved tie perfection. He and Luke made their unhurried way towards the lift.

'What does this tell us?'

'That they want something,' said Luke promptly. 'And they won't hurt us until they're absolutely convinced they won't get it.'

By now they were entering the lift.

'Do you think they'll offer us lunch?' enquired Luke, as the doors closed. 'I'm still quite hungry.'

Raymond Parrish was shocked. 'Oh, you don't want to eat here, son. The Portmans are well known to keep the worst table in town. And for heaven's sake, don't touch the wine. Ernesto Portman once served me cheap Bordeaux. With plaice, would you believe.'

Luke threw him an appalled glance. 'No. Surely not.'

'I'm afraid so,' said Raymond Parrish. 'I've never been back since.' He smiled at their escort. 'Well, not voluntarily, anyway.'

'Don't blame you,' said Luke. 'Some things just can't be forgiven.'

The lift stopped. A bell tinged as the doors opened.

The Parrishes continued their conversation in the corridor. 'It's a sad fact of life, Luke – you can't put lipstick on a pig. Even a Portman pig.'

A nearby door was flung open just in time for his remarks to be clearly audible to those awaiting their arrival. As, no doubt, Raymond Parrish had intended.

They entered a large, square room with windows on two sides overlooking the river – obviously an office of some kind, with an enormously overcompensating desk facing them from the far side of the room.

'Mahogany,' said Luke, dismissively.

'Again?' said Raymond Parrish. 'I'm certain that if we opened the window, we would hear the rainforests crying out in condemnation even as we speak.'

Luke glanced around at the office. The over-patterned carpet, the too ornate swags and curtains, the portraits of hopefully dead Portmans on the walls, the glass-fronted bookcase full of never-read classics. *Wuthering Heights*. *The Woodlanders*. *Hard Time*. And a very slim pamphlet on the standards to be maintained while in political office.

'It's all very 20th century, don't you think, Dad? And as anyone who's ever found themselves face to face with the 20th century will attest – that is not a compliment. I don't know anyone here, so I'm assuming these are lower-ranking Portmans. Are they worthy of my notice?'

'I shall introduce them anyway,' said Raymond Parrish. He turned to the assembled group of Portmans. 'Please be aware that today's little gathering still does not mean we will be publicly acknowledging you in future.'

He gestured at the three men standing behind the sad reminder of a once majestic rainforest. 'Luke, allow me to introduce Ernesto Portman – not one of *the* Portmans, obviously – but they do occasionally entrust him with some of their more minor legal matters.'

Ernesto Portman was a small man. Especially when compared with the similarly aged but far more imposing Raymond Parrish. From his pursed mouth to his long thin nose, everything about him looked small and mean. His thinning grey hair was obviously carefully cherished.

'Nice combover,' said Luke, beginning to enjoy himself, because when you can't make a situation any better, you can always revel in making it considerably worse.

'The one on the right is Anthony – Ernesto's oldest son, I believe.'

Anthony was taller than his father. Not that that was difficult. He had fair hair and was chunkily built. If his suit had been less sharply cut and he wore less jewellery, he might have been considered handsome.

Luke tilted his head to one side and grimaced. 'Trying just a little bit too hard there, Anthony. We can't all be Luke Parrish.'

Anthony took an angry step forwards. 'Shut up, Parrish.'

Unfortunately for Anthony, Luke had barely started. He'd had a bad, bad day. Time to start spreading it around. And – a handy Time Police tip here – when violence is certain to occur, make sure to be the one starting it.

'Oh, look,' he said brightly. 'An angry Portman.' He made the classic *come on, then – come and have a go if you think you're hard enough* gesture. 'Come on, sonny, I'm just in the mood.'

At a gesture from his father, Anthony Portman stopped dead.

Luke grinned. 'You know, I'm certain that as a fully qualified member of an all-powerful organisation with far-reaching powers and a remit that permits us to do pretty much as we please, I should be making strenuous efforts to behave in a responsible and mature manner in order to bring this matter to a peaceful resolution.' He paused for breath. 'But – as you said – these are only Portmans.'

'*Minor* Portmans,' corrected his father. 'Please pay more attention, Luke.'

'Sorry, Dad.'

Raymond Parrish brushed imaginary dust from his sleeve. 'I don't know, Ernesto, whether you received specific instructions to kidnap me and accidentally brought a member of the Time Police along for the ride – but . . .'

'Excuse me,' said the third Portman, his face bright red with anger.

'Oh, dear me, where are my manners?' said Raymond Parrish, who knew exactly where his manners were and had no intention of disturbing them. 'I seem to have overlooked Bradley. Again. My only excuse is that everyone does it. Luke, the one on the left is Bradley – sometimes referred to as the runt of the litter.'

'You know, Dad,' said Luke, not bothering to lower his voice, 'I've heard malicious people say Anthony isn't actually Ernesto's son – and obviously one shouldn't listen to spiteful rumours, even when one was the one to start those spiteful rumours – but now that I've actually met him, I think they might be right. Bradley, on the other hand – definitely Ernesto's. Although by a different wife, I believe.'

'Portman wives don't last long,' said Raymond Parrish.

Luke nodded. 'I hear they've formed a support group. They meet every month to discuss the dubious benefits of Portman wifehood, eat and drink the good food and wine they never got to enjoy when living under the Portmans' roof, and to congratulate each other on their escapes.'

He looked at Bradley. 'I gather Evangelina expensively slipped through your fingers last year, Bradley. Bad luck. Although not for her, of course. What was she – your third? Fourth? Gotta say, it's going to cost your dad an absolute packet to buy you the next one. Word's got out about you and your nasty little habits, you know. I doubt money will be enough.'

Bradley scowled. 'I see someone's finally given you the good kicking you deserve, Parrish.'

Luke smiled slightly. Anything more was still painful. 'I don't know why you're assuming I lost, Bradley. You should see the other bloke.' Which, he decided, gave the right impression without actually telling a lie. He waited hopefully, but neither of the younger Portmans rose to the bait. And Ernesto simply smiled.

'I expect you know why I've requested this meeting, Raymond.'

Raymond Parrish looked around. 'Did you hear a request for this meeting, Luke?'

'Nope.'

'Nor I.'

Ernesto tried the smile again. 'Raymond, I . . .'

'I know exactly why I'm here, Ernesto. It's because your failure in this matter is beginning to cause major concern and now you've had to resort to more drastic methods before senior members of the family become completely exasperated by your feeble efforts. In the interests of our long . . . association . . . I should perhaps advise you that you are, at this exact moment, in even more trouble than you realise. The best you can hope for is that I immediately remove myself and my son – *the Time Police officer* – leaving you not only to contemplate the error of your ways, but almost completely unharmed. And your charming office, too.'

'Please don't choose that option,' said Luke to Anthony.

Anthony bristled. 'Yeah? Seriously?'

Raymond Parrish put a hand on his son's arm and looked across at the older man. 'Allow me to save a life today. My son was not in the happiest mood even before he climbed into your car. Rein in your offspring, Ernesto. For their own sakes.'

'You never let me have any fun,' complained Luke.

'Well, perhaps later. If you are a very good boy.'

Luke put his hands in his pockets and grinned. 'I was hoping to be a very bad one.'

Ernesto came from around his desk. 'There really is no need for all this hostility, Raymond. Can I offer you any refreshment?'

'Good God, no,' said Raymond Parrish, shuddering. 'Do you still serve your guests that excruciating Merlot? The one that tastes like burned tin?'

Ernesto compressed his lips but said nothing.

Luke was listening with only half an ear. He wasn't the first officer to find himself outgunned and outnumbered, but, fortunately, the Time Police have a procedure for this sort of thing.

First, carry out the basic Time Police threat assessment. OK – what could he use? The desk was only for show. No papers, keyboards, or com devices marred its gleaming emptiness. Nothing there that could be utilised. There were matching chairs scattered around – heavy wooden affairs. If he could lift one, he could definitely do some damage. If he could lift it. The main problem was that although there were ostensibly only three Portmans in the room, he was prepared to bet any number of their former escorts were ready and waiting on the other side of the door. With reinforcements as well. At the first signs of any trouble, a small army would be here in seconds.

He eyed the long-dead Portmans on the wall. If he was very lucky, Ernesto and his sons might very soon be joining their ranks. He was just in the mood but, sadly, Time Police procedures or not, this room was lacking in anything that might come in useful as a weapon. Perhaps deliberately so. Luke never more bitterly regretted leaving behind his sonic, his baton, his string, his knife, his blaster, his other blaster . . . He had nothing with him. He wasn't even in uniform.

With one ear on his father disparaging Portman hospitality, he slipped his sunglasses into his top pocket and stood in the approved Time Police manner. Feet slightly apart. Weight evenly distributed – ready to move in any direction at a moment's notice. Hands relaxed and by his sides. All right. While he and his father were sensibly close together and could watch each other's backs, all three Portmans were standing foolishly far apart. He'd take out Anthony first, because he was the biggest threat. And the biggest prat. Assuming he himself was still on his feet after that, he'd go for Bradley, because Bradley would be too stupid to take any action unless specifically directed to do so. Ernesto could safely be left to last. He was well known to have a sadly non-fatal heart condition. Although fingers crossed . . .

The thing not to do . . . the one thing not to do . . . was to think about how much this was going to hurt him. One blow to the face and he'd be down. The same with his ribs. A sensible man would smile and placate and await his opportunity. Except that the longer they were here, the worse their chances were, so he crossed his fingers and grinned at Anthony Portman, who was going down no matter how much it hurt. Hanging on by his fingertips though he might be, Luke was still a Time Police officer. Time to make a few Portmans wet themselves.

He cut across Ernesto. 'Do any of you realise how much trouble you're in? You've kidnapped a Time Police officer. You can have no idea of the shedload of shit about to descend upon you.'

Ernesto smirked. 'On the contrary, officer, we simply offered

371

you and your father – old friends of the family – a lift. Out of the kindness of our hearts.'

Raymond Parrish brushed imaginary dust off his sleeve. 'And it's simply a coincidence that today I was without my team.'

'We've waited weeks for this opportunity. Which, I hope, will tell you how eager we are that this meeting should take place. *And* we were concerned for Officer Parrish, who looks to have recently sustained some serious injuries.' He spread his arms. 'Where is the gratitude?'

'I have no idea,' said Raymond Parrish vaguely, looking around. 'Why don't you ask your people to start looking for it – something that should keep them occupied indefinitely – while my son and I continue with our plans for the day.'

He turned back towards the door, incidentally giving Luke a little more room and positioning himself with his back to a nearby wall. Anti-kidnap training. Luke was relieved to see his father had at least paid some attention.

Ernesto was nodding. 'Of course. I understand you must both be very busy men. I shall only keep you a moment and then you can be on your way.'

'We'll be on our way now, I think.'

Ernesto walked back around the desk and opened a drawer. Luke stiffened but he only pulled out a document. 'As I said, Raymond, in a moment.'

Raymond Parrish was amused. 'Ernesto, never tell me you've finally grown a set. Are you actually attempting to force me to do something?'

'Harshly expressed, Raymond, but you've left me very little choice. You are a very difficult man to pin down. My people

372

have been trying for a meeting with you since well before last year.'

'And I keep telling you I have no interest in meeting your people. Delightful though I'm sure they are. And since I am fairly certain I know what you want, let me end your suffering by informing you, categorically, once and for all, that I have not signed in the past. I will not sign now. I will not sign in the future. To simplify things for the hard of understanding – or the Portmans, as they are generically known – I will never sign.'

Luke turned to his father. 'Normally I wouldn't interfere – especially since you seem to be doing such a good job by yourself, Dad – but since I've been dragged here against my will, I do feel I have a right to know. What will you never sign?'

'Divorce papers,' said Raymond Parrish, briefly.

'Ah,' said Luke, who would be torn apart by wild horses rather than admit he hadn't a clue what was going on. 'I see.'

One by one, Ernesto laid the documents on the desk. 'You have only to sign these, Raymond.'

Raymond Parrish smiled. 'You have only to send them to my office.'

'You send them back. Unsigned. Every time.'

'And still you fail to take the hint.'

Ernesto Portman changed tack. 'Raymond, I appeal to you. This unfortunate situation has remained unresolved for far too long. For the sake of everyone, let us agree to draw a line beneath it and move on.'

'And as I have repeatedly told you, Ernesto – when I hear this from Alessa, then I shall comply. But – as I have repeatedly told you, Ernesto – I want to hear this from Alessa herself.

Arrange a meeting – allow me to speak to my wife – and I shall happily carry out her wishes.'

'Alessa's health . . .'

'Is a very convenient excuse. I suspect she wishes this divorce as little as I do, which is why you keep her from me. Give it up, Ernesto, and return my wife to me.'

Ernesto appeared to think this over. 'I will speak with her doctors and comply with their advice. In the meantime, sign the documents and let us all make new beginnings.'

Raymond Parrish was firm. 'Not until you take me to my wife and I am satisfied she is acting of her own free will.'

There was just the veriest fraction of a pause. Luke opened his mouth and then closed it again.

Ernesto produced a pen. 'Sign the documents, Raymond, and I am sure something can be arranged.'

'Never going to happen.'

'Are you sure? These are difficult times. Especially for you. The recent scandal over your involvement in the illegal activities at a certain Site X really didn't do your share price any good at all, did it? How many millions were wiped off the value of your companies? And suppose you were to suddenly vanish from public sight. People will say you ran away. A sure sign of guilt. And even if they don't – for how long, do you think, can you afford to be absent from the helm of Parrish Industries?'

Raymond Parrish yawned. 'One of my many talents is the ability to employ and retain first-class staff. Much though it pains me to admit it, I suspect my absence will make very little difference. Even if you attempt to keep us here forever.'

'Yeah, I really don't advise that,' said Luke. 'The kidnap

374

and imprisonment of a Time Police officer isn't something even you'll be able to buy your way out of, Portman.'

Ernesto Portman smiled. 'Well, I admit you are an unplanned surplus, Officer Parrish, but it will be interesting, I think, to see precisely how much effort the Time Police put into reacquiring their prodigal son.'

'More than you might think, actually,' said Luke, who had no high hopes of this.

'Are you sure? Is it not possible they'll just post you as AWOL, heave a deep sigh of relief and carry on as if you've never even crossed their threshold?'

Luke's stomach churned. That was actually extremely likely. The sudden realisation that, with the possible exception of his father, there wasn't a single person on the planet who would come looking for him was rather a cold slap in the face.

Casually, he shifted his weight to bring himself another half step closer to the door. Time to move things on a little.

'Serious word of advice, Bradley, you should leave before things get rough.' He paused, apparently struck by a new thought. 'Although, rumour has it that's just how you like it, especially when enjoying a spot of uphill gardening on the Heath. Not you, of course, Anthony. Word on the street is that you no longer enjoy a spot of any sort of gardening – uphill or otherwise. According to Annabelle Lowestoft anyway. The more generous among us – of whom I am not one – ascribe your stifficulty to steroid abuse. In fact – and I think everyone here will enjoy this little joke – so limp and useless is Anthony's dick that people have taken to calling it Bradley.'

Both brothers turned identical shades of purple. Anthony raised one meaty fist.

'Enough.'

Ernesto's voice cracked across the room. Both of his sons stopped in their tracks. There was a moment's silence during which the only thing audible was Anthony's heavy breathing.

Ernesto smiled tightly, his determination not to take offence strained to its limit. 'He's very rude, Raymond. He reminds me of you.'

'He's a fine boy,' Raymond Parrish said, smiling. 'We're all very proud of him.'

Recent events – and Lt Grint – had dealt Luke a series of heart-stopping hammer blows. And here was another. For one brief moment, he found himself without words.

Raymond Parrish hadn't finished.

'So sorry to hear about young Eric, by the way, and this is a genuine enquiry: did he take his own life in an attempt to evade justice? Or was his life taken from him to prevent him sharing his knowledge of your illegal Time-travelling organisation?'

Ernesto Portman did not so much as flinch. 'According to recent reports, Raymond, you are far more knowledgeable about such things than I. I hear your organisation supplied most of the component parts for the mysteriously named Site X. Should it not be *you* sharing your knowledge with the Time Police?'

He appeared to notice Luke again. 'Or is that perhaps what I have interrupted today? A private briefing, perhaps? The son updating the father? And vice versa.'

Luke turned to his father. Another half step nearer the wall and a better position. 'Let's go, Dad. I'm hungry. And we have a great deal of secret information to exchange.'

'As I said,' began Ernesto Portman.

'And as I said,' interrupted Luke. 'Kidnapping a Time Police officer is a very serious offence carrying a minimum sentence of fifteen years and believe me, I will be very happy to press charges. *And* I strongly suspect the rest of your worthless family won't hesitate to rid themselves of embarrassments like you. They'll sell you down the river, Ernesto, and your idiot offspring, too. But by all means give it a shot. We in the Time Police are famed for enjoying a good laugh.'

There was a short silence and then, ignoring the warning from his father, Anthony surged forwards. He was taller and heavier than Luke, who shifted his weight to the balls of his feet, ready and waiting.

Anthony had obviously been well instructed by professionals. Luke, on the other hand, had spent a fair amount of time being beaten up in the corridors of TPHQ and knew, none better, not to stand around waiting for others to make the first move. While Anthony sensibly went for his face – as expected – Luke closed in under his attempted blow, hooked his leg behind Anthony's calf, and used both their momentums to swing him around and down and smash his face into the, unfortunately for Anthony, very solid wooden desk. The crunching noise was probably Anthony's nose. And possibly a few teeth as well. Damage to the fine old desk – minimal. The Revenge of the Rainforests, perhaps.

Leaving Anthony to fall to the floor under his own steam, Luke whirled around and seized Bradley who, as expected, had been too slow to move and was still facing in the wrong direction. Ignoring the pain in his ribs, he got one arm around Bradley's throat and forced his right arm up behind his back. Almost to breaking point. Bradley shrieked in pain. Luke pulled him close and leaned heavily on him. Instinctively, Bradley braced himself. Good. Now Bradley was holding them both up and Luke could concentrate on the next threat. Because any minute now . . .

The door flew open. Luke pulled Bradley even closer. As a prop, he was proving useful. Sadly, since he was a good six inches shorter than Luke, as a body shield, he was about as much use as a crocheted condom. Luke braced himself. Four men piled into the room. Each of them brandishing a weapon. This was probably not going to end well. He looked around for his father.

Raymond Parrish was standing calmly in the centre of the room, one arm around Ernesto's throat and the other holding an uncapped fountain pen to Ernesto's carotid artery. Twin streams of blue and red stained Ernesto's previously immaculate collar. The much taller and more powerful Raymond Parrish was pulling Ernesto almost off his feet. Ernesto was clawing uselessly at Raymond Parrish's forearm, his face darkening as he struggled for breath. Raymond Parrish, on the other hand, was maintaining his usual polished poise. Except that his tie, once again, had become slightly disarranged. For which heads would roll.

The office was suddenly full of big, black-suited men all with very unfriendly expressions. There was a lot of shouting along the lines of *release the prisoners*, *put your hands in the air* and other unhelpful instructions, all of which were completely ignored.

'I am a member of the Time Police,' said Luke. 'Sadly, I have something in my hands at the moment, but if one of you would be kind enough to shoot Bradley here, I shall be able to show you my official ID.'

378

The shouting went away. Although the guns remained.

'That's better,' said Raymond Parrish. 'Perhaps we should all take a moment to step back?'

'No need,' said the biggest man – one of their original escort, Luke thought. The other three were almost as big. And at that moment they were joined by the chauffeur – another big man. The Portmans obviously didn't hire any other sort. Luke had a horrible feeling the next ten minutes were really going to hurt.

'I am Officer Parrish of the Time Police,' he said again, feeling the point couldn't be made too strongly. 'Kidnapping and threatening an officer of the Time Police is a felony. Stand aside and allow us to exit the building.'

'Or what?' said the man. 'Is it true what they say? That the Time Police can't count. After all, there are five of us' – wisely, he was discounting the Portmans as an effective fighting force – 'against the two of you.'

Luke forced Bradley's arm another impossible half-inch. Bradley cried out in pain.

'I'm sorry,' said Luke, pleasantly. 'You were saying?'

'I'm saying you're not going anywhere. Sorry about this, Mr Portman, but they can't hold you forever. They have no weapons. We have this situation completely under control.'

Faintly, in another part of the building – like a gift from God – there was an explosion. Luke felt the floor shake beneath his feet. And then the screaming started.

32

For a long while, no one moved.

'Not entirely sure what's going on out there,' said Luke, eventually, 'but we all know there's only one organisation who makes that sort of entrance. Now, they don't love me, but they're certainly not going to be happy about your attempt to detain me against my will.'

There was another bang, swiftly followed by the roar of a discharged blaster. And shouts and screaming. And chaos, of course. Yes, folks, the Time Police were definitely here.

'If I might make a suggestion,' said Raymond Parrish. 'Perhaps, for all our safety, and definitely for the avoidance of awkward questions, we should all take a moment to think very carefully about our next moves. Since I have no intention of becoming an unfortunate Time Police statistic, I intend to release my friend Ernesto here. Luke will do the same with Bradley, and we will leave the rest of you to make whatever explanations you think will be most appropriate. Or you can put your weapons away and we can all pretend this is a scheduled business meeting that had somehow slipped my mind.'

This sensible suggestion was wholly disregarded. It would appear that, Time Police or not, the Portman security forces were unwilling to surrender their advantage. Somewhere in the room, a safety clicked off.

Bradley squeaked.

'Sorry, did I hurt you?' enquired Luke, solicitously. 'My bad. Can I suggest you start shouting directions, Dad? Some of my colleagues will almost certainly need all the help they can get to find us.'

'No need for that,' rasped Ernesto. 'My dear friend Raymond is quite correct. An impromptu business meeting. We were all so overjoyed at seeing each other that time just flew by. Stand your men down, Adnan.'

'Sir, I can deal with . . .'

'You heard what I said.'

'Sir . . .'

'I don't want the Time Police all over this building. Just do it.'

Raymond Parrish released Ernesto, who straightened his jacket and tried to smooth his hair.

After a moment, Luke shoved Bradley away from him. Bradley stumbled and would have fallen hard had Adnan not caught him and then roughly pushed him behind a chair and out of the way. Rather the story of Bradley's life.

There was the sound of shouting from the other side of the door. On this side of the door, all guns miraculously disappeared. The Time Police have never been famous for politely asking people to lay down their weapons.

'Quickly,' said Luke, gesturing, and two Portman security men rolled the still very groggy Anthony behind the desk and out of sight.

Not a moment too soon. The door burst open to reveal the

full majesty of Lt Grint, fully armed and armoured, his smoking blaster covering the entire room.

'Oh shit,' muttered Luke. That there wasn't a person in the entire room with whom he was on friendly terms was not an encouraging thought.

And it wasn't just Grint. A much smaller officer stood at his shoulder, covering his rear. They moved into the room in a well-coordinated movement. Textbook stuff. Luke was slightly taken aback to see how well Jane and Grint worked together. That didn't seem right, somehow.

'All weapons on the floor,' said Grint. 'Now.'

It seemed safe to assume the instant obedience gladdened Lt Grint's flint-like heart. Unbidden, Jane backed against the wall where she had a good view not only of the office and its occupants, but of the corridor as well.

Grint kicked the weapons aside. 'Step back against the wall, all of you. Slowly. Officer Parrish – report.'

'Good afternoon,' said Luke, strolling to the middle of the room, but very slowly. With a fully armed Grint within striking distance, he wasn't sure his position had improved any. He gestured towards his father. 'I feel I should point out that although our presence here is entirely involuntary, it is not Time Police-related. It would appear this is the standard Portman method of obtaining a signature on certain . . . business documents. No threat to the Time Police was intended. I was simply swept up in the enthusiasm of the moment.'

Grint raised his visor. 'Are you hurt?'

'Of course not. They're only Portmans.'

If Grint was delighted to hear Luke was unharmed, he hid it well. 'Do you want to press charges?'

'No,' said Raymond Parrish, apparently under the impression it was his decision. 'I don't think so. Officer Parrish had the situation well in hand before your timely arrival – thank you very much, by the way – and we feel that their colossal embarrassment – together with your no doubt hefty bill for wasting Time Police . . . er . . . time – will be punishment enough for the unfortunate Portmans. This has been a minor inconvenience – nothing more. As Luke said, a mix-up over a signature which I am happy to say has now been entirely resolved. Portman and Webber has realised its error and will, I am certain, never make this mistake again. Will you, Ernesto?'

Luke stood very close to Ernesto Portman. 'Consider this a warning. From the Time Police. Your card's marked, Portman.'

He looked over at Bradley, gently massaging his throat. 'It's all over, Bradley. You can come out from behind the chair now and pretend to be a man again.'

Raymond Parrish began to move slowly towards the door. 'Pleasant, is it not, Ernesto, to have sons of which to be proud? Oh, I'm sorry – you only have Anthony and Bradley. How unkind of me to rub it in. Well, never mind. Shall we go, Luke?'

'Whenever you're ready, Dad.'

Lt Grint was not about to relinquish control of the situation. 'Wait for me in the corridor, Parrish.'

'To which Parrish are you speaking?' enquired Luke, unable to resist the temptation.

'Guess.'

Jane stepped aside to maintain safe distance as both Parrishes exited the room. Her visor was still down. Luke had no clue as to her feelings.

As they stepped a few paces down the corridor, he could hear

Grint addressing the assembled room. Standard Time Police bollocking. He took his father's arm and together they moved out of earshot.

'Nice moves, Dad.'

'Thank you,' said Raymond Parrish, straightening his tie. 'I think that should make them think twice about tangling with the Parrish boys in future, don't you?'

Luke cast a glimpse towards Jane, now angled in the doorway so she could keep an eye on happenings in the corridor, and lowered his voice even further.

'Did you notice, Dad?'

'I did indeed.'

'When he wanted you to sign?'

'Yes.'

'They didn't produce Mum because they couldn't.'

'No.'

'I always thought she was here. Well, not here, but with the Portmans, somewhere.'

'Yes.'

'But they don't have her, do they?'

'No, apparently they don't.'

'So who does? If she's not here, then where is she? Where is my mother?'

Raymond Parrish nodded. 'That is a very good question, Luke. Hush now.'

They were joined by Lt Grint, who closed the office door behind him and used the butt of his blaster to bludgeon the door handle into uselessness.

'Well,' said Raymond Parrish. 'Thank you very much, officers, for your timely appearance. Officer Lockland I already know – I hear great things of you, officer – but perhaps you could introduce me to your other colleague, Luke.'

There was a short, but somehow very expressive, pause.

Luke gritted his teeth. 'Dad, this is Lt Grint. He heads up another team and is second in charge of our department.'

Raymond Parrish was not thrown for one instant. 'How do you do, Lieutenant. Luke often speaks of you.'

Grint, unsurprised that great things had not been heard of him, nodded silently, although it is possible that any response would have been inaudible over the impatient whining of his enormous blaster.

Raymond Parrish stared impassively at the still-visored Jane.

'Officer Lockland, I know this is neither the time nor place, but you and I need to have a short conversation as soon as possible.'

Jane made no move or comment.

Grint, however, made a movement which gave them to understand that vacating the premises should commence without further delay.

They took a different route out of the building. It would appear the lift in which Grint and Lockland had arrived was no longer functioning at optimum efficiency.

Their progress, or as Luke referred to it – Team Parrish's progress – through the building was enormous fun. It would be fair to say that, in their own ways, a great time was had by all. Lt Grint's enormous blaster led the way, growling under its breath, warning lights blinking, seeking what it might devour. The blaster was closely followed by Lt Grint himself, in no good mood and not particularly bothered about who knew it.

The Parrish boys strolled casually, occasionally pausing to

inspect a painting or ceramic and make derogatory remarks. Each wore an identical smirk, with Raymond Parrish going so far as to call personal and not always complimentary greetings to the various faces hiding behind half-closed doors. No one attempted to hinder their exit.

Jane marched at the rear, her own blaster raised and ready. She didn't expect to have to use it but she didn't see why Grint should have all the fun.

'Attagirl,' said Bolshy Jane, completely on board with this reprehensible attitude.

They found the public lift on the floor below, crowded with nervous people who, for some reason or other, all scattered at their approach.

The lift doors pinged closed, shutting them in. Jane fretted in the enclosed space, worrying that a message might be sent ahead of them to prevent their leaving.

'We should be so lucky,' said Bolshy Jane, cracking a knuckle or two. 'I could just fancy a quick punch-up. Clear the pipes a bit.'

'Pipes?' enquired Jane, all at sea. 'What pipes? Do I have pipes?'

'You do indeed, sweetie, and you really need to get yours cleared.'

Jane ignored this.

The lift opened into a basement with no apparent exit.

A rumbling sound from Grint indicated his always limited patience had run out. 'This way,' he said, leading Jane and Raymond Parrish along a corridor. The floors and wall were grey. There were no designated door numbers. From the lack of windows Luke assumed they were well below ground level.

Possibly even below car-park level. This was obviously an area not designed to be seen by the public.

Luke paused thoughtfully, looking up and down the corridor. Something someone had said was nagging at his brain. Something very recent. He frowned, then shrugged. Jane, the last of the group, was just disappearing around a corner. Luke made haste to catch up, but when he too turned the corner, there was no sign either of his colleagues or his father. He wheeled about. This new corridor was as featureless as the last one. However, there was a pair of double doors at one end and he headed towards these. They were locked. And undamaged. Lt Grint had obviously not passed this way. His attitude towards locked doors was well known.

Undeterred, Luke turned around, intending to retrace his steps. Grint would have noticed he was gone by now. Probably. He surveyed the corridor ahead of him. He'd turned left before, so down here and turn right. Or should it be left again? For God's sake, this was the sort of thing that usually happened to Matthew, whose mother was well known to have the sense of direction and general purpose of a plastic bag in a high wind.

He turned right. No, this wasn't his corridor, either. There were no doors at all here. Except for just one, down at the end. Another lift, perhaps. He strode forwards at exactly the same time as a man in medical scrubs emerged, carrying a tray.

'Hold that door,' shouted Luke.

The man looked around, saw Luke, dropped his tray with a crash and groped for the heavy-duty taser hanging from his belt.

Luke Parrish was not in the mood. His right hand went for the taser. His left hand jabbed his only two fingers into the medic's eyes. The medic yelled and relinquished the taser.

Luke pushed him hard and the momentum carried them both into the room. Two swift punches, one to the kidneys and one to the jaw, ended Medical Man's resistance.

Luke blew on his throbbing knuckles and contemplated a job well done.

Until someone hit him over the head with the tray.

388

33

Outside in the car park, meanwhile, the three quarters of Team Parrish – the ones who, according to Lt Grint, possessed at least a rudimentary sense of direction – had just become aware that twenty-five per cent of their party was missing. Lt Grint, on the verge of powering down his blaster, abandoned that action as frivolous and unnecessary and looked around. 'Where is he? Lockland?'

They looked at each other, identical thoughts crossing their minds. That Luke Parrish, having no desire to return to the shambles that was his career in the Time Police, had made himself scarce on purpose.

'He was behind me,' said Jane, looking around. 'And then he wasn't. Mind you, it's a bit of a warren back there – he's taken a wrong turning, that's all. I'll go back and get him.'

Grint opened his mouth, considered his options and closed it again. It made sense for him to remain outside with Raymond Parrish who, in the scheme of things, was slightly more important than his useless shit of a son. Actually, in the scheme of things, blue-green algae was probably more important than Luke Parrish. Grint was tempted to push off and leave him here, but his instructions were to return Officer

Parrish to TPHQ, and return him he would. Whether Officer Parrish liked it or not.

He nodded. 'Be quick. I don't want to give them time to regroup.'

Jane pushed open the door and found herself back in the maze of grey corridors. Tilting her head, she thought she could hear voices somewhere off to her left. Pulling her blaster from her rip-grip patch, she made her way very cautiously along the corridor. There was an open door at the end. She was careful to make no noise but it was unlikely any of the occupants of the room would have heard her anyway.

The first occupant was lying spark out on the floor and showing no interest in anything at all.

The second occupant, one Luke Parrish, was sitting on the floor, rubbing his head and complaining bitterly. He broke off when he saw her standing in the doorway.

'Jane. Thank God. Get your clothes off.'

Not for the first time – or the last – Jane paid him no attention at all. She hadn't bothered when he was team leader so she certainly wasn't going to start now.

'That's the ticket, sweetie,' said Bolshy Jane. 'Fire up your blaster and laminate his sorry arse to the ceiling.'

Jane raised her blaster. 'I can see you've had a bad day, Parrish, but give me one good reason why I shouldn't make it even worse.'

He was trying to get to his feet. 'No time for that, Jane. Take off your clothes.'

'I keep telling you to kill him,' complained Bolshy Jane. 'You've brought this on yourself. When I think how you've squandered the opportunities . . .'

'Fire truck off, Parrish.'

'Keep your voice down.'

'Your father killed . . .'

'No, he didn't, but I don't have time for that now. I want your clothes.'

'I don't care what you want, Parrish, so just . . .'

Finally heaving himself to his feet, Luke grabbed her arm and physically turned her around.

'Goodness gracious,' said Wimpy Jane.

'Well, I'll be buggered,' said Bolshy Jane.

'What . . . ?' said Actual Jane.

Luke gestured impatiently. 'Jane – for the love of God, give me your clothes.'

Jane pulled herself together. 'I will not.'

Luke closed in.

Back in the car park, the remaining rescuer and rescuee were becoming impatient.

'Obviously, I don't want to interfere with your excellent handling of the situation so far,' said Raymond Parrish, rocking backwards and forwards on his heels, 'but it does occur to me that any moment now we might need to make a quick getaway, and since I lack your particular skill set, I feel my time would probably be most profitably spent ensuring the speed of said getaway. Do you drive at all, Lieutenant?'

Grint shook his head. 'Only qualified on driverless.'

'In that case . . .' Raymond Parrish set off towards the sleek black car parked nearby.

'It'll be locked,' warned Grint.

'I don't think . . .'

Disinclined to waste any time, Grint went to smash the driver's window with the blunt end of his blaster.

Raymond Parrish sighed. 'Cameras, officer.'

'Time Police,' said Grint, a phrase he frequently found settled all disputes, and lifted his blaster again.

Raymond Parrish pulled open the door. 'Actually, not locked. *And* the key card is still in the slot. Nevertheless, an excellent thought and much appreciated.'

Grint grunted and was heading back towards the building when the door opened to reveal Luke and Officer Lockland – who appeared to require Luke's support.

'Lockland?' enquired Grint, sharply.

'She's fine,' said Luke, reassuringly, somehow managing to insert himself between Jane and the ever-present CCTV cameras. 'Just banged her head a little.'

'She's wearing a helmet,' said Grint, gearing himself up for a repeat of the infamous corridor incident.

'She is, isn't she?' said Luke, brightly. 'Could you lend a hand here, please?'

At that moment, a glossy black car reversed neatly alongside with a nonchalant Parrish senior at the wheel.

Luke blinked. 'A getaway car. Yet another nice move, Dad.'

A lesser man might have smirked.

'Everyone inside,' said Luke, wrenching open a rear door.

Jane crawled on to the back seat with a deeply suspicious Grint alongside.

'Give me your blaster, Jane,' said Luke, sticking his head into the car. 'I'll stow it in the boot. We don't want any inadvertent discharges, as Lt Grint would be the first to agree.'

Before Grint could say anything, he seized Jane's blaster and disappeared around the back of the car.

'What's he doing?' said Grint irritably, twisting to peer around the raised boot lid.

Jane sighed softly and sagged against him, puzzling Grint, who looked down in some concern. 'Are you all right?'

Jane nodded bravely.

'Lift your visor, Lockland – let's have a look at you.'

Jane shook her head, whispering, 'I'm fine.'

Behind them, Luke gently closed the boot. Grint frowned and might have said something, but at that moment, Raymond Parrish surrendered the driving seat, saying quietly, 'I think this might be better suited to your talents, Luke.'

Making himself comfortable in the passenger seat, he looked over his shoulder, saying, 'I believe this vehicle is equipped with seat belts. It might be wise to put them on.'

Luke grinned, climbed into the car, slipped on his sunglasses, engaged first gear, let out the clutch and the car moved smoothly forwards. Towards the car park exit. Where the barrier was down.

A uniformed guard stepped out of his cubicle and indicated they were to halt.

Luke frowned, calculating the odds. For one wild moment he actually contemplated driving straight at the barrier. On second thoughts, however, that might not be the best idea. It looked solid. Very solid. Easily solid enough to deter any spontaneous barrier-ramming plans anyone might entertain.

He slowed. Perhaps this was just a formality. Surely there hadn't been time for them to discover . . . and there had been no security check on entering the car park. He came to a stop.

The guard moved around the front of the vehicle, peering suspiciously through the windscreen. Grint's blaster began to whine in anticipation.

'No,' said Luke, quietly. 'This is not the time or place. There's a portcullis and stingers. We won't get six feet. And I suspect the next layer of Portman security will be considerably more efficient and less tolerant than the ones we've just met.'

'We're the Time Police,' rumbled Grint. 'Run him over.'

'Trust me,' said Luke. 'The last thing we need at the moment is any trouble. Got that?'

He wasn't sure if it was his imagination or not, but it seemed to be Jane to whom the guard was paying particular attention. This situation was about to go downhill really fast. Luke had no doubt Lt Grint would prove more than equal to the occasion and normally he'd have no problems with that, but at this moment – at this very moment – a safe, secure, and above all, *immediate* getaway was of paramount importance.

The guard tilted his head as if listening. Someone was talking in his ear. His gaze snapped back to Jane. Luke cursed. Someone was raising the alarm. Not taking his eyes off her, the guard walked around the car to peer at the passengers.

'You – lift your visor.'

Jane stared at him, saying nothing.

'You heard me.'

Luke had adjusted the rear-view mirror and was watching the door from which they had just escaped, fully expecting it to open at any moment and a veritable Portman army appear. They only had seconds left . . .

Grint lifted his blaster.

Jane put her hand on his arm and very slowly raised her

visor. 'I am Officer Lockland of the Time Police,' she said, hoarsely. 'Am I about to have a problem with you?'

That the guard was suspicious was very obvious. And he wasn't giving up. Luke's hands clenched on the steering wheel. They absolutely, completely and utterly *must not be caught*.

He smiled and tried to slow his breathing. 'Good day. My father and I have just finished our meeting with Ernesto Portman. And Anthony and Bradley, of course. An important meeting, obviously. You can see our Time Police escort.' He frowned. 'Should I have collected some sort of parking token on our way out? Or perhaps . . .'

The guard wasn't buying any of it. Grint began to climb out of the car. Any minute now . . .

Without warning, Raymond Parrish collapsed sideways against the door, clutching his chest and grimacing with pain. 'Aaaghh.'

Luke froze for one moment and then shouted at the guard, 'What did you do?'

The guard, six feet away, stepped back, hands held high. 'Nothing. I never touched him.'

'Pills,' gasped Raymond Parrish. 'Right-hand pocket, Luke. Quickly. Quickly.' He doubled over, clenched fists clutching at his chest. 'Aaaggh.'

Luke rummaged in his father's empty right-hand pocket. 'Dad, they're not there. Where are they? What do I do? Dad? Dad?'

But Raymond Parrish was beyond speech. A thin line of saliva appeared at the corner of his mouth and ran down his chin.

Luke shook him. 'Dad . . . Dad . . . tell me. What do I do? Oh God, I don't know what to do. Talk to me. Dad?'

Grint was out of the vehicle. And he'd brought his blaster with him.

Luke was panicking. 'I can't find his pills. Perhaps he doesn't have them. It's their fault. The Portmans. They kidnapped him and he didn't bring his pills with him. I didn't know he was ill and that he needed them. Grint – get us out of here. To the hospital.'

Grint stared down at the guard. 'I am an officer of the Time Police,' he said, heavily. 'And today I am Raymond Parrish's personal escort. Get that barrier up and live.'

The guard stared around. The car park was empty. Although for how much longer? He looked back at Grint. As he later swore to his colleagues – the bastard had grown another three inches during the short time he'd looked away.

Luke gunned the engine and, in a panic he didn't have to simulate, shouted, 'Get that fire-trucking barrier up. Hang on, Dad. I'll get you to the hospital. Why didn't you tell me . . . ?'

And then, miraculously, the barrier was raised. Grint barely had time to leap back into the vehicle. Tyres screaming, the black car roared up the ramp, erupted out of the garage, swerved across the lane reserved for emergency vehicles, the three lanes reserved for cyclists, and narrowly missed illegally mounting the Blackfriars walkway before Luke eventually regained control and returned the car to its designated lane, leaving complete chaos behind them.

'Pull over,' said Grint in a voice that brooked no argument.

'But . . .'

'Now.'

Raymond Parrish sat up and carefully wiped his chin on a spotless handkerchief. 'Naturally I defer to your greater experience, Lieutenant, but in this instance, I think returning to Parrish Industries with all speed will not only seem more natural under the circumstances, but should there be any repercussions from this afternoon's events, we will be able to deal with them more competently from there. I'm almost certain this car will be tracked and what could be more natural than for us to return home where I will certainly be in a position to receive the best care.'

'Doesn't matter, Dad,' said Luke through gritted teeth and making a sharp turn left. 'After a stunt like that, I'm going to kill you myself.'

Unlike their departure from Portman House, their arrival in St James's Square was much less spectacular. Automatic stingers ensured speeds of more than fifteen miles per hour around the square were impossible and while Luke couldn't care less about the continued well-being of their vehicle, he wasn't finished with it yet.

They drew up outside Parrish Industries HQ. Luke knew, without even looking, that all Parrish Industries' extensive camera and security systems would be trained on them, to say nothing of those belonging to the council, the police, national security and all the private armies of their rich and therefore very important neighbours. Scores of eyes would be watching them at this very moment. This was by no means over.

He pulled up but left the engine running, making it clear, he hoped, that he wasn't stopping.

Raymond Parrish went to open his door.

'One moment, please,' said Grint, reminding Luke he wasn't out of the woods yet. Barely emerging from the thicket, in fact. 'What's going on, Parrish?'

'Actually, I'd rather not say.'

'And I couldn't give a flying duck about what you'd rather not do,' said Grint. 'Out of the car. Now.' The words *so I can more easily beat the living shit out of you again* were not spoken but didn't need to be, really.

Luke made no move to obey. 'I really think I should make sure my father gets inside safely. This has been a very upsetting experience for him. He's extremely shaken.'

An impassive Raymond Parrish agreed that he was, indeed, extremely shaken.

'He won't be the only one,' said Grint. 'Out of the car or I'll drag you out.'

There was a certain amount of anticipation in his voice.

Jane put her hand on his arm. 'Not here, sir.'

Grint stared down at her for a long moment. She shook her head. 'Not here.'

Contrary to everything Luke Parrish had ever said about him, Lt Grint was not stupid. 'Parrish, you're AWOL. You're to return to TPHQ in my custody.'

Luke glanced at his watch. 'Give me an hour.'

Grint swelled with wrath. Quite an impressive sight if you'd never seen that before. Or even if you had. Luke's bruises began to throb in anticipation.

Jane bit her tongue. This was Grint's decision. Temporarily, he was her team leader. She'd done what she could for Luke but today she took her instructions from Lt Grint. Who was staring at Luke. Luke stared back. The moment seemed endless and was only broken when Grint finally climbed out of the car. 'One hour, Parrish.'

'One hour,' said Luke.

Jane opened her door. 'Do you require assistance, Mr Parrish? Not you,' she added as Luke opened his mouth.

Ms Steel was already standing at the top of the steps, a security guard on either side. If they were carrying weapons then they were certainly well concealed, but these were very big men, hand-picked from the best, probably, and they bore an air of overwhelming confidence.

Grint curled his lip at these amateurs, saying again, 'Fifty-five minutes, Parrish.'

'I told you – I'll be there,' said Luke.

Raymond Parrish turned to Jane and held out his hand. 'Thank you, Officer Lockland.'

Jane didn't move. 'I've kept my visor down because I find it very difficult to look at you.'

'I understand. I would like to make a short statement to which you do not have to respond in any way. I know I am not the Raymond Parrish who laid information to the Time Police about your parents. You may not be aware that my father was also a Raymond Parrish. It's a family name. He died some years ago so we cannot ask him, but I strongly suspect he is the person to blame for the death of your parents. And before you ask, he would have done it for no better reason than to secure a business advantage over a rival. In his admittedly very weak defence, I suspect the tragic consequences were completely unintended. I shall ask Ms Steel to investigate, but I would not be at all surprised to learn that regular payments have been made to Mrs Lockland. For her silence, of course, but also contributions towards your welfare and education. I also strongly suspect you have never seen a penny of that.'

He smiled slightly. 'I think you have had rather a lot of

information thrown at you today, therefore I shall leave you to think over what I have said and draw your own conclusions. Should you wish to speak to me, ring this number.' He pulled out a business card and wrote something upon it. 'Ms Steel will either put you straight through to me or make the earliest possible appointment.'

Raymond Parrish paused and then said, 'I apologise for my father. He was not a nice man. Neither am I, but I hope I am better than he was. Please accept my most sincere apologies for the wrong done to your family.'

He waited for a moment, presumably to see if a dumbstruck Jane had any comment to make.

Grint hefted his blaster. 'Officer Lockland.'

Jane nodded.

They both turned away and were heading towards the river when Grint stopped dead. 'Your blaster – it's still in the boot of that car. For some reason.'

'As to that,' said Jane, quietly. 'I believe I owe you an explanation. But not here.'

Luke watched until his colleagues turned the corner.

'I have to go, Dad, I'm on the clock.'

'Only if you promise that at some point you will explain exactly what is happening. Exactly why was it necessary to place Officer Lockland's really very modest blaster in the boot?'

'I don't want to implicate you, Dad, but I've discovered the real reason Ernesto didn't want the Time Police all over Portman House and it wasn't anything to do with us.'

'And now you have really piqued my interest.'

Luke grinned. 'Buy me a drink and I shall be delighted to divulge all. In the meantime, I have a car to dispose of.'

Raymond Parrish nodded his approval. 'Always make sure the evidence is safely disposed of, son.'

'I intend to. I think I'll ditch the car somewhere it will cost the Portmans a fortune in time, money and embarrassment to get back. If it doesn't get blown up first. The double yellow lines outside the Ministry of Defence or the forecourt of the new New Scotland Yard, perhaps. What do you think?'

'Commendably imaginative, my boy. Good luck to you. Ah, Lucinda – I hope you haven't been too worried, but we've had such an exciting time.'

'And it's not over yet,' muttered Luke, getting back into the car and pulling away.

Jane and Grint watched the car pass them and disappear into traffic. They walked slowly, side by side, back towards the river. Grint had powered down and shouldered his blaster but managed to look no less menacing. The pavement was quite crowded but still people parted around them.

'What do you think?' said Grint. 'Will we ever see Parrish again?'

'Oh, yes, I'm certain of it,' said Jane.

They fell silent.

Out of nowhere, Jane said, 'The Time Police killed my parents.'

'I know.'

'Do you think I should resign?'

'Did Hay tell you to?'

'No.'

'Did she threaten to throw you out?'

'No.'

401

'Do you want to resign?'

'No.'

Grint shrugged. 'Well, then. Problem solved.'

'Not really. I'm not in a team any longer and I suspect no one will want to work with me.'

'Lockland, what are you doing at this very moment?'

'Um ... retrieving Officer Parrish.' She paused. 'And working with you.'

There was a long silence.

'Point taken, sir.'

They reached the river, walked straight to the head of the queue and boarded a convenient clipper.

Grint steered them both on to the top deck, trusting the sounds of wind and water to keep their conversation private.

'What's going on, Jane?'

'Well,' said Jane. She talked rapidly but quietly.

At the end, Grint stared at her. 'You know I have to report this?'

Jane nodded. 'Of course, sir.'

'Shit . . .'

'I know.'

'This means . . .'

Jane nodded again. 'Would you like me to go with you when you report to Ellis?'

'Never mind Ellis – I'm going straight to Hay. And so are you.'

Luke, meanwhile, had driven – quietly and carefully – to his own apartment. He certainly couldn't afford to be pulled over now.

His apartment was one of the few in the complex with its own designated parking space – something that had doubled the price of the flat – but the space was a long way from the lift doors. Ignoring the signs detailing the massive fines imposed on those parking in other people's spots, Luke carefully reversed into the one nearest the lift. Jumping out, he trotted around the car and opened the boot, again carefully shielding as much as he could from the ubiquitous security cameras, saying cheerfully, 'You can come out now.'

Curled up in the boot, half-naked, covered in a blanket, shaking, dirty, drugged and terrified, Imogen Farnborough squinted up at him.

34

Getting Imogen out of the car proved more difficult than Luke had expected. True, she hardly weighed very much, but her movements were so erratic and uncoordinated that she could do very little to help herself.

Luke wrapped his jacket around her, hauled her into the lift, propped her against the wall like a ladder and stood directly in front of her, masking her as much as he could.

His voice unlocked his front door and he half carried, half dragged her inside. Once the door was closed behind them, however, the strength seemed to leave her completely and she collapsed against him.

'Nearly there,' he said. 'Just a little further.' Kicking open the door to the spare room – the one recently occupied by Jane in her undercover role as Luke's Female Friend Forty-Four – he laid her on the bed, pulled up the covers and instructed her to sleep.

As usual, she ignored everything he said, plucking at his sleeve and attempting to speak.

He shook his head. 'Try to sleep, Imogen. I have to go but I'll be back in a couple of hours. I have to get rid of the car and report in. No one's going to look for you here,' he said – more in hope than in actual belief, but a lot of rich and powerful people lived in this complex and the security was correspondingly robust – 'and then we'll talk about what to do next.'

She tried to clutch at his sleeve, slurring, 'No. Wait. 'Mportant.'

He sat on the bed. 'What is, Immy? What's important?'

It took her three goes to articulate the words. Her eyes were unfocused. Her movements jerky. This was not just drugs – she was displaying typical signs of being over-tasered. Luke wasn't greatly surprised. This was Imogen Farnborough. She would not have cooperated with her captors in any way and had obviously paid the price.

'Wait a minute, Immy. I'll get you some water. If you promise not to hit me over the head with a tray again.'

She coughed a laugh and closed her eyes.

'Don't go to sleep.'

''Kay.'

The water went everywhere. Neither of them were very steady. In the end, Luke sat her up, wedged her against his shoulder and held the glass for her.

'Sip it slowly. Otherwise it'll all come straight back up again and I'll have to change the bed.'

'Never changed . . . a bed in your . . . entire life, Parrish.'

'And I'm not starting now, so don't throw up.'

She tried to smile.

'Immy – what happened to you? What's going on? You're dead. I saw you die.'

Her voice was little more than a whisper. 'You were there?'

'I was, yes.' His voice cracked a little. 'Immy, they shot you.'

'I was drugged. Heard a bang. I thought . . . I was dead.' She looked around. 'Not sure I'm not.'

405

'You're not,' he said, firmly. 'You were in Portman House. Remember?'

'Not really. Just funny drinks. Made me sleep.' She tried to focus on her scarred forearm. 'They burned me, Luke.'

'Immy . . .'

'No. Listen. Mummy.'

'Mrs Farnborough? What about her?'

'They held me. So she'd do . . .' Her eyelids closed.

'What they wanted?'

'Yes.' Her head fell forwards. Then jerked upwards again. 'Saw Jane. Where's Jane?'

'Gone. I had some daft idea about swapping identities and getting you out as her, only she refused to take her clothes off.'

'Always was . . . brains of your . . . team.'

'We all have our strengths. I've always thought that while Matthew has the technical skills, and Jane the brains – it's me that brings the style and charm.'

'Fire . . . truck off, Parrish.'

Luke sat thoughtfully. The involvement of Mrs Farnborough changed everything. Eventually, he roused himself. 'Listen, Immy. I have to go.'

She struggled to keep her eyes open. 'No.'

'Yes. I have to report back to TPHQ. I'll admit – I don't know what to do next. I was going to keep you here, but that leaves your mother too exposed.'

He chewed his lip, formulating and discarding various ideas. His original plan had simply been to smuggle Imogen out of the building wearing Jane's uniform and shove Jane – gently – into the boot. Jane's refusal to take off her clothes had stymied that

406

plan, but they'd improvised. Time Police training had finally paid off, but no need to tell them that.

The priority had been to get Immy away somewhere safe until he could make more permanent arrangements. Jane, he knew, would report to Grint, who would report to Hay, but he'd hoped for at least a short head start.

The involvement of Imogen's mother, however, changed everything. It was his duty to report this. That a member of the government was acting under duress. But that would expose Imogen to the Time Police. And they'd already executed her once. How and why Imogen was with the Portmans of all people was something he would have to think about when he had time. His main concern was that he could be nursing her back to health so the Time Police could execute her all over again.

And Imogen herself – the Portmans would be looking for her. She was their key to controlling Mrs Farnborough. If they got to Imogen . . .

He toyed briefly with the idea of enlisting his father. If Luke had known then what he knew now then he could have unloaded Imogen at Parrish Industries HQ. She would almost certainly be safer there than here. But that still wouldn't solve the problem of Mrs Farnborough. He sighed. It always came back to Mrs Farnborough.

He looked down to see Imogen watching him. She'd always known what he was thinking. Often before he did. 'Mummy,' she said.

'Immy, I can't tell them about your mother without telling them about you.'

'Not 'mportant. Do it, Luke.'

He patted her shoulder. 'I'll think of something. You just leave everything to me. Jane's not the only one with a brain, you know.'

But Imogen had fallen asleep. He had no idea whether that would make things easier or not.

He laid her down gently, pulled up the covers and left, closing the bedroom door behind him. Pulling out his com, he tapped in a code. His com informed him Mrs Farnborough's number was unreachable. Which did not surprise him. Standing in the kitchen, he switched on the coffee machine and thought for a moment. Then he laughed and pulled out his com again.

A familiar voice answered.

He grinned. 'Lola. Darling. Guess who.'

Thirty minutes later, a smartly dressed woman with long blonde hair, carrying a small overnight bag, presented herself to the concierge in reception and asked for Luke Parrish.

The concierge – who knew her well from Luke's former occupancy – replied that as far as he knew, Mr Parrish was not currently occupying his apartment.

'I think you'll find he is,' said Lola, confidently.

The concierge picked up the phone, spoke briefly, and informed her that yes, Mr Parrish was not only available but was on his way down to greet her.

'Lovely,' Lola said, smiling.

The lift door pinged open to reveal the recently discussed Mr Parrish, who immediately flung his arms wide. 'Lola!'

'Darling!'

Everyone looked away for a few minutes. Lola's extreme affection was matched only by her lack of public inhibitions.

Eventually they drew apart. Lola patted her hair back into place. 'Darling. How are you? The most dreadful rumours are flying around town. Actual rehab? You poor thing. And your face. Whatever did they do to you? Although I have to say that underneath all that, you appear to be as handsome as ever.'

Luke smirked. 'I am, aren't I? Are you coming up?'

'Darling, I do hope so.'

She flashed the concierge an enchanting smile and followed Luke to the lift.

Once inside his flat, he lost no time in introducing the semi-conscious Imogen to his glamorous guest. Lola, to her credit, drew back and stared at him suspiciously. 'Luke, what *have* you been doing?'

'It's not what it looks like, I promise you. Help me to undress her.'

'For God's sake, Parrish,' said Imogen sleepily and tried to pull up the sheets.

Lola didn't move. Her expression was nowhere near as friendly as it had been. 'Sorry, darling, but I've always made it a rule that everyone in bed with me must at least be conscious. All sorts of trouble otherwise. And even if the lady sobers up, I should warn you – this sort of thing doesn't come cheap. And neither do I.'

'You never did.'

'Well, no, but I add a couple of noughts these days. Going up in the world, you know.'

'What – as opposed to going down?'

She laughed, showing perfect teeth. 'Naughty boy. You haven't changed a bit. I, on the other hand, am very nearly respectable now.'

'Pull the other one.'

'Delighted to, but that'll add yet another nought.'

'Well, that's not very respectable.'

'Oh, but it is. I move in the very best circles these days. Not only have I shagged at least half the Cabinet in the last six months, but the Archbishop of Canterbury herself came to my birthday party. She's a game old bird, isn't she? Drank us all under the table.'

'Indiscreet as ever, I see.'

'Only to you, darling.'

'Good. Can you get these clothes off Imogen? Help me clean her up and then put your clothes back on her.'

'Darling boy, you are losing your grip. I remember when you would have had my clothes off in no time at all and sometimes you weren't even in the same building as me.' She sighed. 'Those were the days.'

'They were, weren't they, but she's . . . you know . . . unconscious. Or as good as, and I don't want to be accused of . . . tampering.'

Lola regarded the drowsy Imogen. 'I can get those off her easily enough. I'll need you to help me dress her, though. Take the weight and so on.'

Luke nodded. 'OK.'

Undressing Imogen was the easy part. They stared in silence at the taser burns and then Lola unpacked her suitcase. As she said, how fortunate that all her clothing was designed to drop off if anyone so much as took out their credit card, and then to drop back on again equally quickly should there be an unfortunate knock on the door. Redressing Imogen was rather a struggle but they got there in the end. In fact, by the time they'd finished, Imogen was sitting up and taking notice.

She squinted. 'Is that Jane?'

Lola blinked. 'Who's Jane?' She looked around. 'How many more women do you have up here, Luke?'

'Just my two favourites,' said Luke tactfully.

Lola surveyed Imogen with an expert eye. 'Coffee?'

Luke sighed. 'Oh, yes. Please.'

'Not you, darling.'

Two cups of coffee later and Imogen could stand. She squinted down at her neat silk dress and matching jacket. 'What am I wearing? How long have you been cross-dressing, Parrish?'

'They're mine,' said Lola. 'And this is probably the moment to hand you the wig.'

Imogen squinted some more. 'Is that a dead cat?'

'No,' said Lola patiently. 'Hold still.'

There was a little bit of a struggle to get it on over Imogen's partially shaved head, but again, they got there in the end.

'Brilliant,' said Luke. 'You look just like Lola.'

'No one looks like me, darling,' said Lola. 'I am unique.'

'True,' said Luke. He looked at Imogen. 'Are we ready?'

'Bit unsteady on my feet,' said Imogen.

'I have that effect on women,' said Luke. 'No one will be at all surprised. Lola, you know what to do.'

'I do, darling. We have only to agree the price. And let me be clear – this is not the moment to pinch the pennies.'

Luke sighed. 'Ten thousand.'

Lola laughed merrily at his amusing little joke.

'Twenty.'

Lola fixed him with a reproachful eye. 'Darling . . .'

411

'Twenty-five. Top offer.'

'Per night.'

'What?'

She grinned.

He sighed. 'Oh, all right, then.' The problem of finding the money could be addressed later. 'Now, you know what to do?'

'Stay here until you come back. Enjoy the facilities offered. If the Portmans or the Time Police turn up – delay everyone for as long as possible. If I'm arrested – call your father.'

'No clients or the deal's off.'

'No problem, darling. A night or two of lying around drinking champagne and watching cheesy holos is just what the doctor ordered.'

Luke had the forethought to make sure he picked up his credit card. Over the years, Lola (surname never known) had been Luke's female friend Numbers Nine, Nineteen, Thirty-one, Thirty-three and Thirty-Eight. She'd visited on many occasions. She knew how everything worked. She was, he knew, honest – brutally so, sometimes – but she was also fatally addicted to vintage champagne. A habit Luke had no intention of funding. Or even the means to do so.

'Just lie around and enjoy yourself. And remember – don't answer the door to anyone but me.'

'The concierge?'

'They won't know you're here. Officially, you're leaving the building with me. Spin it out as long as you can, Lola.'

'At twenty-five k a night, darling, I'm here till the end of the millennium.'

Imogen had woken up again. 'Are you disguising me as a call girl?'

412

'Um . . .'

Imogen grinned wonkily. 'Oh, cool.'

Luke had his arm around Imogen's waist as they emerged from the lift into the car park.

'If you could manage to look as though you've been thoroughly and spectacularly rogered, then that would be great. Just for the cameras. Yes – that's perfect.'

'You are so dead, Parrish. I'm going to drown you as soon as we get outside.'

'You wish. As soon as I let go, you'll be flat on your face. Smile, now – you've just had the fire-trucking of a lifetime.'

'I'm going to rip out your heart and grind it beneath my heel.'

'That's the ticket. The car's just here. In you get.' He looked at his watch. 'My hour's up so I'm going to have to exceed the speed limit. On the other hand, I'm a Time Police officer on Time Police business in a Portman car. Once again – no downside.'

Despite Luke's best efforts – some of which were quite spectacular – they arrived some twenty-five minutes after Grint's deadline.

Luke pulled up at the rear of TPHQ, retrieved Jane's blaster because he didn't want to get her into trouble, and helped Imogen out of the car.

'This way.'

'What about the car?'

They looked at it, doors wide open, skewed across the road and surrounded by a complex web of double yellow lines. A Corporation notice sternly forbade parking at any time – the emergency services would require access to the fire hydrants.

To say nothing of being within car-bombing range of the Time Police. This was possibly the most illegally parked car in history.

'Well, that's caused a lot of trouble for a lot of people, I suspect,' said Luke, surveying his effort with satisfaction. 'I'll tell you something, Immy, it'll be a long time before the Portmans try anything against the Parrishes again. I bet my dad's lawyers are making their lives a living hell even as we speak.'

Imogen hung back, looking up at TPHQ. A building even more intimidating from the back than the front. 'Speaking of a living hell.'

Luke took her hand. 'I know. But just tell them what you know . . .'

'And they'll execute me again.'

'I don't think so, Immy. They're going to be far more interested in what you have to say than filling you full of bullets. Trust me. And if the going gets tough, then we'll summon the even tougher.'

'Your dad, I assume.'

'Correct. Come on, now. Don't be afraid. I . . . I let you down before but I never will again. Trust me.'

'All right,' said Imogen. 'I will.'

Luke sighed. 'Now I know you're heavily drugged.'

Their entrance into TPHQ was spectacular. Or would have been had they been able to gain access. The building appeared to be in lockdown.

'It's me,' announced Luke Parrish in ringing tones, banging on the front door and attracting a great deal of attention from both inside and outside TPHQ. 'Officer Parrish for those who don't know me. Reporting in after a brief but exciting spell of AWOLness.'

He banged again. A very reluctant Officer Curtis unlocked the door. 'What do you want, Parrish?'

Luke lurched inside. 'This is my friend Lola. My *very* good friend Lola.' He waved an erratic arm at their surroundings. 'Thought I'd show her around.'

Imogen was leaning heavily on his arm, her long blonde wig slightly askew, giving her a raffish look that Lola herself might have envied.

Like Queen Victoria, Officer Curtis was not amused. 'Parrish, what the fire truck are you playing at? Are you pissed?'

'As a newt,' said Luke. ''S the only thing that makes this place tol'rable.' He gestured around the atrium with his other erratic arm, raising his voice. 'You don't have to be pissed to work here, but it certainly helps.'

There were half a dozen officers present, detailed – unusually – to prevent anyone exiting the building, rather than guarding against unlawful access. Since neither was happening, they were bored out of their skulls and slightly resentful at having to patrol an empty, echoing atrium. No one looked particularly amused.

'So sick of this arsehole,' muttered Curtis. 'I'll get Ellis down here.'

'No no no no no no no no no no no,' said Luke, wagging an erratic finger. 'Don't want Ellis down here. Doesn't like me, you know.'

'Definitely Ellis, in that case,' said Curtis, opening his com. He looked at his colleagues. 'And if Parrish throws up on the floor, then rub his nose in it.'

415

Luke turned to Imogen, rocking on his heels. 'This is going well. Told you it would work.'

'Perhaps,' said Curtis, with awful sarcasm, 'you and your . . . friend . . . would like to begin your tour of the building in Interview Room 2 over here.'

'Ex'llent idea,' said Luke. 'Is it Wednesday? Will there be waterboarding? Hey . . .' He turned to the watching officers. 'That could be our new motto. Forget all this *Protecting the future to* . . . whatever it is – we could have *Wednesday is waterboarding day at fun-loving TPHQ*. Anyone know how that would sound in Latin?'

'For God's sake, get him out of here.'

Luke and his very good friend Lola were hustled into a small room where good things very rarely happened.

'Thank God,' said Luke, as soon as the door was closed. 'Believe it or not, I was running out of offensive remarks. Good . . .' he consulted his watch, 'evening, Officer Curtis. If Grint and Lockland have returned, then I think you'll find Hay is expecting us.'

Officer Curtis was not inclined to cooperate. Standing squarely in front of Luke, he leaned forwards until their faces were only inches apart. 'Give me one good reason why I shouldn't give you another good hiding right now.'

'Because,' said Imogen Farnborough, pulling off her wig and dropping it on the floor, 'if you lay one finger on Officer Parrish, I shall give you the kicking of a lifetime. In case you haven't recognised me, I'm that bitch Imogen Farnborough. Back from the dead to ruin your day. And possibly your year, as well. Now take me to Commander Hay or I start screaming.'

'Immy . . .' said Luke, and whether this was exasperation

at her revealing her identity or astonishment at her defence of him was never clear.

'I don't think,' began Curtis and never got any further. No one did.

For those interested, the secret of a successful scream is to expel most of the air in your lungs – because that makes for a much better scream – open your throat, stabilise your neck – because we don't want any pulled muscles, do we? – clench your fists – because arm movements can be very helpful in this sort of situation – and bend your knees.

Imogen did all that. And then screamed. Had there been windows they would have shattered.

'Jesus,' said Luke, reeling backwards. 'Some warning next time, Immy.' He waggled a finger in his ear and turned to a stunned Officer Curtis. 'She's very good, isn't she? Professionally trained, you know. Plus, a natural aptitude, I suspect.'

Imogen closed her mouth, breathed in, breathed out and screamed again. Sadly, barely had she got going than the door was flung open to reveal Lt Chigozie. 'What the fire truck . . . ?'

Scowling at the interruption, Imogen prepared to go again.

Chigozie held up his hands. 'No. Stop. For God's sake. Commander Hay asks if you could spare her a moment. And you, Parrish.'

'Success,' said Luke. 'Thank you for your assistance, Officer Curtis. Have a nice day.'

Curtis scowled. 'Shift your arse, Parrish. Before I shift it for you.'

Chigozie held out his hand. 'Your com.'

Curtis stepped back. 'What?'

'I'm taking everyone's. You never saw this woman.' He paused and then added inaccurately, 'Or heard her, either.'

Two armed officers escorted them to the lift.

'I expect they think we don't know the way,' confided Luke to Imogen, who was, by now, very pale. 'Buck up, Buttercup. Nearly there.'

'I so loathe you, Parrish.'

He took her hand. 'Oh good. You're feeling better.'

Their guards followed them into the lift, along the corridor and into Commander Hay's office. Also present were Captain Farenden, Major Ellis, Lt Grint and Officer Lockland.

'Oh look,' said Luke, brightly. 'The gang's all here.'

35

Commander Hay stood up. 'Please come in, Miss Farnborough. Lt Grint and Officer Lockland have briefed me on the circumstances of your rescue this afternoon. Do sit down.'

Imogen planted her feet in a manner very reminiscent of her mother. 'Last time I sat down for the Time Police, you executed me.'

'That is unanswerable,' said Hay, quietly, 'but please sit down anyway. You are far from well. I have asked the doctor to attend. He will be here in a moment.'

Imogen laughed, genuinely amused. 'You're going to nurse me back to health before executing me for a second time?'

'Actually,' said Luke, pulling out a chair for her, 'I've heard that if an execution fails then the . . .'

'Then the authorities do it again,' interrupted Hay, seating herself. 'The wording specifically emphasises *until dead*. However, Miss Farnborough, I have no interest in executing you for a second time. Not now – not in the future. Unless you do something to deserve it, of course.'

Imogen sat up. 'This is just a joke to you, isn't it?'

'I assure you I am not joking. I give you my word – there will be no attempt at a second execution.'

419

Imogen stared for a moment and then said, 'All this is unimportant. You have to tell my mother. They were using me to manipulate her. You have to tell her I'm all right. Well, not all right, but that she doesn't have to do as they say any longer.'

'I tried to speak to Mrs Farnborough,' said Luke. 'The number was unreachable.'

Hay nodded. 'It is. However, this solves the mystery of why she let us down so badly.' She frowned at Imogen. 'The bill failed because Mrs Farnborough voted against it.'

'With respect . . . ma'am,' said Luke. 'Mrs Farnborough thought her daughter was dead, then discovered she wasn't and was then informed she would be if she didn't do as they commanded. I think this is an occasion for understanding rather than condemnation.'

Commander Hay regarded him. 'A very valid point, Officer Parrish.' She appeared to reflect for a moment. 'Lt Grint, take Officers Lockland and Parrish and bring in Mrs Farnborough. I want her here. Safe. I'm sorry I can't let you have anyone else at the moment. I need to maintain security here, but as soon as more personnel are cleared, I'll send back-up. Now, please. Before . . .'

She stopped.

'Before the Portmans decide to cut their losses and eliminate a dangerously credible witness,' said Imogen, bleakly. 'My mother.'

'Yes. Prep for immediate departure, Lieutenant. Officer Parrish will join you in a moment.'

Grint jerked his head at Jane and the two of them left the room.

This last effort had finished Imogen, who seemed to collapse

420

in her seat. It was at this moment that the doctor entered, took one look and then said, 'I'm going to ask you to vacate your office for ten minutes, ma'am. Just while I examine the patient. I don't think she should make the trip down to MedCen just yet.'

'I have no intention of sending her to MedCen at any time,' said Commander Hay. 'No offence intended, doctor.'

'None taken, ma'am. Given recent events – a wise decision.'

Hay stood up. 'We'll reconvene in your office, Captain. Miss Farnborough, I shall leave you with our doctor for a few minutes.'

Back in Captain Farenden's office, Hay took the visitor's chair. Major Ellis propped himself against a table. Luke stood, exposed, in the middle of the room.

Commander Hay began. 'Well, when I said we were to shake the tree, I had no idea Miss Farnborough would fall out.' She frowned at Luke. 'Was there some reason you and Miss Farnborough didn't return with Lt Grint?'

'Well, to be honest,' he said, 'I didn't know about Mrs Farnborough at that stage and I had no intention of handing Imogen over to the very people who shot her in the first place. Plus, I had one or two little things to do – get her clear of Portman House, install her in my old flat, hire a very high-class call girl, dispose of a stolen car in such a way as to cause maximum consternation and expense to everyone involved – all that sort of thing, and . . .'

'You hired a prostitute?' said Major Ellis, faintly.

'I did not,' said Luke indignantly.

'You said . . .'

Luke glanced nervously over his shoulder. 'For heaven's

421

sake, don't let Lola hear you calling her a prostitute. She's got a hell of a temper on her. She once beat up two yobbos she found torturing a cat. I don't mind saying I was terrified. And then she made me pick it up and carry it back to her place and the thing bit me. The cat, I mean. Not Lola. Although she will if you're prepared to pay extra. I had to have shots. Because of the cat, not Lola. Their bites are poisonous, you know.'

He paused for breath. Expressions were not encouraging.

'But why hire a high-class call girl in the first place?' enquired Ellis, seemingly unwilling to let the subject drop.

'I don't know any other type,' said Luke, simply, causing Captain Farenden to stare fixedly at his desk calendar.

'Of course,' said Hay, gravely. 'Just one point, Officer Parrish, and I think we all know what the answer is likely to be, but should I be offering Time Police protection to Mr Raymond Parrish as well, since he too was involved?'

'A kind thought, but he's probably kicking Portman arse at the moment and won't take kindly to being distracted.'

'As you wish. Join Lt Grint, officer.'

Luke shot out of the door.

Ellis stood up. 'With your permission, ma'am, I'll continue with the investigation. The sooner I can free up officers for you . . .'

'Yes, thank you, Major.'

He too left the room.

'You're frowning, Charlie.'

'Parrish and Lockland, ma'am? Together?'

Hay frowned herself and then said slowly, 'Did it strike you, Charlie, that the Officer Parrish with whom we've just spoken was not quite the Officer Parrish we've previously known and not loved very much?'

He blinked. 'Now you come to mention it . . . and he called you ma'am, ma'am.'

'Yes . . . I wonder. Anyway, Mrs Farnborough knows him. Which may or may not prove helpful. *And* it's an excellent opportunity to see if Lockland and Parrish can still work together.'

Captain Farenden grinned. 'I'm certain Lt Grint is more than capable of keeping things on track.'

Hay stood up and went to her window, staring out at the night sky. Before her, London was lit up like Fairyland. She sighed and rested her weight on the windowsill. 'It is still today, isn't it?'

'It is, ma'am, yes. And it's not over yet, is it?'

'Nowhere near, I'm afraid. Keep trying to contact Mrs Farnborough, would you? If you can get through, tell her if she has a panic room to go there now. Failing that, arm herself with whatever is likely to do the most damage and wait for us to arrive. Under no circumstances is she to leave the house or let anyone in.'

'Yes, ma'am.'

'Where's Major Callen?'

'On his way back from Glasgow and still in the air. Delta Zero One has just passed our outer marker. Ten minutes at the most.'

She sighed. 'I'm reluctant, but I don't have a lot of choice. Have him diverted to Mile End. Back-up for Grint and his team if necessary.'

'Yes, ma'am.'

*　　*　　*

The pod containing Lt Grint, together with Officers Lockland and Parrish, landed in Mile End, setting down near the Tube station. They made no attempt at concealment, leaving the pod uncamouflaged and conspicuously parked, although there were few people about at this time of night.

Most properties in this area of London had been divided into flats, but Mrs Farnborough, recipient of a Cabinet minister's pay, supplemented by the dividends from some canny investments, together with the income from a small estate in Rushfordshire, had an entire house to herself.

'Right,' said Grint, as they piled out of the pod and set off at a trot. 'What have we got on the layout of the house? Lockland, do you have a floorplan?'

'No need,' said Luke. 'I've been here many times.'

There was a silence.

'Look,' said Luke, angrily. 'This is important. If you want to play silly buggers then that's fine with me, but can we do it after we've safely retrieved Mrs Farnborough? Which is, after all, the whole point of the mission.'

Jane stared at her trusty notebook and refused to catch anyone's eye.

'All right,' said Grint, eventually. 'Report.'

'Three storeys. Kitchen in the basement. Four reception rooms on the ground floor. Four bedrooms and three bathrooms on the first. No access to the attics that I know of. Small garden to the rear with no direct access from the street. No knowledge of a panic room, but that doesn't mean there isn't one.'

'Where is she likely to be?'

'At this time of the night? Living room – ground floor front, or bedroom – first floor rear.'

'Number of people in the house?'

'Again, at this time of night – probably only one. Our target. Assistants and secretaries go home at six. She's always insisted on it.'

'Security team?'

'Withdrawn, probably. As an ex-member of the government, she's not entitled.'

'So almost certainly alone?'

'Yes.'

'In that case, regard anyone not our target with extreme prejudice. Lockland, you're with me. Parrish, can you get in through the rear?'

'Done it many times when smuggling Imogen back from somewhere she shouldn't have been.'

'I meant are you fit enough?'

'Yeah. Easy. I'll go over a couple of walls and straight through the French windows.'

Grint regarded him. 'Can you actually climb a wall?'

Luke regarded him straight back again. 'Fortunately for you – yes.'

'Then go.'

Luke peeled off into the dark and Jane followed Grint. They turned sharp left into a quiet street. Mrs Farnborough's house was third on the left. The street lights were on and a few lights showed in nearby buildings, but they were mostly in the bedrooms. People were preparing for a peaceful night's sleep.

They should be so lucky.

Jane wondered how late it was, but there was no time to look at her watch. She sighed. This day seemed endless.

'You knock,' said Grint as they halted at the bottom of a flight of six shallow steps. 'I'll cover you.' He opened his com. 'Parrish, where are you?'

'Still scrambling over a couple of garden walls,' panted Luke. 'Go ahead – I'm nearly there.' He hoped his voice didn't betray the fact that he just might have slightly overestimated his wall-climbing abilities. Three walls down, two to go and his ribs were definitely complaining. But, he reasoned, getting his leg over yet another one and dropping to the ground on the other side, it was taking his mind off his current predicament and giving him a reason – a good reason – to shove everything that had happened today to the back of his mind. At some point, he knew, he was going to have to think about the events of the last twelve hours, but being included in this mission had given him an excellent reason to shelve all that for the time being. It would be fair to say there had been a seismic shift – actually, several seismic shifts – in his thinking today. Everything would have to be dealt with at some point. But not now. He wondered how Jane was coping. He was quite prepared to bet she was doing better than he was. And she had Grint.

He scrambled over the last wall. Nearly there.

Jane ran lightly up the steps, took two deep breaths to calm down and rapped sharply on the knocker, trying to sound urgent but not violent. She remembered to stand back and hold up her ID for the camera.

There was no response. The door remained firmly shut.

'Perhaps she isn't in,' said Jane.

'Or we're too late,' said Grint, grimly. 'Parrish?'

'Yeah, I'm in the garden. No signs of any forced entry. Ready when you are.'

'Wait until I give the word.'

'Roger.'

Jane crouched and pushed open the letterbox. 'Mrs Farnborough. This is Officer Lockland with the Time Police. Officer Parrish is here as well. We've come to take you to safety. Are you able to open the door?'

Silence.

She stepped back and looked up. The house was completely dark. Were they too late? She looked over her shoulder. 'No response, sir.'

'Step back, Lockland.'

Jane stepped back, pulled down her visor and turned her head away. Grint's blaster whined and then roared. There was a boom, a sudden, acrid smell, and pieces of burning wood exploded across the porch. Grint shut down his weapon while Jane booted aside the remains of the door. Raising her own recently returned blaster, she stepped across the threshold, her headtorch illuminating a wide passage. On her right, a flight of stairs led downwards – to the kitchen, she supposed – and on her left, more stairs led up to the bedrooms.

'I'll search downstairs,' said Grint. 'Parrish, you take the ground floor. Lockland – upstairs.'

Jane set off up the stairs, her torch lancing through the darkness. 'Mrs Farnborough, this is Officer Lockland. Can you show yourself, please?'

There was no response. Jane began to have a very bad feeling about this.

The screech of tearing wood, together with the sound of

tinkling glass downstairs indicated that Luke had arrived and that, coincidentally, the French windows had come to the end of their useful life.

The stairs ended at a broad landing which stretched left and right. A wooden floor, a carpet runner, paintings on the walls, two occasional tables with lamps. Neither switched on. Everything looked in perfect order. No signs of intruders. No signs of a struggle. She could see three doors. Luke had said Mrs Farnborough's bedroom was at the back. She turned left.

The last door was slightly ajar. Jane had no idea whether this was good or bad. She said softly, 'Mrs Farnborough, I'm coming in.' Which would alert anyone in the room, good or bad, but Jane was of the opinion it was better to be shot at by a professional than a terrified amateur. Although this was Patricia Farnborough – hunting, shooting, fishing Patricia Farnborough – who could probably wield a 12-bore shotgun before she could walk.

Jane flipped off her headtorch and engaged her night vision. Using the tip of her blaster, she slowly eased open the door. The curtains were undrawn and the faint light filtering through the window showed this was a bedroom. She took stock. Bed to the left, flanked by wardrobes. Dressing table on the far wall. Empty fireplace with an armchair and low table set to one side. Sofa with some kind of coffee table under the window. What looked like a bookcase on the third wall. Carpeted, meaning she could move quietly. A faint smell of talcum powder. Jane remained on the threshold, careful not to present a silhouette to anyone lurking within. Using her night vision, she scanned the room. Either that was a very large, very peculiarly shaped armchair or . . .

Mrs Farnborough sat motionless, showing no reaction at all to Jane's presence. Jane drew back against the wall. Someone was coming up the stairs. Luke, she thought. The footfalls weren't heavy enough for Grint.

'It's me,' he said softly, coming up behind her.

'She's in here,' whispered Jane. 'Alone, as far as I can see. But . . .'

'Yeah?'

'Not moving.'

Luke swore.

'I'll check the other rooms. Give me two minutes.'

She could hear him moving from room to room and finally back to her side. 'All clear.'

Jane entered first, watching where she put her feet and scanning for booby traps, ambushes, hidden trip hazards and the like.

Luke bent over the motionless figure. 'Oh, shit.'

No, thought Jane, in anguish. Please no. Not now we've got Imogen back. Surely someone today deserves a happy ending.

He shook her gently. 'Mrs Farnborough? Jane – a light.'

Jane lifted her visor and snapped on her headtorch again. Luke was examining Mrs Farnborough, feeling for a pulse. He raised an eyelid, peered carefully and then straightened up. 'No.'

'No? You mean she's dead? Did she take her own life?'

'No. She's alive. She's just out cold. Drunk. Can't you smell it?'

Jane was astonished at the vast wave of relief that washed over her. 'Thank God.'

'Yeah – come on. We need to get her out of here.'

'How? I know I can't lift her. Can you?'

'Probably not. And she'll be a dead weight, so probably not even both of us together. Fortunately, we know someone who can though, don't we?' He turned his head, calling, 'Lt Grint. Paging Lt Grint. Your services are required.'

The stairs creaked heavily as Grint made his way up. He paused in the doorway. 'Is she dead?'

'Unconscious.'

'Has she taken something?'

Jane shook her head. 'No sign of tablets or needles. I doubt she would try to kill herself. They'd have no reason to keep Imogen alive if she did that. Luke thinks she may just be drunk.'

Grint sighed. Of the three of them, he was by far the most battle-hardened officer here. Sadly, of the three of them, he was also the only one capable of lifting Mrs Farnborough. If they encountered any difficulties . . . He sighed again, pulled Mrs Farnborough out of the chair and heaved her over his shoulder. Jane primly arranged her skirt for maximum decency.

Luke nodded his approval of Grint's action. 'Great way of making sure she doesn't choke on her own vomit.'

As usual, Grint ignored him, setting off for the door. 'Parrish – you go first. Lockland at the back. This might be easier than we expected.'

He froze in the doorway. They all did. There had been a sound downstairs . . .

Grint backed into the bedroom and, with not a great deal of respect for a former member of the government, none too gently shed his load. Jane switched off her torch and snapped down her visor. Luke slipped behind Mrs Farnborough's armchair. Jane took up position in the shadow of a wardrobe. Grint

430

knelt beside the sofa. They all levelled their weapons at the door and waited.

There was another sound somewhere in the dark. As if someone was crunching their way over the remains of the front door. Jane glanced at Grint. They – whoever they were – could only get up the stairs one at a time. The stairs were a pinch point. If they could take advantage of that . . .

Grint nodded, whispering, 'Parrish, you stay with Mrs Farnborough. Her safety is paramount. Back-up will arrive. Lockland and I will hold them off as long as we can. Lockland – with me.'

They slipped away into the dark.

Again, Luke felt a twinge of . . . something. Yes, he wasn't match fit and it made sense for him to stay here with Mrs Farnborough, but there was something in the way Grint and Jane fitted together so well . . .

The hall was suddenly full of sound and light. Figures poured through the shattered front door, firing as they came. Two, three, four of them. Jane leaned over the landing banisters, firing short, sharp controlled bursts, and they pulled back.

'Nice work, Lockland,' said Grint, moving to cover the stairs. 'Keep them pinned down as long as you can.'

'Movement in the garden,' said Luke, who had been checking the window. 'More coming through the back.'

'Stay where you are,' commanded Grint. 'You're our last defence.'

Gunfire erupted again.

Luke cast a swift look around. All the furniture here was old – antique even – but very solid. He overturned the coffee table with a crash.

'What's going on in there?' demanded Grint.

'Building a barricade. Somewhere for you to fall back to.'

Grint grunted. 'Good thought.'

Another blast of gunfire and bullets cut him off.

Luke put his shoulder to the sofa and heaved with all his might. It shifted perhaps one inch. Possibly two. His ribs, however, felt as if they had burst into flames and tried to exit his body through his lungs. Nor had it done his groin a great deal of good, either. OK – not the best idea. Forget the sofa.

Using the overturned table and just about everything he could carry or drag, he barricaded Mrs Farnborough into a corner, finally, and probably redundantly, covering her with her own bedding. Four fat pillows plugged any possible gaps.

He stepped back, trying to ease his aching ribs. Despite his best efforts, it genuinely looked as if a four-year-old had built a fort in his parents' bedroom. He moved to the window again, checked the charge on his blaster, and waited.

Blaster fire was criss-crossing the building, lighting up the house and the street outside. Lumps of burning plaster rained down upon Jane and Grint. The lower part of the banisters were alight. Pictures fell off the walls with every impact. Valuable ceramics exploded expensively.

Jane could hear Grint yelling at her to fall back. He himself was crouched halfway up the stairs, somewhat exposed, but spraying continuous blaster fire from left to right across the hall. The curtains never stood a chance.

'Clear,' shouted Jane, achieving the relative safety of the landing. 'Now you, sir.'

She laid down the same covering fire as he raced up the stairs, two at a time, flames at his heels. Part of his uniform was smouldering.

Three figures crashed through the front door again, kicking aside burning debris as they came. Jane could see more shadowy outlines on the steps outside. And, according to Luke, there were more around the back. How long before the opposition decided it would be quicker and easier simply to take out the entire house? And the neighbours, as well. Just to be on the safe side. Well, with luck, the neighbours would all be on the line to the emergency services. How long before the civilian police arrived? Or even their own promised back-up from TPHQ? Everyone must surely be aware a war was being fought at the house of a former government minister. She took a moment to check her charge.

Luke shoved the butt end of his blaster through the window and opened fire on whoever was in the garden, doing his best to ensure they would not be, as the Time Police delicately phrased it, taken from behind.

'Fall back to the bedroom,' yelled Grint.

'Luke, I'm coming in,' shouted Jane, and the next moment she was in the room with him. Grint crouched in the doorway, ready to deal with anyone coming along the landing.

'More incoming,' shouted Luke. Two figures lay face down in the little garden but the rest were piling through the remains of the French windows and into the house.

At least five or six of them, thought Jane. Not too bad. We can deal with that.

The grenade came straight through the shattered window.

'Grenade,' shouted Luke, who bent, grabbed at it left-handed, straightened up and in the same movement tossed it straight back out again. 'Get down.'

Everyone threw themselves to the floor. The grenade

exploded in mid-air, blowing in what was left of the windows and covering everyone with the latest look in broken glass, plaster, splintered wood and bits of curtain.

Luke, closest to the windows, lay face down, ears ringing and temporarily unsure who he was. Or where. Or when. Or why. Or anything, really.

Jane lay nearby, struggling to reach her blaster – as she thought – but in reality, simply pawing at the carpet and wondering whose arm that was.

Lt Grint lay almost completely buried under one of the world's most substantial wardrobes. It was probably the only thing in the house that weighed more than he did. He lay crushed and unable to move, watching three dark figures cautiously making their way up the stairs. He strained again. The wardrobe still didn't move. He was completely pinned down.

The three figures reached the top of the stairs. Grint could see their red laser beams slashing through the dust-laden air. When the red dots reached him . . . well, that would be the end of it. The end of everything . . .

Jane . . .

The three figures inched forwards along the landing, weapons covering everywhere. Doing everything right. The part of his mind still working approved their professionly . . . professionality . . . professionalness . . . ness.

He strained again. The wardrobe moved. Just very slightly. This was good. He could heave it to one side and leap to his feet . . . just in time to have his head blown off as they came through the door. If he could just get a hold on his blaster . . . he could take out the first two . . . first one definitely . . . and Jane could perhaps . . .

434

What Jane could perhaps have done they never found out.

With exactly the same sort of primeval roar and general disregard for property frequently showcased by Godzilla in his relationship with Tokyo, Mrs Farnborough shoved aside the sofa that had so endangered Officer Parrish's reproductive equipment, and emerged – really the resemblance to Godzilla was quite amazing – from the shattered remains of Officer Parrish's fort. Either taking in the situation at a glance – or, more likely, too stewed to know what she was doing – she effortlessly grabbed a substantial Louis XVI repoussé coffee table – a rather nice piece with Corinthian column legs and concave under tier – and bellowing, 'God for Harry, England and St George,' charged at the figures in the doorway. Straight over the top of Lt Grint, who, for one brief moment, found himself bearing the weight not only of the former wardrobe but of a former Cabinet minister as well.

She was an astonishing sight. Her hair stood on end. Her clothing was dishevelled. There was a sudden strong smell of Le Courvoisier. If the Home Counties had ever got down to producing their own Valkyries, this is exactly how they would look.

What should have happened, of course, was that the three intruders aimed and fired simultaneously, thus annihilating both the table and its ululating wielder.

What actually happened was that they hesitated just that one second too long. The table – by now an unstoppable force – caught the first two square amidships and propelled them out of the door, along the landing and backwards into the third member of the team. Feeling the floor disappear beneath his feet, he teetered precariously, arms flailing, instinctively grabbing at his colleagues. Gravity won, as it always does, and the entire tangled mass – intruders, Valkyrie, hastily co-opted table – all tumbled heavily down the stairs to land at the bottom with a thud that made the whole house bounce and, incidentally, dealing the already heavily damaged banisters their death blow.

It probably hadn't been her intention at the time, but Mrs Farnborough could not have more effectively blocked the stairs had she sat down and carefully – and soberly – planned such a thing. The combination of jumbled limbs, unconscious people, broken banisters and wedged table comprised an insurmountable barrier to the two other intruders cautiously emerging from a back room.

'Stop pissing about,' said a third, appearing up the kitchen stairs. 'Burn them. Burn the whole bloody house down.' He raised his weapon.

It's very possible that the whine of their overcharged blasters would have been impressive had it not been completely drowned out by a sudden deafening clatter from outside. Brilliant, bright white light illuminated the interior of the house, showcasing the damage inflicted by both sides. If she survived the night, Mrs Farnborough was probably not going to be happy.

The clatter drew even closer. Dust, smoke, plaster and sparks swirled through the air, further obscuring visibility. Swooping white lights dazzled people's eyes, causing many to believe they were undergoing some sort of religious experience and wishing they'd been kinder to their mothers. The noise was eardrum-bursting. And then . . .

436

'THIS IS THE TIME POLICE. LAY DOWN YOUR WEAPONS AND SURRENDER OR WE WILL OPEN FIRE. LAY DOWN YOUR WEAPONS AND SURRENDER. NO FURTHER WARNING WILL BE GIVEN.'

The enhanced voice bounced off the walls, echoing down the street and over the rooftops. Those few inhabitants of this quiet suburban street not already convinced the end of the world was at hand immediately changed their minds as a hail of gunfire raked the street outside. Lumps of paving slabs cartwheeled into the air. A street lamp buckled. A manhole cover exploded, flinging shrapnel in all directions. Someone's house alarm went off. And then another. The helicopter hovered only feet above the streets, the downdraught from its rotors causing massive damage to any object weighing less than the Albert Hall. Armoured figures leaped from the chopper, firing as they came.

Lt Grint's view was obviously somewhat limited, but it would seem their back-up had arrived.

The clatter withdrew slightly as the helicopter backed up and away to provide cover as the Time Police poured in through the front door, weapons roaring and just looking for trouble.

A voice shouted to retreat, as those who still could attempted to exit via the former French windows, where they ran straight into the welcoming arms of Lt Chigozie and his team.

Lt Fanboten paused at the bottom of the stairs and looked at the tangle of arms, legs, furniture, banisters . . . 'Good God.'

The heap moved slightly as those unfortunate enough to be at the bottom fought for air.

'Someone lend me a hand here.'

Slowly, and with many comments along the lines of 'I think this leg belongs to that arm over there,' followed by 'Unlikely – that leg's female. And that one's a wooden spindle,' the pile was resolved into its component parts. Three illegals, one female former cabinet minister and a surprisingly undamaged Louis

XVI table. As someone remarked – it had probably survived the guillotine.

Major Callen appeared in the doorway, lifted his visor and surveyed the scene. 'Report.'

'Target acquired, sir.' Fanboten sniffed the air. 'The lady appears . . . a trifle pissed, sir.'

'Tired and emotional, Lieutenant.'

'Sorry, sir?'

'Lesser mortals are pissed, Fanboten. Exalted beings such as members of the government are only ever tired and emotional.'

'Ah. Reassuring to know, sir.'

'Grint and his team?'

'We're just clearing a path to them now.'

Callen led the way up the stairs and paused in the bedroom doorway, surveying the devastation. 'Bring up the medics.'

'Hoi,' said Grint, still in an unsolicited relationship with the wardrobe.

Fanboten bent over him. 'Watcha doing down there?'

'Fire truck off, Fanboten.'

Grinning, Fanboten went to move away.

'Get this fire-trucking thing off me first.'

It took four men to lift the wardrobe. It took two men to assist Officer Parrish to his feet. Jane was lifted, one-handed, by an officer who was actually talking to someone else at the time.

'Well, that's not insulting at all, is it?' said Bolshy Jane. 'Bite his bloody arm off, sweetie.'

'Will you shut up,' said Jane, wearily.

Callen surveyed them all – from a safe distance, because Lockland had once vomited all over him and everyone learns from experience.

439

'Get them back to TPHQ. And Mrs Farnborough. Asap. The chopper can come back for us and the prisoners. Send someone to take back their pod.'

Mrs Farnborough was transported to the helicopter. It wasn't graceful, but as Luke said, she'd never know anything about it.

The pilot strapped them in and revved the engine.

'Right, then,' said Luke, watching the ground disappear beneath them. He surveyed the unconscious Mrs Farnborough, the bleeding Grint and the still-groggy Jane. 'Back for a nice mug of cocoa, I think. Anyone else had a long day?'

36

Commander Hay sat back in her chair and pinched the bridge of her nose. It didn't help. Events at TPHQ were still proceeding. Although in which direction was anyone's guess.

'Give me a sitrep, Charlie. I think I might be losing track.'

Captain Farenden flicked through his scratchpad. 'Major Ellis is clearing officers as fast as he can go, ma'am. His investigation into the attacks on John Costello and Mrs Lockland is still ongoing.' He nodded to her desk. 'His preliminary reports are awaiting your attention. Together with all the relevant footage from security.'

She nodded. 'No matter what else goes tits up today, Charlie, I want Ellis to stay in TPHQ. If anything should happen to me . . .'

'It won't, ma'am.'

'I wouldn't be so sure. It's been that sort of day. Continue.'

'Lt Filbert is in MedCen and unlikely ever to return to full duties. His verbal statement has been transcribed and is also on your desk.

'Lt North, together with Team Two-Three-Five, Meiklejohn and Costello are still in New York, ma'am. Illegally. There will be hell on if that one goes wrong.' Farenden waited but apparently his commanding officer had nothing to say to that.

'Officer Varma is with Dr Maxwell. God only knows what *they're* up to. But I'm sure we'll get to hear about it soon enough. Officer Farrell is in the wind. He could be anywhere. The bill failed and we're broke. Delta Zero One is bringing in Lt Grint and Officers Parrish and Lockland, who are themselves bringing in Mrs Farnborough. No one has been seriously hurt, although there is significant damage to the house and its surroundings, which is probably going to have to come out of our pay. Major Callen is following on with his prisoners. Two dead. One will be very soon. One is not looking good and the rest will probably recover. We'll interrogate them, of course, ma'am, but I suspect they'll have been hired through several third parties and will have no idea who they are really working for. The recently deceased Imogen Farnborough is receiving treatment prior to being installed in our third-floor guest suite.'

Commander Hay stared at him. 'Is that all? Are you sure you haven't missed anything?'

'Actually, ma'am . . .'

'Dear God, Charlie, the question was rhetorical.'

He remained silent.

'Sorry. Bad day.'

'I'll have some sandwiches sent up.' They both eyed the sad, forgotten sandwich on her desk. 'Fresh sandwiches.'

'That sounds good. And coffee. Lots of coffee.'

'Yes, ma'am.'

She took off her spectacles and rubbed her eyes. In direct contravention of medical advice. 'What a day, Charlie. In fact, you'd be hard put to see how it could get any worse.'

'Oh,' said Captain Farenden. 'I'm sure it will.'

As if to demonstrate the power of Fate over lesser mortals, the door opened to admit Lt North. Tired, dishevelled and still in her New York clothes.

'Ma'am – I thought you should know as soon as possible.' She drew herself up. 'I have to report we failed to retrieve all of Tesla's papers. Thanks to John Costello, we were able to gain possession of Tesla's notebook. However, according to Meiklejohn – and I have no reason to believe she's lying – the contents of the notebook were gibberish. All the other documents were taken by Henry Plimpton.'

Hay was very careful to keep all hint of blame and frustration from her voice, merely saying neutrally, 'Where is the notebook now?'

'Destroyed.'

Hay regarded the unfamiliarly dishevelled officer in front of her. 'Well, that's something to be grateful for. Were the other papers gibberish too?'

'Unclear, ma'am. The only other person to have seen them was John Costello.'

'What does he say?'

North set her jaw. 'Nothing. He's dead.' She took a breath. 'He gave his life trying to ensure our getaway, ma'am. I feel that should be recognised in some way.'

Hay nodded. 'I'll see what I can do. Thank you, Lieutenant. Let me have your reports asap, please.'

North departed, passing the sandwiches and coffee in the doorway.

Hay poured and sipped. 'Excellent coffee, Charlie. This didn't come from the kitchens, surely.'

He appeared in the open doorway. 'Do you remember,

443

ma'am, when we both started in our current jobs, you made it very clear there were some things you never wanted to know?'

'Yes,' said Hay, warily.

'This might be one of them.' He went to turn away.

'Dear God, you can't leave it there. Tell me what it is I don't want to know.'

'An illegal coffee machine, ma'am.'

She blinked. 'Is that actually a thing?'

'I believe coffee machines are quite common, ma'am.'

'So what's with the illegal bit? Do illegal machines make better coffee for some reason? Is that why they're illegal? Come on, Charlie, you can't leave it there.'

'Luke Parrish, ma'am.'

'Ah. Yes, of course. Where is it?'

'In the former Team Two-Three-Six's office, ma'am. Sitting on an illegal bookcase and plumbed into an illegal water supply. Well, the water's legal – it's the method of obtaining it that isn't.'

Hay waved these irrelevances aside. 'I want one.'

'Er – that particular machine, ma'am?'

'Only if you can't get me one from elsewhere.'

'Er, yes, ma'am.'

Captain Farenden withdrew to organise the purchase and installation of a smart new coffee machine which would, for the sake of sparing his commanding officer unnecessary trouble and inconvenience, be installed in his own office.

Hay switched on her desk light, sipped her excellent coffee, sighed, and very reluctantly reached for the first of her reports. Silence filled the office as she flicked her scratchpad, scanning the screens. In the act of reaching for a sandwich, she stopped, stared, and then flicked back. Then further back. Then forwards again.

Could it actually be that simple?

She frowned. 'Charlie, are you still out there?'

He appeared in the open doorway. 'I am, ma'am.'

'Did you know Jake Costello is dead?'

'Who? Do you mean *John* Costello?'

Hay regarded him. 'Yes. I meant John.'

'Yes, Lt North told me.'

'And Filbert's still in MedCen?'

'I believe he's being prepped for onward transmission to a civilian burns unit, ma'am.'

'By helicopter?'

'Air ambulance, ma'am. Yes.'

'I suspect he'll never arrive. Get on to MedCen and tell them to hold. Filbert mustn't leave the safety of TPHQ. I'm overriding any medical arguments. And double the guards on his cubicle.'

'Yes, ma'am.'

He vanished.

Hay reached for her com. 'Major Ellis. Meet me in MedCen. Immediate. I think we might be in danger of losing Lt Filbert.'

As a senior officer in the Time Police, Ellis was accustomed to obeying orders without question. Today, however . . .

'Ma'am?'

'Immediately, please, Major. And leave your weapon behind.'

Ellis stood very still. 'Could you confirm your last order, please?'

'Come unarmed.'

445

She shut down her com and stood up to go. Captain Farenden, who had heard every word, appeared in the doorway. 'Ma'am?'

'Mind the shop, Charlie.'

'Ma'am, I . . . Where are you going?'

'You will remain here, Captain. Under no circumstances will you leave this office.'

'Ma'am? Where are you going? What is happening?'

Commander Hay made no reply. She pulled a blaster from her drawer, checked the charge and slapped it on her rip-grip patch.

Captain Farenden drew himself up. 'Commander Hay, I request and require you to . . .'

'No, Captain. You don't. I say again – you will not leave your office. That is a direct order.'

Without giving him a chance to reply, she swept out.

Major Ellis was waiting outside MedCen. 'With respect, ma'am, what's going on?'

'You are my witness, Major. My unarmed witness.'

'Ma'am, you are alarming me.'

She shook her head and pushed open the doors. Four guards surrounded Lt Filbert's cubicle – two facing in and two out.

'Report.'

'The doctor's with him now, ma'am. Checking he's fit to travel.'

'Thank you, officers. You may stand down. Return to your normal duties.'

That they were surprised was evident. 'Ma'am?'

'That will be all, officers. You are dismissed.'

As they left, the doctor appeared. 'The patient is well enough to travel, ma'am, although I'll give him something to make his journey a little easier.'

'Hold off for a moment, please, doctor. I need to speak with Lt Filbert urgently.'

'He's not . . .'

'Now, please, doctor. I promise you this is important.'

He compressed his lips. 'Very well.' Reluctantly, he stepped back.

Hay entered the cubicle with Major Ellis at her shoulder. He edged slightly sideways, taking up a position that would give him a view of the patient, the doctor and his commanding officer.

A heavily bandaged Lt Filbert lay propped up on his pillows. His right arm seemed to be encased in some sort of metal support structure which took the weight and prevented any movement which might cause further harm to his already extensively damaged arm. An unpleasant smell of cooked meat lingered in the enclosed space. His face was grey and his eyes heavy. Drugs, she supposed.

She turned to the doctor. 'Can he understand me? Is he capable of speech?'

His eyes watchful, the doctor nodded.

Hay stood at the foot of the bed, saying softly, 'Well now, Hugh. How are you feeling?'

Filbert nodded. 'Not too bad, thank you, ma'am.' His voice was weak and hoarse but easily understood.

'That's good to hear. Before you're transferred, I need to ask you a few questions. Please listen carefully – this could be the most important thing you've ever done as an officer in the Time Police.'

He struggled to sit up a little. 'Stay still,' said the doctor sharply. He lowered his voice. 'Ma'am, must this happen now?

His arm's a mess. There's massive bone, tissue and nerve trauma. He took a blast at point-blank range. His upper arm is burned right through. It's going to take a lot of very painful, very major surgery and even then, there's no guarantee it can be saved.'

'I promise you this won't take long, doctor.'

Hay smiled down at Lt Filbert.

Behind them all, unseen by anyone, Major Callen, still in flying gear, entered MedCen and stood quietly. Listening.

37

In so much as it was in his nature to do so, Captain Farenden was fretting. He looked up as his door opened. 'Ma'am, what's happ—? Oh, it's you.'

Mikey halted in the doorway. It was very apparent she was the last thing he wanted to see at the moment. 'Yeah. Sorry. It's not important.' She went to go away again.

Captain Farenden pulled himself together and climbed wearily to his feet. 'No. Stop. Sorry. It's just . . . Come in. Is there something I can do?'

She took a reluctant step into the room. 'Sorry . . . Matthew's not here and I . . . There isn't . . .'

He crossed to the door, looked up and down the empty corridor, sighed and closed it. 'I hear you lost your friend.'

Mikey nodded. 'It's stupid. I didn't know him that well. I hadn't seen him for ages. I don't know why . . .'

'It's because he died in front of you. You were there. You saw it happen.' He regarded her for a moment, forcing himself to concentrate on the here and now.

'Mikey, I've read North's report. It was his choice. He didn't do what he did to save Tesla's papers – he knew there was a good chance they were useless. He did it to make sure you got

away. I suspect he thought he was paying his debt. You know –
the Locklands. You should be grateful to him.'

'I'd rather be grateful he was still alive.'

'I understand. I've lost friends, too. Quite a few, actually.'

She looked at him almost as if seeing him for the first time.
'Yes, I expect you have. Does it get easier?'

'No. Nor should it.'

She nodded, staring down at the floor. 'We didn't get
everything we wanted.'

'But you *were* able to retrieve Tesla's notebook. I know it
wasn't what we expected, but you were the one who worked
the problem, Mikey. You took the absolute minimum of information and arrived at the correct conclusion. You were spot-on.
That's quite an achievement.'

Mikey shook her head. 'But the contents were rubbish. We
could have let Henry Plimpton have it. Jakey died for nothing.'

'He died doing a good thing, Mikey.'

'His last words were for Jane. About her parents. He was
sorry he couldn't save them.'

'I think she would like to hear that. Do you know if he had
any relatives? Anyone we should notify?'

'I don't think so. He was like so many of us. Completely
alone.'

'Hey.' Farenden touched her forearm. 'You're in the Time
Police now. None of us are alone.' He looked around at the
writing still on the wall. 'Although sometimes we wish we
were.'

She managed a smile.

'Get yourself something to eat. Write your report. Have a
drink in his memory.'

450

'Yeah. Thanks. I will.'

'I mean it, Mikey. Just because we spent years trying to kill you doesn't mean you're on your own here. If you have a problem – come and talk to me about it. Get the old person's perspective.'

Mikey surveyed him critically, blinking the tears away. 'You're not that old.'

'Thank you for noticing. Did you see Commander Hay at all on your way up here?'

'No – should I have?'

'No. I just wondered.'

Down in MedCen, Commander Hay was careful to make her voice calm and quiet.

'I shan't keep you long, Lieutenant. Just a few points to clear up. Meiklejohn was with the prisoner when Varma brought him in, was she not? To the best of your knowledge, did Meiklejohn have the opportunity to speak to anyone between the Pod Bay and security?'

Filbert moved his head fractionally. 'No. As far as I know she came straight from the Pod Bay with all the others.'

'She was present when the prisoner was registered?'

'Yes. The prisoner was registered and they all went off to clean themselves up.'

'They were all together? At all times?'

'Yes.'

'This is very important, Lieutenant – did anyone – anyone at all – have the opportunity to speak to them on the way? Was Varma so keen to register her prisoner that she took her eye off the ball, perhaps?'

He shook his head again. 'No. Varma made a point of keeping them all together. What's this about?'

'There seems to be some doubt about Meiklejohn's actions when she actually arrived in security. Did she speak to the prisoner? Did she say anything at all?'

Filbert closed his eyes.

'Lieutenant.' Hay spoke sharply. 'Hugh. Stay with me.'

The doctor made a movement of protest, caught Ellis's eye and subsided.

A note of doubt entered Filbert's voice. 'Well, I wasn't in the Pod Bay, of course, so I don't know . . .' He tailed away; his eyes unfocused in an effort of recollection. 'Yes, now you come to mention it, Meiklejohn *was* a few seconds behind everyone else, so I suppose it's possible she might have said something to someone then, but no, she didn't speak the whole time she was in security.'

'You are absolutely certain Meiklejohn played no part in the registration?'

'No. None at all.'

'That she never said a word.'

'No.'

Commander Hay struck swiftly and surely.

'So why did you call the prisoner Jake?'

Filbert's eyes flew open. 'What?'

'All our records show him as John Costello. Occasionally he used the alias James Costello. Or Jack. Never Jake. No one else in TPHQ knew him by that name. And yet you called him Jake.'

'I heard Meiklejohn call him that.'

'You've just told me that Meiklejohn never spoke during the

time Varma was registering the prisoner. You said she wasn't even present for most of it.'

'I was mistaken. Meiklejohn *was* with all the others. They all came in together and there was a lot going on. I heard her call him Jake.'

'Not according to the tapes.'

'But . . .' He stopped.

'Yes?'

'Nothing.'

'You were going on to say you'd what . . . doctored the tapes?'

'Of course not.'

'I've seen the log entry. The prisoner was registered as John Costello. Which was the name Varma knew him by. As did I. As did everyone. Even Captain Farenden didn't recognise the alias. And yet you, Lieutenant, called him Jake. Is it possible you'd heard of him before? From Henry Plimpton, perhaps?'

'I . . . no . . . Where are you getting all this from?'

'Do you know, having read the transcripts, I suspect you and John Costello were not unknown to each other.'

'I don't . . .'

'And, of course, he's a link between you and Henry Plimpton. When Two-Three-Six brought Plimpton in last year, you made sure you were his interrogating officer, didn't you? You let Varma make a start with the interrogation – just to make things look good – and then you moved in yourself. For your instructions. Because you were the person Henry Plimpton wanted to contact. To give and receive information.

'You're the one who attacked Costello. What a shock for you when you found him standing in front of you in security.

And about to be offered amnesty if he told us everything he knew. You had to shut him up pretty quickly, didn't you? You meant to kill him but you didn't have time to finish him off. You just had to keep your fingers crossed he didn't remember the actual attack.

'You're the one who tampered with our records – including those relating to Lockland's parents – because the one thing you had to conceal, above everything else, was the fact that you were the officer whom Mrs Lockland contacted all those years ago.'

If possible, Filbert had turned an even muddier shade of grey.

'You were panicking by now, weren't you? You must have thought yourself safe and then, suddenly, not just one but all your dirty little secrets are about to come to light. First Costello – who knew you – and then old Mrs Lockland herself. That was why you killed her. You had to. Officer Varma is persistent and would have got there in the end.'

Filbert was gabbling. 'Are you mad? I was wounded in the attack on Mrs Lockland. I tried to save her. You've seen the footage.'

Hay's voice dripped contempt. 'How stupid do you think I am? You turned the blaster on yourself. At point-blank range. You had to. You would have been number one suspect, otherwise. And even shooting yourself worked to your advantage. Yes, it's a nasty wound, but it would have bought you an honourable discharge. Medals. Approbation. Compensation. Full pension. On top of whatever Henry Plimpton has been paying you.'

She sighed heavily. 'And the clincher, of course. Only you could have arranged the fake execution of Imogen Farnborough.'

454

With deep satisfaction, she saw the sick look in his eyes. 'Oh yes, we know it all. A staged execution at Droitwich. What cover story did you use? Did you tell them Farnborough was going under deep cover somewhere and needed to be officially dead? You arranged for the "body" to be released, supposedly to her mother, but in reality, to a member of the Portman family. Which confirms that the Portmans and Plimpton are not unknown to each other. I suspect they now know that I know. I wonder how long they'll let you live. Certainly not long enough to testify against them.'

Filbert's good arm scrabbled at the covers as if he was trying to get out of bed. 'This is lies. All lies. None of this is true. You have no proof.'

Hay's voice was deadly. 'Let me lay it out for you. Raymond Parrish senior told Mrs Lockland about her daughter-in-law's activities. She told you. You told Henry Plimpton. He killed the Locklands and stole their pod. What else have you told him over the years?'

For a moment her rage spilled over. *How much damage have you done? How many are dead because of you?*

She took a deep breath. 'And then – shock horror – not only is the Lockland business revived, but Mrs Lockland is actually brought in for questioning. She'll recognise you as soon as she sees you. You take very good care to stay clear until you can get Varma out of the way and then in you go. I wonder if she thought you'd come to get her out. Well, she got that wrong, didn't she? I'm guessing Mrs Lockland wouldn't have identified you but, knowing her, you'd have been paying out for the rest of your life and you couldn't risk that, could you?

'So in you go – she looks up – but before she can say anything, you supposedly see someone in the doorway. You throw yourself at this supposed intruder. You "grapple" with them. All carefully out of camera shot because the cameras are designed to monitor the interrogation room, not the doorway. Something that will be rectified at the earliest opportunity. You've cleared Ellis and North out of the way. You've sent Varma to investigate what triggered the alarms – a stroke of luck for you, but I'm sure you'd have thought of some way of getting rid of her. You were quite anxious for her to take a break, weren't you? You don your own helmet which you left just outside the door, straight back in and snap Mrs Lockland's neck. You kick the helmet down the corridor. Then you shoot yourself – I hope it hurt a very great deal – and take care to collapse in the doorway so the cameras concentrate on the door opening and closing and miss the fact there's no one escaping down the corridor. Everything flung together at the very last moment, but nonetheless brilliant for all that.'

'No. This is rubbish.'

Hay swept on. '*You* betrayed Nuñez and Klein when they were investigating Site X. To their deaths. The only reason you didn't betray Lockland and Parrish as well is because I never told anyone I was sending them in.'

'I didn't do any of this. I'm innocent.'

'Hugh Filbert, you are under arrest for . . .'

'You can't do this.'

'I can and I am. This is your one chance, Filbert. Tell me everything about Henry Plimpton and I'll commute your sentence. You won't enjoy it, but at least you will have a sort of life. Otherwise . . .'

'You don't have a single shred of evidence against me and I'm not saying any more.'

'I don't care. Have you forgotten for whom you work? Remember the good old days? When evidence was something only lesser organisations bothered with?'

She smiled and it wasn't pleasant. 'Major Ellis, I would like you to organise a team and a clean-up crew to Droitwich. They are to shut it down and arrest everyone there pending investigation.'

Ellis had to clear his throat. 'Yes, ma'am.'

'Could you see to that now, please, Major. And, doctor, I'd like you to find somewhere else to be for a few minutes. Go somewhere with witnesses.'

The room suddenly went very, very quiet.

'Ma'am? What are you doing?'

'Cleaning up our mess.' She pulled out her blaster. 'I'm afraid, Lt Filbert, that you did not survive your injuries.'

She took aim at his damaged arm. The blaster began to whine.

Ellis swallowed but said nothing.

Not so the doctor. 'Ma'am, I protest. I am a doctor. This is a medical facility. No matter what he's done, I cannot – will not – stand by and watch a helpless patient murdered in his bed. Not in my MedCen.'

Still unnoticed at the other end of the ward, Major Callen backed noiselessly out of the door. He pulled out his com. 'This is Callen. Who's in Logistics?'

'Oti, sir.'

'Listen carefully.' He fired off a set of instructions.

'Now, sir?'

'Yes. I'm in MedCen. Bring it to me. I'll meet you halfway. Top priority.'

'Yes, sir.'

Callen shut down his com and began to run.

Back in MedCen, a deeply conflicted Major Ellis was, for the first time in his life, contemplating disobeying a direct order from his commanding officer. Now he knew why Hay had insisted he come unarmed. No blame could come his way. She was about to shoot a man as he lay helpless in his bed. This was murder. On one level his mind knew this was the best way. No trial – no trace. Filbert died of his wounds. How sad. No one would ever know. On another level, this was a step back to the bad old days of Colonel Albay. This was not how Commander Hay operated. Yes, it was the best thing to do – the easiest thing to do – but it was wrong. So wrong. What should he do?

Nothing. This was the whole point of the Time Police. Desperate situations call for desperate measures. An organisation not constrained by the law was much stronger than one that was. But – and this always happened, no matter how good the intentions, how pure of purpose – sooner or later absolute power corrupts absolutely. Sooner or later that organisation steps over the line. It always happened. It had happened many times under Albay. And now it was happening again.

He swallowed hard and opened his mouth to end his career in the Time Police.

The door crashed open behind him making him jump. He looked around to see Major Callen trundling in a flatbed on which reposed a large wooden crate. With airholes. And on top of the crate, what looked like a personnel file.

'Good evening,' said Callen, cheerfully. 'Sorry I'm late, Commander. I've only just got in. Doctor, I do beg your pardon.' He gestured to the trolley. 'These things aren't as easy to handle as you'd think and I'm afraid I've taken rather a large chunk out of your wall. By the way, Grint and his team have suffered minor injuries and will probably require some attention.'

The doctor opened his mouth and then closed it again, plainly on the horns of a dilemma. Ashen-faced, Filbert had fallen back on his pillows.

'Now then,' said Callen, seemingly not noticing the tension in the room. He picked up the file and opened it. 'Let's see, shall we? Yes, here we are. Filbert, H. Five foot eleven and twelve and a half stone.' He peered at Filbert. 'You've put on weight, Lieutenant. Your file needs updating. Well – it did. Not really important now, is it?'

He peered at Hay over the top of the file. 'Delta Zero Two is being prepped for departure as we speak, ma'am. Flight plan filed and cleared. For this particular mission the call sign will be Ghost One and, according to the designated protocols, all records will be expunged immediately afterwards.'

He closed the file and handed it to Major Ellis. 'Commander Hay, as officer commanding the Time Police, I must ask you, formally, to confirm now that I am to proceed according to Black Directive Zero Zero Seven.'

There was a long pause. No one moved. Then Hay said, 'Very well, Major. I so confirm.'

'Thank you, Commander. Doctor, Major, I am obliged to tell you now that everything you see and hear is covered by Black Directive Zero Zero Seven. Please confirm you have been so advised.'

Major Ellis, who had discovered the file was blank, drew himself up and very carefully did not look at Commander Hay. 'I so confirm.'

The doctor looked at Commander Hay, whose nod was almost imperceptible, and said, reluctantly, 'I so confirm.'

'What?' said Filbert. 'What's going on?'

'Well,' said Callen, suddenly cheerful, 'I'm rather glad you asked me that because I've never done one of these before and I've always wanted to. If everyone could listen very carefully, please. From this moment onwards, Lt Filbert no longer exists. Doctor, you will cease all treatment forthwith. Please have the patient's medical records sealed and sent to me for disposal. Should anyone ever question you about the events of this evening, your official response will be that you were not here at the time and can neither confirm nor deny events.'

Callen turned to Hay. 'Everything is in place, Commander. The loadmaster informs me the interior of Ghost One has been rigged to carry cargo.' He gave the crate an affectionate slap. 'We are cleared for take-off in . . .' he glanced at his watch, 'Thirty minutes from now Ghost One will fly east along the Thames, using the emergency airway, and then follow the coast northwards. Purpose of flight has been designated as an emergency resupply mission. Apparently one of those environmental Arctic expeditions is experiencing some minor difficulties. Not that that's anything to do with us, of course, because some twenty minutes before arriving at its official destination, Ghost One will report severe engine problems which will necessitate jettisoning its cargo – a single crate – over the North Atlantic.'

460

He eyed Filbert, who had gone so white that his skin looked transparent under the harsh lights.

'My calculations lead me to believe the time between being thrown out of the helicopter and impacting the water will be approximately two minutes.' He smiled at Filbert. 'I wish it could be longer, but we can't always get what we want, can we? Although I suspect that for you, it will be the longest two minutes of your life. And the last.'

Filbert appeared to be beyond words. And he wasn't the only one, reflected Ellis. He found he was being addressed.

'Ellis, if you can lend a hand here. If we remove the lid then we should be able to . . .'

With a feeling that all of this was happening to someone else, Ellis stepped up.

Callen turned towards the doctor. 'With respect, doctor, you might not wish to be here.'

'I don't,' said the doctor.

'I believe you will find Grint and his team in one of the treatment rooms.'

The doctor turned on his heel and left the cubicle. A door banged somewhere.

'Right,' said Callen. He peered down into the crate and then looked critically at the patient. 'We'll have to take that cage thing off his arm otherwise we'll never get him in. Do you know how it works?'

'No,' said Ellis. 'No idea.'

'Well, we'll just unscrew everything until it drops off, shall we?'

'The arm or the support?'

'Does it matter?'

Ellis considered this. 'No, I suppose not.'

They bent over the patient, who shrieked, 'Don't touch me. Don't touch me.'

'Making a lot of noise for someone who doesn't exist,' said Callen.

'I'll tell you. I'll tell you anything you want to know. Just don't touch my arm.'

'Can you hear something?' said Callen to Ellis.

Filbert raised his voice to a scream. 'Help me. Someone help me. For God's sake.'

'Gentlemen,' said Hay, quietly. 'I think you can desist.'

'I applaud your humanity, Commander,' said Callen, 'but I suspect as soon as we do desist the prisoner will change his mind again.'

'No. No, I won't. Just don't touch my arm.'

'Well, that's very disappointing,' said Callen. 'I was rather enjoying myself.'

'That's what I find so concerning,' said Hay.

Callen perched on the bed, ignoring Filbert's moan of pain. 'Let's do a deal, shall we? You tell Major Ellis everything – and I do mean everything – and I'll come back in an hour. If Major Ellis assures me you're playing nicely, then I might instruct Ghost One to stand down. But then again – I might not. We just don't know, do we? Don't you find uncertainty quite exciting, former Lt Filbert? I shall leave you now with Major Ellis. Commander, may I walk you to your office?'

She nodded curtly and they left the cubicle.

'Well,' he said, opening the door for her as they exited MedCen. 'I thought that went very well, didn't you? I'm certain he'll cooperate. It's a shame MedCen is underground. I could have flown the chopper around the building a couple of times. I'm sure that would have jogged his memory wonderfully.'

Commander Hay stopped dead.

'Is something wrong, Commander?'

She clenched her teeth. 'I have no idea why I let you live.'

'Well, that's a little harsh. I thought it was rather brilliant improvisation given such short notice. Ghost One? Black Directive Zero Zero Seven? A little credit, please, Commander.'

'Credit where it is due, Major, you've hardly solved my problem. What do you propose we do with him now? I can't keep him here. I don't want this building under attack for a second time, and Plimpton will move heaven and earth to silence him.'

'Once again, my brilliance astounds even me. I shall have him taken to the Tower. Where we hold all traitors. I shall convey him there myself. By helicopter, no less. Imagine how he will enjoy the trip.'

'You bastard . . .'

'All in all, I think he'll be happy to tell us everything he knows. Has ever known. And would have known in the future.'

She shook her head, not looking at him. 'I would have shot him. In his bed. I would have murdered a helpless man.'

'I know you would.' Callen spoke very gently. 'And it would have been the quickest and safest thing to do. Leadership frequently entails making unpleasant decisions so others don't have to. They can continue their blameless lives in complete ignorance of the actions taken to ensure they *can* continue to live their blameless lives in complete ignorance. You stepped up. With Droitwich so compromised you didn't have a choice.'

He smiled a crooked smile. 'I couldn't let you do that to yourself, Marietta.'

The lift door opened. 'After you, Commander.'

Meanwhile, a very wobbly Mrs Farnborough had been discreetly whisked away to the guest suite.

Someone else's problem, thought Jane, handing in her weapon for recharging before heading to MedCen. But a nice surprise for mother and daughter when they both awoke.

The doctor regarded them all without enthusiasm.

'Didn't we chuck you out only a couple of hours ago, Parrish? We don't do air miles, you know.'

'Where's . . . ?' said Grint, and made not particularly flattering gestures indicating Mrs Farnborough.

'Safe,' said the doctor. 'Let's have a look at you all. You first, Lockland – in here.'

None of Jane's cuts and bruises were deemed to be serious.

'Anything else?' enquired the doctor.

Jane hesitated. There might never be a better opportunity.

'Actually,' she began. And stopped.

The doctor paused in the act of disposing of the soiled dressings. 'Yes?'

'Well . . .'

'Yes?'

'Um . . . well, I wanted to ask . . . um . . . how normal is it to hear voices? You know – actual voices?'

The doctor pursed his lips. 'In this place? Perfectly normal. I hear voices all the time. *Doctor, I think I've got rabies. Doctor, I'm bleeding again. Doctor, should it do that? Doctor, I'm*

464

sure it's got bigger. Doctor, look what happens if you poke it. Doctor . . .'

'Yes, I see,' said Jane, hastily.

'Why? Are you hearing voices?'

'Perhaps,' said Jane, cautiously.

'It's a yes or no question, Lockland. It's like being pregnant. Either you are or you aren't.'

'Yes, I am.'

'Pregnant?'

'What?' shouted Luke from just outside the door.

'Did you hear that?' said the doctor. 'Is that the sort of voice you mean?'

'No,' said Jane, lowering her own voice. 'I only hear them sometimes.'

'Uh huh,' said the doctor, showing a disappointing lack of interest. 'And what do these voices say?'

'Well, mostly they're advising me to kill Luke Parrish. Am I going mad?'

'Good God, no. We all hear voices telling us to kill Luke Parrish.'

'I can still hear you, you know,' shouted Luke. 'Nothing wrong with my hearing.'

'We know that,' shouted the doctor. 'It's usually your under-standing that is at fault. Lockland, go away. You're perfectly normal. For this place, anyway. Lieutenant – you're next.'

Jane waited outside until Lt Grint emerged.

Like Jane, once the covering of dust, dirt and smoke had been washed away, there was comparatively little damage underneath. A wooden splinter had torn open his cheek, which had been glued back together again and a dressing applied.

Luke, emerging from another treatment room, eyed this with interest and enquired whether Grint shouldn't be wearing one of those lampshade collars they gave to dogs. 'You know, to stop him worrying at his stitches.'

Grint, on his way towards the door, stopped in his tracks. The world might have held its breath. Jane certainly did.

And then he started walking again. 'Parrish, you're an arse-hole.'

'And proud to be so.'

Grint pushed open the door and disappeared.

Luke turned to Jane. 'I think he's warming to me. What do you think?'

38

Two hours later, Commander Hay was still at her desk.

'All right, Charlie. Give me an update, please.'

He yawned. 'Sorry, ma'am.'

'I feel that way myself. Is it still today?'

'If you mean, are we still within the same twenty-four-hour period, ma'am, astonishingly, yes.'

'Longest day ever.'

'Although it hasn't been dull, ma'am.'

She glared at him.

'I beg your pardon. Just attempting to lighten the burden.'

'Why?'

'It's in my job description.'

'Given your activities over the last few months – not least wantonly and recklessly plunging the Time Police into a financial apocalypse – I wonder if now might not be the ideal time to review this fabled job description of yours.'

'By all means, ma'am.'

'But only after the update from which you have failed to divert me.'

'As you have pointed out, ma'am, it has been a long day

and my skill set is certainly not as . . . vibrant . . . as it was this time yesterday. However, forging manfully on . . .'

He consulted his scratchpad. 'Officers Farrell and Varma have returned to the fold. Bringing with them a number of former Plimpton employees – the interviewing of which should be extremely interesting. I think. Given the actions of Dr Maxwell, it might also be appropriate to send another note of thanks to St Mary's, ma'am.'

Hay groaned. 'Must I?'

Captain Farenden beamed. 'I have already drafted one up. To save you the bother. You have only to sign it.'

There was silence from the other side of the desk.

'Moving swiftly on, ma'am . . . we now know the probable location of one of Henry Plimpton's remote sites. A clean-up crew is on site as we speak.'

'What have they discovered?'

'No trace of Henry Plimpton or his men. The site has been completely abandoned and no one has any clue as to where they've gone.'

'Well, it's Roanoke. That's about par for the course.' She frowned. 'I suppose it's too much to hope they fell prey to . . . how are we going to designate whatever it was?'

'I thought we could just refer to it as local forces, ma'am. Anyway, there was no damage to the settlement – other than that inflicted by Dr Maxwell, of course. All evidence points to Henry Plimpton leaving in a hurry, and we hope to acquire some very useful odds and ends.'

'Including four former employees, I gather.'

'All of whom are proving to be extremely cooperative,

ma'am. Officer Varma acted on her own initiative and offered them a partial amnesty as an incentive.'

'Do we actually prosecute *anyone* these days?'

'Well, not as many as we used to, ma'am, but that's because our role is now preventative rather than punitive.'

Hay sighed. 'I enjoyed punitive. It was easier.'

'I think we all did, ma'am, but times change.'

She sighed again. 'What else?'

'We now have a definite link between the Portmans and Henry Plimpton. Plus, their involvement in the kidnapping of Imogen Farnborough and blackmailing a member of the government.'

'Twenty-four hours ago, I'd have put my money on it being Raymond Parrish. Despite having no hard evidence at all.'

'You would not have been alone, ma'am.'

'I suspect we'll have even less success proving anything against Portman and Webber than we had with Parrish Industries. Still, we'll give it a go.'

He nodded. 'Moving on . . . Lt Grint was slightly wounded during what he refers to as the "scuffle" at Mile End. He will recover. If, indeed, he has not already done so. Parrish and Lockland are also more or less unharmed – however, given his original injuries, Parrish has requested and been granted five days' leave, most of which he intends to spend with his father.'

Hay nodded. 'Interesting.'

'Mrs and Miss Farnborough are safely ensconced in the third-floor guest suite. Miss Farnborough is sleeping off the effects of her confinement. Mrs Farnborough is just sleeping it off. Officer Rockmeyer is providing discreet security from an armchair at the end of the corridor, although that might no longer be necessary.'

'I think we'll take no chances,' said Hay.

'As you wish, ma'am. Major Ellis has shut down his investigation and people are resuming their normal duties. A massive breakfast for everyone and then we should be good to go. And last but definitely not least, I have arranged for you to address the security department later today. To explain Lt Filbert's "death".'

'Yes, we'll need to manage the situation quite carefully. The official line is that Filbert died quietly of his injuries. It's all very sad and I will, however reluctantly, have to accord him full honours.'

'Ma'am . . .'

'I know what you are going to say, but it won't do morale any good for the truth to come out. And if the world thinks he's dead – including Plimpton, of course – then we might buy ourselves a little time.'

Captain Farenden consulted his scratchpad. 'Just to put your mind at rest, I have a contact at the Tower who confirms Filbert's safe arrival.'

Hay stared at him. 'You know someone at the Tower? Why am I asking? Of course you do. A Beefeater, I suppose.'

'Uncle,' said Captain Farenden, briefly.

'Good grief, Charlie . . .'

'I fail to see anything disreputable in having an uncle, ma'am.'

'I'm sure your uncle is delightful. It's the nephew who is so irritating.'

'I'm sure you will feel more able to combat this supposed irritation after a good breakfast.'

Hay mournfully considered her cold coffee. 'I didn't get to

finish my coffee. I wasn't able even to start on the sandwich. The second sandwich.'

'Allow me to sprinkle a little joy along the path of your working day, ma'am. Accessing our non-existent budget, I have ordered a brand-new, top-of-the-range, all-singing, all-dancing coffee machine. To be delivered and installed later today. However, given your understandable reservations concerning our perilous financial state, do I gather you would like me to cancel the order?'

'Actually, I was considering trading you for the coffee machine.'

'Hastily changing the subject, ma'am, Officer Lockland is here. You wanted to speak to her.'

'Ask her to come in, please.'

Jane nervously seated herself, obviously expecting yet another bombshell.

She got it.

'Officer Lockland, I regret to inform you that your grandmother, Beatrice Lockland, has been killed. While in our custody. To the outside world we are calling it a heart attack. I'm afraid I can't yet divulge the name of her killer. I can assure you this is for operational reasons rather than any attempt to instigate a cover-up.'

Hay sat back. 'I'm sorry it happened here. As you now know, we were blameless in the matter of your parents – something else to lay at Henry Plimpton's door – but not in the death of your grandmother. On behalf of the Time Police, I offer my sincere apologies.'

Jane seemed more bewildered than upset. 'Should I be sad? I don't feel sad.'

'No, I don't think you should feel sad. Nor do I think you should feel guilty because of that. Take a while to think of her, if you like, but don't beat yourself up if you can't find any happy memories. She was, I suspect, a deeply unhappy woman. It is to your credit that you did not allow her unhappiness to overwhelm you. Think of this as the end of your old life. I believe new chapters are beginning to open up for you, Officer Lockland. A whole new life. I encourage you to make the most of it.'

'Yes, ma'am.'

To Jane's surprise, Lt Grint was waiting for her as she exited the lift. She smiled at him. He did not, however, smile back.

'Lockland, I heard your grandmother died.'

Jane nodded.

'I'm . . . sorry. If you're upset, I mean. Not because . . . although I am if you are.'

Accustomed to Grint's conversational style, Jane nodded. 'I'm absolutely fine, thank you.'

'Glad to hear it.' He nodded in turn and walked away. Ten paces later he halted, stood for a moment then turned and came back.

'Jane . . .'

She looked up at him. 'Yes?'

Not looking at her even a little bit, he said awkwardly, 'Nothing must ever happen to you, Jane.'

Jane stared at the ground, unable to speak. Then she nodded.

Grint walked away.

39

'How are you feeling?' enquired Raymond Parrish as they boarded the helicopter.

'Stiff,' said Luke. 'And sore.' He watched the ground fall away beneath them. 'Where are we going?'

'Wiltshire.'

'For any particular reason or is it just Wiltshire's lucky day?'

'After consultation with Commander Hay, I have been able to procure suitable accommodation for Mrs and Miss Farnborough as they recover from recent events. I would welcome your opinion. It's a nursing home – a very pleasant place – very discreet but with excellent security. And peaceful – which is, I think, a primary requisite for both of them after the events of the last few months.'

Luke nodded, and spent the rest of the journey with his chin on his chest, trying to keep his thoughts at bay.

The pilot set them down smoothly and began to shut things down. 'Will you be requiring me, Mr Parrish?'

'No, thank you, Miles. We might be a while – make sure they feed you.'

'Yes, sir.'

'Nice place,' commented Luke, looking around.

It was indeed a very nice place. Other than birdsong and the tinkle of an unseen fountain, there was utter silence here. No sounds of traffic – on the ground or in the sky. An air of tranquillity pervaded.

The garden was as beautiful as only an English garden can be in early summer. Long lawns led up to an ancient, E-shaped, three-storey building, covered in ivy. Sunshine winked off mullioned windows. Brightly coloured flower beds bordered the gravel drive. Five or six garden seats had been grouped in the shade of an ancient elm. Several people were sitting there, either reading or just enjoying the fine day.

'Most of the facilities are around the back,' said Raymond Parrish. 'Spa, cinema, arts centre. This way.'

They climbed a set of ancient stone steps. The front door stood wide open, giving a glimpse of a large, square hall with a gleaming wooden floor.

'You were saying about security?' murmured Luke.

'I warned them of our arrival. Ah – Dr Summers. How are you?'

A tall, rangy-looking woman with grey hair and wearing a white coat was coming down the stairs towards them. Luke took off his sunglasses.

'Mr Parrish, welcome. Both of you.' She peered professionally at Luke's face.

Raymond Parrish shook hands. 'How are things, doctor?'

'Good. We're very pleased. But first things first. I believe you wanted to inspect the rooms. Do come this way.'

She led them down a long corridor painted in a pleasant shade of creamy yellow. The same wooden floor shone. Bright pictures lined the walls. In fact, everything was highly polished and immaculate. Prettily coloured curtains flapped gently at the open windows. There was certainly no hospital smell here.

'Nice flower arrangements,' commented Luke, passing a console table displaying an exuberant mixture of summer flowers.

'Thank you. We grow our own and every fortnight there is a small competition for those who enjoy flower arranging. A very successful therapy. Except on the occasions when we have flower wars, of course.'

'Flower wars are a thing?' queried Luke.

She laughed. 'Oh, very much so. One tweaks a rose at one's peril.'

Luke found himself with an urge to tweak. Just to see what would happen. Resolutely, he put his hands in his pockets.

They had arrived at the end of the corridor. Two doors faced them from behind an empty nurse's station. 'And here we are. Two bedrooms with a shared lounge between them, together with a small courtyard garden in which they can sit if they so wish. There is no outside access – everyone must pass this station which will be manned at all times.'

She opened the first door to reveal a pleasant room, square in shape and looking out over a walled garden. In the centre, a tiny fountain reflected the sunlight.

'The other bedroom is exactly the same with the lounge between them. We don't allow electronic devices, of course, but there are holos, music, books. Anything they want will be provided – within reason, of course. We have a strict no drink or drugs policy, but I don't think that's likely to be a problem in this case.'

Raymond Parrish had stepped out into the sunshine and was looking up. 'Drones?'

'Not a problem here.'

'Don't tell me,' said Luke, unable to resist. 'There's a small competition for those who enjoy bringing down the occasional drone. Catapults, trebuchets, boomerangs and so forth. A very successful therapy.'

The doctor laughed. 'Roof-mounted lasers, actually. But the staff are very competitive. There is an actual league table about which I, of course, know nothing.'

'Ah.'

'These are very pleasant rooms,' said Raymond Parrish.

'And quiet. And at the end of the corridor, as you saw. There's no reason for them to meet our other guests unless they so choose. Which we will encourage, of course, but in their own time. The Time Police have forwarded their medical records. I suspect both ladies will be somewhat fragile to begin with.'

Raymond Parrish nodded. 'This is all very satisfactory, Dr Summers. I am certain you and your excellent staff will work your usual magic.'

'I see no reason why not. I suspect Miss Farnborough will require the most care and attention. Would I be correct in assuming, however, that Mrs Farnborough will want to remain here until she is completely satisfied her daughter will recover?'

'That is very probable, yes. Both ladies can, of course, stay for as long as they wish.'

'Understood, Mr Parrish.'

Luke wandered out into the garden. Sunshine bounced off the walls. He felt an overwhelming urge to sit under the tree in the corner and just close his eyes . . . listen to the fountain . . . watch the little goldfish. He wondered if Imogen would consider taking him on as a roommate.

476

'. . . taken a while to establish the correct dosage,' the doctor was saying. 'But I think we have it now. Obviously, nothing is certain, but I'm quietly confident we will see a continued improvement.'

Her bleeper went off. Frowning, she consulted the read-out. 'And now, if you will excuse me . . .'

'Of course, doctor.'

'Do you mind making your own way . . . ?'

'Not at all. Good day, doctor.'

She strode away.

Luke opened his eyes. 'Do you have medical qualifications I don't know anything about, Dad?'

Raymond Parrish shook his head. 'I did once hold a first-aid badge at school, if that is the sort of thing you are referring to.'

'Only I'm not sure what qualifies you to dictate the length of their stay.' He paused. 'You're paying for it, aren't you?'

'Well, I could do, but I'm not. There will be no bill.'

They began to retrace their steps back along the highly polished corridor.

'Dad, this place won't be cheap.'

'Irrelevant. I own it.'

Luke stopped dead. 'You own a nursing home? When did that happen?'

'They do good work here.'

'For overpaid politicians and drug-addled celebrities, I suppose. A nice little earner.'

'There are fifteen beds here. Seven are set aside for private patients. Their fees pay for the other seven National Health patients. We still manage to make a small profit every year.'

Arriving back in the hall, Raymond Parrish indicated they should climb the stairs.

'Hold on,' said Luke, pausing. 'You said fifteen beds.'

'I did, didn't I?'

At the top of the stairs, a broad landing ran left and right. Raymond Parrish turned left and tapped lightly on a half-open door at the very end. Someone called to come in. Luke paused outside, unsure.

This was a large, sun-filled room – half bedroom, half sitting room – with tall windows letting in the light. Pictures, ceramics and books were everywhere. A small piano stood in one corner and an artist's easel in another. The impression was of a pretty, feminine room. A bowl of fresh rose petals filled the room with their scent.

Sitting at a small table by a window overlooking the garden, a nurse and another woman wearing a long white linen dress were playing chess.

'Good morning,' said Raymond Parrish, quietly.

The nurse smiled. 'Here's Mr Parrish come to see you, my dear. Just in time for me, thank goodness.' She smiled at Raymond Parrish. 'You have saved me from utter annihilation.'

Raymond Parrish walked forwards. 'Alessa, my dear. How are you? You look delightful, as always.'

Luke remained just outside the door, rooted to the spot. For the life of him he could not have moved.

The woman in the white dress lifted her face to be kissed. 'Raymond. How lovely to see you. I was hoping you would come today – I want to show you around the gardens. I have big plans for a water garden, you know.'

'I do know,' he said. 'But before we do that – I've brought

478

you a visitor today. This is Luke. You remember him, don't you?'

She twisted in her chair. Luke, still unable to move, stared. Memories tumbled, one after the other. She looked so different. Her face was thinner and her hair had turned grey, but her eyes – a little puzzled just at this moment – were as blue as ever. He tried to remember when he had last seen her, but his mind refused to cooperate.

'Oh – how lovely.'

It was very obvious she hadn't the faintest idea who he was. Luke turned to his father. His voice cracked. 'Dad . . .'

Raymond Parrish put his hand on Luke's shoulder. 'It's all right, son – just give her a moment. She'll recognise you in a little while.'

'How long . . . ? How could you . . . ? Why didn't you tell me . . . ?'

'I never lost sight of your mother. Not for one moment. I took her to a number of establishments before discovering this one. The regime has suited her. They were, however, having financial issues, and rather than risk them closing and having to find Alessa somewhere probably not as good, I bought the place outright. It's been a long, hard road over the years, but Dr Summers thinks they've finally got the medication right. There's been a marked improvement over the last six months or so and it's been maintained. I didn't want you to see her until . . .' He turned away to look out of the window.

Alessa Parrish stood up, her eyes shining. 'Luke? Luke, is that you?'

Nurse Suti whisked herself out of the room. Raymond Parrish followed her out and closed the door.

'Mum . . .'

He walked into her arms and the room was very quiet for a long time.

'Look at you,' he said, forcing himself to sound cheerful. 'Even prettier than ever.'

She laughed. 'You are so tall. I think they give you too much food at that school of yours.'

'It's all right,' said Raymond Parrish, coming back into the room. 'It will take her a moment or two to orient herself. Just be a little patient.'

Luke nodded. 'I've left school, Mum. I'm in the Time Police now.'

'How exciting. What are the Time Police?'

'Um . . . well, we make sure people behave themselves.'

She laughed and even Luke had to smile.

'If you remember, Alessa, he was awarded a commendation. I told you about it. Do you remember?'

Her eyes clouded. 'No, I . . . Yes, I do. You were there.'

'Well done. I was, yes. He looked very smart in his uniform. You should ask him for a picture.'

Fortunately, before Luke could annihilate his father on the spot, Nurse Suti appeared to ask if they would be staying for lunch.

Alessa Parrish clapped her hands. 'Oh, yes. Do stay. And then I can show you my plans for the water garden.'

Raymond Parrish smiled. 'We shall be delighted to stay for lunch, Nurse Suti. Thank you.'

On their way back to London, Raymond Parrish turned to his son. 'You must have many questions.'

480

'I do, Dad. After which I might well pitch you out of this helicopter. For how long have you and Mum ... I mean ... The way Ernesto was talking, I thought she was living with the Portmans and ...'

'Oh no. He was bluffing. She never went back to the Portmans. The sad truth, Luke, is that she wasn't always as well as you saw her today. Not for a long time. Dr Summers has achieved some remarkable results, although I do think the peace and quiet and pleasant surroundings have played their part as well. And she was encouraged to develop an interest in the gardens, which has helped enormously. And she has a talent for it, as you saw.' He paused. 'It is unlikely she will ever leave there. The outside world is too much for her. You do understand that, don't you?'

Luke nodded. 'But I can visit?'

'I go every week. Sometimes twice. You are very welcome to accompany me. Or make your own arrangements. You must remember that, occasionally, she might not be able to receive visitors, but do not allow yourself to be alarmed by that.'

'I understand.' He hesitated. 'Dad, you've had all this ... you've had to do this by yourself and ...'

'Well, firstly, I felt – and still feel – that Alessa would not benefit from returning to live with her Portman family.'

'And secondly?'

'Secondly, it is my privilege to care for my wife. I do not begrudge a single penny or a single moment.'

Luke found himself with nothing to say. How dark had been the struggle? Deceiving the world. Deceiving the Portmans. Watching and waiting for any small signs of recovery. How deeply must his father love his mother? A lesser man might have consigned a mad wife to the attic, to live alone, abandoned . . .

SHIT!

Luke sat bolt upright in a tangle of flailing arms and legs.

The pilot looked over his shoulder, saying sharply, 'What's going on back there?'

'Nothing. Nothing. Everything's fine. Shit. Dad, how long before we get back?'

'Why do you ask?'

'Lola. I forgot Lola.'

'Oh,' said Raymond Parrish. 'You know Lola, do you? How is she?'

Luke had his second severe shock of the day. *'You know Lola?'*

'My dear boy, everyone knows Lola.'

'I think I meant – in a professional capacity.'

'I have employed her services on several occasions. She is very talented.'

Luke regarded his parent. 'You – and Lola? You come straight from visiting Mum and tell me you've been with Lola?'

'She speaks fluent Mandarin and is a very shrewd negotiator. She has several times represented me abroad. Why, what did you think I used her for?'

'Er . . . um . . .'

'And while we're on the subject, what did you mean by, "I forgot Lola"?'

'Dad, I might need a loan. Will need a loan. A very large loan.'

'For what purpose?'

'I used her to help me get Imogen Farnborough out of my flat and I . . . kind of . . . forgot her. She's been there all this time.'

Raymond Parrish seemed amused. 'Well, she certainly doesn't come cheap. How much are we talking about?'

Luke glanced at the pilot. 'Can he hear us?'

'Every word,' said the pilot. 'Health and safety requirement. Constant contact with the passengers.'

'How much?' repeated Raymond Parrish.

'Um . . . twenty-five thousand.'

The helicopter wobbled.

'Good heavens,' said Raymond Parrish.

'Per night.'

The helicopter nearly dropped from the sky.

Raymond Parrish regarded his son more in sorrow than in anger. 'Luke, my boy . . .'

The pilot laughed all the way back to London.

Epilogue

A week later, peace and quiet had, more or less, returned to Commander Hay's office. A mug of very excellent coffee sat on her desk alongside a plate of chocolate biscuits. She sat at her desk with a number of reports spread in front of her, quietly making notes for the next senior officers' meeting.

After a while, she lifted her head and listened. A moment later she got up and went to the door.

Captain Farenden, already halfway across his office, turned his head. 'Already on it, ma'am.'

'Great heavens, Charlie. I can hear the shouting from all the way up here. Check for survivors and report back.'

'Yes, ma'am.'

Ten minutes later he returned.

'Well?'

'Three broken ribs, ma'am.'

There was a silence. 'Well? Don't just give me the beginning.'

'Actually, ma'am, that was the end. The beginnings of this particular incident occurred back in some prehistoric time and place beyond the ken of man.' He remembered his audience. 'Or woman.'

'Oh God.'

Normally, at this point, Captain Farenden would intervene with words of calming explanation, emphasising the situation was by no means as bad as it could have been, and to have hope for the future. Conspicuously, on this occasion, that did not happen.

Commander Hay flattened her data stack and adjusted her glasses. 'Just tell me, Charlie.'

'Well, it all began when Miss Meiklejohn . . .'

'I've changed my mind. Go away.'

'No, I think you'll enjoy this one, ma'am.'

'Three broken ribs?'

'And some minor damage to Time Police property, ma'am.'

'How minor is minor?'

'Well, certainly not major, ma'am. Nothing to be recorded on the official inventory, anyway.'

'Let's hear it. What has she done?'

'Nothing. Nothing at all.'

Commander Hay regarded him shrewdly. 'Was it done *to* her?'

'No, no, ma'am. The whole thing was just a series of unfortunate events.'

'Which I might actually hear about if my adjutant gets a move on.'

'Yes, ma'am. Well, Officer Lockland had put in a request for Miss Meiklejohn to come up with some sort of . . . indoor facility. You know, after John Costello fell over her in 1746.'

Hay frowned. 'Was that in her report?'

'Not her written one, ma'am, no.'

'So, moving swiftly to the point . . .'

'Lockland and a few other female officers – well, most

of them – and a good number of male officers as well, approached . . .'

'Yes, yes, we've done all that. Were their requests successful?'

'Indeed, ma'am. Miss Meiklejohn produced a facility in near record time.'

'A flash in the pan, perhaps?'

Captain Farenden regarded her. 'Actually, ma'am, the saying *a flash in the pan* refers to . . . but I can see that's not important right now. To continue – Lt Grint, to whose pod fell the honour of the thunderbox's inaugural appearance, refused point-blank to have people crapping in his pod. His words – not mine. Therefore, on arrival in whenever it was they had jumped to, he insisted it be deployed outside. Officers Curtis and Rockmeyer volunteered to erect a small canvas-draped edifice around it – for privacy and to protect users from the elements.'

He paused, but no comment was forthcoming so there was nothing to do but carry on.

'In almost less time than it takes to tell, the thunderbox was assembled, the edifice erected, two toilet rolls hung from dinky pieces of string and . . .' He paused. 'And a polite notice requesting all officers to sit.'

Hay nodded. 'Ah – the problem of perpetually poor pee-pointing at the porcelain.'

Captain Farenden nodded. 'I think you'll find this interesting, ma'am – did you know that most European men pee sitting down? In fact, in Switzerland standing up to pee is illegal after 10 p.m.'

'What? Why?' said Hay.

'Apparently social pressure is playing a large part in changing men's peeing habits around the world.'

'Why are we even discussing this?' She paused. 'Hang on – even in America?'

'No one knows how they pee over there, ma'am. Or even whether they pee at all.'

'What a shame North wasn't briefed on this. She could have returned with valuable intel.'

'Which we would never have been able to use, ma'am, owing to the fact we have never actually jumped to America, have we?'

Hay groaned. 'If anyone ever finds out, I'll be in front of a Select Committee. Again.'

'Allow me to divert your mind from such a possibility, ma'am.'

'Back to the thunderbox?'

'Indeed. There wasn't a lot of wood about, so the edifice was, perhaps, a little on the not very tall side. There was no option other than to sit. A circumstance that caused some muttering among the ranks of those possessing the Y chromosome. Apparently, the phrase *stand-up guy* has several meanings.'

'I still fail to see how . . .'

'Picture the scene, ma'am.'

'Must I?'

'A dark, dark night lit only by a gibbous moon.'

'A *what*?'

'Officer Curtis staggers from his sleeping module, eyes half closed, and enters the thunderbox.'

'Oh God, tell me there wasn't a badger in there.'

Captain Farenden blinked his way back to the real world. 'A badger? No. Why would there be a badger?'

'That happened to me once, you know.'

'Not a badger, ma'am, no. Although a badger would probably have been easier to deal with.'

'Have you ever dealt with an enraged badger, Charlie?'

'Well, not as such, ma'am, but you're interrupting my story.'

'My apologies, Captain.'

'Not at all, ma'am. Anyway, picture the scene. A cold, cold night. Officer Curtis is sleepily preparing himself as he approaches the focus of the night's drama.'

'Too much information, Charlie.'

'Sorry, ma'am, but it's necessary to set the scene.'

'Yes, Officer Curtis is fumbling away as he . . .'

'Please, ma'am. No man is comfortable with the word *fumbling* in these circumstances. He enters the thunderbox, remembers to crouch low to avoid concussion, manoeuvres himself into position, lowers himself gently and carefully . . .'

Captain Farenden stopped.

'Yes? And?'

'And finds himself sitting on the naked lap of Officer Rockmeyer, who had earlier visited the facility for a similar purpose.'

'Didn't Rockmeyer think to call out?'

'Alas, ma'am, the edifice being a trifle snug and he being a trifle sleepy, he'd leaned against the wall, closed his eyes only for a moment . . . and dropped off.'

'Off the seat?'

'Off to sleep, ma'am. He was therefore unaware of the presence of Officer Curtis until Officer Curtis's naked buttocks came to rest gently upon his . . . lap. There was mutual horror.'

488

'I'll bet.'

'Apparently the night resounded with screaming and recriminations from both parties. Meanwhile, the rest of the teams, having been violently aroused from their blameless slumbers, tumbled from their pods, weapons raised, looking for dinosaurs, wolves, tigers, dragons or, in Lockland's case – a seagull.'

'A seagull? Well, I've heard they can be nasty. Nothing like an enraged badger, of course.'

'If we could move on from the enraged badger, ma'am.'

'I'd love to but it still haunts my nightmares. However, in the interests of eventually ascertaining whose ribs were broken . . .'

'Yes, ma'am. Well, people got themselves more or less sorted out, but only then did they notice the two officers, still with items of clothing at half-mast, locked in an apparent death match.'

'Were they blind? Put them all down for the Observation and Surveillance refresher course soonest.'

'Yes, ma'am. Well, there was a certain amount of derision and mockery from the male contingent. Female officers made a few uncomplimentary hand gestures.'

'You did say it was a cold night.'

'Indeed, ma'am. Order was restored by Lt Grint threatening to shoot anyone not back in their sleeping module within the next ten seconds. Which they were. The only exception being Officer Curtis who, as he explained, still hadn't had the opportunity to . . .'

Hay put her head in her hands. 'You are making all this up.'

'If only, ma'am.'

'Not our finest hour.'

'We don't really have finest hours, do we? The occasional satisfactory second is about all we can aspire to.'

'The broken ribs, Charlie.'

'Yes, well, sadly for Officer Curtis, the night was not yet over.'

Commander Hay regarded him. 'I hardly dare ask.' She brightened. 'Oh wait – was there an enraged badger after all?'

'No, ma'am. No badger. At no point does a badger – enraged or otherwise – appear in any of this sorry tale.'

'There's no need to shout.'

Captain Farenden breathed deeply. 'No, ma'am.'

'I think we left Officer Curtis preparing for Midnight Evacuation 2.0.'

'Yes, ma'am. And, following Lt Grint's strict instructions that, in future, no one was to enter the facility without one, he took a torch.'

'Wise.'

'Actually, ma'am, as things turned out – no.'

'Oh, dear God, Charlie.'

'I should perhaps explain that the facility is a simple box with a hole in the top and a catchment area underneath. Miss Meiklejohn has plans to modify and improve the design . . .'

'Get to the point.'

'. . . on successful completion of planned field trials. The point I am making, ma'am, is that a handy shaker was provided for . . .'

'A handy shaker?'

'To sprinkle Miss Meiklejohn's patent-pending substance down the hole, ma'am. To prevent odours and . . . facilitate . . . breakdown.'

'Your commanding officer has just lost the will to live.'

'I'm sorry to hear that, ma'am. Do you wish to be alone during your final moments?'

490

'Just tell me who broke whose ribs and why.'

'Of course, ma'am. Well, as he prepared himself for another attempt, Officer Curtis inadvertently shone his torch down into the hole. Just briefly, you understand, and . . .' He stopped.

'And what?'

'Something moved.'

'What?'

'Something moved, ma'am. Down in the depths.'

Commander Hay sat back. 'I may never visit the lavatory again.'

'You are not alone, ma'am.'

'And neither, I gather, was Officer Curtis. Don't keep me in suspense, Charlie. What the hell was it? For God's sake, don't tell me someone out there has sentient poo. Although, on consideration, I could easily believe we possess officers whose bowel movements are more intelligent than they are.' She shook herself. 'Why are we even talking about this?'

'Ribs, ma'am. You wanted to know.'

'Forget it. I no longer care.'

'I've nearly finished.'

'No rush, Charlie. I've already decided to skip lunch.'

'To continue, ma'am. For the second time that night, the air was rent with dreadful screams.'

'I have to say, your narrative style is definitely deteriorating.'

'Officer Curtis once again erupted from the thunderbox, this time screaming, "Eyes! It's got eyes! It's got eyes!"'

'Eyes?'

'There was massive consternation, ma'am.'

'I can imagine. What was it? To whom did the eyes belong?'

'Alas, ma'am, we'll never know. Lt Grint, somewhat prickly

at having his beauty sleep disturbed for the second time that night, discharged his blaster into the thunderbox, which ignited, exploded, disintegrated and so forth on the spot. Officer Curtis disappeared behind a tree to fulfil his destiny and everyone else went back to bed. The rest of the night was, thankfully, undisturbed.'

He got up to go.

'So whose ribs were broken?'

'Officer Curtis, ma'am.'

'In the fight with Officer Rockmeyer?'

'No. Here in TPHQ.'

Hay was bewildered.

'On his return to TPHQ, Officer Curtis celebrated his eventual relief with a beer and a bag of nuts and one went down the wrong way. He choked. Lt Grint, still somewhat miffed at the complete dog's breakfast his mission had deteriorated into, performed the Heimlich manoeuvre with enthusiasm and . . . well, he's a big man. They reckon they heard Curtis's ribs crack from right across the other side of the bar. He was not a happy officer.'

'Something you could have reported in approximately four seconds.'

'But that would have deprived you of the . . .'

'Leave my office, Captain.'

'Yes, ma'am.'

THE END

492

Author's Note

I'm sure there are many among you who think I just throw these books together over a weekend when there's nothing much on the telly. Which, let's face it, is most weekends.

Not so!

I spent ages on the internet trying to work out how long it would take a wooden crate containing a twelve-and-a-half-stone man to fall from heights of five, ten or fifteen thousand feet. I'm sure I've heard the expression 'thirty feet per second per second' somewhere – which means as little to me as does the ridiculous sentence, 'Don't eat all that chocolate at once.'

Because my maths is spectacularly bad, I came up with a variety of answers, ranging from ninety seconds to over five minutes, and at that point I made the mistake of consulting my brother, the cowfearing eminent author. He sent me pages and pages of graphs, technical information and obscure formulae, all of it utterly incomprehensible to my tiny author brain. Out of gratitude for his kindness, I'm sending him a cow.

Anyway, I was pretty much stuck – murdering someone by stuffing them into a crate and hurling them out of a helicopter obviously wasn't as easy as I had anticipated – and I was on the verge of giving up and just having him shot instead when . . .

bored to tears one weekend – because, coincidentally, there was nothing on the telly – I found myself watching *The Grand Tour*. And there were Clarkson, May and Hammond dropping a Citroën 2CV from a height of five hundred feet. And from a helicopter, no less.

I rewound, grabbed a pen and paper and solemnly – I swear this is true – counted the seconds the car took to travel five hundred feet downwards.

Nine seconds.

Nine seconds to drop five hundred feet.

Ninety seconds to drop five thousand feet.

One hundred and eighty seconds to drop ten thousand feet.

Two hundred and seventy seconds to drop fifteen thousand feet.

Never mind all this *per second per second* stuff – I decided to go with ten thousand feet and three minutes. If anyone argued I'd say there was a headwind. Or thick cloud. Or something. As the Time Police themselves would say, 'Close enough for government work.'

Massive thanks to Messrs Hammond, May and Clarkson, without whom I'd have had to go with a boring gunshot wound.

Another Author's Note

Well, this is just typical, isn't it? I send off my manuscript and sit back in the usual happy – well, slightly less grumpy than usual – glow of author satisfaction and it appears that Headline have people who can do actual real maths. Who knew? You'd think they'd have proper jobs to get on with, but no, they all sat around discussing how long it would take to kill someone using a helicopter and a crate. Anyway, someone who actually knows what they're doing calculated it would take only fifty-five seconds for a crate to plummet earthwards. Which is no good to me at all. Has anyone ever heard a Bond villain cackle, 'You have only fifty-five seconds to live, Mr Bond'?

Fifty-five seconds is no use to man nor author.

Normally I make every effort to make sure my books are factually correct – yes, Australia, I'm still sorry about the euca-lyptus tree – but I really wanted the dramatic impact of at least two minutes before, as my editor so elegantly put it – *splat*.

So – author confession – I've deliberately lied. I have made a small concession in the interests of accuracy – I've shifted the time from three minutes to two. Two minutes seems an entirely reasonable time to hit the ground from ten thousand feet.

While we're on the subject, researching the maximum flying

height of military helicopters while living in interesting times isn't always a smart thing to do. Heed my words.

Anyway – that's the story of Major Callen's big scene. My excuse is that he's a complete bastard and would happily lie his head off about how long from being thrown out of the helicopter to . . . splat. He lies to everyone. Except one person, perhaps.

Happy reading.

Acknowledgements

As always, thanks to my agent, Hazel Cushion, currently smothered in diamonds and prosecco on her YACHT (can you tell I'm not bitter?) and cruising the world's most exotic destinations, and who, despite bad wi-fi, typhoons, monsoons, humidity and heat, still manages to harangue me about everything under the sun on a regular basis.

Many thanks to Zara Ramm, who makes such a wonderful job of narrating my books.

Thanks also to everyone at Headline:

Frankie Edwards – editor-in-chief and mastermind.

Jessie Goetzinger-Hall – editorial assistant and responsible for this book's production. A bit of a poisoned chalice.

Zoe Giles – marketing genius.

Emily Patience – in charge of publicity and general world domination.

Hannah Cause – audio production guru.

Jill Cole and Sharona Selby – copy editor, proofreader and safety nets par excellence.

And many thanks to everyone else involved, including the Sales, Rights, Art and Production teams, all of whom presumably were unable to run away quickly enough.

TEAM WEIRD RETURN IN ...

KILLING TIME

TIME POLICE BOOK 5

Coming Summer 2024.

DISCOVER JODI TAYLOR'S GRIPPING SUPERNATURAL THRILLERS

There are some things in this world that only Elizabeth Cage can see. Important things. Dangerous things.

But what is a curse to Elizabeth is a gift to others – a very valuable gift they want to control. And they'll stop at nothing to do so . . .

Available to order now.

To discover more about

JODI TAYLOR

visit

www.joditaylor.online

You can also find her on

Facebook
www.facebook.com/JodiTaylorBooks

Twitter
@joditaylorbooks

Instagram
@joditaylorbooks